A
Nearly
Normal
Family

A
Nearly
Normal
Family

M. T. EDVARDSSON

Translated by

RACHEL WILLSON-BROYLES

CELADON
BOOKS

NEW YORK

A NEARLY NORMAL FAMILY. Copyright © 2019 by M. T. Edvardsson. English language translation copyright © 2019 by Rachel Willson-Broyles. All rights reserved. Printed in the United States of America. For information, address Celadon Books, 175 Fifth Avenue, New York, N.Y. 10010.

www.celadonbooks.com

Designed by Steven Seighman

ISBN 978-1-250-20443-1 (hardcover)
ISBN 978-1-250-23112-3 (international, sold outside the U.S., subject to rights availability)
ISBN 978-1-250-20442-4 (ebook)

Our books may be purchased in bulk for promotional, educational, or business use. Please contact your local bookseller or the Macmillan Corporate and Premium Sales Department at 1-800-221-7945, extension 5442, or by email at MacmillanSpecialMarkets@macmillan.com.

Originally published in Sweden in 2018 by Forum as *En helt vanlig familj*

Published in agreement with Ahlander Agency

First U.S. Edition: June 2019
First International Edition: June 2019

10 9 8 7 6 5 4 3 2 1

A *Nearly* Normal Family

Prologue

The district courthouse is in downtown Lund, kitty-corner from the police building, a stone's throw from Central Station. Anyone who lives in Lund passes the courthouse regularly, but most go their whole lives without setting foot inside the building. Until very recently, that was true for me as well.

Now I'm sitting on a bench outside Courtroom 2, and the monitor in front of me informs me that a trial is under way in a homicide case.

My wife is inside, on the other side of the door. Before we walked into the courthouse and went through security, we stopped on the stairs outside and held each other. My wife squeezed my hands so hard they trembled and she told me it is no longer up to us, that the decision is in someone else's hands now. We both know that isn't entirely true.

The loudspeaker crackles, and I am struck by an acute wave of nausea. I hear my name. It's my turn now. I wobble as I rise from the bench and a security guard opens the door for me. He nods, but his expression doesn't betray a single thought or emotion. There is no room for that here.

Courtroom 2 is larger than I'd expected. My wife is squeezed in among the audience members. She looks tired, exhausted. There are traces of tears on her cheeks.

An instant later, I see my daughter.

She's pale and thinner than I remember; her hair looks tangled and wispy, and she looks at me with dull eyes. It takes all my strength not to run over and throw my arms around her and whisper that Dad is here, that I'm not going to let go of her until this is all over.

The presiding judge welcomes me, and my immediate impression of him is favorable. He looks alert, yet there is something sensitive about him. He appears to be both sympathetic and authoritative. I don't think the lay judges are likely to oppose his ruling when it comes. What's more, I know he, too, is a father.

Since I'm a close relative of the defendant, I'm not allowed to take the oath. I know the court must hear my testimony in full knowledge that my daughter is the defendant in this case. But I also know that who I am, and not least my occupation, means that the court will consider what I have to say to be trustworthy.

The lead judge gives the defense attorney the floor. I take a deep breath. What I'm about to say will affect so many lives for so many years to come. What I'm about to say might decide everything.

I still haven't decided what I'm going to say.

PART ONE

THE FATHER

A man will be satisfied with good by the fruit of his words,
And the deeds of a man's hands will return to him.

<small>PROVERBS 12:14, NEW AMERICAN STANDARD BIBLE</small>

1

We were a perfectly ordinary family. We had interesting, well-paid jobs and an extensive circle of friends. We kept active in our free time thanks to our interest in sports and culture. On Fridays we ate takeout in front of *Idol* and dozed off on the sofa before the voting was over. On Saturdays we ate lunch downtown or at a shopping center. We watched handball or went to the movies; we enjoyed a bottle of wine with good friends. We fell asleep each night cuddled close together. Sundays were spent in the forest or at a museum, having long talks on the phone with our parents, or curled up on the sofa with a novel. We often rounded off Sunday evenings sitting up in bed with papers, binders, and computers strewn everywhere, preparing for the upcoming workweek. On Monday nights, my wife went to yoga and on Thursdays I played basketball. We had a mortgage, which we dutifully made payments on; we sorted our trash and used our blinkers and kept to the speed limit and always returned library books on time.

This year we took vacation late: early July to mid-August. After several lovely summers in Italy, we had spent the last few years scheduling our international trips in the wintertime so we could spend summers relaxing at home and going on shorter excursions along the coast to visit friends and relatives. This time we also rented a cottage on the island of Orust.

Stella spent just about her whole summer working at H&M. She was saving up for a long trip to Asia this winter. I still hope she manages to go.

You could say that Ulrika and I rediscovered each other this summer. It sounds like such a cliché, almost too cheesy; no one believes it's possible to fall in love with your wife all over again after twenty years. As if the years raising a child were merely an aside in our love story. As if this is what we've been waiting for. But that's how it feels, anyway.

Kids are a full-time job. When they're babies you're waiting for them to become independent, and you spend all your time worrying that they'll choke on something or fall on their face. Then comes preschool and you worry because they're out of your sight, because they might fall off a swing set or fail their next checkup. Then they start school and you worry that they won't fit in, won't make any friends, and everything is homework and riding lessons, handball and pajama parties. They start high school and there are even more friends, parties and conflicts, talks with tutors, all the chauffeuring around. You worry about drugs and drinking, that they'll end up in bad company, and the teenage years go by like a soap opera at 190 kilometers per hour. Then suddenly you're standing there with an adult child and you think you'll finally get to stop worrying.

This summer, at least, we managed several long runs without worrying about Stella. Family life had never seemed so harmonious. Then everything changed.

One Friday in August, Stella turned eighteen—I had booked a table at our favorite restaurant. Italy and Italian cuisine have always been close to our hearts, and there's a little place in the Väster neighborhood that serves divine pasta and pizza. I was looking forward to a quiet, cozy evening with my family.

"*Una tavola per tre,*" I said to a waitress with deer eyes and a pierced nose. "Adam Sandell. I have a reservation for eight o'clock."

She looked around anxiously.

"One second," she said, walking off through the busy restaurant.

Ulrika and Stella turned to me as the waitress fussed at her colleagues, gesturing and making faces.

It turned out that whoever had accepted my reservation had accidentally written it down for Thursday.

"We thought you were coming yesterday," the waitress said, scratching the back of her neck with her pen. "But we'll figure it out. Give us five minutes."

Another party had to get up while the staff dragged an extra table into the dining room. Ulrika, Stella, and I stood in the middle of the crowded restaurant, trying to pretend we didn't notice the annoyed glances shooting our way from every direction. I almost wanted to speak up, point out that it wasn't our fault—it was the restaurant's mistake.

When our table was finally ready, I hurried to hide my face behind my menu.

"Apologies, apologies," said a man with a gray beard, presumably the owner. "We'll make it up to you, of course. Dessert is on the house."

"It's no problem," I assured him. "We're all only human."

The waitress scribbled our drink order on her pad.

"A glass of red wine?" Stella said.

She looked at me for permission. I turned to Ulrika.

"It's a special day," my wife said.

So I nodded at the waitress.

"A glass of red for the birthday girl."

After the meal, Ulrika handed Stella a card with a Josef Frank pattern.

"A map?"

I smiled mischievously.

We followed Stella out of the restaurant and around the corner. I had parked her present there that afternoon.

"But Dad, I told you . . . it's too expensive!"

She brought her hands to her face, gaping.

It was a pink Vespa Piaggio. We'd looked at a similar one online a few weeks earlier and, sure, it was expensive, but in the end I had convinced Ulrika we ought to buy it.

Stella shook her head and sighed.

"Why won't you ever listen to me, Dad?"

I held up one hand and smiled.

"A thank-you will do."

I knew Stella wanted cash most of all, but it felt so boring to give money as a present. With the Vespa she could get downtown easily and quickly, to go to work or visit friends. In Italy, every teenager drives a Vespa.

Stella hugged us and thanked us several times over before we all headed back into the restaurant, but somehow I felt disappointed.

The waitress brought our comped tiramisu and we all agreed that we couldn't eat another bite. And then we ate it all up anyway.

I had *limoncello* with my coffee.

"I have to head out now," Stella said, squirming in her seat.

"Not already?"

I looked at the time. Nine thirty.

Stella pressed her lips together as she continued to rock back and forth on her chair.

"A little while longer," she said. "Like ten minutes."

"It's your birthday," I said. "And the store doesn't open until ten tomorrow, does it?"

Stella sighed.

"I'm not working tomorrow."

She wasn't working? She worked every Saturday. That's how she'd gotten her foot in the door at H&M. A weekend job had turned into a summer job and more hours.

"I had a headache all afternoon," she said evasively. "A migraine."

"So you called in sick?"

Stella nodded. It wasn't a problem at all, she told me. There was another girl who was happy to take shifts.

"That's not how we raised you," I said as Stella stood up and took her jacket from the back of her chair.

"Adam," Ulrika said.

"But why such a hurry?"

Stella shrugged.

"I have plans with Amina."

I nodded and swallowed my displeasure. This was just the way eighteen-year-olds were, I supposed.

Stella gave Ulrika a long, heartfelt hug. I, however, only managed to rise halfway before she put her arms around me and our embrace was awkward and stiff.

"What about the Vespa?" I asked.

Stella looked at Ulrika.

"We'll get it home," my wife promised.

Once Stella was out the door, Ulrika slowly wiped her lips with her napkin and smiled at me.

"Eighteen years," she said. "How does it go so fast?"

———

Ulrika and I were both totally beat when we got home that night. We sat in our respective corners of the sofa and read as Leonard Cohen crooned in the background.

"I still think she could show more appreciation," I said. "Especially after the incident with the car."

The incident with the car—it already had a name.

Ulrika made a sound of disinterest and didn't even look up from her book. Outside, the wind had picked up enough to make the walls creak. Summer was heaving a sigh, taking a breath; August was almost over, but I didn't care. Autumn has always appealed to me, that feeling of a fresh start, like the first phase of new love.

When I put down my novel a little while later, Ulrika was already asleep. I gently lifted her head and placed a pillow underneath. She moved restlessly and for a moment I considered waking her up, but instead I went back to my reading. It wasn't long before the print grew blurry and my thoughts wandered. I drifted off with a great lump in my chest over the chasm that had opened between Stella and me, between the people we once were and the people we had become, between the images I had of us and reality as it looked now.

When I woke up, Stella was standing in the middle of the room. She was shifting back and forth as the gentle moonlight illuminated her head and shoulders.

Ulrika had awakened too and was rubbing her eyes. Soon the room was full of sobs and gasping breaths.

I sat up.

"What's wrong?"

Stella shook her head as the tears ran huge and wet down her cheeks. Ulrika threw her arms around her and when my eyes adjusted to the darkness I realized that Stella was trembling.

"It's nothing," she said.

Then she left the room with her mother and I was left behind with an uneasy feeling of emptiness.

2

We were a perfectly ordinary family, and then everything changed.

It takes a long time to build a life, but only an instant for it to crumble. It takes many years—decades, maybe a lifetime—to become the person you truly are. The path is almost always circuitous, and I think there's a reason for that, for life to be built around trial and error. We are shaped and created by our trials.

But I have trouble understanding the point of what happened to our family this autumn. I know it's impossible to understand everything, and there is a greater purpose to that as well, but I still can't find the deeper meaning in the incidents of the last few weeks. I can't explain it, not to myself and not to anyone else.

Maybe it's the same for everyone, but I imagine that because I'm a pastor I'm held accountable for my view of the world more often. In general, people have no problem calling my philosophy of life into question. They wonder if I truly believe in Adam and Eve and the virgin birth, that Jesus walked on water and brought the dead back to life.

In the beginning of my Christian life, I frequently went on the defensive and began a debate about the questioner's own views. I sometimes argued that science is just one more religion among many. And I certainly had doubts; I found myself wavering in my convictions now and then. These days, however, I am secure in my faith. I have accepted God's blessing and I let His face shine over me. God is love. God is longing and hope. God is my refuge and my comfort.

I like to say I'm a believer, not a knower. If you start to believe you *know*, be wary. I think of life as a state of constant learning.

Like the great majority of us, I consider myself to be a good person. That sounds arrogant, of course, if not self-important or superior. But I don't mean it like that. I'm a person with an abundance of failings, a person who has made innumerable mistakes and errors. I am acutely aware of this, and the first to admit it. What I mean is that I always act with good intentions, out of love and care. I have always wanted to do the right thing.

The week that followed Stella's eighteenth birthday wasn't much different from any other. On Saturday Ulrika and I biked to the home of some good friends on the other side of town. That's one of the advantages with Lund: it's small enough that you can bike from one side of the city to the other in just twenty minutes.

I took the opportunity to ask a cautious question about the previous night's incidents, but Ulrika assured me that Stella wasn't in any trouble, that it was some boy problem, the sort of thing that commonly afflicts eighteen-year-olds. There was no need for me to worry.

On Sunday I spoke on the phone with my parents. When the topic of Stella came up, I mentioned that she was seldom at home these days, at which point Mom reminded me of how I had been as a teenager. It's so easy to lose perspective.

On Monday I had a funeral in the morning and a baptism in the afternoon. It's such a strange job I have, where life and death shake hands in the foyer. In the evening, Ulrika went to yoga and Stella locked herself in her room.

On Wednesday I officiated a lovely marriage ceremony for an older couple in our congregation who had gotten to know each other as they grieved their former life partners. A moment that truly touched my heart.

On Thursday I twisted my ankle playing basketball. My old friend from handball, Anders, now a fireman and father of four boys, accidentally stepped on my foot. Despite the injury, I managed to remain on the court for the whole game.

When I biked to work on Friday morning, I was tired. After lunch I buried a man who had only made it to forty-two. Cancer, of course. I never get used to the fact that people younger than I am can die. His daughter had written a farewell poem but couldn't get through it, with all her tears. I found it impossible to keep from thinking of Stella.

On Friday evening I felt unusually worn down after a long week. I stood at the window and watched the end of August sink into the horizon. The solemnity of autumn had a foot through the door. The last of the grill smoke vanished up over the rooftops in curling columns and patio furniture was emptied of cushions.

At last I took off my clerical collar and I wiped my sweaty neck. When I leaned against the windowsill, I accidentally knocked our family photo to the floor.

A crack appeared across the glass, but I put the photo back anyway. In the picture, which is at least a decade old, I have a healthy glow and something playful about my eyes. I recalled that we laughed just before the photographer snapped the picture. Ulrika is smiling with her mouth open, and in front of us is Stella, with rosy cheeks, braided hair, and a Mickey Mouse shirt. I stood at the window for a long time, gazing at the photograph as the memories swelled in my throat.

After a shower, I made a casserole with pork tenderloin and chorizo. Ulrika had bought new earrings, small silver feathers, and we shared a bottle of South African wine with our meal, then rounded out the evening with pretzel sticks and a game of Trivial Pursuit on the sofa.

"Do you know where Stella is?" I asked as I undressed in the bedroom. Ulrika had already crawled under the covers and drawn the blankets to her chin.

"She was going to see Amina. She wasn't sure if she would be coming home."

This last bit slipped out of her like a minor detail, although Ulrika knows exactly what I think about hearing that our daughter *might* come home on a given night.

I looked at the clock; it was quarter past eleven.

"She'll get here when she gets here," Ulrika said.

I glared at her. Sometimes I think she says things just to provoke me.

"I'll text her," I said.

So I wrote to Stella and asked if she was planning to sleep at home. Naturally, I didn't receive a response.

With a heavy sigh, I got in bed. Ulrika immediately rolled over onto my side and slipped a hand onto my hip. She kissed my neck as I stared at the ceiling.

I know I shouldn't worry. I was never the neurotic type when I was young. The anxiety crept up on me when I had a child, and it only seems to increase with each passing year.

With an eighteen-year-old daughter you have two options: either you drown under the constant worry or you refuse to think about all the risks she seems to love taking. It's simply a question of self-preservation.

Soon Ulrika was asleep on my arm. Her warm breath rolled over my cheek like gentle waves. Now and then she gave a start, a quick, electric movement, but soon sleep enfolded her again.

I really did try to sleep, but my head was occupied with thoughts. My exhaustion had given way to a state of manic brain activity. I thought of all the dreams I'd had throughout the years, many of which had changed and others of which I still hoped to fulfill. And then I thought about Stella's dreams and was forced to accept a painful truth—I didn't know what my daughter wanted from her life. She stubbornly claims that *she* doesn't even know. No plans, no structure. So unlike me. When I finished high school I had a very clear image of how my life would take shape.

I know I can't influence Stella. She's eighteen and makes her own decisions. Ulrika once said that love is letting go, letting the person you love fly away, but it often feels as if Stella is just flapping her wings without taking off. I had imagined something different.

No matter how tired I was, I couldn't fall asleep. I rolled onto my side and checked my phone. I had received a response from Stella.

On my way home now.

It was five minutes to two when I heard the key in the lock. Ulrika had moved to the very edge of her side of the bed and was facing away from me. I heard Stella padding around downstairs: water running in the bathroom, quick steps into the laundry room, more water running. It felt like an eternity.

At last I heard her footsteps creaking on the stairs. Ulrika gave a start. I bent over to look at her, but it seemed she was still asleep.

I was beset with mixed feelings. On the one hand, I was annoyed that

Stella had let me worry; on the other, I was relieved that she had finally returned home.

I got out of bed and opened the bedroom door just as Stella went by in only her underwear, her hair a wet tangle at her nape. Her back was a glowing streak in the dim light as she opened the door to her room.

"Stella?" I said.

Without responding, she slipped through the door and locked it behind her.

"Good night," I heard from the other side.

"Sleep tight," I whispered.

My little girl was home.

3

On Saturday morning I slept late. Ulrika was sitting at the breakfast table in her robe and listening to a podcast.

"Morning!"

She pulled her headphones down to hang around her neck.

Although I'd slept in later than usual, I still felt disoriented and spilled some coffee on the morning paper.

"Where's Stella?"

"At work," said Ulrika. "She was already gone when I woke up."

I tried to dry off the paper with a dishrag.

"She must be exhausted," I said. "She was out half the night."

Ulrika aimed a smile at me.

"You're not looking particularly energetic yourself."

What did she mean by that? She knew I couldn't sleep when Stella wasn't home.

We were invited to a late lunch at the home of our friends Dino and Alexandra on Trollebergsvägen. A late lunch meant alcoholic beverages, so we biked into town. As we reached the Ball House sports center I spotted a police car; fifty meters on, at the roundabout next to Polhem School, were two more. One had its flashing lights on. Three officers were walking briskly up Rådmansgatan.

"Wonder what's going on," I said to Ulrika.

We parked our bikes in the courtyard and took the stairs up to the apartment. Alexandra and Dino met us in the hall, where we got past the pleasantries. It had been a long time. How were things?

"Isn't Amina home?" Ulrika asked.

Alexandra hesitated.

"She was supposed to have a match, but she's not feeling very well."

"I don't understand what it could be," Dino said. "I can't recall her ever missing a handball match."

"It's probably just a regular old cold," Alexandra said.

Dino made a face. I was probably the only one who noticed.

"As long as she's healthy again by the time school starts," Ulrika said.

"Right, she wouldn't miss that even if she has a fever of a hundred and four," Alexandra said.

Ulrika laughed.

"She's going to make a fantastic doctor. I don't know anyone as diligent and thorough as Amina."

Dino puffed up like a peacock.

He had every right to be proud.

"So how's Stella?" he asked.

It was a perfectly reasonable question, of course. But I think we hesitated to respond for a moment too long.

"Just fine," I said at last.

Ulrika smiled in agreement. Perhaps that answer wasn't far from the truth after all. Our daughter had been in a good mood that summer.

We sat on the glassed-in balcony and enjoyed Dino's pitas and mini pierogis.

"Did you hear about the murder?" Alexandra asked.

"The murder?"

"Right here, by the Polhem school. They found a body there this morning."

"The police," Ulrika said. "That's why—"

She was interrupted by the squeak of the balcony door. Behind us, Amina peered through the crack, her eyes glassy, washed out and colorless, a shadow.

"Oh sweetie, you look awful," Ulrika said, with no tact whatsoever.

"I know," Amina croaked; she seemed to be clinging to the balcony door to keep from falling over.

"Go back to bed."

"I suppose it's only a matter of time before Stella comes down with the same bug," I said. "Because you two were hanging out last night, weren't you?"

Amina's expression froze. It only took half a second, maybe tenths of a second, but Amina's expression froze and I knew immediately what that meant.

"Right." Amina coughed. "Hope she's okay."

"Now get back to bed," said Ulrika.

Amina pulled the door closed and dragged herself back to the living room. Lying is an art that few people fully master.

4

If it weren't for our daughters, Ulrika and I probably never would have become friends with Alexandra and Dino.

Amina and Stella were six when they ended up on the same handball team. Most of their teammates were a year older, but it wasn't very noticeable. Both Amina and Stella showed a winner's instinct early on. They were strong, stubborn, and unstoppable. Amina, in contrast with Stella, also had an unusually gifted sense for executing planned strategies and plays.

During those first practices, Ulrika and I sat on the bleachers in the sweaty gym and watched our little girl run herself absolutely ragged. We had seldom seen her so free and happy as she was on the handball court. Dino was single-handedly coaching the girls' team; he was extremely engaged, passionate, and generous, and gave the little handball players lots of love. But there was one problem: his body language. He displayed explosive joy through gestures and expressions when one of the girls succeeded on the court, but he was equally free when expressing his distress if something went wrong. Naturally, this was a matter of concern to Ulrika and me, and we discussed it after every practice. I suggested we talk to the other parents or perhaps go to the club council. We really liked Dino as a coach. Maybe he was simply unaware of how his body language could be interpreted.

"It's better to talk to him personally," Ulrika said, and after the next practice she walked up to Dino, who, rumor had it, had once played handball on a pretty high level himself.

I hovered in the background as Dino listened to Ulrika. Then he said, "You seem to have a knack for this. Would you like to be my colleague?"

Ulrika was so taken aback that she couldn't respond. When she finally managed to speak, she pointed in my direction and said that I was the one who actually knew anything about handball and would make an excellent assistant coach for him.

"Okay," Dino said, looking at me. "The job is yours."

The rest, as they say, is history. We led that team to win after win, traveled around half of Europe, and brought home so many trophies and medals that there wasn't room for them all in Stella's bookcase.

Amina and Stella were quickly compatible on the court. With finesse and cleverness, Amina got the ball to Stella, who tore herself free from the line without ever yielding until the ball was in the goal. But that winner's instinct had its downsides. Stella was only eight when things went off the rails for the first time. During a match at Fäladshallen, she received a pass from Amina, smooth as butter, and found herself alone with the goalie but missed the breakaway. Quick as a wink, she caught the ball as it bounced back and threw it full force at the goalie's face from three meters off.

Chaos ensued, of course. The coach and parents of the opposing team rushed the court and fell upon Stella and me.

She didn't mean to. Stella never aimed her rage at anyone but herself. Upset by the missed goal, she had simply reacted impulsively. She was full of regret to the point of being crushed.

"I'm sorry, I wasn't thinking."

This became a recurring phrase. Almost a mantra.

Dino liked to say that Stella was her own worst enemy. If only she could conquer herself, there would be no stopping her.

It was just that she found it so darned difficult to control her emotions.

Aside from that, it was easy to like Stella. She was thoughtful and had a strong sense of justice; she was energetic and outgoing.

Amina and Stella soon lived in close symbiosis even off the handball court. They were in the same class, bought similar clothes, listened to the same music. And Amina was a good influence on Stella. She was charming and quick, caring and ambitious. When Stella began to slip, Amina was always there to get her back into balance.

I only wish Ulrika and I had taken Stella's problems more seriously. That we had reacted earlier. I'm ashamed to admit it, but apparently our greatest hurdle was our pride. Ulrika and I both considered it a radical failure to turn to the institutions of society. It may seem egotistical, but at the same time it's very human, and it might not have been entirely misguided. We had demanded a lot of ourselves, to be the best parents we could be, but we were unable to live up to our own requirements.

Perhaps it never would have had to go as far as it did.

5

When we biked home from Alexandra and Dino's, the police cars were still at the school. It was frightening, that something like this could happen so close by. Apparently the body had been found at a playground by an early-bird mom who'd brought her small children to play. I shuddered at the thought.

Ulrika hopped off her bike in the driveway and hurried for the door.

"Aren't you going to lock it up?" I called.

"Have to pee," she mumbled, digging through her purse for her keys.

I led her bike across the paved path and parked it next to my own under the metal roof. I realized I had forgotten to cover the grill and found the protective casing in the shed.

When I came inside, Ulrika was standing on the stairs.

"Stella's still not home. I called, but she won't pick up."

"I'm sure she's working late," I said. "You know they're not allowed to have their phones on them."

"But it's Saturday. The store closed hours ago."

That hadn't occurred to me.

"I'm sure she just went somewhere with a friend. We'll have another talk with her tonight. She needs to get better at keeping us in the loop."

I put my arm around Ulrika.

"I got such a terrible feeling," she said. "When we saw all those police. A murder? Here?"

"I know. It makes me feel uneasy too."

We sat down on the sofa and I looked up the latest news on my phone, reading it aloud to her.

The victim was a man in his thirties, a local. The police were being very secretive about the incident, but one of the evening papers said that a woman who lived nearby had heard fighting and shouting outside her window during the night.

"This kind of thing doesn't happen to just anyone," I said, as if I, and not Ulrika, were the expert. "I'm sure it's alcoholics or drug addicts. Or gang crime."

Ulrika breathed calmly against my shoulder.

But I wasn't saying this to relieve her anxiety. I was convinced it was true.

"I was planning to make carbonara."

I stood up and kissed her cheek.

"Already? I don't think I could manage to eat as much as a piece of arugula right now."

"Slow food," I smiled. "Real food takes time, honey."

As the bacon sizzled in my carefully selected olive oil from Campania, Ulrika came thundering down the stairs.

"Stella forgot her phone."

"What?"

She paced restlessly back and forth between the kitchen island and the window.

"It was on her desk."

"Well, that's odd." The carbonara was at such a critical stage that I couldn't look away from it. "Did she forget it?"

"Yes, didn't you hear me? It was on her desk!"

Ulrika was nearly shouting.

It was certainly unusual for Stella to leave her phone at home, but there was no reason to overreact. I stirred the carbonara swiftly as I turned down the heat.

"Forget the pasta," Ulrika said, tugging at my arm. "I'm seriously worried. I just called Amina, but she isn't answering either."

"She's sick," I said, just as I realized the carbonara was going to be a failure.

I slammed the wooden spoon down on the counter and yanked the pan from the burner.

"Maybe she left her phone at home on purpose," I said, battling whatever was bubbling up in my chest. "You know her boss has been getting after her about it."

Ulrika shook her head.

"Her boss hasn't been getting after her. She gave the whole staff a warning about using their cell phones at work. Surely you don't believe Stella would voluntarily leave her phone at home?"

No, of course that didn't sound likely.

"She must have forgotten it. I'm sure she was in a hurry this morning."

"I'll call around to her friends," Ulrika said. "This isn't like her."

"Shouldn't you hold off on that?"

I rambled on, something about how we'd been spoiled by modern technology and constant access to our daughter, always knowing where she was. There was really no reason to get all worked up.

"I'm sure she'll come flying through the door any moment."

At the same time, I started to have a nagging feeling in my stomach. Being a parent means never being able to relax.

When Ulrika padded up the creaking stairs, I took the opportunity to slip into the laundry room.

There I was. Surely it wasn't just a coincidence? I opened the door of the washing machine and pulled out the damp clothes. A pair of dark jeans that I had to turn right side out to confirm that they belonged to Stella. A black tank top that was also hers. And the white blouse with flowers on the breast pocket. Her favorite top that summer. I was holding the blouse in one hand and fumbling for a hanger. That's when I saw it.

Stella's favorite top. The right sleeve and front were covered in dark stains.

I looked up at the ceiling and said a silent prayer. At the same time, I knew God didn't have a thing to do with this.

6

Throughout the years I have frequently encountered the false assumption that a belief in determinism is simply a natural by-product of my belief in God, as if I must consider my free will to be limited by God. Of course, nothing could be further from the truth. I believe man to be the living image of God. I believe in man.

Sometimes when I meet people who say they don't believe in God, I ask which god it is they don't believe in. They often proceed to describe a god I certainly don't believe in either.

God is love. It's wonderful to find someone you belong with. It might be God, it might be another human being. It might even be both.

Ulrika and I were young when we met and since then there has been no other alternative. We were both new to Lund. Thanks to my powerful but naïve dream of becoming an actor, I joined the skit group at the Wermlands student union, and Ulrika moved into the union's student apartments later that winter. She was the type of person who attracts attention without taking up too much space, who shines without being blinding.

As I fought to chip away at my Blekinge accent and rid my skin of pimples, Ulrika sailed into every imaginable university scenario as if she clearly belonged in each one. I plastered the city with posters that read *No EC, No Bridge* while Ulrika became procurator of the student union and aced all her law exams.

Late that year, when we found ourselves attending the same corridor party, I finally got up my nerve. To my surprise, Ulrika seemed to enjoy my company. Soon we were spending all our time together.

"I can't believe you're going to be a pastor," Ulrika said on that first eve-ning. "You could be a psychologist or a political scientist or . . ."

"Or a pastor."

"But why?" Ulrika eyed me as if I were begging to have a healthy limb amputated. "You're from Småland, huh? It's in your blood?"

"Blekinge." I laughed. "And my parents have very little to do with it. Aside from the fact that they sent me to Sunday school, of course, but I think that was mostly just for the free babysitting."

"So you weren't brought up a Christian?"

I laughed.

"I was actually a die-hard atheist until I started high school. I was a mem-ber of Revolutionary Communist Youth for a while; I went around quoting Marx and wanted to rid the world of religion. But you grow out of all that dogmatic stuff. In time I grew more and more curious about different out-looks on life."

I liked the way Ulrika was observing me as if I were a riddle she wanted to solve.

"Then something happened," I said. "In my last year of high school."

"What?"

"I was on my way home from the library when I heard a woman scream-ing. She was by the edge of the harbor, jumping up and down, waving her arms. I ran over."

Ulrika leaned forward. Her eyes widened.

"Her daughter had fallen into the cold water. There were two more children. They were on the quay, screaming. I didn't have time to think. I just threw myself into the water."

Ulrika gasped, but I shook my head. I wasn't telling her this to portray myself as some sort of hero.

"Something happened just then. The second I hit the water. I didn't quite understand what, at the time, but I know now. It was God. I felt Him."

Ulrika nodded thoughtfully.

"It was like a bright light came on in the dark water. I saw the little girl and got hold of her. My body filled with strength—I've never felt so strong, so determined, nothing could stop me from saving that child. It was almost effortless. Something supernatural pulled the girl up over the edge, made me blow life back into her. The mom and the little sisters were standing next to me, screaming, as water poured from the girl's mouth and she came to. At the same time, God left my body and I returned to my regular self."

Ulrika blinked a few times, her mouth open.

"So she made it?"

"Everything turned out okay."

"Incredible," she said, giving me her amazing smile. "And ever since, you've known?"

"I don't know anything," I said firmly. "But I believe."

7

On that Saturday night when our lives were about to change, I turned to God. I was worried about the stained blouse in the washing machine. I made the snap decision not to mention it to Ulrika. Those stains could be from anything, it didn't necessarily mean much, and there was no reason to subject Ulrika to further anxiety. Instead I closed my eyes and prayed to God, asking Him to take care of my little girl.

I was leaning against the kitchen island and swirling a glass of amber-colored whiskey in my hand when Ulrika came bounding down the stairs.

"I just talked to Alexandra," she said, out of breath. "She woke Amina. Apparently she was shocked to hear that Stella never came home."

"What did she say?"

"She doesn't seem to know anything."

I swallowed all the whiskey.

"Should we call her colleagues at H&M?" I asked.

Ulrika placed Stella's phone on the counter.

"I already tried. She only has Benita's number saved, and Benita didn't know who was working today."

I sighed and muttered. My anxiety was mixed with irritation. Wasn't Stella aware of what she put us through? How we worried about her?

When the phone began to jump on the counter, both Ulrika and I lunged for it. I was faster, and hit the green button.

"Yes?"

I was met with a deep, slightly guarded male voice.

"I'm calling about the Vespa."

"The Vespa?"

My head was spinning.

"The Vespa that's for sale," the man said.

"There's no Vespa for sale here. You must have the wrong number."

He apologized but insisted that he hadn't misdialed. There was an ad on-line with this number, and a Vespa for sale. A pink Piaggio.

I grunted something about a mistake and hung up.

"Who was that?"

Ulrika sounded eager.

"She's planning to sell the Vespa."

"What?"

"Stella put out an ad."

We sat on the sofa. Ulrika sent a group text asking anyone with any information about Stella to text back. I poured another whiskey and Ulrika put Stella's iPhone on the table in front of us. We sat there staring at it, and every time it buzzed we bounced up. Time stood still as Ulrika scrolled with her thumb.

A few of Stella's friends texted back; some seemed mildly worried, but most of them stopped at stating they knew nothing.

When I googled Stella's phone number, I found the ad straightaway. She really had put the Vespa up for sale. Her birthday present. What was she up to?

"Should I take my bike and go looking for her?"

Ulrika wrinkled her nose.

"Isn't it best to stay here?"

"This must never happen again. Doesn't she understand how much we worry?"

Ulrika was close to tears.

"Should we call the police?" she said.

"The police?"

That seemed excessive. Surely it couldn't be that bad.

"I have some contacts," Ulrika said. "They could at least keep their eyes peeled."

"This is ridiculous!" I stood up. "That we should even have to . . . I'm so . . ."

"Shhh!" Ulrika said, one finger in the air. "Do you hear that?"

"What?"

"Ringing."

I stood stock still, watching her. Both of us were sick with worry. Soon a long signal echoed through the house.

"The landline?" Ulrika said, standing up.

No one ever calls the landline.

8

We never planned to have Stella. She was a wanted, welcome baby; eagerly awaited and beloved long before she took her first breath. But she wasn't planned.

Ulrika had just received her Master of Law degree and was about to start a clerkship when, one evening, she sat down across from me, placed her hands over mine, and looked deep into my eyes. Her smile was restrained as she shared with me the fantastic but overwhelming news.

I had one year left in my education and another year as a curate after that. We lived in a one-room apartment in Norra Fäladen and survived on loans; our situation was far from optimal for bringing a child into the world. I realized, of course, that Ulrika had doubts; there was an anxious hesitation behind that initial, effervescent joy, but a whole week passed before either of us even said the word "abortion" aloud.

Ulrika was rightly worried about practicalities. Money, housing, our education, and careers. We could always wait a few years to start a family; there was no reason to rush into it.

"With love, we can do anything," I said, bringing my lips to her belly.

Ulrika made some financial calculations; meanwhile, I bought tiny socks that said "My Dad Rocks."

"You're not antiabortion, are you?" she'd asked even during those first intoxicating days of our love, five years earlier, when we'd hardly left the student apartment at Wermlands Nation.

"Absolutely not," I responded.

I'm certain my belief in God filled her with doubt and fear. It was easily the greatest threat to our budding, fragile relationship.

"I never dreamed of a pastor," she said on occasion. Not to hurt me, not at all. It was just an ironic comment on the mysterious ways of the Lord.

"That's okay," I would reply. "I never dreamed of a lawyer."

Not once did I seriously consider not having the baby. At the same time, I inserted doubt in my conversations with Ulrika, to seem open to all options. It didn't take long, though, before we were united in our decision.

Before the birth we took classes and practiced breathing together. Ulrika had morning sickness and I massaged her swollen feet.

With one week left before her due date, Ulrika woke me at four in the morning. She was standing at the foot of the bed, wrapped in a blanket.

"Adam! Adam! My water broke!"

We took a taxi to the hospital and it was like I didn't understand what was happening, how much was at stake and how much could go wrong, until Ulrika was lying on a stretcher in front of me and writhing in pain while the midwife snapped on her long rubber gloves. It was as if I had gathered all my fears and anxieties into a hiding spot deep inside, and it had all been released, all at once.

"You have to do something!"

"Let's have a sit, Dad," a nurse said.

"Take it easy," said the midwife. "Everything is going to be fine."

Ulrika was hyperventilating and swearing. As soon as a new contraction hit, she pressed herself upward, screaming and flailing.

I held Ulrika's hand tight. It was relentless; her whole body was shaking.

"We have to get the baby out now," the midwife said.

"You can do this, honey," I said and kissed Ulrika's hand.

She stiffened and her body tensed like a spring. The room grew perfectly silent and I could almost feel the wave of pain that crashed through her body. Ulrika thrust her pelvis in the air.

"Help me, dear God!"

And the midwife yanked and tugged and Ulrika roared in long, primal jolts. I held her tight and swore to God that I would never forgive Him if this didn't end well.

Silence fell over us like a blanket. You could have heard God snap His fingers in that moment. The longest second of my life. Everything that meant anything seemed to hang in the balance. My mind was devoid of thought, but I still knew this was the instant when it would all come to a head. In the silence.

Then, as I peeked out, I saw it. A bloody, blue clump on a towel. At first I didn't understand what it was. A moment later, the room was filled with the most beautiful infant's cry I had ever heard.

9

Stella's face flickered through my mind as I rushed into the kitchen after Ulrika. Although our little girl was eighteen now, the face I always pictured was that of a child.

Ulrika grabbed the landline phone from the wall. Not once during the call did I take my eyes off her.

"That was Michael Blomberg," she said after she'd hung up.

"Who? The lawyer?"

"He has just been appointed to represent Stella. She's with the police."

My first thought was that Stella had been the victim of a crime. Hopefully it wasn't anything serious. I even had time to think that it was okay if she'd been robbed or assaulted. Anything but rape.

"We have to go, right away," Ulrika said.

"What's going on?" I thought about the peculiar call and the ad online. "Is it the Vespa?"

Ulrika looked at me like I was nuts.

"Forget about the damn Vespa!"

On her way to the door she ran into my shoulder.

"What did Blomberg say?" I asked, but she didn't respond.

Ulrika snagged her coat from the rack and was headed for the door when she suddenly wheeled around.

"I just have to do one thing," she said, walking back into the house.

"Come on, what did Blomberg say?"

I trailed her through the kitchen. As she reached the doorway she turned around and fended me off, her arms straight out.

"Wait here. I'll be right back!"

Taken aback, I stood in the doorway, counting the seconds. Soon Ulrika returned and shoved past me.

"What did you do?"

Once again I saw Stella's face before me. The toothless laugh, the little dimples in her soft cheeks. And I thought about everything I'd wanted for her that had never come to be.

It's so easy to believe that the best is always yet to come. I suspect that's a deeply human fault. Even God instructs us to yearn.

Why don't we ever think about how quickly time passes, while it is passing?

Stella's first word was "abba." She used it for both me and Ulrika. These days, most Swedes associate the word with pop music, but in Jesus's language, Aramaic, it means "father."

I had four lovely autumn months of paternity leave with Stella, and I watched her personality emerge day by day. The other parents at our congregation's children's group often remarked that she was the very definition of a daddy's girl. I don't think I understood the significance of this until it was too late. To some extent, my whole life has been one big *esprit d'escalier*. I haven't managed to capture a single moment. I've always had terrible timing.

I am doomed to yearn.

10

We were standing in the entryway. My hand on the lock. Ulrika's whole body was shaking.

Why had Michael Blomberg called? What was Stella doing at the police station?

"Tell me," I said to Ulrika.

"All I know is what Michael said."

Michael Blomberg. It had been several years since I'd heard his name. Blomberg was well-known in more than just legal circles. He had made a career as one of the country's foremost defense attorneys and had represented defendants in a great many high-profile cases. His picture had been in the evening papers and he was called upon as an expert on TV. He was also the man who had once taken Ulrika under his wing and paved the way for her success as a defense attorney.

Ulrika was breathing hard. Her eyes were darting like frightened birds.

She tried to squeeze past me and out the door, but I caught her, held her in place between my arms.

"Stella is in police custody."

I heard what she said, the words reached me, but they were impossible to comprehend.

"There must be some mistake," I said.

Ulrika shook her head. A moment later, she collapsed against my chest and her phone crashed to the floor.

"She's suspected of murder," Ulrika whispered.

I stiffened.

The first thing I thought of was Stella's stained top.

———————

Ulrika called a taxi as we hurried to the street. Outside the recycling station she dropped my hand.

"Hold on," she said, stumbling in among the recycling bins and containers.

I stayed put on the sidewalk and heard her coughing and throwing up. Soon a black taxi appeared.

"How are you feeling?" I whispered as we put on our seatbelts in the back.

"Like shit," Ulrika said, coughing into her hand.

Then she typed on her phone with both thumbs as I rolled down the window and bathed my face in the fresh air.

"Can you go a little faster?" Ulrika asked the driver, who grumbled a little before stepping on the gas.

My mind turned to Job. Was this my trial?

Ulrika explained that Michael Blomberg was waiting for us at the police station.

"Why him?" I asked. "Isn't that an awfully big coincidence?"

"He's an extraordinarily talented attorney."

"Sure, but what are the chances?"

"Sometimes things just happen, honey. You can't control everything."

I don't want to say I disliked Blomberg. I don't like speaking badly of others that way. Experience tells me that when you dislike someone on such vague grounds, the problem often rests with you.

I tipped the driver and then had to jog up the stairs to the police station, where Ulrika was already pulling open the door.

Blomberg met us in the lobby. I'd almost forgotten what a big man he is. He came lumbering over to us like a bear, his jacket flapping around his stomach. He was tanned and wearing a blue shirt and an expensive suit, and his slicked-back hair curled at the back of his neck.

"Ulrika," he said, but he stepped right up to me and shook my hand before he embraced my wife.

"What's going on, Michael?"

"Take it easy," he said. "We just concluded the interrogation and this nightmare will be over soon. The police have come to an extremely hasty conclusion."

Ulrika sighed heavily.

"Stella was identified by a young woman," Blomberg said.

"Identified?"

"Perhaps you heard that a body was found on a playground over by Pilegatan?"

"And Stella was supposedly there? On Pilegatan?" I said. "There must be some mistake."

"That's exactly what it is. But this girl lives in the same building as the man who was murdered and claims to have seen Stella there last night. She thinks she recognizes Stella from H&M. That seems to be all the investigators have."

"That's ridiculous. Can she really be in custody on such flimsy grounds?"

I thought back to the night before and tried to remember the details. How I had lain awake, unable to sleep, waiting for her; how Stella finally came home and showered before slipping into her room.

"Is she detained?" Ulrika asked.

"What's the difference?" I asked.

"The police have the right to take someone into custody, but in order to keep them there a prosecutor must order detention," Blomberg said. "The lead interrogator just has to brief the prosecutor on duty and then Stella will be released. I assure you. This is all a mistake."

He sounded far too confident, just as I remembered him, and that worried me. Anyone so free of doubt is certain to lack attention to detail and engagement as well.

"But why such a rush to bring her in?" I asked. "If they don't have anything else to go on?"

"This case is a real hot potato." Blomberg sighed. "The police want to act quickly. The fact is, the victim isn't just anyone."

He turned to Ulrika and lowered his voice a notch.

"It's Christopher Olsen. Margaretha's son."

Ulrika gasped.

"Mar . . . Margaretha's son?"

"Who's Margaretha?" I asked.

Ulrika didn't even look at me.

"The dead man is named Christopher Olsen," Blomberg said. "His mother is Margaretha Olsen, a professor of criminal law."

A professor? I shrugged.

"What does that have to do with anything?"

"Margaretha is very well-known in legal circles," Blomberg said. "Her son has also made a name for himself in a number of circles. A successful businessman, he owns real estate; he sits on lots of boards."

"Why would that matter?" I said, my irritation mounting.

At the same time, I recalled my own words, that this sort of thing only happens to alcoholics and drug addicts. That had certainly been an assumption full of prejudice, but it was also based on empirical evidence and statistics. Sometimes you have to close your eyes to the exceptions to keep from going under.

"Maybe it shouldn't matter," said Blomberg. Reading between the lines, it was clear that it *did* matter, and that he wasn't sure there was anything wrong with that fact.

"Margaretha Olsen's son," Ulrika said. "How old is . . . was he?"

"Thirty-two, I think. Or thirty-three. Deadly force with a bladed weapon. The police are being very tight-lipped with the details. During the interrogation, they were mostly interested in Stella's whereabouts yesterday evening and last night."

Yesterday evening and last night?

"When was this man murdered?" Ulrika asked.

"They're not sure, but the witness heard arguing and shouting just after one o'clock. Were you awake when Stella got home?"

Ulrika turned to me and I nodded.

There I'd been, tossing and turning, unable to fall asleep. The text I'd sent, without receiving a reply. So my worry hadn't been unfounded. I thought of how Stella had come home and clattered around in the bathroom and laundry room. What time had it been?

"There must be someone who can give her an alibi," I said.

Both Ulrika and Blomberg looked at me.

11

Michael Blomberg offered to give us a ride home. The late-summer evening was offering up short-sleeve weather and people were strolling around the streets of Lund as if nothing had happened. Dogwalkers and party people; people on their way out or home or nowhere at all; night-shift workers and insomniacs. Everyday life wasn't about to stop just because our lives had been knocked off balance.

As we pulled up at our house, Blomberg wondered if there was anything else he could do. He said it would be no trouble for him to stick around for a while.

"There's no need," I assured him.

Ulrika remained standing in the driveway for a moment to talk to him as I hurried into the bathroom. My whole body felt warm and my mouth was dry as sawdust. I drank straight from the faucet and sponged my forehead with water.

It was way past midnight when I went to the kitchen to find Ulrika sitting with her head in her hands. Despite the hour and my protests, she was soon calling around to every contact she had with the police, some journalists, and lawyers, anyone who might know something or be able to help. I sat across from her, scouring the internet for information about the incident on Pilegatan, about Christopher Olsen and his professor mother.

Time and again I looked at the clock. The minutes were dragging by.

Once a whole hour had passed, I could no longer sit still.

"Why aren't we getting any answers? How long could this take?"

"I'll call Michael," Ulrika said, standing up.

There was a creak on the stairs and I heard her closing the door to her office. I brooded, my thoughts gnawing at my brain, all the creepy-crawlies of anxiety under my skin.

I walked aimlessly through the kitchen, out to the entryway, and back again. I was holding the phone in my hand when it rang.

"It's Amina."

She sobbed and cleared her throat.

"Amina? Is something wrong?"

"I'm sorry," she said. "I lied."

Just as I'd suspected. She hadn't seen Stella on Friday after all. They had talked about hanging out, but it never happened.

"I didn't know what to say when you asked," she said. "I lied, but only for Stella. I thought maybe something . . . I wanted to check with her first."

I understood. There was no reason to get upset with her. It was a white lie.

"But there must be someone else who can give her an alibi," Amina was desperate to add. "This is totally insane!"

It truly was surreal. At the same time, it was becoming more and more clear that this was reality. I pictured Stella locked up in the cold, squalid cell where they put murderers and rapists.

Ulrika came down the stairs at a jog.

"The prosecutor has given the order to remand Stella," she said.

"Remand her?"

My heart was pounding. I broke out in a sweat.

"They're holding her in jail."

"How is that possible? There's no evidence!"

"It may have to do with the investigation. Things the police want to check up on before she is released."

"Like an alibi?"

"For one."

I didn't know what we should do. My body was in an uproar. I could only manage to sit down for short periods, then I had to get up and move around. I walked through the house like a zombie, all around the house in my stocking feet.

As the sun sent its first tentative rays across the eastern horizon, we still knew nothing. The lack of sleep had made my brain fuzzy.

At last Blomberg called. I stood across from Ulrika in the kitchen and held my breath.

Her answers were brief and mumbling. She stood there with the phone pressed to her ear even after the call had ended.

"What did he say?" I asked.

Ulrika was looking at me and yet her gaze was elsewhere.

"We have to leave the house."

Her voice was thin as a spider's silk, about to break.

"What? What's going on?"

"The police are on their way. They're going to search the house."

My thoughts went immediately to the stained blouse. It couldn't be blood, surely? Of course there would be a sensible explanation. It must be as Blomberg had said, rash decisions and misunderstandings.

Stella could never . . . or could she?

I stole into the laundry room and lifted the pile of clothes I'd shoved the top under. My hands stiffened.

It was gone.

"What are you doing?" Ulrika said from the kitchen. "We have to get going."

I desperately dug through the other piles of clothing but didn't find a thing. The clotheslines were empty. The top was gone.

"Come on!" Ulrika called.

12

The future was always bright, but in a glistening, almost blinding way, like the winter sun through billowing mist. There was no worry, even if our paths weren't yet laid out before us. I recall tiny Stella, with baby teeth and pigtails.

And then I recall a very uncomfortable parent-teacher conference at preschool when Stella was five.

The teacher, whose name was Ingrid, first reported on all the activities, crafts, and educational games they had done during the autumn and winter. Then she took a deep breath, paged through her papers at random, and seemed unsure of where to focus her gaze.

"A few parents and children have approached us with concerns," she said without looking at us. "At times Stella can be quite dominant and she gets . . . angry. If things don't go her way."

This sounded familiar, of course, although I suppose we had been hoping it wasn't as obvious at preschool as it was at home. I immediately felt both embarrassed and defensive when I learned that other parents had aired opinions about my daughter.

"I'm sure it isn't that bad? She's only five."

Ingrid nodded.

"A few parents have brought it up with the school director," she said. "It's important for Stella to receive help for this, both at school and at home."

"What? Who are those parents?" Ulrika said.

"Could you give us an example?" I asked. "What is it that Stella does wrong?"

Ingrid paged through her documents.

"Well, in role-playing games, when the children play pretend, Stella very much wants to control the others."

Ulrika shrugged.

"Isn't it sometimes good that someone takes on the role of leader?"

"We know Stella can sometimes seem domineering," I said. "The question is how much we should try to stifle it. As Ulrika said, leadership qualities can be a very good thing—that she's direct, a driving force."

Ingrid scratched intensely at her right eyebrow.

"Last week, Stella said she was like God. The other children had to obey her, because she was like God and God is in charge of everything."

I felt Ulrika's eyes boring into me from the side. Stella had spent quite a bit of time at church with me; she had shown interest in my work and was already asking existential questions, but I would never dream of providing her with neatly packaged solutions or clear-cut answers. Furthermore, I would never touch upon God's omnipotence even in my daughter's absence.

"We'll talk to Stella," I said curtly.

In the car on the way home, Ulrika pointedly turned off the radio, one finger poking at the panel on the dashboard.

"It's crazy, the opinions people have about other people's children."

"It's nothing to worry about," I said, turning the music back on. "She's only five."

I had no idea how quickly time would pass.

13

On Sunday afternoon I was sitting in a spartan interrogation room at the police station, waiting to be questioned. I was given strong coffee in a mug; the minutes passed slowly, painfully, and my skin felt itchy.

The chief inspector finally arrived; her name was Agnes Thelin and she was wearing a conciliatory expression. She claimed that she knew exactly how I must be feeling. She had two sons around Stella's age.

"I know you're feeling scared and sad."

"Those aren't words I would use."

Above all, I was angry. It might sound strange, at least in retrospect, but I was probably in the midst of the "shock" stage. I'd put fear and sorrow on hold and was focusing on my survival, on my family's survival. I would get us out of this.

"What is it you're looking for?" I asked.

"What do you mean?"

"I mean how you're searching our house. All the police who are going through our belongings this very minute."

Chief Inspector Thelin nodded.

"We're looking for forensic evidence, which can be lots of different things. It's possible that we'll find something that's to Stella's advantage, something that corroborates her story. Or we might find nothing at all. We're trying to figure out what happened."

"Stella has nothing to do with this," I said.

Agnes Thelin nodded.

"We'll take it one step at a time. Can you start by telling us what you did last Friday?"

"I was at church almost all day."

"At church?"

She made it sound like the last place on earth she would visit.

"I'm a pastor," I explained.

Agnes Thelin gaped at me for a moment, then came to her senses and busied herself with paging through her documents.

"So you were . . . working?"

"I had a funeral that afternoon."

"A funeral, okay." She scribbled a note. "What time did you return home?"

"Around six, I should think."

I told her that I had showered and prepared a pork casserole, then ate it with Ulrika. After the meal we played a game of Trivial Pursuit on the sofa and then went to bed. Stella worked until quarter past seven and had been planning to meet a friend in town afterwards.

Agnes Thelin asked if I'd been in contact with Stella that evening and I told her that I had sent a text, but I didn't remember what she responded, or even whether she responded at all.

"Is it typical for Stella not to answer texts?"

I shrugged. "You have teenagers."

"But we're talking about Stella right now."

I explained that it wasn't unusual at all. She often answered sooner or later, but later was common. Sometimes much later. Nor was it unusual for the response, when it arrived, to consist solely of a smiley face or a thumbs-up.

"Who was the friend?"

I had to swallow.

"What do you mean?"

"Who was the friend Stella was planning to meet? The one she was going out with?"

I stared down at the table.

"Stella had told my wife she was going to meet up with her friend Amina. But we've asked Amina, and they didn't see each other on Friday."

"Why do you think Stella was lying?"

Her choice of words was infuriating.

"She wasn't lying. Amina told us they had been planning to meet up, but plans changed."

"What do you think she did instead?"

I didn't answer. Why would I speculate? Surely my thoughts didn't mean much.

"Do you know what she did instead?" Agnes Thelin asked.

That was a more reasonable question.

"No."

Agnes Thelin flipped through her papers again in silence. It probably only took a few seconds, really, but it was enough for the silence to seem meaningful, somehow.

"What kind of phone does Stella have?" the chief inspector asked.

I explained it was an iPhone, but that I always get the models mixed up. It was white, in any case, I could tell her that much.

"Does she have more than one of them?" Agnes Thelin asked.

"More than one? No."

Obviously the police would find her phone in our house, and take it into evidence. For a moment I wondered if I should mention to Thelin that Stella had forgotten her phone at home, but I decided not to. It sounded strange for an eighteen-year-old to forget her phone. As if it meant something was wrong.

"Do you know if Stella has access to pepper spray?"

"Pepper spray? The kind the police use?"

"Exactly. Does Stella have a spray bottle like that?"

"Of course not. Is that even legal?"

I felt nauseated.

"What time was it when you went to bed on Friday?" Agnes Thelin asked.

"Eleven, maybe a little after."

"Did you fall asleep right away?"

"No, I couldn't sleep."

"So you lay awake for a long time?"

I drew a breath. My mind was whirling. Fuzzy images of Stella as a little girl, a proud teenager, a grown woman. My little girl. Our family: Ulrika, Stella, and me. The photograph on the windowsill.

"I lay awake, waiting for Stella. I suppose it doesn't matter how old your child gets, you never stop worrying about them."

Agnes Thelin nodded. I think she understood.

What happened next is hard to explain.

I hadn't planned it. I had come to the interrogation with every intention of sharing what I knew. Not once had I considered deviating in the least from the truth.

"So you were awake when Stella came home?"

Agnes Thelin's eyes were large and inviting.

"Mmhmm."

"I'm sorry?"

"Yes," I said, my tone sharper. "I was awake when Stella came home."

"Do you have an idea of what time that was?"

"I know exactly what time it was."

What is a lie? Just as there are different sorts of truths, there must be different sorts of lies. White lies, for example—I've never shied away from those. Better a kind lie than a hurtful truth, I've always thought.

But of course, this was different.

"It was eleven forty-five when Stella came home."

Chief Inspector Thelin stared at me and the Eighth Commandment twisted in my gut like a snake. The Bible says that he who tells a lie must perish. But at the same time: my God is just and forgiving.

"How do you know that?" asked Agnes Thelin. "So precisely, I mean."

"I looked at the clock."

"What clock?"

"On my phone."

There's a verse in the Gospels that says a house divided cannot stand. I realized I had forgotten about my family. Neglected it. Taken it for granted. I hadn't been the father and spouse I should have been.

I still knew nothing about what had happened when that man lost his life on the playground on Pilegatan, but I knew one thing with full certainty: my daughter is no murderer.

"And you're sure that it was Stella coming home?" Agnes Thelin asked.

"Of course I am."

"I mean, you couldn't have been hearing something else?"

I smiled with certainty. Inside, I was going to pieces.

"I'm sure. I talked to her."

"You talked to her?" Agnes Thelin exclaimed. "What did she say? Did anything stand out?"

"Not at all. We mostly just said good night."

Agnes Thelin refused to take her eyes from me.

The snake twisted in my belly once again. An overwhelming sense that this wasn't really me, it was someone else saying all these things in the stuffy interrogation room.

In his first letter to Timothy, Paul writes that someone who doesn't take care of his own family has abandoned his faith in Jesus. I hadn't taken care of my family well enough. This was a chance to correct my mistakes.

I thought, *This is what families do. They protect each other.*

14

After the interrogation, I called Ulrika. She had just swung by the house, but the police were still there.

"They seriously think Stella did something," I said. "This is a nightmare!"

"What did you tell the police?" Ulrika wanted to know.

"I told them I know exactly when Stella came home on Friday. I explained that I was awake and spoke to her."

Ulrika didn't say anything for a moment.

"What time was that?" she asked.

I drew in a breath. I hated lying. Especially to my wife. But I saw no other option. I couldn't drag Ulrika into this. She didn't know; she had been asleep when Stella arrived home. How could I tell her I had lied to the police?

"Eleven forty-five," I said.

It didn't feel as awful as I'd feared. As if my own resistance was worn down a little more each time I uttered the lie.

Ulrika explained that she was on her way to meet a police investigator she knew. There was nothing I could do for the moment. Nothing to do, and so much that needed to be done. I walked briskly over to Bantorget. The sun was sharp and forced my eyes downward. The voices around me seemed shrill and accusatory. I sped up. It was like the whole town was full of staring eyes.

I am adamant in my belief that nothing could be as difficult as being a parent. All other relationships have an emergency exit. You can leave a lover, and most people do at some point, if love ebbs away, if you grow apart, or if it no longer feels good in your heart. You can leave friends and acquaintances along the way, and relatives too, and even siblings and parents. You can leave and move on and still make it out okay. But you can never renounce your child.

Ulrika and I were young and inexperienced at life when Stella came into the world. I suppose we knew it would be tough, but our anguish was mostly bound to worldly things like lack of sleep, difficulty breastfeeding, and getting sick. It took quite some time for us to realize that the hardest part of being a parent is something completely different.

I grew up in a family steeped in the 1970s values of freedom and solidarity. Rules and demands hardly existed. Good sense and inherent morals were enough.

"Does it feel good in your heart?" my father asked me when, at the age of ten, I was caught pulling my sister's hair so hard great clumps came out in my hand.

That was enough to make me cry with shame and guilt.

I tried the same thing on Stella a few times.

"Does that feel good in your heart?" I asked when her headmaster called to say she had thrown another girl's hat up onto the roof of the school.

Stella stared back at me.

"My heart doesn't feel anything. It's just beating."

For almost ten years, Ulrika and I tried to give Stella a sibling. At times, our whole lives revolved around this missing part, taking up all the energy we could spare. We went to war, both of us armed with the worst kind of determination to win. We told ourselves that a little plus sign on the pregnancy test was the solution to everything.

We couldn't see what was happening to us, how we were digging ourselves into a pit of guilt, shame, and inadequacy.

The last couple of years, we were so into our battle against nature and each other that we probably forgot what we were fighting for. I've read about soldiers in the trenches in World War I who eventually forgot who they were at war with and started shooting at their countrymen.

———

Late that Sunday afternoon, the police finally vacated our house. When I returned home, Ulrika was off being questioned by Chief Inspector Agnes Thelin, and my stomach crawled with discomfort as I unlocked the door and slowly walked through room after room. I could have no complaints when it came to the police's degree of care; what traces they had left were few in number and hardly noticeable. But the feeling of having had my private life invaded gnawed at me.

I walked around the first floor and inspected the laundry room, the hall, and the living room; I even opened the woodstove and peered in. Then I went upstairs to Stella's room. I stood in her door for a moment and was struck by how empty it felt. The police must have seized quite a lot of her belongings.

I stood before the window in our bedroom for a while, gazing at the photograph I'd broken. I let my index finger glide across the picture and it felt good in my heart. There's nothing more important than family.

Outside the window, dusk was bathing the land in a thin layer of darkness. My eyes followed the glimmering string of streetlights off to the horizon and I thought about how mercy comes to the patient. The righteous hold to their way.

I noticed that a few neighbors were standing across the street and pointing at our house. I pulled down the blinds with a crash. Even as I did so, I decided to call the chairman of the parish council and take sick leave. He sounded honestly sorry for me; he shared a few words of comfort and advised me to stay home as long as I needed to and told me not to worry about the congregation.

When I called Ulrika, her interrogation had just come to an end.

"It's not as simple as Blomberg first thought," she said.

Her voice seemed to come in waves. I couldn't tell whether the connection was bad or Ulrika was about to burst into tears.

"What do you mean?"

A few pops came over the line. I heard her gasping breaths.

"The police must have found something in our house. The prosecutor has just submitted a request for detention."

15

Michael Blomberg's office was three floors up in one of the fanciest buildings on Klostergatan, just a stone's throw from the Grand Hotel. Come Monday morning, Ulrika and I were all but hanging from the lock. The lack of sleep was clearly reflected in my wife's face. Although I hadn't gotten a wink of sleep in the last forty-eight hours either, my exhaustion was the least of my concerns. There was too much else going on inside of me.

We were served coffee under the high ceiling with its plasterwork and flourishes, while Blomberg tucked his thumbs into his back pockets and shuffled his shiny leather shoes on the floor.

"The detention hearing will be at one."

I felt butterflies. Finally, we could see Stella.

"The police found a footprint at the scene of the crime," Blomberg went on, scratching his neck. "From a shoe the same size as Stella wears, with the same pattern on the sole."

I squeezed Ulrika's forearm.

"Is that all?" I asked. "The only evidence? Did they find anything when they searched our house?"

"It's too soon to say. Some of what they seized from your residence has been sent to the lab for forensic analysis."

"Doesn't that usually take time?" I asked.

"It won't take more than a few days to get answers," Blomberg said. "What we're dealing with here is what's called investigative detention. In blunt terms, it means that they'll keep Stella in jail while the police wait for an answer from the lab. It doesn't take much to get someone detained for reasonable suspicion."

"Just for a footprint?"

Blomberg looked at Ulrika as if he thought she should chime in. As if it was her job to explain things to her dim-witted husband.

"I think you need to be prepared for Stella to remain in jail."

It sounded so fateful. So resigned. I looked at Ulrika, who just nodded in confirmation. What was going on?

"Who's the prosecutor?" Ulrika asked.

"Jenny Jansdotter."

"She's supposed to be good. One of the best."

It was hard for me to tell whether this was an advantage or disadvantage for us. I'd never needed to immerse myself in the legalities involved with deprivation of liberty. Most people, happily, never have reason to do so. Even though I'm married to a lawyer, my knowledge was basic at best. Now I know how little evidence it takes to keep a person under lock and key. I had heard the opposite many times—despairing police officers claiming that the suspect was set free before they had the chance for an arrest, the general view that the Swedish justice system was broken and would rather protect the rights of suspects and convicts than deal with the suffering of victims. Demands for tougher punishments and stricter measures. I'd worked in jails before and had shared these thoughts myself. There had never been a reason for me to shift perspective.

"What's more, the prosecutor has a witness. The neighbor," Blomberg said, leaning across the desk to read from the document. "My Sennevall."

He sounded so calm, as if this was something that must simply be accepted. Shouldn't he be furious? Want to take action?

"The witness," I said. "How can she be so certain it was Stella she saw? She doesn't know her."

"She claims to recognize Stella from H&M."

"Recognize her?" I muttered.

Ulrika elbowed me in the side.

"What does Stella say?"

Blomberg cleared his throat and ran his hand through his hair. Once again he turned to address Ulrika directly. With every passing second, I became more convinced of his incompetence.

"After closing time, Stella and a few colleagues went up to the Stortorget restaurant. They ate and had a glass or two of wine. Around ten thirty, Stella left the restaurant. All of her colleagues have confirmed this. She said nothing about where she was going, but everyone assumed she was going to bike home."

"But she didn't?"

"Stella herself says she biked over to Tegnérs and went around to a few other pubs in town. She doesn't remember exactly where she was at any given point in time."

Ulrika and I exchanged glances. This didn't sound like a very solid alibi. In fact, it seemed evasive, the sort of thing a guilty person would say. Why hadn't she made an effort to remember more details?

"There must be something more she can recall," I said. "There must be other people who saw her. She knows half the city."

Blomberg glanced at Ulrika, whose response was to stretch and gaze past him and out the large window.

"Do we know anything else about the timeline?" she asked. "That witness, Sennevall, said she heard screaming and fighting around one o'clock?"

"That's right. The first reports mentioned just after one in the morning, but now they're waiting for the medical examiner's report before nailing anything down."

Ulrika looked at me.

"If it's determined that Christopher Olsen died at one o'clock, that means Stella has an alibi."

"That's correct."

My vision swam.

"And not just any alibi," the star attorney went on, a smug smile on his face. "Everyone I've spoken with says you're the personification of honesty, Adam."

I swallowed heavily.

16

The custody hearing took place right after lunch. I had passed by the county courthouse in Lund thousands of times, that unusual façade with its irregular shale siding and copper details, the little clock tower out front. Now, for the first time, I stepped through the doors and was forced to empty my pockets. I stood in the entry like a crucifix as a security guard patted me down. Once inside, Ulrika and I sat on a cot-like bench in the corridor to wait. The air was thick.

Each time the door opened, we flew up, causing the security people to startle until finally they told us to take it easy.

At last Stella arrived, flanked by two uniformed men. She just hung there, a slender ghost between the broad-shouldered guards. Didn't even look our way. Ulrika dashed up and threw her arms around her but was quickly fended off by one of the uniforms.

"Stella! Sweetheart!"

I tried to force my way between the guards to touch my little girl, but one of the large men put out both his bulging arms and blocked my path.

"It'll be over soon, Stella," Ulrika said.

Stella was pale, her eyes sunken, and there was something else about her, something I'd never seen before. She was resigned. The exhaustion in her face was the kind you only see in people who have acquiesced, abandoned themselves to their fate, or, in this case, to the system. People who say, "Do what you want with me." You can see it in their eyes, how all the life has been sucked out.

I've met others who capitulated. People so thoroughly drained of purpose and volition that they can no longer muster up the strength even to inflict harm upon themselves.

As Stella was guided into the courtroom, I was flung down into a limbo of uncertainty. I'm still suspended there in midair, kicking for my life, grasping for stability.

The courtroom was no larger than a living room. The presiding judge was paging through some documents as we took our seats in the gallery. Blomberg pulled out a chair for Stella and as she tried to sit down she looked like she'd gone to pieces, as if her body were no longer articulated, and Blomberg had to hold on to her with both hands.

Ulrika and I squeezed each other's hands. Our little girl was just five meters away from us and we weren't even allowed to touch her.

The prosecutor entered, wearing heels that could be heard from all the way down the hall. Springy steps in expensive clothing, tinkling jewelry around her neck and wrist, the body of a gymnast: short, slim, fit, and bowlegged. Her glasses had square, black frames and her hair was slicked down, not a strand out of place. She arranged her documents in three prim stacks on the table, straightened their edges with her ruby-red nails, and then shook hands with Blomberg and Stella.

I hardly had time to understand that the hearing had begun before the presiding judge ruled that it would take place behind closed doors and a bailiff explained that Ulrika and I needed to leave.

"That's my little girl!" I shouted right in his face.

The guard glared at my clerical collar in surprise.

Love is a human's most difficult task. I wonder if Jesus understood what He was asking of humanity when He urged us to love our neighbor as we love ourselves.

Can you keep loving a murderer?

As I sat there outside the courtroom, during that first detention hearing, the thought grew stronger and stronger. It had tried to force its way into my mind earlier, but this was the first time I dared to linger on it. The thought that Stella might be guilty.

The stains on her blouse. They might be from anything. But why hadn't anyone seen Stella? Someone who could say where she had been, what she had been doing. There was a gap of several hours on that Friday night. What had she done in that time?

I have sat across from abominable killers and promised them the unconditional love of God. Human love is of a different type. I thought of Paul's words about love that rejoices when truth wins out, love that is faithful no matter the cost.

For my family. That's what I was thinking. I have to do whatever it takes for my family. Far too many times I had failed in my endeavors to be the world's best spouse and father. Suddenly I had the chance to mend my ways. I would do everything I could to protect my family.

By the time the door to the courtroom opened again, my body felt so heavy that Ulrika had to help me up and inside. Before us sat Stella, her face buried in her hands.

Ulrika and I clung to each other like two people drowning in rough seas. The door closed behind us and the judge's gaze swept the room.

"Stella Sandell is under reasonable suspicion for murder."

No parent ever expects to hear their child's name in that context. No one who has held their child to their chest, all tiny floundering feet and gurgling laughter, could have imagined this. This happens to other people. Not to us.

I held tight to Ulrika's hand and thought, *This isn't the kind of parents we are*. We aren't substance abusers; we're academics, high earners. We are in good health, both physically and mentally. We're not a broken family from a marginalized area with social and economic problems.

We were a perfectly ordinary family. We weren't supposed to be the ones sitting there. And yet there we were.

17

After the detention hearing, Ulrika and I waited in silence outside Blomberg's office. I stood up, then sat down, then stood up again. Walked over to the window with a sigh.

"Where is he?"

Ulrika was sitting perfectly still, staring at the wall.

"When can we talk to Stella?" I asked. "It's inhumane to keep her isolated like this."

"That's how it works," Ulrika said. "She'll be under restrictions as long as the investigation is ongoing."

At last Blomberg came bustling in. The orange-peel skin on his cheeks was even redder now. He spoke rapidly, like a wind-up toy.

"I've got all my people checking out Christopher Olsen. It turns out he had more than one skeleton in his closet, if you'll pardon the expression."

I didn't, but I was far too curious to speak up.

"Tell us!"

"It's easy to make enemies as a businessman," Blomberg said. "But in Olsen's case, they're not just any enemies. Apparently he's found himself in hot water with some Poles whose rap sheets are as long as the Gospels."

I made a skeptical face. That sounded like something straight out of a bad police procedural.

"It's about a property Olsen purchased last spring. The Poles have a pizza place on the ground floor, and Olsen was eager to get rid of it. I imagine it didn't do him any favors when it came to the rent he could have charged."

"But the method hardly suggests a mafia hit," Ulrika said.

"Who said anything about the mafia? I'm talking about Polish pizza bakers. But it gets even better."

I disliked the whole concept. In my world, the police were the ones who handled homicide investigations, not lawyers. What's more, it didn't feel at all right to cast suspicion on the victim like this.

"Just six months ago, charges were filed against Christopher Olsen for repeated instances of assault and rape. A preliminary investigation was opened, but after a few months the prosecutor decided to close it due to lack of evidence." Blomberg paused for effect and eyed us. "The accuser was Olsen's ex-girlfriend. According to her, Christopher Olsen was a violent tyrant who ruined her life."

I could see the change in Ulrika as everything brightened.

"She never obtained redress?"

"No," Blomberg said.

"She may be out for revenge."

Blomberg nodded.

Ulrika turned to me.

"Do you understand what this means?"

Blomberg's plan was to present an alternative perpetrator in order to create reasonable doubt about whether Stella was guilty. The Polish pizza bakers were one option, but Christopher Olsen's ex-girlfriend seemed to be much more relevant.

"But she might not have anything to do with this," I said to Ulrika as we sat on the sofa that night, unable to sleep. "Wouldn't it be better to leave this sort of thing to the police?"

She looked at me like I was nothing but a dumb pastor.

"This is the kind of thing lawyers do."

"But isn't it enough to prove that Stella is innocent? What if a different innocent person ends up in a fix? She's been assaulted and raped, and now—"

Ulrika stood up.

"This is Stella we're talking about. Our daughter is locked up in a jail cell!"

She was right, of course. Nothing was more important than getting Stella out as soon as possible. I drank the rest of my whiskey and walked over to the woodstove. When I opened its glass door, the heat flew up into my face and I had to wait a moment before jabbing the poker into the ash, sending it whirling. Curls of smoke swirled up around my head.

"Do you love me?" I asked without looking at Ulrika.

"Why, honey, of course I do." She reached for me and touched the back of my neck. "You and Stella, I love you both above everything else."

"I love you too."

"This is a nightmare," she said. "I've never felt so powerless."

I sat down and put my arm around her.

"Whatever happens, we have to stick together."

We kissed.

"What if she . . . ," I said against Ulrika's cheek. "Do you think she might . . ."

Ulrika recoiled.

"Don't think like that!"

"I know. But . . . her blouse."

I had to know what had happened to it. Ulrika must have taken the top. And if so, she would definitely have noticed the stains; they were impossible to miss.

"What do you mean?" she said.

"The stains on her blouse," I said.

"What stains?"

She looked at me as if I were delirious.

Hadn't she moved the blouse? If not, the police must have found it. My heart was pounding as Ulrika placed her hand on my arm.

"We know Stella was home when that man died."

And she left it at that.

18

I didn't get a wink of sleep on Monday night. My mind went round and round. What had Stella done?

I vacuumed, scrubbed the floor, and cleaned the kitchen cabinets until I was dripping with sweat and feeling more and more bewildered. Frightened of my own thoughts. Stella, my little girl. What kind of father was I, to breathe even a whisper of doubt about her innocence? The oxygen caught in my throat like phlegm and I had to go out to the garden to fill my lungs with fresh air.

Ulrika had shut herself into her office. Several hours later I found her asleep, her head between her arms on the desk. Next to her was an empty bottle of wine and a glass that was still half full. I gently stroked her hair, inhaled the scent from her nape, and left her to sleep on.

The next morning I sank down at the kitchen table, exhausted. I began to flip through the paper and came face-to-face with a picture of the playground where Christopher Olsen had died. Had Stella been there on Friday night? Had she . . . Why? I shook off my thoughts and went up to see Ulrika.

"I'm going to go there. I want to see it with my own eyes."

"See what?"

"The spot. The playground."

"I don't think that's a good idea at all," Ulrika said. "It's best for us to stay as far away from everything as we can."

Instead I looked around on the internet.

Thus far there was only limited information about the murder, but it was clearly only a matter of time, probably just hours, before people would be posting about it in forums, before it would be chatter on social media. Stella would in all certainty be stamped as guilty. Where there's smoke, there's fire, people would say. The gossip would be extra delicious given that a pastor's daughter was involved.

The power to condemn belongs to the people, no matter the opinion of the legal system, and the court of popular opinion hardly has the same evidentiary requirements as a court of law. I have only to look at myself. How many times have I felt doubt when a suspect is freed for lack of evidence?

I kept googling, but words and images were not enough. I needed to see it with my own eyes, stand at the center of it.

I didn't tell Ulrika where I was going. She seemed so certain that Stella had nothing to do with what had happened. I climbed into the car with my chest constricting.

My phone rang when I was halfway into town; the screen told me it was Dino.

"The police questioned Amina. I'm not happy that she is being dragged into this."

His words came quickly, and there was an unusual harshness to his voice.

"What did they ask about?" I wondered aloud, but Dino wasn't listening.

"What if word gets out at the medical school that Amina is involved in a murder investigation? That won't look good."

"Dino, stop! My daughter is suspected of murder! Amina isn't the one we should be feeling sorry for here."

He abruptly fell silent.

"I know, I know. I'm sorry, I just don't want anything bad to happen to Amina because of something . . . something she has nothing to do with."

Naturally, he didn't mean any offense. Tact and discretion are not Dino's strong suits. I can't even count all the times I've had to smooth things over after one of his hasty reactions or harangues on the handball court. But this time I was under stress as well. To say the least.

"So do you believe Stella had something to do with it?" I asked.

"Of course not, but we're talking about medical school here. Amina doesn't know a thing about what happened last Friday."

"But Stella doesn't either, does she?"

"It's just so typical, that this would happen *now*. It's not like this is the first time Amina has gotten into trouble because of . . ."

He never completed that sentence. He didn't need to. I hung up on him with a trembling index finger.

I stopped the car outside the Ball House and walked the last little bit. I found the playground behind a hedge alongside the allotment gardens. All that was left of the police barrier was a forgotten scrap of blue-and-white tape tied to a lamppost. Inside the playground, a girl full of bubbling laughter had pumped her swing so high that one shoe had flown off. Her dad was nearby, his arms outstretched before the slide, where the girl's little brother was hesitating before taking the plunge.

A memorial had been set up along the hedge behind them. Candles, roses and lilies, photographs and cards bearing final greetings. Someone had written the word *WHY?* in capital letters, in red on a black background.

The girl made a flying leap from the swing, grabbed her shoe, and put it back on her foot all in one movement; she rocketed for her father with a joyful shout.

"Shhh," he whispered, glancing my way.

I stood with my head bowed before the flowers and candles and said a short prayer for Christopher Olsen.

I had only seen his face on my computer and phone screens, a few photographs from an article and a corporate presentation. Now I saw him for the first time in a different way, in the context of a private life, as a human being of flesh and blood, a person whom others missed and grieved. In the largest portrait, he was looking into the camera with sparkling eyes and a smile that seemed a blend of happiness and surprise, as if he had been startled by the photographer. Death is seldom so tangible as when you can see how alive a person once was.

I was overwhelmed by a brutal feeling of helplessness. Everything felt so hopelessly terrible. A young man, a stranger, had been robbed of his life here in the crunching gravel. There were still signs of blood.

How could anyone believe for even a second that Stella could have been involved? I looked at the pictures of Christopher Olsen. An obviously attractive young man with happy eyes full of promise for the future. This was a senseless tragedy.

I hurried back to the sidewalk and peered down Pilegatan.

Why did that neighbor claim to have seen Stella here last Friday? Who was she, and how could she be so sure of herself? If she was lying on purpose, someone needed to inform her of the potential consequences.

And if she wasn't lying? What if Stella had been here?

I found the yellow turn-of-the-century building Christopher Olsen had lived in at the end of the street. I gazed up at the beautiful windows and elegant balconies. Then I tried the door. It was open.

I didn't know if there were any legal reasons I couldn't talk to the witness. From a moral standpoint, of course, it was utterly reprehensible, even if I promised myself I wouldn't try to influence the girl. I just wanted to understand what she had seen. And she had to realize that Stella was a real person with loved ones who were about to go to pieces with worry. Someone had to make sure she knew this wasn't a game. She needed to see that I existed.

19

I slowly made my way up the stairs, stumbling a little as I went. I stopped on the first landing and read the nameplates. There it was: *C. Olsen,* in script on shiny metal. There were two more apartments across from his door. To the right lived someone called Agnelid, and on the left-hand door was a hand-written nameplate that said *My Sennevall.* I recognized the name immediately.

The doorbell jangled and I tried to think of what to say. I had to make her understand why I was here. Soon I heard scuffing footsteps on the other side of the door; the floor creaked, but then everything was as quiet as it had been before. I rang the bell again.

Was she standing behind the door listening?

"Hello?" I said, my voice low. "Is anyone there?"

I heard the lock turning, and very slowly the door opened. The crack was so narrow that I had to lean to the side to catch a glimpse of the figure inside.

"Hi. Sorry for just showing up like this."

I couldn't see much more than a pair of eyes glowing in the darkness.

"My name is Adam Sandell."

"Okay . . ."

"May I come in?"

She cracked the door a little more and stuck out her nose.

"Are you selling something?"

Her voice sounded like a child's.

"I just want to ask a few questions about Stella," I said. "I'm her dad."

"Stella?" She seemed to be thinking back. "That Stella?"

"Please, I have to know."

With great hesitation, she undid the security chain and held open the door so I could step into the dimly lit hall. There was a cap on the hat rack, and a windbreaker and an umbrella hung from the hooks. Otherwise the hall was perfectly empty.

"You're My, aren't you?" I asked. "My Sennevall?"

The girl backed into the wall and fixed me with a jittery glare. She was small and dainty, with hair that hung like a veil to her waist. She couldn't have been much older than Stella.

"I don't know what you want from me," she said. "I've already told the police everything."

"I won't stay long," I promised, craning my neck to see into the apartment.

The walls were bare, and a lone floor lamp cast a dull light over the otherwise dark room. In front of the window was a dark-blue wingback chair that could have used some rehabilitation. I couldn't see a TV or computer. On the IKEA bookcase were a few mismatched porcelain figurines, the kind you find at flea markets. There was no desk, no chair, no other furniture. Just an unmade twin bed in the corner.

"Okay, but tell me why you're here," said My Sennevall.

I didn't quite know why I was there myself.

"Could you just tell me where you saw her? I need help understanding what happened."

My Sennevall blinked a few times.

"I usually sit by the window there," she said, pointing at the wingback chair. "I like knowing what's up."

"What's up?"

"What's going on."

That sounded odd. What sort of person was she?

"When you saw Stella . . . ," I began, "are you sure it was last Friday?"

She snorted at me.

"The first time was at eleven thirty."

"The first time?"

She nodded.

"Stella came zooming up on her bike. She yanked open the door down there and ran inside."

My Sennevall took a few slow steps into the room, stood by the chair, and pointed out the window. She had an excellent view of Pilegatan.

"Then I saw her again. About half an hour later. She was standing down there on the sidewalk, across the street. Under that tree."

Half an hour later? So My Sennevall had seen this person she believed to be Stella not just once, but twice on the same night.

"How can you be so sure it was Stella you saw? Do you know her?"

She bowed her head.

"I know she works at H&M. I said so to the police right away."

She looked at me again. My Sennevall certainly seemed peculiar, but there was nothing to suggest she was lying. I was sure she had seen someone last Friday, and she was convinced it was Stella. I found myself thinking that she didn't look like a liar. A bizarre thought.

"Do you know everyone who works at H&M, or just Stella?"

She snorted at me again.

"I am uncommonly good at remembering faces," she said, looking out the window. "I have a very good memory overall. I notice things that other people miss."

"I'm sure you do," I said.

"I've seen your daughter at H&M lots of times. When the police showed me a picture, I was one hundred percent sure. They said it's unusual for witnesses to be so convincing."

I stooped a little to re-create the perspective she would have had when sitting in the chair and found that it afforded a full view of the sidewalk across the street.

"Then I woke up because a guy was screaming. Or howling. At least it sounded like a man."

"When was that?"

"I had just gone to bed, so it must have been around one o'clock."

Just as Blomberg had said. One o'clock.

"I always go to bed at one. Anyway, I ran over here to the window and watched for a while. I didn't see anything, but I'm pretty sure the sounds were coming from the playground over there."

I tried to imagine what it would look like in the dark. To be sure, there were several streetlights along the sidewalk, but even so it couldn't be easy to make out details in the middle of the night.

"How can you be so sure it was her?" I asked. "You understand you might destroy someone's life, several people's lives, if you identify the wrong person, don't you? You have to be totally sure."

"I am. I told you that."

It sounded so naïve, almost like she was out of touch with reality. It seemed completely insane that Stella was locked up in a cell based on a claim made by this woman.

I had to restrain myself. All I really wanted was to grab My Sennevall and give her a good shake.

"You don't know Stella! You've only seen her in the shop where she works. How can you say you're so sure?"

My Sennevall met my gaze. Her eyes were full of sympathy.

"It wasn't the first time Stella was here."

20

One day, when the girls were fourteen, Amina came to see me in the church hall. She stood in the doorway on trembling summer legs, looking as if the world might swallow her up at any second.

"Pastors have confidentiality, right?"

As soon as she spoke those words, I knew that things were going to change. Her frightened doe eyes seemed to reflect life hanging in the balance.

Amina has truly been a big part of Stella's upbringing. There have been times when Stella was at the Bešićs' house as often as she was at home with us. Amina didn't have any siblings either, and although we never discussed it with Dino and Alexandra, Ulrika and I suspected they—like us—had never managed to get pregnant again.

"What's going on?" I asked, placing a hand on Amina's shoulder.

In many respects I consider myself something of an extra dad to her.

"You have confidentiality, right?" she asked again. "Whatever I say, you can't tell anyone else?"

"That depends on what you're going to say."

I asked her to have a seat and offered her orange juice and Ballerina cookies. Before we got to the point, we spent a few moments discussing everything and anything else: how school was going, about friends and handball, and about her dreams. Then she said she'd come about Stella.

I waited two days, and then I had to bring it up with Ulrika.

"Drugs?"

My wife just stared at me. She appeared to be waiting for me to take it back, say I was only joking.

"That's what Amina says."

"And why would Amina tell you something like that?"

She truly did not want to believe it.

"I suppose she's scared," I said.

In the days that followed, Ulrika was firing on all cylinders. She contacted the principal and the school nurse, who arranged for drug testing.

"You can't fucking make me," Stella said, and tried to break loose outside the clinic.

"Of course we can," said Ulrika. "You're not of age."

People stared in curiosity as Stella continued her noisy protests in the waiting room. I tried to hide my face as best I could, but in the end it was all so awkward that I had to drag Stella into the lab and explain that we couldn't wait any longer. Ulrika held Stella's hand tight as the nurse guided the needle into her arm.

A few days later, we got word by phone. There were traces of cannabis in Stella's blood.

"Why?" Ulrika repeated time and again. "Why?"

She paced tight circles around Stella and me at the kitchen table. Now I was the one who felt like a defense attorney.

"Because nothing ever happens," said Stella.

This soon became her default response.

"Everything is so boring. Nothing ever happens."

Ulrika stared at her, quaking, one hand fisted and level with her hip.

"Drugs. Stella! You were doing drugs!"

"It was just weed. I wanted to try it."

"Try it?"

"It makes things more fun. Just like wine, for you."

Ulrika banged her fist on the table hard enough to make our glasses jump. Stella rose and unleashed a long string of Bosnian curse words she must have picked up from Dino.

When I got in bed that night, Ulrika had turned her face to the wall.

"Honey," I said, touching her back gently.

Her only response was a sob.

"It's going to be okay," I said. "We'll fix this. Together we'll get through this."

She gazed at the ceiling.

"It's my fault. I've been working too much."

"It's no one's fault," I said.

"We have to get help. I'll call the teen psych clinic tomorrow."

The psych clinic?

"What must people think of us?" I said.

One evening later that week, I spotted Amina as I was on my way home. I recognized her pink jacket with its fluffy white collar and let go of the handlebars to wave, but Amina didn't respond to my greeting. She slowed down until she was standing still next to a large electrical box, and I realized something must be wrong.

As I approached, the shadows on her face became clearer. I hoped until the last moment that I was mistaken. Amina raised her hand to her cheek in a futile attempt to hide her plight as I braked and leaned forward over the frame of my bike.

"Oh, Amina. What happened?"

She turned her face away.

"Nothing," she said, striding away from me. "I thought pastors had confidentiality."

After two weeks we secured an appointment at the clinic for pediatric and adolescent psychiatry. By then we'd already had a conference at school with teachers and the principal, the counselor, the nurse, and the psychologist. I felt like the biggest parental failure in the world.

The therapist at the clinic had a handlebar mustache so long it curled at the ends. It was hard to look at anything else.

"I like to say that a teenager problem is always a family problem," he said, bending across the low, round table and making his necklace of black beads dangle.

As soon as either Ulrika or I tried to bring up our opinions on the matter, he cut us off by raising one hand in the air.

"Now let's not forget about Stella's perspective. How do you feel?"

Stella stared at her feet.

"Don't care."

"Come on, Stella . . . ," Ulrika and I tried.

"Uppuppupp," said the counselor. "She has the right to feel however she feels."

My fingers itched. This wasn't my little girl, sitting there with her arms crossed and a recalcitrant look on her face. This was some completely different person. I wanted to grab her by the shoulders and shake her.

"Please, Stella," said Ulrika.

My tone of voice was always harsher.

"Stella!"

But Stella continued to mutter her way through the appointments.

"You don't understand anyway. There's no point. I don't care."

I slowly became resigned to what had happened—our daughter had smoked marijuana. It was no disaster. But the drugs were just one symptom of Stella's many issues, and it was frustrating that we couldn't help her. At home, Ulrika and I were always walking on eggshells. The tiniest misstep could spark an explosion. Stella's eyes would darken, and she would scream and throw things.

"It's my life! You aren't the boss of me."

At its worst, we saw no other option than to lock her in her room until she calmed down.

In the late autumn of that year, we exchanged the mustachioed man at the clinic for a mild woman with fiery hair. She gave us tasks to practice at home. Tools, she called them. We needed tools. But when Stella didn't get her way and turned the whole world upside down, it didn't matter what tools we whipped out.

During one examination, it was determined that Stella suffered from a lack of impulse control. According to the redhead, this was something that could be improved.

I confided in my colleagues, who were wonderful and supportive. "Teenagers aren't easy." Even so, I couldn't help but suspect that some of them seemed a little too satisfied—relieved, somehow, that even I had cracks in my façade.

However, the results from Stella's subsequent urine tests came back negative and I was starting to see a light at the end of the tunnel.

21

That night, Ulrika and I were on opposite sides of the sofa. We were battling against time and the wound that had been laid open in the heart of our little family. The air was stifling, full of everything we didn't say to each other.

I couldn't stop thinking about My Sennevall. Her words had poisoned me with dread. She was so sure that it was Stella she had seen on Friday because it wasn't the first time Stella had been to Christopher Olsen's home.

Around two, Ulrika fetched another bottle of wine. On her way back she stumbled and had to catch herself against the wall.

"Maybe we shouldn't have any more to drink," I said.

"'We'?"

I shrugged.

I have preached in several of my sermons on how it so frequently takes tragedy or catastrophe for people to come together and be united, for us to truly stop what we're doing and devote ourselves to one another. In misfortune we rediscover each other and become aware of what it means to be a human among other humans. In sorrow, we need each other more than ever.

"Adam, please, don't tell me what I'm allowed to do," Ulrika said. "My daughter is a murder suspect."

She swayed again, then sat back down on her side of the sofa. I took a deep breath. We were a family—we had to stick together. There was no room for lies or secrets.

"You know what? I think Stella knew that man."

"Christopher Olsen?"

I nodded as she sipped her wine.

"What makes you think that?"

"I suppose it's just a feeling I have."

Ulrika gazed at me, wide-eyed.

Should I tell her everything? Reveal that I had spoken with My Sennevall? I was terrified that Ulrika wouldn't understand. She would fly into a rage and think I had tried to influence My's testimony. It's a matter of honor for her, of course. If she found out, she might even feel duty-bound to report my little stunt to the police.

"What did we do wrong, honey?" I asked. "How could this happen?"

Ulrika's eyes became shiny.

"I've never been enough," she said, almost whispering. "I'm a bad mother."

I moved closer.

"You're a fantastic mother."

"Oh, Stella's always been a daddy's girl. Everyone said so. It was you and Stella."

"Stop it." I reached for her, but she turned her back on me and clammed up. "You and Stella have had a wonderful relationship. Recently . . ."

She shook her head.

"Something has always been missing."

"Maybe it has to be," I said, although I wasn't sure what I meant.

When sleep finally came to us, there on the sofa, it was fitful and fragmented. I kept waking up, my body aching, wondering where I was and trying to figure out what was real and what were only phantoms from my feverish dreams.

Ulrika was half-reclining beside me, whistling as she breathed, eyelids fluttering. Sometime during the morning I cuddled up close to her so I could feel her presence in my dreams.

The next time I woke up, she was gone. I rushed to the kitchen. The morning light was streaming into the quiet house. I ran up the stairs and flung open the bedroom door. The bed was empty. An instant later, I heard her in Stella's room.

"The results from the lab are in. There will be another custody hearing today."

She was standing in the doorway with hunched shoulders and dark circles under her eyes.

"What does that mean?"

"A person can be detained either 'under reasonable suspicion' or 'for probable cause.' I would say the difference is considerable. It doesn't take much to detain someone during an investigation if they're under reasonable suspicion, but the standard of proof is much higher to detain them for probable cause."

The words rattled in my head.

"According to the prosecutor, there is strong evidence against Stella. She wants to increase the level of suspicion."

More suspicions? My heart skidded.

"What did they find?"

22

Ulrika and I never spoke about the guilt and shame that resulted from having a daughter smoking pot and getting into trouble. We kept mum about the hours at the psychiatric clinic, made persistent proclamations about the future, and told everyone, whether they wanted to listen or not, that the most important thing was the welfare of our child, as if we seriously thought that set us apart from other parents.

Ulrika worked fewer hours that fall. She spent more time at home, but she was at least as busy as she had been before.

One night I woke up and heard her typing away. I sneaked into her office and found she was sitting there in the dark wearing only her underwear. Pounds had melted off her in the past few months, and in the faint light of the desk lamp I noticed she had angry red streaks and blisters just below the edge of her bra.

Shingles, the doctor told us the next day. He refused to prescribe sleeping pills but was prepared to have her take sick leave.

"You have to think of yourself, honey," I said, helping her apply calamine lotion to the rash.

"I have to think of Stella," she replied.

For Stella, though, life seemed to be carrying on at full speed. I suppose that's just how it is when you're fourteen, you don't have time to put your existence on standby. You have to keep up or you'll end up behind or left out. I frequently thought of Dino's words, about how Stella was her own worst enemy. That she had to win the battle against herself. At times it appeared the only way she won that match was by forfeit.

"I am so over it! I don't care."

That spring, the redheaded counselor was replaced with a younger version of the same, a woman who was convinced that therapy could solve just about anything, at least until Stella exploded in the middle of a conversation and drowned her out with curse words. Then we were placed with a family therapist, a young man from the north with bangs and a smile full of concern, who urged us to "freeze the situation" whenever Stella had an outburst.

"Stop and talk about how you're feeling and how it ended up like this."

A few days later, Stella threw a sandwich at the fridge after Ulrika and I told her she wasn't allowed to attend a party in Malmö.

"You're killing me!" she shrieked. "What's the point of living when you're not allowed to do anything?"

I stood up and threw out my arms like a hockey referee.

"Let's freeze this situation."

"Oh my *god*!"

Stella ran for the hall, but I quickly blocked her way.

"I can't even deal!" Stella said, rushing past Ulrika and up the stairs. The door slammed behind her and I sighed at my wife in disappointment.

"She *has* to deal," I said, leaning against the kitchen island. "All three of us have to deal."

"I don't understand what's going on," Ulrika said.

Neither of us did. At the age of five, Stella had sat for hours with puzzles that were much too hard for her. Her preschool had never seen anyone with so much patience. These days she couldn't even sit down and concentrate for ten minutes.

But every time the psychologists brought up ADD or ADHD, Ulrika went on the defensive. She never gave them any concrete reason for her reaction, but to me she confessed that she was terrified that a diagnosis would stigmatize Stella and somehow become a self-fulfilling prophecy.

"When I was little, the adult world constantly told me I was a good girl."

Her face twisted as if she had tasted something nasty. I didn't quite understand what she meant.

"'Good girl,' they said, patting me on the head. 'Ulrika's such a good girl.' In the end I had no choice but to become that good girl everyone was expecting."

I had never thought about it like that before.

Sometime in middle school, Stella stopped coming with me to church. I didn't make a big deal about it; I saw it as a perfectly natural form of rebellion. Children become teenagers earlier these days, kicking their way free from their parents even before puberty. There was nothing strange about the fact that Stella wanted to become independent. Furthermore, I would never dream of foisting my belief in God upon her.

As the years passed, it became increasingly common for Stella to blame religion for all the misery in the world; she was scornful and dismissive of people who believed in anything but strict atheism. I realized, of course, that there would be nothing to gain from challenging her views. I had once been like her. But the distressing thing was, I was convinced that she was doing all of this to hurt me. It was taxing. It's painful to watch your child change and move in a direction you never could have predicted.

Considering Stella's negative attitude toward the Church, it came as a surprise when she wanted to attend confirmation camp.

As a newcomer to the congregation, one of my first projects had been to get a good confirmation group off the ground. Along with the neighboring congregation, we found the perfect camp location by Lake Immeln, on the border with Blekinge, and by chance we also managed to recruit a young deacon named Robin as camp director.

The camp was an immediate success, and leading up to Stella's year we received inquiries from teens and parents all over the city. I knew that a great deal of our popularity had been thanks to Robin, who was young and charming but not without depth, so I allocated an exorbitant portion of the congregation budget to hire him as director once more.

Of course I noticed how the confirmand girls looked at him; I realized that his charm concealed certain dangers, but the fact was, I was simply too naïve to hear any warning bells.

"I think we should let her go to confirmation camp," I said one evening in April as the wind was blowing hard enough to shake the walls.

We were sitting around the dinner table, the whole family gathered together for once. A week had passed without a major outburst.

"For real?"

Stella threw her arms around my neck.

"You are so the best," she said with her mouth full. "I love you, Dad!"

"Let's see what Mom says first."

Ulrika was chewing with great focus. She had just been hired on as assistant counsel for the defense in what would become one of Sweden's most infamous trials. She'd thrown herself headlong into the task, going from working too much to working even more.

"What am I supposed to say?"

She took a few sips of milk and stared at me.

"Say I can go," Stella said, still hanging over me.

"Please," I said with a rather foolish smile.

I will confess that to a certain extent I viewed the confirmation camp as an opportunity for Stella to discover new value in Christian fellowship. A chance to open up and find herself. Perhaps, I hoped, this might be the start of a path toward return. A way for Stella to come back, but also a path for me, back to the daughter I missed.

"Of course you can," Ulrika said at last.

It felt like this could be a turning point.

One Friday in August, Stella boarded a bus in the church parking lot. Ulrika had missed her flight from Stockholm, but I stood there waving as the bus backed out. Stella's smile took up the entire back window. She never waved back.

23

On Wednesday afternoon we were back in the courthouse. Ulrika walked ahead of me through the metal detector at security. When it was my turn, the frame began to beep and blink. All eyes were on me, but the guard quickly discovered that I had only forgotten to take off my necklace.

Michael Blomberg hardly had time to give us a proper greeting in the corridor. His forehead was dripping with sweat and the knot of his tie looked sloppy. Was he really the right man to defend Stella?

I could barely feel my feet as we walked into the courtroom. Stella was already inside, and from behind she looked like anyone, a typical teenage girl, a young person with her whole life ahead of her. Only when I saw her listless gaze did reality catch up with me. Nothing about this was normal.

The custody hearing began, and this time neither party demanded closed doors. Prosecutor Jenny Jansdotter had the floor. She spoke rapidly and with no hesitation.

"Based on the new forensic evidence that has emerged in the investigation, I hold that the level of suspicion against Stella Sandell has risen."

I couldn't take my eyes off Stella. It was so awful that she was sitting there, just a few meters away from me, and I still couldn't talk to her. All I wanted was to hug my little girl.

According to the lab results, the footprint the crime-scene technicians had secured next to the site of the murder came from the same kind of shoe that Stella was wearing when she was apprehended. It was not possible, however, to determine whether the print had come from Stella's shoe in particular.

The crime-scene analysis had also indicated clear traces of capsaicin on the victim's body, which likely meant that Christopher Olsen had been sprayed with pepper spray.

"Several of Stella's colleagues have revealed during questioning that Stella always carried a can of pepper spray in her purse," the prosecutor said.

That seemed preposterous. Why would Stella walk around with pepper spray?

Moreover, Jansdotter explained, the police technicians had secured a great many traces left by Stella in Christopher Olsen's apartment on Pilegatan. Strands of hair, flakes of skin, and clothing fibers.

"Stella has been unable to explain these discoveries. Furthermore, she has not provided any cohesive account of her activities during the night of the murder."

Ulrika had my hand in a tight grip, but I didn't dare look at her.

The prosecutor said that they were still awaiting information from the medical examiner in order to map out the sequence of events in detail.

It felt like watching a TV show being filmed. Despite my wife's legal career, I've only ever visited a courtroom a few times, and in those instances, too, I felt like I was at some sort of performance, something taking place on a stage before an audience, something that would be over at a given time. Sort of like a wedding or a funeral. It's not until you're personally involved in the story that it stops being theater. When it's about your own life. Your family.

"The investigators have also discovered evidence on Christopher Olsen's computer," the prosecutor said, paging through a stack of documents. "Here we have a great number of chat conversations between Olsen and Stella Sandell. Conversations indicating that Stella and Christopher knew one another and likely had an intimate relationship."

I felt ill. Horrible images flashed through my mind.

Blomberg hardly raised a single objection when he took the floor, and with that the judge stated that the court would deliberate. This time, the security personnel followed Stella straight down to the underworld. There was a passage that led from the courtroom down to the basement of the jail, and the door closed behind them without a backwards glance from Stella.

"Why doesn't she say something?" I said to Ulrika. "Why . . . ? Why is she just letting them do this?"

It almost appeared that Stella was buying everything that was said. As if she were merely part of the act.

"There's not much she can do," Ulrika said. "She's probably as shocked as we are."

I didn't even want to consider any other alternative.

After just ten minutes we were summoned back into the courtroom and the judge declared that the court had decided to detain Stella with probable cause on suspicion of homicide.

We headed straight for Michael Blomberg's office on Klostergatan. The celebrity lawyer walked across the groaning hardwood floors with heavy steps and a wild expression.

"It's scandalous how worthless this investigation is. Both Jansdotter and the police seem to have blinders on; all they can see is Stella."

"Why didn't you say anything in court?" I asked.

Blomberg stopped short.

"What do you mean?"

He turned to Ulrika, as if she were the one with opinions, not me.

"Why are you just accepting this?" I said. "Shouldn't you be protesting? She has an alibi! Why didn't you say anything about her alibi?"

Blomberg waved dismissively.

"That wouldn't be of any use right now. There's too much circumstantial evidence against Stella, and the ME hasn't determined an exact time frame for the murder yet."

"But the witness," I said. "My Sennevall. She heard fighting outside her window around one o'clock."

Blomberg looked at Ulrika.

"Well, that's true," my wife said. "What have you learned about this Sennevall woman, Michael?"

Blomberg sank down at his desk.

"She might not be the most competent witness. My Sennevall lives her life in a window. Literally. She only goes out to buy groceries or see her therapist; otherwise she sits there spying on her neighbors. She's totally in the know about what goes on in the neighborhood."

"That sounds like a really good witness," I said.

"Not really—this girl is the very definition of mental illness. She has every phobia and neurosis you've ever heard of."

I could just about have predicted as much.

"But that doesn't really matter, does it?"

Both Blomberg and Ulrika squirmed.

"You might not think so," said Blomberg.

"What about Olsen's ex-girlfriend?" Ulrika asked. "Have you dug up anything more on her?"

Dug up? I didn't like the sound of that. I associated it with gossip and slander, bad journalism in celebrity magazines. As if we wanted to find a scapegoat at any cost.

"I think we should put all our money on the ex-girlfriend," said Blomberg. "Linda Lokind."

"Is that her name?"

Blomberg snapped up a piece of paper from his desk to check.

"Yes. Linda Lokind, of Tullgatan 10."

"Have you spoken with her?" Ulrika wondered.

"She's not exactly a chatterbox. She says she's already told the police and the prosecutor everything, but no one believes her. I've tried to get a copy of that statement, but it seems to be stamped confidential. But I'm sure we'll sort that out. We'll have to go through the court instead."

"How long is that going to take?" I asked.

Blomberg clicked his pen.

"Calm down now," Ulrika said, patting my arm.

"Calm down? What do you mean, calm down? If this Lokind has a motive, it ought to be in everyone's best interest to interrogate her! Aren't the police supposed to work 'broadly and objectively'?"

"The police have interrogated her," Blomberg said, tossing his pen on the desk. "For information."

"Evidently that's not enough," I said. "And when can we see Stella? We need to talk to our daughter!"

I was halfway out of my chair.

"Stella is on full restrictions," Blomberg said. "She's only allowed to speak to me."

"She's only eighteen," I said.

"Unfortunately, age doesn't matter," Blomberg replied.

"She's a child!"

I didn't mean to shout. It just happened. I could feel my pulse in my fists and Ulrika took a firm grasp on my wrist.

"Not according to the law," Blomberg said cautiously.

"I don't care about the law. I want to see my daughter!"

My ears were ringing. Even the bearlike Blomberg looked a bit frightened as I yanked myself away from Ulrika's clutches and flew out of my chair.

"Make sure that Stella tells the police everything. No more secrets or nasty surprises. Innocent people don't lie."

24

I hadn't told Stella that I was planning to visit during confirmation camp. Maybe that was stupid of me. Of course I should have mentioned it, but to me it was an obvious thing to do. I was the pastor of one of the organizing congregations, the camp had been launched on my initiative—naturally I wanted to visit the youngsters.

When I arrived at the camp, the confirmands had just finished grilling hotdogs. Several of them had changed into swimwear; some were up to their waists in the water, shivering; others were jumping in from the dock. The two female camp counselors were watching from under a tree, while Robin was splashing around in the lake, his hair wet, a delighted grin on his face.

I lingered up on the grassy slope for a while. It was like standing in front of a piece of art. The happiness and fellowship painted the scene in the loveliest of colors.

The kids didn't have time for me. Several of Stella's classmates said hello, but most of them barely noticed my arrival.

I walked down to the counselors under the tree and shook their hands. They told me everything was going fantastically well. The group was wonderful to work with, and there had already been a number of interesting and openhearted conversations.

None of them mentioned Stella, which I took to mean that she, too, was behaving herself. I had already made up my mind not to worry, but now that it became clear to me that nothing had gone wrong, I noticed relief washing through my body.

But things changed when Stella realized I was there.

She came wading out of the lake with her wet hair hanging in thick ropes. Once on the beach, she wrapped a towel around her body.

When she caught sight of me, her eyes went dark.

"What are you doing here?"

"I'm just checking in on everyone."

I attempted a gentle smile.

"Let me be!"

She vanished up the hill with flip-flops slapping.

Robin convinced me to stay for dinner. There was a separate room where we could sit and Stella wouldn't have to see me.

The cooks at the camp were truly skilled, and the food was exquisite. After dinner I asked if it would be okay to stick around for a while. I would soon be heading for home, but there were a few things I needed to prepare before services the next day.

"Of course," Robin said.

After a few hours of obligatory socializing, it was pleasant to be alone with just my computer and my own thoughts. I'm a fairly social person, but at heart I would probably consider myself an introvert. I've always held privacy to be holy, even within my own family. The right to one's own space in life is, to me, as important as the opportunity to open up and speak about everything. I think it's been a frequent help to Ulrika and me that we've always had the chance to retreat and have some alone time. A requirement to constantly share everything can so easily become stifling. It's often said that people are herd animals, but we mustn't forget that we have the need for solitude as well.

As I completed my preparations, dusk began to steal over the lake. Time had flown by, and my undertakings had been more demanding than I'd expected. And since Ulrika was working in Stockholm, there was no real reason for me to rush home. All that remained was to bid farewell to Robin. I was hoping to avoid Stella to keep from annoying her even further. It was largely thanks to Robin that the camp was having such success once again, there was no denying it. I was so pleased that everything had gone well. A great weight had lifted from my chest, and I enjoyed every crisp breath on my way across the courtyard.

The camp was held at a conference retreat center that was made up of three separate long buildings. The main building contained the dining room, kitchen, and common room; directly across the courtyard was the dormitory. Not far off, partially hidden behind the trunks of tall beeches, was the smallest building, where the counselors slept when they weren't on night duty.

The confirmands appeared to be enjoying free time. Some were out on the lawn, but most of them were keeping to the dormitory.

"Have you seen Robin?" I asked one of the female counselors.

"I think he went to the counselors' cabin."

I hurried through the small grove of trees. The teens' laughter echoed off the evening sky.

I approached the door and knocked. There was no response. Perhaps Robin was on the toilet? Or in the shower? I tried the handle, but the door was locked. Surely he hadn't fallen asleep?

I rounded the corner of the building and peered through the window, but all I saw was an empty bed. With little hope, I moved on to the next window. The curtain was down, but I could see faint light coming from inside thanks to a small gap. Robin must be sleeping. I leaned forward to knock but was startled as I realized I could see straight into the room through the gap. There, in the dark, sat two people who were staring at each other in panic.

That brief glimpse was all it took. Three years have passed, and I can still evoke that unpleasant image whenever I want. Presumably it will never go away.

The image of Robin and Stella scrambling to get their clothing back in place.

25

By Thursday morning, Stella had spent five nights under lock and key. I pictured her on a dirty bed in a cramped, dark jail cell and my heart ached. During breakfast I paced back and forth across the kitchen, harping on all my worries.

"Stop that," Ulrika said. "Dwelling won't help."

"Then what should I do?"

"I'm going to work," she said. "Maybe that would make you feel better too."

It would at least help me think about something else. I reported myself healthy again over the phone and walked over to the church hall. September is like Advent for this university town. After the summer lull, the streets are full of giddy students trying to find their way, confused, consumed with putting their identities on display. Wobbling cyclists everywhere, GPS voices in their pockets, twenty-year-olds with answers to all of life's difficult questions in their leather briefcases or Fjällräven backpacks. Lund never recovers until October, when the worst of the coquetry has settled, after people have exchanged saliva during orientation and the very strangest of newcomers have been reabsorbed back into their hometowns. This is the downside to a university town as much as it is its charm. To be invaded, each autumn, by fresh dreamers and do-gooders, to shed its skin for a few weeks of Indian summer before the leaves fall. Love it or hate it, you never quite get used to it.

My colleagues were in the church-hall kitchen and their voices carried into the entryway as I hung up my coat.

"I was shocked at first, but when I gave it some thought, well . . ."

"She's always had a terrible temper."

It was impossible not to hear what they were saying.

"They haven't set limits. There's only one language a girl like Stella understands."

"Ulrika and Adam have been too tolerant."

I stood stock-still in the entryway, taking in their words.

"Of course it's not Stella's fault," said Monika, one of the deacons. "She's only a child, or at least a teenager."

They were silent for a moment. I closed my eyes and felt myself slowly rising from the ground and floating. Then they went on:

"Stella's seen a psychiatrist before, you know."

"That doesn't surprise me."

"She's always had some sort of mental health issue. Even as a little girl, there was something different about her."

Silence again. Someone coughed.

I like my colleagues. I have always depended upon them, always felt their trust and love. Ever since I started with this congregation, large parts of the operation have undergone positive changes, and I'm sure most people would agree that is largely to my credit. I was so unprepared to be slandered in this manner that it was as if my mind went numb. Like a zombie, I walked straight into the kitchen and joined them at the table.

"Why . . . Adam!" Monika exclaimed.

Five pairs of eyes stared at me, huge and mute, as if they had just witnessed the second coming of the Lord.

"You're not supposed to be at work, are you?" they chorused.

"I have a wedding this afternoon."

"But we assigned Otto to that," said Anita, our administrator.

"Didn't you see that I reported myself healthy again?"

She blushed.

"We didn't think you . . ."

I examined each of them, one by one, and waited for someone to make excuses, but all that came out were broken sentences.

At last Monika stood up and took my arm. She has been with the congregation since the days of Saint Ansgar—she's the glue that holds us all together, the rock we all cling to in every situation.

"Come," she said, leading me slowly down the corridor as my brain continued to run on idle.

We sat down across from each other in the low easy chairs in her office. Monika placed her ring-adorned hands on my knees and leaned forward with her gentle cat eyes.

"Where do you think we went wrong, Monika?"

She took me by the elbows and shook her head slowly.

"You didn't do anything wrong," she said. "God has a purpose. Something we haven't discovered yet."

Part of me wanted to tell Monika and God to go to hell, but luckily I came to my senses and thanked her for her concern instead.

"Now go home and get some proper rest. Take care of Ulrika," Monika said, hugging me. "I'll be praying for you two. And for Stella."

In that moment her words felt so petty. Almost fake.

But I do wish I had followed Monika's advice.

There was too much crawling around under my skin. My thoughts seemed to take shape behind a thick curtain of fog, and my heart was scratching at my ribs like a terrier. My body was telling me to run, to keep from congealing into a single painful present, so I ran—or walked, at least—mile after mile until my back was soaked with sweat.

I walked all the way downtown, and as I left City Park I wondered how everything would have turned out if we'd reported Robin to the police. He had raped Stella, and we had let him get away with it. What signals had that sent to our daughter? What sort of parents were we?

My pulse was pounding indignantly in my neck, and my muscles were twitching. I sped up as I passed the dog park at Södra Esplanaden.

When I saw the street sign for Tullgatan, I felt a stabbing in my chest. I stopped and stared.

This was where Christopher Olsen's ex-girlfriend lived. Blomberg had read us her address. I couldn't just walk by.

26

It was in many ways Ulrika's decision not to file a police report on Robin. I don't mean to blame her—it was my choice too—but I likely wouldn't have hesitated to report him if it hadn't been for Ulrika's objections.

I shoved him up against the wall in the counselors' cabin, my fist hanging in the air, but at the last second I managed to control myself. I dragged Stella off through the grove of trees and sat her in my car. I still don't recall anything about the drive home.

Ulrika thought we should take Stella to the hospital immediately, but I was of the opinion that we had to call the police first.

"He raped her," I said. "Even if Stella did follow him to the counselors' cabin. Whether or not she initiated it."

Ulrika was dashing back and forth in the kitchen.

"I don't know what's best," she said.

"You can't mean to say that Stella is responsible in any way. She's a child."

"Not in the eyes of the law. She's fifteen. The age of consent in Sweden."

Ulrika stopped by the window. Her shoulders were shaking.

"I know how this sort of trial goes," she said. "I've personally been involved in several of them."

I'd almost repressed the memory, but a few years earlier Ulrika had defended a guy who was on trial, along with a few other young men, for gang rape. There had been an outcry when all of them were acquitted.

"They'll come after her hard," said Ulrika. "Every detail will be scrutinized. What she said, how she acted, what she was wearing."

"Stop," I said. "She's the victim here."

"I know that. Everyone knows that. But in court, who did what is crucial—what sort of initiative Stella took, how she behaved before and after the incident. Anything that can sow even a kernel of doubt will be dissected by the defense attorney."

I went over to the window and placed my arms around her waist.

"We can't let that happen. That can't be what happens."

Ulrika stroked my arm.

"I don't know if it can happen any other way."

Later that night she shared with me some of the many horrid details the girl was pushed to share during the gang-rape trial. It was shocking. I wouldn't consider myself particularly naïve, but the fact is, I felt physically ill once I learned how this sort of trial unfolds. Sure, we've all read and heard about lawyers who ask rape victims how short their skirts were and how much alcohol they'd had to drink, but still, I had dismissed these instances as extreme exceptions. Only now did I understand it was more or less the standard practice in such cases.

I'd never thought I would advise anyone, much less my own child, not to file a police report, not to trust the system, not to let justice take its course, but now that I was starting to understand what would be demanded from Stella, what she would be forced to endure, I found that I had to reconsider.

"What's the most important thing here?" Ulrika asked before we fell asleep. "That Stella makes it past this relatively unscathed, or that Robin doesn't go unpunished?"

As if those outcomes were in direct opposition. Why couldn't we have both? Today I wish I had challenged the black-and-white picture Ulrika had painted for me, that I had stood my ground and made sure that justice was served.

We failed Stella unforgivably.

27

I walked up to the first door I found on Tullgatan. I just wanted to check.

Perhaps Linda Lokind was sitting there inside even now. Christopher Olsen's former live-in girlfriend. Blomberg seemed certain that she had something to do with the murder.

My heart beat faster as I read the last names next to the intercom. Jerbring, Samuelson, Makkah. No Lokind.

I walked to the next door.

If nothing else, Linda Lokind could help me understand. She could tell me about Christopher Olsen. Maybe she had some idea about how he and Stella had met and what had transpired between them.

At the third door, I found it. Lokind, second floor. I stared at the name for a long time and my heart pounded even faster. What was I *doing*?

I tried the door. Locked. Leaning forward, I peered into the stairwell. What would I say? How could I introduce myself without scaring her? Without seeming crazy? What if she called the police?

I glanced through the names on the intercom again and settled on I. Jönsson. It sounded friendly, somehow. I pressed the button, and when a croaking voice said "Hello?" I explained that I had a delivery of flowers for a neighbor who wasn't home. I. Jönsson buzzed me into the stairwell right away.

I stopped two floors up and rang the bell.

I recalled my visit to My Sennevall and wondered how I could make things go more smoothly this time. It had already been crossing a line to visit Sennevall, but this was an even greater overstep. If it came out that I'd tracked down Linda Lokind . . . was it possible that she was dangerous? In the worst case she was a revenge-fueled killer; in the best case she was a psychopath liar who had falsely accused her ex of the most horrifying things. I had every reason to be cautious.

When a surprised woman opened the door, I recoiled. This could hardly be her. The woman before me looked like a model.

"Linda?" I said.

"Yes?"

She peered at me, suspicious.

"I need to talk to you."

"Who are you?"

I pointed at my clerical collar.

"May I come in for a moment?"

She gasped. "What happened? Is it Mom?"

"It's about Christopher Olsen."

Right away, Linda Lokind's expression relaxed.

"Okay," she said, letting me in. "But I've already said I don't want to get involved."

Her apartment was bright and spacious. The wall of the corridor that led to the bedroom was covered with a world-map decal, and on the floor below it stood a meter-high glass vase in the shape of a bottle with a single lily in it. The bookcase held a few fitness books held up between colorful decorative elephants. It was all bathed in the light of a giant, modern chandelier.

"Could we have a seat?" I asked, pointing at the dining table in front of the French balcony.

"Why? What do you want?"

She had stopped in the doorway with her hands on her hips.

"I represent the Olsen family," I said, pulling out a chair for myself.

It was as if the plan had been there all along. I just needed to set it in motion.

"I told you, I don't want anything more to do with this."

"Just sit down for a little bit," I begged. "I'm here because the family deserves a dignified closure."

"What family? Margaretha?"

"That's right." I nodded quickly. "Christopher is no longer with us. All we want is for the truth to come out."

"What do you mean?"

Of course I hadn't expected her to confess to the murder, but it was interesting to observe her reactions. I've always been good at exposing liars.

"What happened between you and Christopher?" I asked.

"Margaretha knows what happened. I told the police everything."

She sat down at last, a reluctant grimace on her face.

"Can't you tell me again?" I asked.

"That police officer. Agnes Thelin. She didn't believe me. I tried to ask for someone else, but no one listened."

Linda Lokind was undeniably an attractive woman, but beneath her smooth skin and well-proportioned face I sensed something else: a self-conscious and ambivalent little girl. How old could she be—twenty-two, twenty-three? I was quite certain she wasn't telling the whole truth, but I was almost as certain that she wasn't a cold-blooded killer.

"I understand it's difficult for Margaretha to accept, but her son is a psychopath. *Was*, I mean. Chris was a sick psychopath."

According to Linda, everything had been just fine for the first two years. Or at least, she'd lived her life believing that this was the case. Later on she had realized there had been hints of darkness all along: secrets, betrayals, infidelity. But it took almost two years for the façade to start crumbling.

Linda fell head over heels when they first met. Chris Olsen was handsome, charming, intelligent, and sociable. It quickly went from a passionate crush to love and plans for a future together. Too quickly, she now knew. Perhaps she would have seen the warning signs in time if she hadn't thrown herself headlong into the relationship.

"Stop blaming yourself," I said. "Our hearts and our brains can both be good guides. Only in hindsight is it easy to see which paths you never should have taken."

She smiled. Although she was hiding something from me, I felt an immediate soft spot for her—that bald naïveté and her keen longing for sympathy.

"When he hit me the first time, I swore to myself it would never happen again. I wasn't that kind of woman. I don't know how many times I told myself that."

"I don't think anyone considers themselves that kind of woman."

She nodded. Her smile had vanished; her eyes were shiny.

"It sounds stupid, but really, Chris was wonderful too. When he wasn't violent. Every time I thought it was the last time, that it would never happen again, that I would leave him. But then everything would turn around and I would feel hope again. Maybe this time. If I just give him another chance. Idiotic, right?"

"Not at all."

I believed her. I'd heard similar stories from other women in the same situation.

"I haven't experienced it myself, but I've met many violent men through my work. I understand that it's just one side of them. No person is solely one thing or the next."

"It would have been so easy to leave," Linda said, wiping her pinky finger under her eye. "I'll never forgive myself for staying. I'll never be able to see myself as the person I thought I was. You have no idea how awful it is for your whole self-image to come crashing down."

She was right. I couldn't understand. Not back then, at least.

"But Chris was a pig who deserves to rot in hell. He abused me and cheated on me and then he left me. You can read all about it in the interrogation with the police. I can't deal with going through it all again. Anyway, it doesn't matter anymore."

"For Margaretha's sake . . ."

Linda looked straight at me.

"I really don't care. I'm not sorry that Chris is dead."

Her eyes were cold as ice. It was clear that she meant what she said, and for the first time I thought perhaps she had been involved in the murder after all. Maybe there had been multiple killers? Maybe she had hired someone to do it?

"I'm not a bit surprised, either," she said. "I'm sure he did the same thing to her."

I tried to ignore my curiosity; I folded my hands and looked at her, but this time there was no continuation. Linda pursed her lips and let her gaze wander to the window.

"To whom?"

"Stella. The girl who did it."

What did she mean by that? How did she know Stella's name?

"She's only a teenager. I guess she did what I should have done a long time ago."

I couldn't help the images that came to my mind. The glint of a knife, stabbing and stabbing; Christopher Olsen's lovely smile twisting into a scream of pain. Dazed, I tried to erase Stella's face from the scenes. It couldn't be true.

"Why would you say that?" I managed to say.

"What?"

"Why do you think Stella did it?"

Linda looked at me in surprise.

"She's the one who was arrested for it."

"Do you know her?"

She shook her head.

"I hope she gets off."

I was struck dumb. Could it be true that Christopher Olsen had attacked Stella, or victimized her somehow? If he had, why hadn't she told the police? What if Stella was the true victim in this mess?

"How is Margaretha doing?" asked Linda Lokind.

I had sunk into my thoughts and didn't respond.

"It must be terrible," said Linda. "I liked Margaretha. Or at least I didn't have anything against her. She was always nice to me. It's not her fault that Chris is a psychopath."

"No," I said, although I was inwardly hesitant. Didn't Margaretha bear some of the guilt? She was his mother, after all.

"What about Stanne? What does he say?"

I scratched the back of my neck. Who was she talking about?

"Stanislav?" Linda said.

Her eyes went sharp and narrow. I felt cornered.

"You said you represent the Olsen family. Don't you know who Stanislav is?"

"Of course."

Linda pushed back her chair and took a few hasty steps backward.

"Who are you, really? You never told me your name."

"I didn't?"

A name popped into my mind immediately, but I was reluctant to utter it. How many times can you allow yourself to lie? Sooner or later you'll cross the line of decency and dignity, no matter how noble the purpose of the lie may seem.

"I want you to leave now," said Linda.

She had backed up against the wall beside the large glass vase. She looked frightened, but there was still something wild in her eyes, something that seemed to border on madness.

"I'm leaving right now," I said, hurrying past her. "Thanks for your time."

She slipped over to the doorway to keep an eye on me. She held her phone in one raised hand, ready to make a call with a single push of a button.

I crouched down in the cramped hall to put on my shoes. I had tied one and was about to switch feet when my glance landed upon the shoe rack next to me. There must have been seven or eight pairs on it, but there was one in particular that captured my attention.

Fingers trembling, I managed to tie my other shoe, then stole another look at the rack.

No doubt about it—on the rack stood a pair of shoes identical to Stella's. Might they even be the same size? The same shoe that had left the footprint at the scene of the crime. The same kind of shoe Christopher Olsen's killer had been wearing.

28

I hurried through downtown, my thoughts buzzing like a nest of wasps. So Linda Lokind owned the very same brand and style of shoes as Stella. And that look in her eyes when she backed up against the wall. Distant and lost, but also full of rage. She had truly looked like someone who might suffer a fit of insanity. At the same time, her theory that Christopher Olsen had assaulted Stella ached in the back of my head. I couldn't ignore the fact that this was a conceivable scenario. Had that bastard harmed Stella?

I walked faster, my steps falling so hard that they echoed off the asphalt. Not again. It couldn't be true. At the same time, it wasn't at all difficult to imagine Stella's violent reaction, how she would fly into a crazy, blind rage; use a knife that happened to be at hand. But why? Outside the building, on a playground. And where had the knife come from? And why on earth wouldn't she have told the truth to the police?

I considered consulting Ulrika about this line of reasoning, but I was afraid she would dismiss my ideas as fantasy and try to make me reconsider my actions. She seemed to have a completely different opinion about how we could best help Stella. I didn't understand how she could trust Michael Blomberg so completely. He may have been extraordinarily qualified, and he was certainly capable, but it didn't feel like he was sufficiently engaged. Why was Stella still in custody? And we still hadn't been allowed to see her.

Instead I decided to talk to the police. This could not stand. Anyone could see that Linda Lokind would be able to provide knowledge in this investigation. Why was Stella locked up when Linda was the one who had motive?

I increased my speed until I was nearly running up Stora Södergatan. As I reached the Stäket restaurant and the Färgaren parking garage, my phone rang in my pocket. It was my mother. She spoke breathlessly, and some of what she said was lost, but there was no mistaking her general message.

Everyone knew.

The evening papers had published online articles about Stella. This afternoon there had even been a brief story on the radio news. She hadn't been mentioned by name—respect for journalistic ethics hadn't fallen completely by the wayside, at least—but they had generously given enough clues that anyone who wanted to know her identity didn't have to put in too much effort to find out.

"Aunt Dagny already called to ask if it's true," Mom said.

She sounded so shaken.

"Tell her the truth. The police have made a mistake."

As soon as we hung up, I slipped into the small alley beside the parking garage to find an out-of-the-way spot. I walked straight through the building and out the other side. Then, on a bench outside the Katedral School, I devoted half an hour to self-destructive googling. First I read what had been written in the papers, and then I moved on to shadier sites. The information ran the gamut from general facts about Stella and our family to flat-out lies and crazy speculation.

She showed a lot of promise at handball, but she couldn't control her temper.

She was probably waiting for him on the playground. Olsen was worth millions, it must have been planned.

I read it all and just wanted to scream. It was so out of touch with reality. And the people who were typing these comments in front of their screens were the same folks I might meet on the street, in church, maybe even in a courtroom.

I had to talk to the police. As I walked up Lilla Fiskaregatan, I called and notified Agnes Thelin that I was on my way. She relayed that I was welcome to drop by.

I was stopped several times on my walk by curious people who wanted to talk to me. I was forced to stand there, surrounded by people who knew who I was but whose names I had long since forgotten, as bikes whooshed past and the Romanian man outside Pressbyrån played the theme from *The Godfather* on his accordion.

A woman from my congregation was out walking a puppy and stopped me.

"How are you doing?" she asked with mournful eyes. "It must be a mistake. The police are making fools of themselves."

I usually have no trouble standing before a full congregation and leading a service or greeting every single person I meet. I'm happy to stop and exchange a few words, listen to a fellow human, and try to say something sufficiently polite and wise. But this was different. I felt suffocated.

In the end I panicked, hid my face, and hurried over to Bantorget, then under the viaduct and up to police headquarters.

Chief Inspector Agnes Thelin met me outside her office. She offered me coffee, but my hand was shaking so hard that the spoon fell to the floor when I tried to stir in the sugar.

"How are you doing?" she asked.

"I finally got a little sleep last night."

Agnes Thelin nodded and gave me a warm smile.

"I hoped you would be in touch, Adam."

What did she mean by that?

"I thought *you* would be in touch," I said with a certain edge to my voice. "It feels like we're not getting any information whatsoever."

Agnes Thelin poured milk into her coffee.

"The investigation is at a delicate stage. We're working very hard to find out what happened."

"Are you?" I said, crossing my arms. "Are you really? Are you working 'broadly and without preconceived notions'? Because one might easily think you'd already made up your minds."

For an instant my vision went fuzzy. I bent forward and brought my hands to my forehead.

"Are you okay?" Thelin asked. "I understand this must be wearing on you."

I glanced up and tried to compose myself. I must not appear to be crazy.

"Linda Lokind," I said. "Why aren't you taking a closer look at her?"

Thelin sipped her coffee.

"Naturally, we are looking at everything that might be relevant in this case," she said, running a finger over her lips.

"Are you aware that Linda Lokind has a pair of the exact same shoes as Stella's? The same ones that left a print at the scene of the crime?"

The chief inspector nearly spat out her coffee.

"What? How do you know that?"

"How I know isn't really the important thing here, is it? Someone told me. The question is, why haven't you investigated it? Why haven't you searched Linda Lokind's place?"

Agnes Thelin wiped her mouth with a napkin.

"I am unable to discuss the preliminary investigation with you, but I guarantee—"

"Your guarantees aren't worth much to me right now! I'm getting the impression that you don't know what you're doing."

"I'm sorry you feel that way," said Agnes Thelin. "But it's not true."

I took a deep breath.

"Linda Lokind was abused and denigrated by Christopher Olsen for several years. When she finally dared to report it, you didn't listen to her and closed the investigation. She had every reason to take the law into her own hands. She wanted to take revenge on the man who destroyed her life. Could there be a clearer motive? Furthermore, she owns the exact same shoes that the killer was wearing. Can you explain to me why she should walk free while my daughter is locked up and isn't even allowed to talk to her parents?"

Agnes Thelin glanced at the door. It was clear she was having a hard time defending herself.

"This is starting to look an awful lot like corruption," I said. "A miscarriage of justice."

"I understand it may seem frustrating, but we know a lot more than you do, Adam. You have to trust that we're doing our best to arrive at the truth."

"Then why don't you tell me what you know?"

She scratched her nose.

"I can tell you this much. There may be good reason not to give too much credence to what Linda Lokind says. We've done an exhaustive inquiry into the accusations she made against Christopher Olsen, and the preliminary investigation was closed for lack of evidence. There was nothing to suggest that she was telling the truth about what happened."

"Are you suggesting that Linda Lokind is lying about all of this?"

Agnes Thelin bit her lower lip.

"I'm just telling you what was found in the investigation."

29

Agnes Thelin waited as I stirred my cup of coffee.

Could it be true that I had been duped by Linda Lokind? Was she the actual crazy one here—had she reported Christopher Olsen for abuse and rape in order to get revenge?

"Isn't it generally true that domestic abusers go free more often than not?" I asked.

"It can often be a challenge to find evidence that will hold up in court," Agnes Thelin admitted. "But in this particular case, there were so many uncertainties that I advise you to take Lokind's statements with some reservation. Unfortunately, I can't say any more than that."

She didn't have to. She was sure that Linda Lokind had been lying about Christopher Olsen. I, too, was convinced that Linda was hiding something.

"But that doesn't really change anything. If Linda Lokind was prepared to direct false accusations against her former partner, she might very well have resorted to violence as well. Can't you see that?"

Agnes Thelin tried to hide a sigh behind one hand.

"I hear what you're saying, Adam."

I clenched my teeth. She heard what I was saying but wasn't planning to do a thing about it.

"When did you last talk to Stella on the phone?" she asked.

What did that have to do with anything?

"I don't really recall. We hardly ever talk on the phone. I've stopped calling; she won't answer anyway. It has to be text or Messenger."

"You said you had contact via text on Friday night."

"No, not contact. I sent a text, but I didn't get a response."

"Are you sure of that?"

I kept my answer to myself. Had the police managed to re-create Stella's texts? Or would it come to seizing my phone and searching it? There was certainly no reason to be caught in a lie that might not even turn out to be important in the long run.

"I don't actually recall. Maybe she responded; maybe not."

The chief inspector cleared her throat.

"When did you last see Stella's phone?"

Huh? I turned away to keep from showing my surprise. Hadn't the police found Stella's phone? I'd assumed it was confiscated when they searched our house.

"I'm sorry. I don't remember."

Agnes Thelin jotted down a note in her file.

"Have you seen the phone since Stella was apprehended?"

What did this mean? Where could Stella's phone be, if the police hadn't found it?

"No," I replied.

Agnes Thelin let a sigh escape through her nostrils.

"This is important now, Adam. Do you remember what Stella was wearing when she came home Friday night?"

Sweat sprung to my underarms.

"Is this an interrogation? Do I even need to answer your questions?"

Thelin just looked at me.

"I'm useless at that stuff. My wife is always annoyed; I never notice when she buys new clothes."

Agnes Thelin gave a forced smile.

"But you talked to Stella when she came home? You saw her clothes?"

"Yes, sure."

"And you didn't notice anything different? Stains, or something like that?"

I was sweating even more.

"It was dark. I don't really recall . . ."

Not remembering, of course, is not the same thing as lying. I was trying to squeeze myself through every loophole I could find. Meanwhile, Thelin paged through her documents, her fingers tense.

"When did you first hear of Christopher Olsen?"

"Last Saturday," I said honestly. "When I found out you had taken Stella into custody."

"So you'd never heard his name before?"

I rubbed at my eyes.

"Not that I know of."

"It's a simple question, Adam. Had you heard of Olsen before, or not?"

"No, I hadn't."

"So Stella never mentioned his name. Did she ever talk about someone who might have been Olsen? A boyfriend? Did you know that she was seeing someone?"

"Stella didn't have a boyfriend. Ask anyone! As I understand it, she only met up with Christopher Olsen on a few rare occasions. Why would she want to hurt him? It's not logical."

"Human behavior isn't always logical."

"But mostly it is."

Agnes Thelin took a sheet of paper from her desk.

"Listen to this," she said, reading aloud. "*I think about you 24-7. I want you so much.* Or this: *You are the handsomest, sexiest being on earth. So freaking glad I met you.*"

A clump of disgust slid up my throat. Was she really allowed to do this? It felt so wrong, against the rules—immoral, to say the least.

"These are chat messages Stella sent to Christopher Olsen. We found several more like them on his computer."

I made fists under the desk and pressed them against my thighs.

"How do you know Stella wrote those? Anyone could have hacked her account."

Thelin ignored me.

"I know how this must feel, Adam. But it's going to be okay; we're going to get through this together."

"What are you talking about? You don't have to get through anything. You can go home tonight and hug your boys. My daughter is the one who's locked up in a cell!"

"I know, I know. But the only way to move forward now is to be brave enough to tell the truth. Were you really awake when Stella came home?"

"Yes."

I fought to keep my breathing calm and slow.

"What time was it then?"

I took a deep breath.

"Quarter to midnight," I said with as much self-control as I could muster. "Exactly eleven forty-five."

Agnes Thelin gave a brief nod and pushed her chair back from the desk. The legs of the chair scraped against the linoleum floor. She ended up about a meter away from her desk, where she leaned back and gazed up at the ceiling.

"Adam, Adam," she said. "I understand why you're doing this. Perhaps I would do the same."

I didn't say anything. She had no idea what it was like to be sitting here.

"Our children mean everything to us," she went on. "Stella is your little girl. It's horrible to find out you can't protect your own child."

Once again, I thought of Job.

"I'm not out to judge you," said Agnes Thelin. "But I don't think this is the right way to go about things. This isn't right, Adam."

I closed my eyes. Is it not right to protect your child? Your family? Can it ever be wrong?

"I think we're done here," I said, standing up to leave.

Agnes Thelin sighed and stared after me.

I had to get hold of Amina.

I looked up her number and called. After one ring, an automated voice informed me that the number was no longer in service.

30

I hurried toward the arena. The girls' practice would be over any minute. With any luck I would find Amina there.

Normally, I love walking into the arena. This time, when I pulled open the door and my nostrils filled with the stuffy smell of late summer sweat, all I felt was discomfort. A few teenage boys in their workout clothes were hanging around in the cafeteria, and a woman breezed past me on her way to the parking lot. My discomfort suddenly became overwhelming. The looks, the questions—the fact that everyone knew. Because they did, didn't they? Everyone had so many opinions, they thought they knew, they had ready-made theories. My brain was clouded and my heart was pounding all the way up in my throat. I couldn't stand the thought of being forced to encounter people I knew.

I stumbled back out to the bike racks and hid behind a tree. There I stood, my back pressed against its rough trunk, shielded from the world and furious at the situation.

After a while, the girls streamed through the door. Amina's teammates. I peered out without revealing my hiding spot.

At last Amina came toward the bike rack. She secured her gym bag to the luggage holder and was just about to bend over and unlock her bike when I said hello.

"You scared me!"

She leaped back.

"I'm sorry, I didn't mean to. I tried to call, but . . ."

"My phone got stolen."

She coiled the cable lock in her basket and backed the bike out of the rack.

"Can we have a chat?" I asked.

"I have to go home," she said without looking at me. "I'm ridiculously busy and school starts in four days."

"I can walk with you for a bit," I suggested. "If you walk your bike."

She sighed and guided her bike with both hands on the handlebars, moving so fast that I had to jog to keep up.

"Why don't you want to talk to me?" I asked.

"What? We *are* talking."

I followed her onto the pedestrian bridge over Ringvägen. Amina's eyes were fixed on a point far ahead and she was still striding at full speed.

"Do you know something, Amina?"

She didn't respond.

"Please, you have to tell me everything," I said.

"I don't know anything!" she snapped. "I told the police everything."

I took a few quick steps and came up alongside her.

"You knew that Stella was spending time with Christopher Olsen, didn't you?"

"Yes," she said curtly as we walked into City Park.

"Were they a couple? Did Stella have a relationship with that man?"

We had just passed the café when she stopped and looked at me.

"No, nothing like that. They met each other out a time or two and knew each other sort of in passing. That was all."

Her eyes flashed in the half darkness. She had taken one hand from the handlebars, and the bike wobbled.

"Had you met him too?" I asked.

She turned around again, took a firm grip on the handlebars, and pushed the bike ahead of her down the gravel path.

"Amina!" I said, my voice overly harsh. "Stella is in jail! Have you ever been in a jail? Do you know what one of those cells looks like?"

I almost got run over by a jogger with headphones who muttered "fuckin' old people" at me as I tried to catch up again. Amina slowed down a tiny bit. Silent tears flowed down her cheeks, and my heart ached. My first instinct was to embrace her like a child, like the child she still was to some extent. Instead I begged her to forgive me.

"I'm not doing so well, Amina. This is all driving me crazy."

"I know," she said between sobs. "I feel like shit too."

"Please tell me," I begged.

31

Amina and I have always had a special relationship. There have been times when Amina preferred to turn to me instead of her parents. I'm quite sure I know things about her that no other adult is aware of.

It was almost four years ago now. Late autumn, after confirmation; the girls were in ninth grade and we were on top of the regional standings for senior girls.

One morning, I discovered Roger Arvidsen standing on the steps of the church hall. He looked dejected and confused in his fur hat.

Roger Arvidsen looked older than he really was. He had recently turned fifty, but poor hygiene and bad genes combined with a sedentary lifestyle, smoking, and constant coffee-drinking had made him look old. He looked in poor shape, with brownish teeth, multiple chins, and dirty fingers. The neighborhood kids called him the Monster.

Each Sunday, Roger dutifully came to church with his mother, with whom he also lived. I quickly made it a habit to converse with him for a bit each time we met, since I suspected he wasn't used to being noticed by anyone but his mother. There was no denying that Roger wasn't particularly gifted, but he seemed to be a kind and timid person who deserved to be treated well.

Not once had Roger sought me out on his own, and when we spoke I often had to draw him out. So I realized straightaway that something was wrong when I saw that he was standing on our steps without his mother.

I asked if I could be of service in any way.

Next thing I knew, Roger was sitting in my office, still wearing his fur hat, his teeth chattering. His story hurt me, physically.

Roger explained that he had been visited by a young girl on two occasions. Both times, his mother had just left home to play bingo. He knew the girl wasn't alone. He had seen her friend down at the front door, keeping a lookout.

The girl had asked if he wanted to invite her in for coffee, so Roger did. That was how he had been raised. When you had visitors, you offered them coffee. The first time, they just talked for a while and then the girl disappeared again. But the next time, she asked Roger out of the blue to take off his pants. He refused, of course. He had no idea what the young girl was up to, but he wasn't dumb enough to believe she was horny for him. After some persuasion, Roger did allow the girl to sit on his lap. She photographed the two of them on her phone.

"Then she wanted a thousand kronor," Roger explained. "If I didn't give her a thousand kronor she would show people the pictures and report me to the police. She said everyone would think I was a pedophile. There are already rumors about me."

So he had given her one thousand kronor. I found it difficult to blame him for that particular action, at least. He was hardly the first person to buy his way out of false allegations.

But now he had received a note in his mailbox—the girl was demanding another thousand kronor, or else she would give the photos to the police.

"I don't want anything bad to happen to her," he said. "It's just as much my fault."

I resolutely stood up and assured Roger that I would take care of it right away.

He didn't even need to say her name. It was obvious whom we were discussing.

I told Monika, the deacon, that I had a migraine, then went home and banged on the door to Stella's room until she let me in.

"What the hell have you done?"

And I never curse. Seldom had Stella looked so flattened. She made no excuses, just confessed and swore up and down that she would return the money immediately and apologize. It was just a stupid idea that had gone off the rails. Nothing like it would happen ever again.

I didn't mention any of it to Ulrika. On one hand this felt like a deception—you're expected to share this sort of thing with your spouse. On the other hand, I was sparing her; what she didn't know couldn't hurt her. In hindsight, I have to admit that much of my reasoning here revolved around shame. I couldn't come to terms with what Stella had done, and I didn't want anyone else, not even my wife, to know about it.

When I saw Roger in church the next Sunday, I took him aside after the service. Once again I had to drag the words out of him.

"Did you get your money back?"

"Oh, yes."

"All of it?"

"Yes."

"And Stella apologized? Did she seem genuinely sorry?" I asked.

"Yes." Roger nodded again and shifted back and forth. "But it wasn't her."

"What?"

He lowered his head.

"It wasn't Stella who did it," he said. "It was the other one, the little dark one."

32

Amina and I walked side by side through City Park. We had nearly reached Svanegatan and could hear the hum of traffic.

"I was there the first time Stella met Chris," Amina said. "It was at Tegnérs. He seemed like a perfectly ordinary guy. Nothing sketchy about him. Except he was pretty old, but we didn't know that at first."

"When was this?"

She shrugged.

"A few months ago."

"But what was Stella doing at his place? The police found evidence that she was there."

"She probably just went home with him."

I regretted asking. I didn't want to know any more.

"An after-party, maybe?" Amina said. "I don't really know. I haven't seen Stella for over a week, since the weekend before last."

Her bike tipped and I readied myself to catch it in case she lost her grip.

"Did you see Christopher Olsen that time too?"

Amina straightened the handlebars.

"Yeah, that Friday."

"That was Stella's birthday."

"We were only with him for a little while, then Stella and I took off for Stortorget and had a glass of wine. I had a match on Saturday, so nothing too crazy."

"And you haven't seen each other since? But you've talked, haven't you? Texted each other?"

"Not exactly. But she did message me on Friday. We were supposed to meet up that night, but I had practice and I wasn't feeling all that well. Then on Saturday I ended up with a fever."

"So you don't have any idea what happened on Friday?"

She was quick to shake her head. I felt doubtful.

"Then what did you tell the police? When they questioned you?"

"The truth, obviously. I couldn't lie, could I?"

I didn't respond.

Over the years I've learned that lying is an art form, a skill some people have mastered while others never will. Like other talents, I'm sure you can improve with practice and hone this skill, but essentially it seems to come down to a certain innate disposition. Stella has always been a good liar. Even in elementary school I had a hard time pinpointing her lies. They were sometimes about the most banal things.

"Have you cleaned your room yet, Stella?"

"Yes, Dad."

One time it would be true; the next she would lie to my face. It was impossible to determine when she was telling the truth.

I presume Amina isn't a skilled liar at all. After the incident with Roger Arvidsen she begged me for forgiveness, sobbing, and got me to promise never to tell Dino and Alexandra. A promise I kept, naturally.

She wasn't succeeding in her lie this time either. I had no doubt that she was hiding something. Who was she trying to protect? Herself or Stella?

Or me? Did she believe I couldn't handle the truth?

We took a left onto Svanegatan. A car sped by, going much too fast.

"Amina, do you think that Stella . . . ? Do you think Stella did it?"

She stopped short.

"No! Stella didn't do anything! You aren't thinking . . . ?"

I didn't know. How could Amina be so certain?

"Please," I begged again as she mounted the bike for the last fifty meters home. "I have to know."

"Know what?"

"Everything."

"I don't know everything either." Amina put her feet on the pedals and pedaled one revolution. "I don't know any more than you do. And neither does Stella, presumably."

She waved over her shoulder as she biked home.

I knew she was lying.

33

When I came home that evening, Ulrika was standing in the bedroom and gazing out the window. My mind was sluggish. Every muscle in my body ached as if I had just climbed a mountain.

"What are you looking at?" I asked.

She didn't respond. As I put my arms around her waist, I discovered that her face was full of shadows; her tears seemed to have hollowed out her cheeks and dried her lips.

"Honey," I whispered.

"Where have you been?"

Her voice was a tremor.

I explained that I had been sent home from work, off sick at least another week. Ulrika didn't react. Her eyes seemed devoid of life. Everything outside the window was darkness. Black, impenetrable murkiness.

"You've heard of Job, right?" I said.

"I'm familiar with the name."

I rested my chin on her shoulder, but she jerked away without warning and turned around.

"You don't seriously think this is a trial from God?"

I no longer knew what to think.

"Job was the most honest man on earth," I explained. "But the prosecutor pointed out that it's easy to believe in God when your life is as great as Job's was."

"The prosecutor?"

"Some translations use that word. It's a euphemism for Satan."

In the midst of all this misery, I glimpsed a smile on my wife's face.

"As a defense attorney, I have no argument there."

As I related the story of Job—how God allowed Satan to take away everything he owned, to take the lives of his livestock and his ten children, to make him very sick—Ulrika nodded in recognition.

"So you're Job?"

It was hard to tell whether she was trying to be funny or just scornful.

"Certainly not. Anyway, Job's wife thought he should turn his back on God after everything that happened to him. Do you know what Job said in response?"

"No, what did Job say?"

"He said that if we accept all the good things from God, we must also be prepared to accept the bad."

Ulrika replied with a snort. I wasn't quite sure what it meant.

Then she sighed.

"We can't keep living here."

"What?"

Ulrika gazed past me and out the window again.

"Did you see the news online today?"

"Yes, Mom called."

"Lund isn't exactly a big city. What's more, you and I have relatively public lives here."

We kept staring into the darkness.

"Aren't you being a little overdramatic?" I said.

"You have no idea. I've seen it happen so many times. People forced to flee, to give up their lives and start over somewhere else."

"So you think Stella's going to be convicted?"

She looked at me as if I were a child she was about to disappoint.

"Maybe not by the justice system. It's too early to predict that right now. But it doesn't really matter. It's the court of public opinion that really counts. In general, people don't care about the court's decision."

I couldn't accept this.

"You're exaggerating."

"Not at all. One week in jail and you're as good as guilty in people's eyes. Even if Stella is freed of all suspicion, a seed of doubt will always remain in those who know who she is. At least as long as no one else is convicted of the crime."

It sounded so cynical. Maybe it was bitter wisdom learned from almost twenty years in the criminal justice system—and there certainly was some truth in her reasoning. I only had to look at myself. How many times had I taken for granted that a suspect was guilty even though the courts came to the opposite conclusion? If Stella was freed but no one else was convicted of the murder, surely many people would doubt her innocence.

"You're serious? You want us to move away from Lund?"

Ulrika nodded.

"Michael offered me something up in Stockholm."

"Michael?"

"Blomberg."

I blinked a few times. The darkness outside the window lingered in my vision like a shadow.

"What kind of thing?"

"He's got a job for me, a big case that'll take a long time, several months. The firm has an apartment downtown, for overnights; we can stay there till we find a place of our own."

"We're moving?"

She put her arms around my neck.

"It's not going to be good for us to stay in this city."

The warmth of her body softened me.

"What about Stella?"

"Stella will come with us, of course. Until she takes off for her Asia trip."

"But she's locked up."

"After the trial," Ulrika said, nuzzling my neck.

"After . . . ?"

"There's nothing we can do about it right now. In all likelihood it will go to trial."

"You think so?"

I twisted my torso away, but Ulrika held me tight and pressed my cheek to her chest.

"But we know she's innocent," I said.

"We don't know anything, honey."

"What do you mean?"

I extracted myself from her arms. She looked so desperately tired. This was sapping us more than I ever could have imagined.

"She has an alibi!" I said. "Stella has an alibi."

Ulrika reached out her hand.

"Honey, I was awake too when Stella came home last Friday. I know exactly what time it was."

Something shattered inside me. Why hadn't she said anything? She had known I was lying to the police.

What else did she know? I thought of the stained blouse and Stella's phone.

"What really happened to Stella's cell phone?"

"What do you mean?"

"I thought the police seized it, but that's not what happened. What did you do with it?"

"I . . . I . . ."

Although she was looking at me, it was as if her gaze floated off. I felt lonely and abandoned, and I had to bite my tongue to keep from saying something I would come to regret.

"What did you do with her phone?" I asked once more.

She stroked my cheek.

"The phone is gone," she said.

I gasped. What had she done? Had she dumped Stella's phone somewhere? If this got out, her career would be ruined.

"How did things end up for this Job?" she asked softly.

"It was a happy ending. God gave him ten new children."

I forced a smile and Ulrika kissed me.

"We have to stick together now, honey," she said. "You and Stella and me. We have to stick together."

I had the strong sensation that she too was hiding something from me. Even my wife.

34

Blomberg called on Monday. Could we come in to his office that afternoon? He had news for us.

"I suppose there's no such thing as good news in this situation," I said to Ulrika.

I held her hand tight on the short walk from the parking lot to Klostergatan.

Maybe Ulrika was right. We should leave Lund. I've always liked Stockholm; it could be our sanctuary.

But of course we couldn't just leave Stella in Lund. As long as she was jailed, we would stay here. I would not compromise on that.

We turned the corner onto Klostergatan and stopped outside the front door. I caught a faint whiff of alcohol as I kissed Ulrika. In the elevator on the way up to Blomberg's office, she took a compact and lip gloss from her purse and spiffed herself up in the mirror.

"Have a seat," Blomberg said; for once he was wearing an ordinary T-shirt. It was unusual to see him so dressed down. It was almost embarrassing. As if he were naked.

"I told him about your job offer," Ulrika said.

Blomberg smiled at me. I found it unpleasant that he and Ulrika had discussions when I wasn't around.

"You said you found something new," I said.

"So I did," said Blomberg, sitting down across from us with his legs spread. "As I mentioned, Chris Olsen has quite the lengthy résumé. But I also found some things that a person would tend not to include in a résumé."

"Like what?" I asked.

"This dude was involved with some fairly shady deals—we're talking real monkey business here." Blomberg nodded and looked pleased with himself. "I told you about the Poles with the pizzeria, right? Turns out Olsen also had a big outfit that depended on cheap labor from Romania. People he housed in some goddamn barn in the countryside while they worked like dogs to fix up properties for Olsen's firm."

"That sounds terrible."

"People like Olsen buy up ramshackle buildings and flip them for ridiculous sums."

"But what does this have to do with the murder?" I asked.

Blomberg gave a huge smile.

"Well, it seems some of the Romanians were grumpy about the conditions and claimed that Olsen was trying to cheat them out of dough. Some of their compatriots we chatted with were convinced that they were the ones who killed Olsen."

"What? Do the police know?"

"I've informed Agnes Thelin, but Jansdotter is the one leading the preliminary investigation."

"Agnes Thelin." I snorted.

Ulrika looked at me in surprise.

"We're still checking up on the Poles as well," said Blomberg. "We've got two names to have a closer look at."

It seemed so anticlimactic. Was that all? I didn't put much stock in Blomberg's private investigations. It's the job of the police to investigate homicides.

"When can we see Stella?" I asked.

Blomberg's neck turned red.

"I want you to know that I tried. I truly have done everything in my power, but that fucking Jansdotter refuses to let you see Stella."

"This is a complete miscarriage of justice. Should we contact the evening papers? Or maybe that investigation show would do an episode?"

Blomberg shook his head.

"It's way too early for anything like that. Until there's been a conviction, they won't be interested."

"You have to talk to Amina Bešić," I said. "I'm sure she's hiding something."

Blomberg fingered his necklace.

"Hmm, I don't know . . . ," said Ulrika.

I assumed she was afraid that this would upset Dino and Alexandra.

"I've tried," said Blomberg. "The police questioned her as well, but it doesn't seem she knows anything of importance."

"She does," I said.

Ulrika elbowed me in the side.

"This is Amina we're talking about. Why would she lie?"

"I know she's lying!"

But I couldn't say more, since Ulrika must not find out that I had spoken with Amina. She would never understand—she would only be furious, sure that I had crossed a line.

"It's still the case that Olsen's ex-partner, Linda Lokind, is the most interesting for our purposes," said Blomberg. "It turns out that Lokind has a history of anxiety and depression. She first sought psychiatric treatment as a teenager and since then she's been bouncing from clinic to clinic more or less continuously."

This didn't exactly surprise me. Linda Lokind was a young woman with a damaged self-image. She reminded me in many ways of other women I'd met who were victims of domestic abuse. I knew Linda had lied to me, but I was uncertain of the extent. Could her entire story of Chris Olsen's violence really have been fabricated? A terrible way of getting revenge on her cheating former boyfriend? I doubted that Linda Lokind was capable of doing something like that. But that meant she had to be hiding something else.

"It's completely absurd that the police aren't properly investigating Lokind," I said. "You have to push them!"

"It's becoming more and more common for this sort of thing to land on attorneys' desks," said Blomberg. "I want you to know my people are capable. But we need to get something concrete on Linda Lokind to move forward."

Something concrete?

"Her shoes," I said.

Ulrika and Blomberg stared.

It just slipped out of me. We needed something concrete, and I knew what it was.

"What shoes?" Blomberg asked, leaning forward.

I sighed and felt Ulrika stiffen beside me. There was no way out but to reveal the truth.

"Linda Lokind has the same shoes as Stella. The same kind of shoes that left that print at the scene of the crime."

Blomberg raised his eyebrows.

"How do you know that?"

I looked at Ulrika. Her face was impassive.

"I went to her house."

Both of them seemed to hold their breath as I told them about my visit to Linda Lokind's place on Tullgatan. I had seen those shoes close up and was one hundred percent sure of myself.

Silence fell and I found myself caught between the piercing glares of the two lawyers.

"What is wrong with you?" Ulrika burst out. "You went to her house?"

"I had to do something. Stella is in *jail*! I can't just sit around and watch as our lives come crashing down!"

Ulrika didn't say anything. Blomberg looked at her, and then the two of them dropped their eyes. Naturally, they understood me.

35

I took another walk through the neighborhood, this time with a cap on my head, eyes on the ground, scared I might have to stop and chat with someone. I dashed around the corner and into the driveway and closed the door behind me.

Ulrika was hunched over her desk, wielding a highlighter over a heap of documents.

"What is that you're working on?" I asked.

"The Stockholm case Michael gave me. It helps me take my mind off things."

I didn't know if that was such a good idea. Why should we think about other things when Stella was in jail?

"Close the door behind you, please," said Ulrika.

I curled up on the sofa and took out my phone. My hands were shaking. I could hear Ulrika's voice from upstairs. She was on the phone.

I poured a whiskey, drank it down, and poured another. Back on the sofa I googled for new information about what the media was now calling the "playground murder."

I started with the websites of the evening tabloids, but soon allowed myself, against my own better judgment, to be led into the gladiator arenas of the internet, where I was forced to acquaint myself with the most horrid types of speculation about Stella. Someone who claimed to have had a brief relationship with her declared in all seriousness, for the entire world, that Stella Sandell was "a perverted sleazeball" and there could be no doubt that she had murdered the thirty-two-year-old. Others writing in the same forum clearly knew Stella personally, which made the whole thing that much creepier. One contributor, who went by the screen name Grrlie, gave a detailed account of things that had happened during Stella's school days. According to Grrlie, Stella was an *ADD kid who thought she owned the whole world*, but this person still considered it highly unlikely that she would have killed anyone.

It was horrifying to read and yet I couldn't tear myself away. Against all odds, it was possible that something useful would turn up. On several occasions I felt like I was a bystander, my hands tied, watching as my little girl was carted off to slaughter.

There wasn't much gossip about the victim. Someone declared laconically that he had been both rich and attractive. Another called him a "typical psychopath," which made me think of Linda Lokind. Was this where she'd picked up Stella's name?

I drained the last few drops of the whiskey and leaned my head against the armrest. I really needed to get some sleep. I blinked a few times and tried to close my eyes even as I kept paging through the feed on my phone.

It started with an anonymous comment.

Bet her dad did it. The pastor. He probably found out his daughter was fucking Chris Olsen.

I sat up and eagerly scrolled down with my thumb.

My thoughts exactly. The dad! wrote one user who called himself Meow76. He soon found agreement in several others.

Everyone in Lund knows what type of person Adam Sandell is, wrote Misspiggylight. *He's always been weird.*

In his next comment, Meow76 had copied and pasted my personal information. My full name, address, and phone number. Age and birthdate.

My chest was roiling. This was slander!

I grabbed my computer and hastily composed an email to the contact address of the forum in which I threatened to take legal action. Then I took screenshots and began to formulate a police report.

Ulrika came downstairs and I heard her open the wine fridge.

"Come here, honey!" I called.

After she read my email to the forum, I showed her the screenshots.

"This is slander, isn't it?"

I pointed at the screen.

"Doubtful," said Ulrika. "And whether it is or not, it hardly falls under public prosecution."

"What does that mean?"

"That your report won't lead to anything but a closed preliminary investigation."

On Friday morning, two weeks after Chris Olsen's murder, I woke up later than usual, disoriented and unsure what time it was or whether I'd slept for an hour or a whole night. When I hobbled down the stairs, Ulrika was leaning against the kitchen island in a terrycloth robe, her hair freshly washed. Two cups of coffee were steaming in front of her.

"The ME's report is in," she said. "They have established the time of Christopher Olsen's death as between one and three A.M."

My heart leaped.

"That means . . ."

Ulrika nodded.

"Cause of death, blood loss from penetrating trauma," she stated matter-of-factly. "Two lacerations and four stab wounds."

Whoever killed Christopher Olsen hadn't just stuck him with a knife. It could hardly have been self-defense. Someone had stabbed him multiple times. There must have been tons of blood.

I thought of Stella's stained blouse. Sure, Stella could become angry when she lost control. And it could happen quickly. But surely she couldn't kill another human being.

"This kind of excess violence typically indicates that it was personal," Ulrika said. "It's likely that the perpetrator felt strong hatred toward the victim."

"Like a vengeful ex-girlfriend?"

"For example."

Ulrika blew on her coffee.

"Michael and I also talked about the apartment."

"What apartment?"

"The one for overnights in Stockholm. We can move in next week. We won't have to bring anything but the necessities."

I burned my tongue on the coffee.

"Already? But . . . shouldn't we think this all the way through?"

"I've made my decision," she said curtly. "I can't turn down this case."

"But surely you're not saying that we should leave Stella?"

"We're not allowed to see her anyway! There's nothing we can do before the trial."

"You've already given up!"

"On the contrary, Adam. I've devoted my whole life to criminal justice. You're going to have to trust me."

I approached her. I got so close that I could feel the warmth of her breath.

"Let me go!" she said.

I looked down and discovered that my hands had grabbed her by the forearms.

"I'm sorry, I didn't mean to."

Ulrika backed away.

"You're becoming . . . I feel like I don't know you."

"What are you trying to say?"

"We have to stick together, honey. We're a family."

I squeezed my fists against my thighs.

"I'm doing everything I can to keep this family together. You're the one shutting me out."

"Michael is a skilled defense attorney," said Ulrika. "He's got a strategy, but he can't reveal all the details to us. We have to trust him. He's already broken his vow of confidentiality, don't you understand that?"

"I don't trust Blomberg."

"We have to, Adam."

She was close to tears.

"What if she did it?" I said. "What if it was Stella?"

Ulrika turned her face away and I stepped close to her again.

"You got rid of her phone. And her top. Why did you do that? Do you think Stella killed that man?"

She placed both of her hands on my chest. Tears were streaming down her face.

"I'm sorry," I said.

Ulrika shook her head.

"You're crazy. You went to her house. Linda Lokind. You went into her apartment, Adam."

"Well, the police aren't doing anything. Someone has to do something!"

"I'm doing something too. Lots of people are doing things, Adam. But not like this. There are better ways."

She dried her tears. I hadn't seen her cry very many times, and guilt was tearing up my insides.

"Alexandra texted me yesterday," she said. "Is it true that you waited for Amina outside the arena?"

I didn't know what to say.

"Did you follow Amina and ask her a bunch of questions?"

"That's not what happened."

I couldn't believe Amina had told her mother. At the end of the day this was good news, because now she would have to confess everything, whatever she was keeping from us. There was no way Alexandra would let her keep mum. It was obvious that Amina was sitting on information that could determine Stella's future.

"You can't keep on like this," said Ulrika.

"What am I supposed to do? My daughter has been accused of murder!"

I thundered out to the entryway and tore my coat from the hook. I flung open the door and let it slam behind me.

36

I walked through town like a boiling cauldron. Staring at my shoes, my feet pounding the ground. I was starting to feel afraid of myself.

Late that afternoon, Ulrika called. I was standing on a gravel path in Lundagård Park with no idea of how I got there or where I was heading.

"I'm sorry, honey," she said. "We can't let this ruin things between us too. It's hard enough as it is."

She had made reservations at Spisen and wondered if we could meet for dinner.

My pulse calmed and I walked slowly past the cathedral. The park benches were full of students sipping Frappuccinos in the late summer sun. Japanese tourists with cameras around their necks and pigeons around their feet were pointing up in fascination at the spires straining toward the sky.

It was sheer coincidence that I ran into Jenny Jansdotter a bit later outside Market Hall. She would later claim that I had followed her somehow, but that was utter nonsense. In fact, I was on my way to Spisen when I caught sight of Jansdotter in front of me. Those twiggy, bowed legs; that springy walk, like she was bouncing forth on her high heels. She was so petite that if it weren't for the heels, the blazer, and the expensive purse over her shoulder you might have mistaken her for a child.

Michael Blomberg's words echoed through my head—Jenny Jansdotter was leading the preliminary investigation. She was the one who guided the actions of the police, who, according to Blomberg, had focused all the attention on Stella as the perpetrator. Why? Was she so absorbed in her work that she'd forgotten real people with real emotions would be affected by her decisions? How could she refuse us the opportunity to see our own child? What kind of person would do something like that? I was honestly curious, and when I saw her crossing Botulfsplatsen I couldn't stop myself. I caught up to her just outside the west entrance to Market Hall.

"Excuse me. Excuse me!"

She whirled around. I think it took a second or two for her to realize who I was.

"This is highly inappropriate," she said.

"I just wanted to ask you something."

She didn't even respond. She whipped back around so quickly that her purse was flung out from her body, and she headed once more for the glass doors of Market Hall.

"Why aren't you investigating Linda Lokind?" I asked, starting after her. "Did you know Lokind has a pair of shoes just like the ones you're looking for?"

She hurried into the building and I had to raise my voice.

"Why can't we see our daughter?"

The prosecutor stopped short and eyed me, cold and impartial.

"You're making yourself guilty of unlawful influence."

"Not at all. I just want to understand why you're doing this."

Jenny Jansdotter shook her head and turned around. In the police report she subsequently filed, she claimed that at that moment I grabbed her arm and tried to stop her. Naturally, this is not true. In reality, I only reached out my hand in one last desperate attempt to make her listen. I did brush her arm, I won't deny that, but I would never have dreamed of preventing her from leaving.

"You're ruining our lives!" I called after her.

People nearby had stopped what they were doing. A forest of curious faces, breathless murmurs, and burning eyes. I put up one hand to hide my face and hurried back out to the sidewalk, toward the cinema.

Later on, the police would question at least ten people, but not a single one of them could corroborate Jenny Jansdotter's story.

37

Ulrika was waiting for me at a window table at Spisen. I sat down right next to her and she rested her head on my shoulder.

"I'm sorry, honey. I'm sorry."

"We're not ourselves."

"I love you," I said.

I felt it so clearly throughout my body. The slightest thought of a future without Ulrika burned painfully.

"Come to Stockholm with me," she said. "There's nothing more we can do here right now. You know I would never, ever abandon Stella, but we're not even allowed to see her. It makes no difference to her if we're here in Lund or somewhere else. We have to think of ourselves as well. I've seen lots of parents in our situation, families ripped apart by this sort of thing."

She was right. As long as Stella was locked up with full restrictions, there was nothing we could do. The worst thing that could happen was if Ulrika and I were driven apart.

"What do you think will happen to Stella?"

"I don't know, but the prosecutor seems determined to bring an indictment."

I pictured Jenny Jansdotter. Should I mention to Ulrika that I'd run into her?

"What do you think happened that night?" I asked.

Ulrika stiffened.

"I don't know . . . I can't . . ."

"Haven't you even considered it?"

"Considered what?" she asked, even though she must have known exactly what I meant.

"The thought that . . . it might have been . . . that Stella did . . . some-thing?"

Deep down I wanted her to say no. It would have been fine with me if she'd flown into a rage and demanded to know how I could allow myself to think such a thing. Better that I was losing my mind than to find that there might be good reason to doubt.

"Of course I've entertained those thoughts. Of course I have—but I re-fuse to allow them to take root."

It sounded so simple. Too simple.

"There is quite a bit of circumstantial evidence," she said. "But overall, the evidence is weak."

As if it were merely a matter of jurisprudence.

She put a hand on my knee and I stroked it slowly. After all these years together, I could feel her skin as I felt my own.

"I just don't understand what Amina is hiding," I said. "There's some-thing she's keeping from us."

Ulrika's hand jumped.

"Why would Amina lie? She's Stella's best friend."

"I don't know. I really don't. I just know she hasn't been completely forthcoming."

"But you seriously believe that Amina is involved somehow?"

"I don't know anymore. I don't know what to believe."

A bit too full and tipsy, we decided to walk to the train. We strolled through town without saying much. People looked at us—some said hello; others turned their backs as we passed and I could hear their whispers. Ulrika had linked her arm in mine and was walking with purpose; she didn't slow down.

I think it was Ulrika's idea to pay a visit to Alexandra and Dino. Since we were in the neighborhood anyway. She thought a little company would do us good and sent a text to let them know we were on our way.

Alexandra met us in the doorway on Trollebergsvägen, her eyes wide.

"Oh, it's you!"

A certain reluctance was hiding behind her surprise. Perhaps Ulrika missed it, because she didn't hesitate to step into their apartment with a big hug for Alexandra.

"We took a chance that you'd be home. I sent a text, but you didn't respond."

Alexandra looked at me over Ulrika's shoulder.

Dino came rambling over, wearing only knee-length shorts and with a beer in hand. When he caught sight of us he smiled and assaulted us with hugs.

"How are you?" said Alexandra. "How is Stella?"

Once we'd given a rundown of the past few days' worth of events, or non-events, Dino herded me into the living room where an agitated soccer commentator was huffing from the wall-mounted flat-screen as peaceful music streamed from the speakers. The balcony door was wide open and the night air drifted in, carrying the mild scents of Indian summer.

"Two to one," Dino said, gesturing at the screen.

"Okay."

I couldn't care less.

"You look tired. No shock there, I suppose," he said. "Here, have a beer."

The cap hissed and I accepted the cold bottle.

"Do you remember we always said Amina was the book-smart one, and Stella was street-smart?" Dino asked. "They complemented each other so well, both on the court and out in the real world."

"Mmhmm."

It was hard to focus when the music was playing and the voice of the commentator was bombarding me even as our wives' voices crowded in from the kitchen.

"Stella's a survivor," said Dino. "A fighter."

I mumbled a response and went over to the speaker with its docking station.

"Is it okay if I turn this off?"

"Sure," Dino said, and I stopped the music.

In the kitchen, our wives were talking about Stockholm. Alexandra said it sounded like a good idea to get away for a while.

I glanced toward Amina's room.

"Is she home?" I asked.

Dino shook his head.

"She's not?"

"No."

He scratched the back of his neck and took a few big sips of his beer.

"Is she in her room?" I asked, pointing at the door.

"No, she's not home."

I stepped over and placed my hand on the door handle.

The truth had to come out.

"What the fuck are you doing? Stop!"

Dino flew off the sofa and an instant later Alexandra and Ulrika came out of the kitchen.

"Amina?" I said, opening the door.

There she was, across the dimly lit room, reading at her desk. She just had time to turn around.

Dino threw himself forward and grabbed at me. Soon he had me in a lock; his arms around my chest, he yanked me back out of the room.

"Stop it!" cried Ulrika and Alexandra.

But Dino didn't stop. He twisted my arm up behind my back so roughly that it almost snapped, and hustled me away.

"What are you doing?" Ulrika shouted.

Alexandra ran up and yanked at Dino.

"Stop it!"

"He is out of here," Dino said, forcing me into the hall, where he jabbed his knee into my tailbone and shoved me up against the wall.

"You're crazy," I said.

"Calm down," Dino hissed.

Through the hubbub I caught a glimpse of Ulrika's terrified expression.

"What happened?"

I tried to respond, but Dino drowned me out.

"He forced his way into Amina's room."

I protested, but it was all in vain.

"What is wrong with you?" said Ulrika.

Dino's brutal treatment made me whimper. I waited for him to respond to Ulrika's question, for some sort of explanation to all this utterly pointless violence. Only when I managed to twist around did I realize that Ulrika's question had been addressed to me.

"You went in her room? Without permission?"

"It wasn't locked," I stammered. "Dino said she wasn't home."

"What is going on, Adam?"

Ulrika brought her hands to her face. Her cheeks were pale.

I didn't understand. All I was trying to do was keep my family from falling apart.

"Adam," Ulrika said. "Please, Adam."

Dino looked at me, pity in his eyes. As soon as he let go of me I swung around, but I stumbled over a pair of shoes on the runner and fell backwards into the door, then landed on my behind.

"She's lying," I managed to say. "Amina knows more than she's letting on."

All three of them looked at me the way you look at someone who's just revealed he is suffering from a fatal illness.

"I feel sorry for you two," said Dino, turning to Ulrika. "But don't make Amina suffer because of this."

Ulrika nodded slowly and Alexandra put her arm around her.

"Of course we've spoken with Amina. She doesn't know anything about what happened."

"I understand," said Ulrika. "I hope you can forgive us. We're not ourselves."

I got my shoes and jacket on and went out to the stairwell. My mind was unraveling. My thoughts galloped by like runaway horses; my ears were ringing and my vision was tumbling over and over. I don't know if I said anything on the way out. I don't remember if I shouted or muttered. It's like a blank spot in my memory when I think back on it. Temporary derangement. I suspect a skilled defense attorney could even get away with an insanity plea.

38

I spent the rest of that weekend tucked in bed with a fever and a raging headache. Even moving from the bed to the sofa sapped all my strength, and I subsisted on soup, toast, and Tylenol.

"Maybe you should get help?" Ulrika said.

I turned off the TV. Every single sound was like a roar in my ears.

"What could a doctor do?"

Ulrika sat down on the couch and stroked my knee.

"I wasn't talking about a doctor."

I pulled the blanket up to my chin.

"Maybe you need someone to talk to," she said.

"And what am I supposed to say? That I've done everything in my power to keep my family together? That I've gone against everything I believed in, all my moral principles? I lied to the police and tracked down witnesses at home and harassed them. I have done everything for my family, but now my wife is convinced that I'm losing my mind."

"I never said that. We're in the midst of a crisis. It's no surprise that we're on the brink of a breakdown."

"We?"

Ulrika was no longer looking at me.

"We all handle crises in different ways."

Early Monday morning, she flew to Stockholm for a few meetings, but also to get the keys to the apartment. I received a text with a selfie and a promise that we would make it through this. She wrote that she loved me and that we would handle it all together.

That morning I called Alexandra and Dino and begged a thousand times for forgiveness for my actions. Could they pass on my apology to Amina? They were understanding and said they hoped this hell would soon be over.

I slowly woke from my torpor. I staggered around the neighborhood with cloudy vision and gelatinous thoughts. Each person I encountered stared at me brazenly. A grizzled man in a duffle coat grunted and shook his head, but when I asked what he'd said, he looked at me, affronted, as if he had no idea what I was talking about.

Ulrika had stacked the entryway full of boxes. She'd already started packing the essentials. I stopped and stared at them, opening one box and rooting through it. A whole life, as I knew it, in eight banana crates. My chest gaped with emptiness.

Three weeks earlier, we had been a perfectly ordinary family.

On Thursday I waited for Ulrika outside the station. She stepped off the airport bus and smiled, squinting into the sun.

We hugged for an eternity, standing there as if in a gap in time, just holding each other—two bodies that belonged together, linked by love, by time and fate. By God? There among swerving buses and bell-ringing cyclists, late students with steaming cups of coffee, academics dashing here and there in pressed clothing, secondhand middle-class citizens. I don't believe we were created for each other, that there was a plan drawn up ahead of time for me and Ulrika, but I believe—no, I know—that time and love have bound us together forever, until death do us part.

We walked close together across Clemenstorget and down to Bytaregatan. Paul's words echoed in my head: He who doesn't take care of his own has abandoned his faith in Jesus.

"How are you feeling?" Ulrika asked.

"Dreadful," I answered honestly.

"I love you, Adam. We have to be strong now."

"For Stella," I said.

Later on we found ourselves once again in the easy chairs in Michael Blomberg's office. He was wearing a baby-blue shirt with big rings of sweat under his arms.

"I've managed to get the preliminary investigation against Christopher Olsen," he notified us, not without a certain hint of triumph in his voice.

"The court bought my line of reasoning, although certain details remain confidential."

He waved a sheaf of papers.

"Get this. It's from one of the interrogations of Linda Lokind."

I leaned way forward in my seat.

"LI: 'This information you've given about Christopher—'"

"Who is LI?" I interrupted.

"Agnes Thelin, the chief inspector," Blomberg said without looking up. "LI stands for lead interrogator."

"Okay, okay."

Blomberg read on.

"'I'm sure you understand, Linda, that these are very serious accusations you have leveled at Christopher. If it's the case that what you've said . . . that some things weren't entirely true, you have to tell us now.'"

"Are you serious?" I exclaimed, throwing out my hands. "Can she really say that? She's arguing that Linda was lying!"

Blomberg gave a heavy sigh and dropped the papers onto the desk.

"I'm sorry," I said. "Go on."

He took a deep breath and kept reading.

"LL—that stands for Linda Lokind," he said with a glance at me. "LL: 'I guess maybe . . . I don't know. Sometimes I'm not sure if stuff really happened or if it's just my imagination. It felt like it happened for real. It honestly did.'"

Blomberg looked at us, his expression serious, before he went on.

"LI: 'Have you said things that aren't true, Linda? All I want is for the truth to come out.' LL: 'I don't know. I don't remember. Everything is, like, blurry, reality and . . . and . . . my dreams.'"

I didn't know what to think. This seemed insane. Wasn't Linda able to differentiate between dreams and reality?

Blomberg folded up the interrogation report and handed it to Ulrika.

"It goes on like that. Linda Lokind doesn't know what really happened and what is just fantasies or dreams. A real fruitcake, in other words. No wonder the preliminary investigation was closed."

Ulrika paged through the document.

"So Christopher Olsen never assaulted Linda?"

Okay, maybe that was true. But that Linda couldn't tell what was a dream and what was reality—I had trouble buying that. In fact, I was certain that she was extremely conscious of her lies. There was something she was hiding. From me, from the police, from everyone. And I had to find out what it was.

39

Ulrika and I left Blomberg's office and zigzagged our way along the narrow sidewalks of Klostergatan. An older man in a khaki-colored overcoat stopped suddenly in front of us, staring at me as if I were a ghost. I passed him quickly, my eyes on the shop windows.

We slipped into a coffee shop, got a table in a hidden corner in the back, and had espresso and cream-and-marzipan pastries.

"You look different," Ulrika said.

"More awake? I actually managed to get some sleep."

She looked at me for a long time, taking in every millimeter of my face. It made me feel safe, as if her eyes were caressing me with warmth and gentleness.

"I know what it is. Your collar," she said. "I'm not used to seeing you without your clerical collar."

I tucked in my chin and looked down at my neck. I'd hardly reflected over the fact that I had taken it off. It wasn't as if I had made a conscious decision. In the past few days, I had simply forgotten to put it on.

"Do you want to read it?" Ulrika asked, placing the preliminary investigation report on the table.

We divided the pages between us and took turns reading. Occasionally we sighed, looking at each other and shaking our heads.

There was no doubt that Linda Lokind seemed like a confused person who constantly gave conflicting information. Based on what came out in the investigation, a person could hardly blame the prosecutor for clearing Christopher Olsen of all suspicion. Linda Lokind's accusations appeared to have been fabricated by a vindictive and mentally unstable partner who had been cheated on and abandoned. But was it really that simple?

When we left the café, Ulrika wanted to make a quick round of the shops downtown.

"I need a new scarf. It'll only take half an hour, max."

"Half an hour?"

She tugged at my arm.

"I don't like it," I said.

"What's that?"

"How people are looking."

"I'll be quick," she promised.

And, muttering, I followed her into Åhléns, crowded my way past people with lowered heads and sweat under their arms. All the while I stuck close by Ulrika. When we finally came back out, I handed a twenty-kronor bill to the shivering woman outside the entrance. She asked God to bless me.

"A quick run to H&M too?" Ulrika said.

"Not H&M. I can't."

"Just let them look."

"But they might ask questions. The staff."

She looked at me and stroked my elbow.

"It will all be over soon. Once we move away . . ."

I steeled myself and walked into the stuffy warmth of H&M just behind my wife; we went straight up the stairs. When I caught sight of a girl from the staff, I darted into the men's department and headed for the back of the store. Using my back as a wall to keep out the rest of the world, I grabbed a few shirts and pressed so close to the racks that the scent of newness tickled my nose.

Several minutes passed as I stood there up against the chalk-line printed garments. Wasn't Ulrika finished yet? I took a step to the side to check.

"Adam? Is that you?"

A single mistake, and she struck immediately. I recognized that shrill voice, the characteristic Betty Boop tone. And sure, if I had to talk to one of the H&M girls, I certainly preferred Benita.

"Hi!" she said, looking at me with a perfect mix of sympathy and delight.

"Hi there," I said, holding back a sigh.

Benita was the same age as Stella and had started working there at around the same time. She had been over to our house a few times, and I liked her. She was a smart, cheerful, openhearted girl who dreamed of becoming a singer. We had said, half in jest and half seriously, that she should audition for *Idol*.

Benita threw open her arms, even as I pulled back, and we ended up in an almost-hug.

"I've been thinking of you all constantly," she said. "How is she doing?"

I looked around the store. It seemed quiet; no one was eavesdropping.

"It's ridiculous," I said. "There is everything to suggest she's innocent, yet the prosecutor refuses to release her. It's almost made me lose faith . . . in the justice system."

"I understand," said Benita. "My cousin was held in jail last summer just because he knew a guy who had shot someone."

I nodded but didn't respond. I didn't understand what that had to do with Stella.

"And it's so awful how she can't work here anymore. But of course, I understand our boss's point of view too. I'm sure lots of customers would have been upset if they recognized Stella, and it would have been, like, bad advertising."

"Hold on. What do you mean? She lost her job here?"

Benita's hand flew to her mouth.

"I thought she told you. Malin wrote her days ago."

"Stella has full restrictions in jail. She's not allowed to communicate with anyone but her attorney."

Benita looked over her shoulder.

"I . . . ," she said, pointing at the registers. "Well, say hi to Stella, anyway. Or, I mean, I hope everything turns out okay."

"It's fine," I said, to spare her.

I didn't look up even once on my way back to the stairs. There was no sign of Ulrika. Halfway down I had to grab the railing. The air went thick and I saw double. Swaying, I made it down the last few steps. All around me were voices, but everything was blending into an indecipherable slurry of sound. A hand touched my arm, but I shook it off, forced my way between the racks toward the door, and crossed the street in front of honking cars. I bent over outside the window of the tourist bureau and took a deep breath, sure I was seconds away from vomiting.

40

I jogged past the pretty little townhouses along Stora Södergatan. There was something I had to do, something that couldn't wait.

I had to get some clarity about what had happened. Had Linda Lokind lied about the abuse, about Christopher Olsen's tyranny? If so, why did she continue to cling to that lie now that Olsen was dead? And why did she claim, in the interrogation, that she got reality confused with dreams and fantasies? That couldn't be true.

After my last visit, I'd been sure Linda was hiding something, but at the same time I recognized so much of what she said from other women who had suffered abuse in intimate relationships.

I didn't believe Linda Lokind was so ill that she couldn't tell the difference between fantasy and reality. Maybe it was something she'd made up when she realized the police weren't taking her accusations seriously. Had she decided to get even with Christopher Olsen on her own instead? It seemed implausible that she would let Olsen get off, after what he had done.

But why had she mentioned Stella? Did she know something about Stella, or had she just read a bunch of nonsense online?

The questions were piling up. I had to know; I couldn't wait.

I was only doing what was right, what would be expected of any father in my situation.

I stopped outside the door to her building on Tullgatan. I have no clear memory of how I got inside, but I repeatedly chanted a prayer as my feet trod heavily up the stairs.

My God is a just and forgiving God.

I knew I was doing the right thing. A family divided cannot stand. He who does not take care of his own family has abandoned his faith.

Linda Lokind unlocked the door and stuck her nose through the small crack allowed by the security chain.

"You again?"

Her gaze flickered in the dim light of the stairwell.

"May I come in? I just have a few more questions I need answered."

She observed me, her forehead creased.

"Hold on a second," she said, closing the door.

I assumed she was just going to undo the chain, but the seconds ticked by and nothing happened. I stood there staring into the closed, quiet door. Wasn't she going to let me in? I waited patiently for a few minutes, then rang the bell again.

Soon her feet padded across the floor. Then silence. I said her name, and at last she let me in.

"Sorry to keep you waiting. I just had to . . . come in."

I hung up my coat and bent down to untie my shoes. Out of the corner of my eye I saw the shoe rack.

They were gone. All the other shoes were still there on the rack, but that particular pair, the shoes that were identical to Stella's, were missing.

"It shouldn't take long," I said when Linda offered me a seat.

She looked at me in surprise and pointed at her neck.

"You don't have . . . ?"

"My clerical collar," I said, feeling for it. "A person can't always be on the job. Sometimes even pastors have to have a private life."

She gave a hesitant smile and sat down.

"So, here's the thing," I said, wondering how to lay it out. "Everything you told me last time I was here, about how Christopher abused you, I believe it. I believe that what you told me is true."

"Great," she said, still looking hesitant.

"But why did you take it all back during the police interrogation? You said you didn't know what was real and what was your imagination. But you *did* know, didn't you?"

"No one believed me anyway."

"So you retracted your accusation because no one believed what you said?"

"Mmhmm."

"Do you have trouble telling the difference between reality and fantasy?"
I asked.

Linda didn't respond.

"The police didn't listen to you," I said. "What were you planning to do
about it, instead?"

She shifted her position in her chair. Gazed around the room.

"Nothing. Or . . ."

"Or?"

She twisted her arm behind her back and scratched her shoulder. There
was nothing to suggest that this woman was crazy, that she couldn't tell the
difference between fantasy and reality. Why had she said such a thing during
the police interrogation?

"I know who you are," she said suddenly.

My thoughts froze.

"What do you mean?"

"I looked into it after the last time you were here."

I opened my mouth, but the words got stuck somewhere on the way out.

"I thought a lot about getting revenge on Chris," said Linda Lokind. "I
don't think I could have killed him, but I thought about various ways to hurt
him. I did do that."

She stared at me.

"I'm sorry," she said at last, her shoulders sagging. "Stella was the one who
killed Chris. I tried to warn her. I know you don't want to believe it, but the
police are right. Your daughter did it."

I couldn't move. I was collapsing inside, drowning in my thoughts, caught
in a vise of darkness.

"You're lying."

She shook her head.

She cautiously folded up the sleeve of her blouse and looked at the clock.

A knock came at the door. Three hard raps.

Linda rose and my legs nearly collapsed beneath me as I followed. The
whole room seemed to be tumbling around.

"I have to go," I said.

Linda walked ahead of me. I stopped in the middle of the living room as
she continued to the hall. I heard her turn the lock. A man's voice echoed in

the stairwell, but I couldn't make out what he said. Meanwhile I hurried for the kitchen, trying to find a place to hide, a way out—I don't know what, exactly.

I could only see Linda's back as she closed the door. Her movements seemed somehow hesitant now. Out of sheer instinct I recoiled, trying to keep out of sight.

The man clomped in without removing his shoes. His footsteps sounded like jackboots against the hardwood floor and without even thinking, I took a quick step to the side and grabbed the neck of the large, bottle-shaped floor vase.

I believe this is deeply human. There's no understanding it if you've never experienced a direct and serious threat to yourself and your loved ones. You make irrational decisions and overstep boundaries as you never would otherwise. A person who can no longer flee must fight.

I lifted the vase off the floor slightly to determine how heavy it was and realized I would have to use both hands. Just as I looked up, the man rounded the corner in front of me. I saw his shiny black boots and my adrenaline pumped out full force.

"Police!"

He threw himself at me.

It all happened so fast—the room spun and shards of glass flew about us like a sudden snowfall. In the next instant I was on the floor with my cheek against the wood and could no longer breathe. It felt like I'd been run over by a car—my back had to be broken—and pain stabbed between my ribs like knives.

"Adam Sandell?" the policeman said in a booming voice.

All I could produce was a whimper.

"Adam Sandell?" he said again and again until I finally managed to confirm that it was my name.

Not until I was yanked up off the floor did I realize that there were two of them. The other officer was standing next to Linda, looking at me with disdain as he took out his handcuffs.

"Do you have any weapons on you?" he asked.

"Weapons? Are you nuts?"

"No sharp objects?"

I was frisked and advised that I would be coming along to the station for questioning. When I asked if I was under suspicion of anything, I was met only with vague excuses. I had to wait until we arrived at the station.

My pleas to loosen the handcuffs were met with silence. The car pulled up behind the police station and I was led across the parking lot like a criminal, flanked by the oversize officers.

41

I had to wait for half an hour before Agnes Thelin entered the small interrogation room. She placed my keys and wallet on the table.

"We're going to keep your phone for forensic analysis," she said, waving an order from the prosecutor.

"Forensic analysis? What crime have I been charged with?"

Agnes Thelin put on an expression of concern, as if she truly cared about me.

"Linda Lokind contacted us back when you came to her apartment for the first time, Adam. She was scared. You ingratiated yourself with her under false pretenses."

"I only happened to be wearing my clerical collar that day."

"You claimed to represent Margaretha Olsen."

I couldn't deny that, although I thought it was a fairly minor overstep. Definitely not the sort of thing that justified the brutality of those officers.

"We decided that Linda should contact us immediately in case of your return," Agnes Thelin continued.

So that's why it had taken her so long to unlock the door.

"But why am I sitting here? Why did they apprehend me? I haven't broken any laws."

"You swung a vase at my colleague."

"Swung? Is that what he claims?"

"He doesn't claim anything. There were four of you in that room."

"But you have to question Linda Lokind again. She confessed to me that all her accusations against Christopher Olsen were true. He assaulted her again and again, and she thought about ways to get revenge."

"I can't discuss details of this investigation, Adam. You have to trust we're doing our job."

"How could I trust you? My little girl is locked up despite the complete lack of evidence!"

"We just received new results from the lab. The crime-scene technicians have discovered small irregularities on the soles of Stella's shoes, and they match the print from the scene of the crime. We are sure that print came from Stella's shoe."

"That can't be true."

"Of course it's true."

"But it could have ended up there any time at all. Stella has an alibi!"

Agnes Thelin made her hands into a pyramid under her chin. Her eyes were a little shiny, but her gaze was steady and firm. I realized that I wasn't going to get anywhere. She had made up her mind. She and Jansdotter the prosecutor had decided that Stella was guilty and that I was a common liar. Nothing I said would change their attitude.

"How are you doing, Adam? You've been overstepping a lot of boundaries recently."

I pressed my hands to my temples to get rid of the constant pounding.

"DA Jenny Jansdotter has filed a police report on you," Thelin went on, taking a piece of paper from the pile on her desk. "You attacked her on the street, shouting and acting threatening."

"Attacked? Threatening?"

My vision flickered. I fumbled around on the table for something to drink. My mouth was full of dust. The light was so bright I had to squint.

"Adam?"

"I want a lawyer."

Contrary to my expectations, it actually felt like a relief when Michael Blomberg lumbered through the door and sat down next to me.

"Trust me," he said, placing one huge paw on my shoulder.

Ulrika had made the arrangements to get him here.

"I did not attack Jansdotter" was all I managed to get out.

"Of course you didn't," said Blomberg. "These charges are completely absurd. You have no reason to worry."

I was stuck in a nightmare.

"I understand that this is awful," said Agnes Thelin, "and that you're not feeling well."

Blomberg's hand shot out.

"I'm having increasing doubts about how you conduct your work around here," he said.

I looked at him. At last he was doing something.

Agnes Thelin went on as if nothing was amiss.

"What I'm going to say now will seem shocking and terrible at first, but in the long run I believe it will come as a relief to you, Adam."

I turned to Blomberg, who fingered the knot of his tie.

"I know you're just trying to protect your daughter," said Chief Inspector Thelin. "But that is no longer possible."

A sudden calm descended over me. I didn't understand where it had come from. The pounding in my forehead ceased and the saliva streamed into my mouth once again. My vision cleared. It was as if the moment had caught up with me at last.

"Yesterday I went to the jail to question Stella again," said Agnes Thelin. "Quite a bit of new information came out."

I pictured what was about to happen, in the span of a few seconds. The future was a movie playing in my head just before it occurred in reality.

"Stella says she did not come home as early as you claim."

"No?"

"She believes it was past one o'clock, maybe closer to two."

"No, that's not right." I shook my head firmly. "She was drunk. She's mistaken about the time."

Second after second vanished. I looked at Blomberg, who looked at Thelin, who looked at me. We knew, all three of us, that this was an act and nothing more. A performance.

"That's not all Stella had to say."

I filled my lungs with air.

"She was there," said Agnes Thelin. "Stella was there on the playground at Pilegatan when Chris Olsen died."

"No," I said. "No, that's not true."

"She has confessed to being there, Adam."

My vision flickered again. The air caught in my throat.

"No," I said over and over. "No, no, no."

"She has confessed."

PART TWO

THE DAUGHTER

*What do you think, would not one tiny crime
be wiped out by thousands of good deeds?*

FYODOR DOSTOYEVSKY, *CRIME AND PUNISHMENT*
(TRANS. CONSTANCE GARNETT)

*He knew that henceforth, all his days would resemble one another,
and bring him equal suffering. And he saw the weeks, months,
and years gloomily and implacably waiting for him,
coming one after the other to fall upon him and gradually smother him.*

ÉMILE ZOLA, *THÉRÈSE RAQUIN*
(TRANS. EDWARD VIZETELLY)

42

The worst part about this cell isn't the rock-hard bed you can hardly flip over in. It's not the dim light. It's not even the disgusting rings of old piss in the toilet. The worst part is the smell.

I have to confess that I was one of those people who thought the Swedish correctional system was a straight-up chain of decent hotels. That it was hardly punishment to be locked up in this country. I believed it was more or less like an after-school program where you could just chill, lie in bed and binge TV series, get fed pretty good stuff, and not have to care about anything.

I said in school one time that I didn't understand why there were homeless people in Sweden, and that I would much rather be in prison than live on the street.

After six weeks in jail I will never again say I want to be locked up, or that I think it's like a hotel.

My room is under one hundred square feet. They call it a room because *cell* sounds more depressing. One hundred square feet is like the size of a horse's stall. It's smaller than most Swedish backyard greenhouses. It has a bed, a desk, a chair and a shelf, a toilet and a sink.

I don't want anyone to feel sorry for me. I'm in here for a reason, and I'm not a victim. I ache all over, I've lost weight, and my thoughts plague me like tinnitus. But there's no reason to pity me. Hell no. Back in middle school I had a favorite expression that I used all the time, and it feels more fitting than ever these days: Don't play with fire if you can't handle the heat.

———

Once a day, you're let out for some fresh air. If you're lucky. Sometimes there's not enough staff, and sometimes they can't come up with an escort to the elevators. Sometimes they mostly don't give a shit which it is.

There's something like a dog park on the roof. All you can do is walk around, back and forth, in small circles. But so what? It's a change. It's something different. You get away from the smell and the trapped feeling for a while. But it doesn't make your thoughts or the sinking feeling in your stomach go away.

One night, rain was pelting down like giant nails, but I trotted around on the roof anyway. Back and forth. It didn't matter that I was freezing my ass off, that the rain stung my cheeks. Anything that is not just flat-out sitting or lying down is gold around here.

Radio, TV, internet? Not a chance. I have full restrictions. I'm not allowed to see, hear, or read anything that isn't directly linked to my case, like detention documents or memos from the court and fun stuff like that. No binge-watching shows, no music, not even a single text. I'm not allowed to make or receive phone calls, and the only person who can visit me is my lawyer.

Three times a week, the commissary cart comes by and I stuff myself with two thousand calories of chocolate and Coke. Sugar is a super-underrated drug, and it's the only one you can get your hands on in here.

Actually, it's incredible how much you can long for the moment when two strangers turn the lock and bring in a tray of food. For the first few days I almost started bawling each time. Just getting to see another person made my whole body rejoice. I darted out of bed and was about to throw my arms around their necks, and then I peppered them with at least fifty questions about everything under the sun just so they wouldn't leave again.

As soon as I'm on my own, my mind starts buzzing. The smell comes back.

I had been here for two days when they sent me to the psychologist.

"I didn't ask to see a shrink," I told the guard.

He stared at me like I was a speck of dirt the janitor had missed.

"It can't hurt."

I think his name is Jimmy. He's got one of those gross goatees that looks like wiry pubic hair on the end of his chin, and his eyes are ice-blue. I one hundred percent recognize him, probably from Étage or some other club.

The guards can be divided into two categories, no problem. Number one: the ones who see this as just a job, something that puts money into their account once a month. Maybe the jail is just a temporary stop on their search for a more rewarding or better-paying career. Number two: the ones who get off on the power. The ones who came here on purpose. Maybe they were rejected from the police academy, probably thanks to the psychologist. They're the ones who like bullying and violence and consider the inmates to be vermin.

You quickly learn to tell the difference. Even though most of them have the same cold eyes, there is a crucial difference between apathy and contempt.

Jimmy is definitely one of the power-hungry ones. It's something about how he looks at you. Sort of from below and above all at the same time. As if he considers himself better than me, superior, even though he knows deep down that it's really the other way around, and that makes him furious. He spends way too much time at the gym. His upper arms are thicker than his thighs, and his neck would look better on a bull. I have such an urge to pin those fat arms to his sides.

He responds to every question with another question.

"Are you joking? What do you think? Do I look like your mother?"

I just want to scream in his face.

If one of us needs a psychologist, it's sure as fuck not me.

I have a theory about psychologists. I'm not saying it's true for all of them, but I certainly have encountered my share throughout the years and so far I haven't run into any exceptions.

Here's the thing: if you get a degree and are fed a bunch of explanatory models and diagnoses, it seems to me like it's pretty much unavoidable that you would later try to apply what you've learned. It would be stupid not to. So you get out of school and greet people—clients, patients, or whoever— with the attitude that you should be able to explain why people are the way they are and do the things they do. A psychologist's job is basically to force the rest of us into one of their templates.

Suggestion: you should do the opposite!

Reason: people are unique.

All those psychologists who came and went. Was that life? All the self-assessments and personality tests. The first thing they start with, obviously, is a rough childhood. It seems to be every psychologist's wet dream to find a broken soul who has repressed a bunch of terrible memories from their childhood.

The bizarre thing about all these diagnoses they throw around is that it's so easy to see yourself in most of them. There's not a single psych test where you wouldn't check off some of the boxes.

For a while I was sort of obsessed with that stuff. Since everyone believed there was something wrong with me, even my own family—or maybe my own family most of all—I tried to get to the bottom of the problem. Everything I read said that it would feel better when you put a label on it, when you could put a name to the problem, when you knew that there were lots of other people dealing with the same thing.

At first I thought I had ADD or ADHD, then Borderline Personality Disorder, Schizoid Personality Disorder, Bipolar Disorder.

I came to the conclusion that it was all bullshit.

I am who I am. Diagnosis: Stella.

There are an infinite number of things wrong with me, I won't deny that. I'm anything but normal. My brain fucks with me twenty-four hours a day. But I don't need any other name for that than my own. I am Stella Sandell. If someone has a problem with me, maybe they're the one who needs therapy.

And it's no secret that psychologists often have their own mental issues. If they don't start out with any, they show up later. Too much Freud would make anyone nuts.

It was while I was reading up on all this that I got hooked on psychopaths. I guess you could say I became obsessed with them. They say it's good to have a hobby, so I replaced handball with psychopathology.

The psychologists I met before I came to the jail were similar in some ways. Most of them were women, many of them were redheads, often with a particular "concerned" look, not infrequently dressed like a high school music teacher. A surprising number of them spoke with a Småland accent.

So as Jimmy the Guard hustles me in to see the jail psychologist, it's not all that easy for me to conceal my surprise.

"Hi, Stella. I'm Shirine." She's dark and pretty and has her hair in two tight braids—a Middle Eastern version of Princess Leia.

"I don't need a psychologist," I say.

I've actually prepared a hailstorm of flashy words like "violation of integrity" and "overreach of power," the kind of stuff that always has some effect on public servants who have underestimated you. But Shirine just sits there like she's fucking Lady on a meatball date and I can't even bring myself to raise my voice.

"That's okay," she says. "I understand you feel reluctant, but I meet with all the teenage inmates here. It's not up to me."

She smiles warmly. She really looks kind, the way you mostly only see in little old ladies and puppies.

"I mean, it's nothing personal," I emphasize. "I'm sure you're great. But I've been to a lot of psychologists."

"I understand," says Shirine. "I won't take it personally."

Then there's silence, the kind I can't handle. Shirine sits across from me, smiling, letting her sympathetic gaze fall upon me.

"So you're going to make me? We're going to sit here for an hour every week and stare at each other?"

"It's up to you, Stella. If you want to talk, I'll be happy to."

I roll my eyes. No chance I'm about to talk, no matter how gentle her brown eyes are and no matter how much she smiles like Lady. What am I supposed to say? I'm never going to tell anyone what I've experienced. No one would understand. I barely understand it myself.

The quiet game starts now.

We sit there looking at each other. Now and then Shirine poses questions I don't answer: "How are you doing in here? Have you gotten to talk to your family? Are you sleeping okay?" The hour passes so ridiculously fast, I almost suspect she's fudging with the time somehow.

"Maybe we'll see each other next week then," she says, rising to summon the guard.

"I'm sure we will," I say, and Jimmy picks me up by the door and herds me like goddamn livestock back through the corridor. He stares at me with eyes of ice as he lets me back in my room.

I hate the solitude. It scares me. Everything creeps so uncomfortably close to you in here. I can't escape my thoughts and feelings when Jimmy turns the lock and leaves me alone with the walls and the smell. Inside, my mind is screaming. I'm about to explode.

I don't know if it's worth it, if I can handle it. I know there are a lot of people who never get out of here alive.

43

They were dressed in civilian clothes, sure, but you didn't need to have watched that many episodes of *Criminal Minds* to figure out that they were cops. Two broad-shouldered clichés wearing guarded expressions, jeans, and running shoes. All that was missing were the walkie-talkies on their belts.

There was only about an hour until closing, and after a pretty busy Saturday the stream of customers had begun to slow to a trickle. I was working the register, taking payment from a gray-haired lady in a denim jacket who had finally decided to pull the trigger on the purple tunic she had come in to finger earlier that morning.

"Receipt's in the bag," I said, handing over the hideous tunic. It would be perfect for her.

The lady lingered at the register, lifting her thick-framed glasses and inspecting the receipt. She almost got run down by the two policemen.

"Stella Sandell? That's you, right?"

I looked at their IDs. The tunic lady's jaw dropped.

"Has something happened?" I asked.

A multitude of potential catastrophes passed through my mind.

"It's not . . . ?"

"We need to talk to you," explained the older officer, scratching at his beard. "I'm afraid you'll have to come with us."

He had kind green eyes and looked like the sort of guy who liked slow food and talking about his feelings even though he must have been born in the fifties. Probably he'd married young and had a wrecked relationship behind him, started dating online once the kids moved out, but belonged to that restless category of people who know the grass is always greener somewhere else, so his romances never lasted more than a couple months.

"Is there anyone who can cover for you here?" asked the other officer. Twenty years younger, but his eyes were much more exhausted. Judging from the cancer-level tan on his face, he had just returned from two weeks in Turkey. He looked like a person who jumps feet first into everything—vacation had to be *vacation*. Late nights, Efes and Raki, card games on the balcony. It would probably take at least a week to recover.

"Anyone who can take over here?" asked the older officer, as if I hadn't heard his colleague.

"It's fine," I said. "We're closing in an hour."

Malin and Sofie both offered to take over my register. Then they stared after me in horror as I followed the officers out.

"What's going on?" Sofie whispered.

I never heard whether she got an answer.

The woman who questioned me was called Agnes Thelin. If I'd seen her around town I don't think I ever would have guessed she was a cop. She looked more like a visual merchandiser or a creative director. She definitely didn't shop at H&M. She probably lived in an architect-designed house with an open floor plan and Danish lighting. She was the kind of person who would never admit that she didn't like sushi. The type who claimed to love brutal honesty but was completely destroyed if someone gave her any straightforward criticism.

I liked her immediately. Maybe because I could identify with her in certain ways.

"What does the name Christopher Olsen mean to you?"

I looked her in the eye and shrugged.

"Do you know him?"

"I don't think so."

Agnes Thelin cocked her head.

"It's a pretty simple question."

I clarified that I know thousands of people, from school and handball, people I meet out or online, friends and friends of friends. Plus, I'm pretty shit at names. Some people, obviously, I know their full names, but other people I only know their first names or nicknames, and some people I have no clue at all.

"Did you say Christopher?"

"Christopher Olsen." Agnes Thelin nodded. "Most people call him Chris."

I considered this.

"Chris? Yeah, I know at least one Chris, I guess. A slightly older guy, right?"

Agnes Thelin nodded. And then—I was completely unprepared—she placed a photo of him on the table and asked if he was the person I was thinking of.

My heart beat harder. I looked at that picture carefully, for a long time. I picked it up and inspected it at close range.

"Yeah," I said at last. "I know him."

"Unfortunately, he's dead," said Agnes Thelin.

I heard myself inhale sharply.

Agnes Thelin told me that some poor mom with small kids had found the body on a playground near Polhem.

"Shit," I said, bringing my hands to my mouth.

I for real thought I was going to puke.

"Did you go to Polhem?" Agnes Thelin asked.

"No, Vipan."

"And you just graduated?"

I nodded and Agnes Thelin shifted a little further back in her chair.

"My oldest graduated from Katedral last summer. He's in London now. My youngest is in his last year of the IB program."

I tried to look like I cared. This was probably a simple trick, getting personal. She was trying to make me want to trust her.

"What does all this have to do with me?" I asked. "Did you have to come get me at work for this?"

"Sorry about that, but it really was necessary."

She was scrutinizing me. I felt a snakelike ribbon of worry wind through my belly. My nausea had turned to something else: a threatening omen; icy, biting fear.

"What is this all about?" I asked.

"Can you tell me what you did yesterday?" asked Agnes Thelin.

"I worked. I worked up until closing. Then we went up to Stortorget to eat. We had some wine and talked."

"We who?"

"Me and some colleagues."

She clicked her pen and made a note.

"What time was this?"

"We close at seven and work until quarter past."

Agnes Thelin wondered how long we had stayed at Stortorget.

"I don't know how long the others stuck around, but I was there for a few hours. I think it was about ten thirty when I headed out."

"Then what did you do?" she asked, resting her pen.

"I . . . I took my bike." I tried to recall exactly what had happened. "First I biked up to Tegnérs. I know I drank a cider at the bar there, but I didn't see any familiar faces. Then I was at . . . Inferno for a little bit, or whatever that place is called. It's kitty-corner from the library."

"Inferno? That's another bar?"

"Yes."

"How much did you have to drink?"

Agnes Thelin sounded like my dad. She had that same typical-parent look. When they claim to be worried, but they just look super fucking annoyed.

"Not that much. I had to get up and work."

She looked at me as if I was lying, which I found offensive.

"It's true. Alcohol isn't my thing."

I happened to think of something Dad likes to say. He maintains it's hard to lie, that most people suck at it. For a long time I thought he was mistaken. Time and again, I proved him wrong. I didn't have any trouble lying at all. In general, people were gullible as shit, I thought.

Until I realized that it might actually be the other way around. That Dad was right. Maybe it wasn't that people will fall for anything. Maybe, in fact, I was exceptionally awesome at lying.

Now I know it's true.

44

When I was little, Dad was my hero. One time, at preschool, Hat-Nisse made fun of my dad. We called him Hat-Nisse because he wore a hat year-round. He laughed at me and told everyone how weird it was to have a pastor for a dad.

I shoved Hat-Nisse backward into a shelf and he cut his head. Dad chewed me out when he heard about it. Of course no one mentioned how it all started, only that I had a fit and pushed Hat-Nisse so hard that he had to go to the ER. And I didn't say anything either.

I've always hoped that Dad would just understand. It seems important that I shouldn't have to explain myself. Maybe there's something wrong with me, something other people don't experience the same way, but I've always felt ashamed to be held accountable for who I am.

Each time Dad didn't understand, I felt disappointed and we drifted further and further apart.

It's awfully ironic that the sides of me that bother Dad most are the things I inherited from him.

There's something to sink your teeth into, Shirine!

I have a theory that the psychologists loved our family. A pastor, a lawyer, and a maladjusted teen. We could serve as textbook examples in their manuals.

One time in school my whole class got bawled out by Bim, our advisor, because we had too many opinions. *Typical millennials,* she yelled. *Always having so many ideas about everything!*

I guess lots of stuff was simpler before, when kids just shut their mouths and obeyed. I've never been that way, and I never will be. I don't think it would matter if I were a teenager in the eighties or now.

When I think back on all those therapist appointments, some of those shrinks sure did display a certain amount of smug schadenfreude. There must be something special about getting a behind-the-scenes peek at an apparently successful family, a lawyer who was on TV sometimes, and a pastor, *ohmygod* a pastor. Just imagine getting to peer into the filthiest corners of our perfect family. Maybe that's what it takes to endure one's own tragic existence at a sad county-run psych clinic.

But I wonder about Shirine . . . she doesn't look at all like them, not the way I remember them.

There was a time when I myself wanted to become a psychologist. I like to think I'm pretty good at seeing through people and understanding and figuring out stuff they may not even realize themselves. I'm a good judge of character. To be honest, this isn't just some idea I have about myself—people have always said so. People turn to me with all sorts of problems: family issues and lame boyfriends. I'm good with people, good at analyzing them.

Another time we were at open houses for the high schools—Katedral, Spyken, and Polhem, the only ones I could imagine attending. There were two guys at Katedral with slicked-back hair and unbuttoned shirts who were telling us about the social-sciences program. When I said I wanted to be a psychologist, they cracked up.

"You know how impossible it is to get accepted to that program?"

It was a slap in the face.

The next week, my counselor confirmed that you needed the highest grades in every subject to become a psychologist. It was one of the most attractive university programs. Would I consider HR instead? It was pretty much the same thing.

I think that's when I decided to say screw it to high school. It wasn't worth it.

How many people do I know who wasted three years of their lives slaving away, and they still only received grades that were average at best? They put their lives on hold; some of them even downed pills and cut their arms to get a B in English. For what? So they can spend their days in a pantsuit?

Bim was actually more perceptive than you'd think. At parent-teacher conferences she told Dad that I surely could have made an A or B in most classes. If I only wanted to.

She was spot on. I *didn't* want to.

I was more into a night out at a club venue with free drinks than an assignment about practical marketing. I prioritized Copenhagen with the girls over a standardized math test. Instead of taking a history exam I hung around Starbucks, making out as if my life depended on it.

It was a conscious choice.

In my third year, when people were starting to talk about university entrance exams and we were invited to open houses at the university, I was busy planning an extended trip to Asia. I was so tired of Lund and Sweden. I devoured YouTube videos from Malaysia and Indonesia and soon that trip became my only goal in life. I longed for adventure, long nights, new people, parties, and nature straight out of paradise. My parents and I agreed we would revisit the university question after my trip.

Bim was an old owl lady who should have retired back in the 1900s. I like to say she was the one who destroyed my academic career, even though obviously that's just a joke.

You could see it in Bim's eyes that she didn't like me. I don't actually care if people don't like me, they have every right not to, but it bugs me when someone is so stupid they can't even hide it. Bim was always going around with this fake smile plastered on her face under her square glasses and downy mustache, grinning too much and saying, "Good morning, boys and girls."

I guess I haven't had too many teachers who liked me. I wasn't the reason they were longing to get back to work on Monday mornings, I guess you could say. I was no model student. It probably would have gone better if I were a guy. They can't help it, boys will be boys, and all that.

"Your dad's a pastor?" Owly Bim asked every time my dad was mentioned. She stared at me as if her whole world was going to pieces. "A pastor? In the Church of Sweden?"

It's all about control.

People never believe that. In their minds, the need for control is a characteristic of that sort of pedant who loses it if a paper ends up in the wrong pile on their desk, the type who sorts their wardrobe by exact shades of color.

People think of organization Nazis with detailed calendars or neurotics who panic if they can't immediately empty their inboxes and go bananas over a few crumbs on the sofa or a dirty kitchen counter. People who keep hand sanitizer in their bags.

But this is a different sort of control. It's about not losing face. Not letting anyone get too close.

It wasn't until I was a teenager that I realized my family isn't the only one with secrets. It had always been so important to Dad to keep up a façade for the rest of the world.

"We'll deal with it when we get home." I don't know how many times I've heard those words. "This is none of anyone else's business."

I was lulled into the belief that our family was unique, that we were the only ones carrying around a bunch of crap that had to be swept under the rug. Maybe it had to do with Dad's work. I suppose pastors are just doomed to live parts of their private lives in secret.

It's sick, but Dad was a die-hard atheist before he got saved. Years ago I found an old column he'd written for his school newspaper. I think he had just started high school. He truly hated religion, and wrote stuff about how Christianity was a fraud, a security blanket that had torn the world apart, and that baptism should be considered abuse of innocent children. He called pastors black-coats and charlatans.

I've wondered sometimes if everything would have turned out differently if Dad had a different career. If he'd been a pencil pusher or middle management or some kind of academic, like normal parents.

To be honest, I think Dad and I are a lot alike. Deep down. I'm also easily consumed by ideas; I can get completely absorbed in something that feels really crucial at the moment. In fifth grade I was the very definition of a Potterhead. I read the books in Swedish and English, watched all the movies at least twenty times, and wrote long fanfics online until my social life just about withered away. A year or two later I went through a period of being addicted to The Smiths and wearing raccoon makeup and spending every waking minute on the Helgon forum for indie kids. There are some autistic traits in our genes. Luckily I decided early on to avoid religion of any kind, unlike Dad.

"Never say never," he liked to tease. "I didn't understand that this was my calling either, until I was eighteen."

"I'd rather scrub toilets," I responded. "I mean, I would rather become one of those New Age women and go on nudist vacations in Ghana and chew khat."

"We'll see." Dad laughed, just nervous enough.

Like every other eighteen-year-old, I've spent hours thinking about the future, about education and various careers. And sure, some jobs are more than just a job. Not like working the register at H&M. You turn on your salesperson smile at five to ten and discard it five minutes after closing. It's not a big part of my identity. I would absolutely jump ship to KappAhl if they offered a thousand kronor more per month. I could just as easily work the register at a hardware store. Who cares? Cash is the only thing I would miss if I lost my job. Which I'm sure I will.

No, I don't think Dad knew what he was getting himself into when he became a pastor. Nowadays he works his ass off to fit into this archetype: the perfect preacher, the perfect father, the perfect human. Just like everyone says we young women try to do. Obviously we're not the only ones.

Clearly it chafes, it hurts, if you don't really fit into that mold. Until, finally, it starts to crack.

Check it out, Shirine. Not a bad psychoanalysis, right? Five years in the psychology program, top grades in all your classes at high school, was it really worth it?

I am my own best psychologist.

I'll never understand people who open up like shaken champagne bottles as soon as someone tilts their head and offers a listening ear. People who bare it all on a blog or on social media; people who tattoo words about how awful they feel on their forearms and torture every soul they run into with their pathetic self-analyses.

I have just one friend, one person on earth who knows all about me and understands everything I feel, think, and do. I wish I could talk to her now. I need her. I don't know what to do without Amina. I don't know if I can manage. Last night I seriously banged my forehead on the wall and screamed so loud it hurt my ears. The only thing that would be worse is if Amina had to be locked up. One afternoon, as the guards were leading me to the elevator, I thought I saw her. I turned around and shouted her name, but behind the black hair hid a strange face. This cell is making me go crazy.

45

Agnes Thelin almost looked apologetic when she explained I was a suspect. My thoughts were like a whirlwind. A suspect? I sank back in my chair and tried to collect myself.

I was still dazed a little while later, when the attorney marched in and demanded to speak to me in private.

"We're going to figure this out," he said, placing his left hand on my shoulder as he squeezed my right hand. "Don't worry."

His hand was large and sticky and he looked like a cross between Tony Soprano and Tom Jones. The size of a bear, tan, gold chains around his neck and wrist. A pigeon-blue shirt with the top three buttons undone. The type of man who drives his SUV all the way to his single-family home even though the neighborhood is supposed to be car free. Who has a grill the size of a camper in the backyard and thinks everything was better when he was young, even though he doesn't feel a day over twenty-three. I'm sure he was high up on the divorced young moms' fuck lists.

"So this is what you look like?" I said.

"What do you mean?"

"I didn't quite remember."

"Have we met before?" the attorney asked.

"I think so."

A light went on in his head.

"Stella *Sandell*. I should have realized. Ulrika's daughter?"

I nodded.

"This'll be quick," he said. "They have nothing on you. Some cops now-adays have awfully itchy fingers. They have their homicide guidebook and stuff to follow. They think the first few hours are totally crucial so they haul in the first best option, for better or for worse."

He sat down, his legs spread wide, and placed his large hands on his knee-caps.

"But they must have something," I said. "They said there was some witness who pointed me out in a photo."

"She can hardly be called a witness. Some silly girl who claims she saw you from a window. In the dark! And she's one hundred percent certain it was you, even though she doesn't know you. No, that's not much of a witness."

I could picture her in my mind. A shady figure in a window on the second floor. Was that really all they had? Was that the only reason I was sitting there?

"They want to continue questioning you as soon as possible," said Blomberg. "You're lucky. Agnes Thelin is one of the most sensible people in this place. Good to talk to."

He stood up and messed with his phone a little, holding it half a centimeter from his nose. Apparently the thought of wearing glasses made him feel old or ugly, or maybe both.

"Forgot my contacts," he mumbled.

My legs felt like overcooked spaghetti when I stood up. The attorney walked ahead of me to the door.

"So what am I supposed to say?"

Blomberg turned around so fast his hair fell down across one eye.

"What do you mean?"

"What should I tell the police?"

"Just tell it like it was."

He looked at me, slowly, up and down, until I pulled my cardigan over my chest. I felt like a show cat. The attorney brought his hand to his forehead and stroked away both hair and sweat.

I stretched.

"Is that all you've got? *Tell it like it was.* That's your strategy?"

Blomberg shrank a bit.

"What are you talking about?"

"You're supposed to be one of these big-shot lawyers," I said. "Haven't you won a bunch of major cases? Didn't you have a better strategy those times either?"

Blomberg threw up his hands.

"What do you want, exactly?"

I had managed to arouse some uncertainty in him. Some philosopher once said that knowledge is power. That is definitely true. Other people's ignorance is also a powerful factor.

"What if I did it?" I said.

Blomberg had transformed completely. He had come marching in here like an alpha male straight out of the tanning bed. Now he looked like nothing but a pale little boy.

I thought of Dad's motto, how lying is a rare skill. Did Blomberg share that belief?

"Why would you have done something like that?" he wondered.

It was, of course, a good question.

46

The book Shirine brings me is three hundred and seventeen pages long. Single-spaced, no room to breathe.

"I thought you might need something to read," she says. "There's not much else to do around here."

I page expectantly through it, my fingers eager. I read the first sentence: *It was a queer, sultry summer, the summer they executed the Rosenbergs, and I didn't know what I was doing in New York.*

Six months ago, I would have laughed. If someone handed me a fifty-year-old book full of long sentences and references I didn't get, I would have assumed it was a bad joke. I can't remember the last time I read a whole book. I've never been able to hold still for long enough. After a few minutes, my thoughts wander off and I completely forget what I've read and I have to start all over. But in here it's different. I long for something that can kidnap my mind for a while. I'm so tired of myself.

"So what kind of book is it?" I ask, as I glance through the blurb on the back.

"It's something of a feminist classic."

I raise one eyebrow.

"Give it a chance. I think you'll like it."

I bring it back to my cell anyway. Then I buy a large Coke and two chocolate bars from the commissary cart. The guard who locks me back in is new, must be one of the temps always coming and going. She stares at me in horror as I reluctantly return to my hundred square feet of smell. The new girl keeps standing there in the doorway, and I feel her eyes writhing across my body like terrified larvae.

"What the fuck is the problem?" I say at last.

Her head jerks back. Her eyes gape.

She looks like a perfectly normal girl. The kind who finishes the social-sciences program with good grades, buys clothes at Forever 21 and Urban Outfitters. In another life, I'm sure she and I could have been friends.

"Nothing," she says, hiding her face with one hand. "It's nothing."

Then she rattles the keys and looks generally stressed out. As the lock clicks, I lie flat on the bed with my mouth stuffed with Daim and Coke.

I open the book and it doesn't take long before I'm hooked. Finally, I can escape myself for a while. A whole different world opens in my mind and I throw myself headlong into it. I never want to come out again, never come back to this fucking cell.

I can't even smell it when I'm reading.

The next morning, Shirine returns to my room.

"I finished it."

I toss the book on the bed, but from Shirine's face you'd think it landed on her toes.

"Already?"

I shrug.

"What happened? Did you like it?"

"It was fucking depressing."

"Yes, that's true."

Shirine's face is heavy with guilt.

I don't know why I don't tell the truth, that I loved the book, that it made me furious and sad, but that I have nothing against feeling furious and sad. I need those emotions. I would never forgive Shirine if she brought me a book full of sunshine.

"Can you get me more books?" I ask.

Her smile travels from eye to eye.

"Of course I'll get you more books."

"Great."

She is about to sit down next to me when the tears well up. I can't explain why. Maybe a thought happened to brush against something that burns.

I press my palms to my face, which aches and stings. And I think about Esther in the book, and that mental hospital.

"Are you okay?" Shirine asks, her voice gentle.

I can't answer her question. No matter what I say, it will sound petty, probably incomprehensible. Presumably egotistical. My life is ruined. Chris is dead and I have made a mess of everything. How will I ever be able to look Mom and Dad in the eyes again? There's no solution now, only escape.

"I want you to leave now," I say to Shirine.

All I deserve is darkness.

47

Amina and I have always been told we're an odd pair. She's so levelheaded and reserved and rule abiding. And I'm constantly taking up space and being loud, always finding some ridiculous rule to break.

But behind these façades, we're a lot alike. I've always seen myself reflected in Amina. Inside, we're the same flesh and blood. We just choose to show different things to the outside world. That's how it works. We all have our secrets, depths and darkness few others are allowed to see. If you only dig a little deeper, it's easy to find some scary shit in every single person. Amina is no exception.

I truly wish she had been there at confirmation camp. I honestly believe things would have turned out differently. Not just camp—everything.

The butterfly effect, it's called. A single beat of a butterfly's wings can have enormous consequences and affect everything that happens.

But Amina didn't even dare to ask her parents if she could come. I'm sure her mom would have been fine with it, but her dad is Muslim. Not that I've ever seen him do anything related to Islam. Rather the opposite. Dino loves beer and would never get it into his head to fast or kneel facing Mecca. Plus, Allah would definitely have an opinion about the four-letter words Dino would bellow at our handball games.

But it didn't matter; Amina wasn't going to ask if she could come to camp. She was Muslim and it was important to say that you were Muslim even though no one really cared. Shit, at home they even ate hot dogs and ribs, but at school she always got her food "pork free."

I'm sure Amina would have stopped me. If only she had been there, at that camp by the little lake. She would have told me what a dumb fucking idea it was. She would have shaken some sense into me, would have been all big-sistery and convinced me to stay in our room and play cards with the other confirmands.

I wouldn't have gone with Robin if Amina had been there.

Maybe I wouldn't be sitting here now.

Butterfly effect.

On summer vacation between seventh and eighth grades, we traveled to some Danish backwater town for a handball championship. As usual we brought home the gold and I was the top scorer. We slept on air mattresses in a sweaty, snore-filled classroom, and on two of the nights there were dances in a tent in the schoolyard.

From day one, Amina and I got stalked by a gang of Croatian guys who were a few years older, with irresistible eyes and muscular arms that made my mouth water. At first we tried playing hard to get. We ignored them or teased them, mostly because that was what we were expected to do, what all girls are always expected to do. But during our last group-stage match, they sat in the bleachers wolf-whistling every time Amina or I got the ball, and that night we followed the Croatians away from the dance. We sat in a big circle down by the beach; gulls were wheeling above the treetops and the waves washed white scum onto the sand. The guys were passing a cigarette around, and it wasn't until it reached my hand that I realized it wasn't a regular one.

"No strong," Luka said in English.

His green cat eyes glittered in the dark. I had wanted him from the moment I saw him. Amina, though, had her eyes on the Croatian goalkeeper.

I took a few drags. I coughed and laughed and the voices around me grew slow and tinny, but otherwise not much happened.

As soon as the joint reached Amina, she began to squirm.

"She doesn't want to," I said.

Luka and the others looked at me curiously.

"You have to respect her," I said, reaching for the joint.

An hour later I was lying on my back in a hidden hollow with Luka kissing my neck full of hickeys before he put his fingers inside me and tried to charm me with lines from porn movies.

———

A summer vacation. When I think back on it now, it feels like an eternity, but it really was just one summer. Our lives shifted into a higher gear and it was like the whole world opened up.

I was fourteen, and everything was an adventure. In my own eyes, I was practically an adult and certainly didn't need any parents interfering in my life. I had more and more trouble controlling my outbursts of emotion and every day felt like a battle.

Mom mostly avoided everything, hiding out, working late, and getting headaches. But not Dad. He would go all over town to chase me down when I didn't come home on time. I knew he went through my pockets, and every night he was standing there in the entryway like a goddamn bouncer.

"Blow," he said, bending over so I could exhale into his face.

"Again."

He sniffed the air like a dog and stared at me with skepticism.

"You haven't been smoking, have you?"

The funny thing was, I'm pretty sure Dad wouldn't have recognized the smell of weed even if you lit a spliff under his nose.

His worry wasn't totally unfounded, though. After the Denmark trip, I'd gotten a taste for weed and soon I was lighting up every day. It rubbed out my thoughts, made me weightless and free.

Ironically enough, I was still more afraid of my mother.

"Promise not to tell Mom," I said, holding Amina in both arms.

"I swear."

"On the Koran?"

"On whatever book you want."

Amina and Mom had always had a special relationship somehow, and that summer it was like they became even closer. I would come home and find them sitting in the yard, laughing at something they could never quite convince me was that funny.

I had gotten to know a group of guys from Landskrona who could get alcohol and pot. They shared everything with me and I felt more alive than ever before. One night I ran away from home and slept under the stars out on the island of Ven. I lost my virginity in a prickly bush and had a two-week relationship with a Danish guy called Mikkel.

It was like everything was dancing and smiley when I filled my lungs with smoke.

"I don't like it, that you're into all of that," said Amina.

"I'm not *into* it," I responded. "It's just for fun. For the summer."

Even though we drifted apart for a while, since Amina preferred to avoid the Landskrona gang, I never doubted our friendship. Amina was always there.

There was just one week left of summer break when I found her waiting outside our house one evening.

"Your dad followed me after practice."

"What?"

I shivered and pulled my jacket tighter. Handball had started up again, but I'd skipped the first practice. I didn't feel like playing.

"What did he do?"

There were tears in Amina's eyes.

"He was pressuring me, asking a ton of questions. Who you hang out with, if you're with anyone, whether you're having sex."

"Whether I have sex?" I seriously couldn't believe my ears. "He asked if I'm having sex?"

Amina nodded.

"And if you smoke and drink and stuff."

"That's just sick. Seriously, that is not healthy."

Amina shifted her weight from foot to foot. Brushed her hair off her cheeks. She was scared. Dad had threatened to blab to Dino, even though Amina didn't drink or smoke or any of that shit. She hardly hung out with those guys. She would rather stay home and watch TV, play handball or basketball, hang out with the guys from our class. Every time she came along to Landskrona, it was for my sake.

It was so unfair for Dad to attack her.

A few days later, we met outside the station. Amina was tired, not wearing any makeup—she looked like a fucking corpse.

"I'm sorry, I'm sorry, I'm sorry," she said.

I took her by the arm and pulled her onto an empty platform. I stroked her hair out of her face and patted her cheeks.

"What's going on? Tell me."

Her breathing was uneven.

"Your dad," she said quietly. "I told him. I had to."

"What did you say?"

She hung her head and cried. I couldn't help it—I shook her shoulders in desperation.

"What did you say to Dad?"

She could only produce a few words at a time.

"I had to . . . he grabbed me . . . hard . . . my arm."

"That bastard!" I said. "What did you tell him?"

She shook her head in despair.

"The weed," she cried. "I told him about the weed."

I stared at her. My best friend since forever ago. My twin soul. The only person who truly knew me.

It was such a huge betrayal. So unfathomable.

"How could you?"

Amina rubbed her eyes.

I watched her as my hand clenched. The muscles twitched and pulled. I couldn't control myself. My fist flew through the air and it was almost like I was watching it from the outside, like it was a movie.

Amina didn't have a chance. My knuckles struck her square in the cheekbone. There was a crunch and it felt tremendous. Better than drugs. I had never felt anything like it.

48

The guards don't knock. The key turns in the lock and an instant later they're standing in my room.

It's Jimmy with the goatee and that new girl, the one who tried to stare me to pieces by the commissary cart the other day. They've come to pick up my meal tray.

"Not tasty today?" Jimmy says with a smile.

I've left a whole sea of baked beans on my plate. I mean, I'm not picky, I eat most stuff. But baked beans, I just can't.

"There's commissary tonight, right?" I ask.

Jimmy's still smiling. He's always walking around with that grin on his face, as far as I can tell. It's not friendly at all. It looks smug, as if he's smiling at his own imagined splendidness.

"We'll see. It's so easy to forget to unlock everyone's door. Isn't it, Elsa?"

The new girl doesn't respond. She barely looks up. She probably wants to avoid getting caught in the middle.

"You heard what he said, Elsa," I say in an exaggeratedly clear voice. "You're my witness. If I'm not allowed to buy anything tonight . . ."

I trail off. It's not worth it. It's impossible to win, with someone like Jimmy.

"You've gotta be kidding me," he says, guffawing.

He hands my tray to Elsa; his smile vanishes and he looks at me with disgust.

"Is it true you stabbed him in the chest over and over?"

I feel the internal struggle. I know exactly what he's after, and I have no intention of giving it to him.

Jimmy turns to Elsa.

"Can you believe that this little chick is a brutal killer?" he says.

Elsa gives him a pleading look that says she wants nothing more than to get out of here, away from the smell, back to her normal world where everything is puppies and rainbows.

But Jimmy doesn't give in.

"You'd never think so, right?" he says. "Right, Elsa?"

Elsa looks down at her feet.

"You can't tell by looking at someone whether they're a killer, can you?"

I appreciate her courage.

"*They*? There's only one person we're talking about here," Jimmy says with a harsh laugh. "Listen, Elsa, I was naïve when I first started working here too. You'll learn. After five years in this place, I've come to realize that's all bullshit. In fact, you can totally tell from looking at someone that she's trash. Most killers look just like you'd imagine: swarthy Travelers, filthy Gypsies. Hardly anything is a surprise."

Elsa's eyes widen. She looks like she wants to crawl out of her own skin.

"Just shut up!" I say to Jimmy.

I simply can't keep quiet. It's a problem I have. People have always told me to keep my mouth shut, back down—you don't have to share every opinion or thought. Lack of impulse control, the psychologists call it. On one test I got, like, the worst possible score. I'm the kind of kid who would swallow the marshmallow in one gulp if I had the chance.

"Who said you could talk?"

Jimmy runs his hand over his goatee and pants right in my face.

"Just let it go," Elsa says behind him.

But Jimmy's not about to let it go.

He's, like, half a meter away from me now, and his eyes are glowing with hatred.

"You dirty murdering cunt. You better think twice before you say a word."

He doesn't know I have zero impulse control. If he did, he wouldn't do this.

"That's enough," Elsa says in an authoritative voice. I think she even tugs at his arm. "That's over the line."

I like her.

"Over the line?" Jimmy whirls around and Elsa is startled. "What fucking line?"

"You aren't allowed to treat—"

"What the hell are you talking about? Are you *defending* this killer whore?"

His arm flings out toward her.

"Calm down," says Elsa.

"Calm down? You'd better think about whether this place is right for you."

I feel for her. It's so clear that she doesn't belong here. She should go back to her life in the white-bread fairy-tale land she comes from, where all the stories have happy endings.

"There are only two sides here," says Jimmy. "Either you're on our side, or you're on theirs."

Then he slowly turns back around to face me.

He ought to know better. He ought to have a much better overview of the situation. He's no rookie, and I'm hardly the only person in here who lacks impulse control.

I size him up thoroughly and aim for a bull's-eye. And in the same instant he turns around, I land a kick right in his crotch.

He groans and doubles over.

Elsa and I look at each other as Jimmy writhes in pain between our feet. Although I make it clear to her that I'm not going to put up any resistance, she takes me down with some sort of judo throw. My cheek is pressed to the filthy floor and her knee is in my back.

So much for that sisterhood. But then again, a good girl never compromises her do-goodiness.

Elsa soon receives help from two colleagues, and after a few seconds of conferring they decide to take me to an observation cell.

They drag me out of the room, and on the way to the elevator I give in and stop resisting. There's no point.

The observation cell is really meant to protect inmates from themselves. It's small and dark, with only a mattress on the floor, and everything you do is observed through a window in the door.

I have to spend the whole night there. It doesn't help when I bang on the wall or scream myself hoarse or threaten to report them.

By morning, when they open the door and bring me back to my room, I haven't slept a wink.

"Welcome home," says the guard who unlocks my room.

The smell invades my brain.

I fall straight into bed and sleep until lunch.

49

I still haven't forgiven myself for hitting Amina. Four years later, the memory tortures me several times each week. What kind of person are you, if you hit your best friend?

An instant after it happened, I cracked. I ran around like a madwoman on a high, shrieking and flailing my arms. I had trouble accepting what I had done. I just wanted to erase the last few minutes and do them over the way a normal person would.

Worst of all: I had enjoyed it. That wonderful, liberating feeling when my knuckles struck her cheek.

Amina sat on the bench next to me with her face in her hands. I pried her arms loose and inspected the screwed-up eye and the reddish-purple lump that was swelling up over her cheek.

"I'm sorry, sweetie! I'm sorry!"

There was no way I could ever fix this, nothing could go back to normal after this. I had ruined it. The only constant in my life, the only thing that was unconditional and truly meant anything—I had destroyed it.

I knelt down and held her hands tight. Passersby stared. A few stopped to ask if everything was okay.

It wasn't. It was fucking far from okay.

I had hit her. I had hurt Amina.

"It doesn't matter," she said. "I deserved it."

"Bullshit! This is all Dad's fault."

"I shouldn't have said anything to him. Can you forgive me?"

"Stop that! You're not the one who should be apologizing here!"

It didn't matter what she said. I realized that you can't forgive someone for this sort of thing. You can say you do, and even believe it yourself, but deep down you will never forget.

We rested our foreheads together and cried.

That winter, I needed Amina more than ever. Mom felt like crap and spent most of her time hiding in her office. Sometimes it seemed like she would rather talk to Amina than me. I got it into my head that she would have liked to trade me for Amina. While I brought disappointment after disappointment, I think Mom saw a lot of herself in Amina, the smart, good girl who never did anything wrong.

At the same time, Dad became more and more paranoid. He went through my pockets, my bag, and my room. He ordered phone records to see who I'd been calling. He went through the search history on my computer and demanded access to all my passwords.

I quickly developed strategies to meet Dad's requirements even as I continued to live a relatively unrestricted life. I was over weed, but there was so much more: guys to kiss, nights to enjoy, parties to have. I let Dad go through my clothes, smell my breath, peer at my pupils, and believe he had insight into everything I was up to. It's much easier to hide something when you give the impression of being transparent.

When the chatter about confirmation camp started going around, my ears pricked up right away. There were a lot of tempting rumors thanks to last year's camp. Alcohol and sex and cigarettes. A ton of ungodly activities. And above all, the icing on the cake, a camp leader called Robin, who was, all sources were unanimous, the hottest being you could imagine.

The Christian elements of confirmation left me completely cold. Of course I didn't believe in God, but neither did anyone else who was going to camp. Most of them didn't care, as long as they got presents and a sweet week of camp. Maybe there was some higher power somewhere, but it had about the same significance in their teenage lives as whether there was life on Mars. I was about the only one who would take any sort of active position the few times questions of belief came up at school, and my hostile attitude toward the church and religion mostly had to do with Dad, of course.

I knew exactly how to lay it out. If Dad was given the tiniest shred of hope that I might develop an interest in the Bible, it wouldn't take much to convince him.

"What do you think?" he asked Mom at the dinner table. It was only a few days before the application had to be turned in. "Should we let her go?"

Mom responded with an empty gaze.

"Don't know. Maybe."

Her standard answer of the past six months. She was sleeping poorly at night, ate like a size-zero model, and wandered around the house like a zombie. I had a hard time dealing with her apathy, not least because I felt responsible for it. Instead of putting my tail between my legs and trying to reach out to Mom, I pulled farther and farther away from her. Even if it was my behavior that had set Mom on a decline, it seemed to me it was her job to fix it.

"You're the one who had me. I never asked to be part of this family."

Childish? Sure, but I was practically still a tween.

When Dad talked about Mom's exhaustion, that she had hit a wall and ought to take time away from work, I protested.

Mom dropped her fork on the floor and took an extra-long time to pick it back up. Dad bit his lower lip.

"She says she'll work less, but she stays up late working every night. Don't you get it?"

I could tell that Dad agreed with me, but he didn't say anything. Was this some sort of strategy? Like, it was better for this to come from me.

In any case, it was soon decided that I would be allowed to go to confirmation camp. Mom and Dad agreed, they claimed, and I set about planning right away.

We brought along a variety of tobacco and alcohol products. When you're only just fifteen, you can't afford to be picky. Someone had filled a shampoo bottle with whiskey and liqueur from their dad's liquor cabinet. Someone else had nabbed half a bottle of mulled wine from their grandma's cellar. And a couple girls had managed to get a wino to buy them a small bottle of Explorer vodka. The cigarettes were hidden in our bags, wrapped in foil, packed up in plastic jars or tin boxes.

I still remember the feeling of freedom in my chest as the bus pulled out of the parking lot.

———

The first few days at camp flew right by. We hardly even had time to think about the bottles at the bottoms of our bags. One late evening I snuck out to the woods with a few guys and smoked three cigarettes in a row and coughed almost until I threw up. Some people hooked up even that first night and made out under the blankets in our dormitory.

There was a lake where we went swimming every day. One morning, Robin was standing there squinting out over the water for a long time, in up to his knees as the sunbeams glittered against his wet chest.

The other girls ran up to the shore, giggling. The lake was still way too cold to stay in for longer than fifteen minutes or so.

I waded slowly past Robin, met his gaze, and smiled. I knew he kept watching me as I continued up to the beach. I took an extra-long time bending over to pick up my towel.

A little further up, in the grass, stood two of the counselors, smiling. I tossed my wet hair and swept the towel around my body before padding back up to camp.

I really should have been surprised, even shocked, to see Dad there. But all I felt was an aching sadness.

He stood there like everything was normal and gave me a hesitant smile. He couldn't even let me have this. Not even this.

I told him to go to hell. Then I ran all the way up to the buildings.

That was when I made up my mind.

A self-fulfilling prophecy, Dad? If chaos was what he was expecting, then chaos he would get.

50

"How are you feeling today?" Shirine asks cautiously.

I don't respond.

She places a new book on the desk in front of me.

"This one isn't quite as depressing as *The Bell Jar*."

I read the back cover and flipped through it absentmindedly.

"I loved it when I was your age," says Shirine.

It seems to be about a seventeen-year-old named Holden who thinks most people are idiots. I like the English title better than the Swedish one: *The Catcher in the Rye*.

"What happened yesterday?" Shirine asks.

Apparently she heard about my night in the observation cell.

"Nothing."

I don't want to talk about it. To be honest, I don't think Shirine quite understands how things work in here. She's not dumb, that's not what I'm trying to say. She's not even naïve. I just think that if you try hard enough to keep your eyes closed you can keep living in denial for as long as you want. Shirine has formed her own impression. She knows how she wants things to be and she basically turns her back on or looks away from anything that contradicts that impression. Swedish jails are good places. People still have rights and are taken care of while waiting to stand trial. In Shirine's world, bullying, assault, and the abuse of power are things you only see in movies.

"I understand that you're having a tough time," Shirine says.

She doesn't understand shit.

The next morning, I wake up with the book on my pillow. Fuzzy images from the night linger behind my eyelids and I have trouble telling the difference between what I read and what I dreamed. I feel like Holden when he wakes up on the couch in the home of his old teacher and the old guy is sitting there stroking his hair. I stand by the sink for a long time, splashing cold water on my face.

It feels really nice when breakfast arrives. The guards are cheerful, and for once the coffee doesn't taste like goat piss.

I'm paging through the book a little as I eat, trying to figure out how far I got before I fell asleep, when the door behind me opens again.

One of the older guards, a woman who looks like she should work at a preschool, peers in with bright eyes and a cheery smile.

"Your lawyer is here, Stella."

"He'll have to wait. I'm having my coffee."

She stares at me, perplexed, without saying anything. At last I get up with a heavy sigh, fold my open-faced sandwich over on itself, and stuff it into my mouth before drinking the last slurp of coffee.

My feet drag as I walk between the guards to the room where Michael Blomberg is waiting.

"I have good news," he says, shaking my hand. "The prosecutor has approved a visit from your parents."

My insides seize.

"What do you mean, approved? Who applied for it?"

Blomberg smiles and pokes himself in the chest.

"Yours truly."

"But . . ."

The snake of worry twists in my belly. Mom and Dad.

"Thanks, but no thanks," I say.

Blomberg leans toward me, concerned. His face goes fuzzy and I feel dizzy.

"What do you mean?"

I take a deep breath and close my eyes.

"I can't handle it," I say, feeling the tears spring to my eyes. "I don't want to see them."

51

I knew Dad was ridiculously fond of Robin. I had heard him praise the man on more than one occasion.

It wouldn't be too difficult to lure Robin into the woods. And once I did, he wouldn't be able to resist me. Then the whole gang of guys would come sneaking up and catch us red-handed. It would be a major clusterfuck.

Dad would freak out, of course. I knew he was still around; his car was parked by the dining hall.

The first part of my plan worked. But once I got Robin in among the trees, hidden from the rest of the camp, I started to have second thoughts. Robin was looking at me in a totally new way when he lifted his arm to touch me. There was a tenderness to it, as if he truly had feelings for me.

"We can't do this," he whispered, touching me with sensitive fingertips.

He was right. I was about to ruin everything for him. He would be finished as a camp director; he'd probably never get a job in the Church of Sweden again. Or worse.

Dad was the one I wanted to punish. Not Robin.

"In a few years," I said, slowly lifting his hand away. "In three years I'll be eighteen."

He smiled.

"Can you wait that long?" I asked.

We still had a few minutes before the guys would come sneaking through the trees. I looked at Robin's longing lips. I wanted to kiss him so much. Just once. What would it matter?

"Your dad," he said, turning his head. "Adam is your dad."

"So what? Are you afraid of my dad?"

"Afraid?" He laughed. "Who could be afraid of Adam?"

"Then what's the problem?"

"Nothing. It's just, you're so different."

He took my hand and led me farther into the trees.

"Come with me."

His teeth gleamed in the dim light.

There was something he wanted to show me. Something in his room in the counselors' cabin. When I pointed out that it was strictly forbidden for us confirmands to be in the counselors' area, he laughed.

"What they won't know won't hurt them."

Ignorance is power.

"What about Dad?" I asked, looking around anxiously.

Robin didn't hear me.

"Come on," he said, unlocking the door.

There were four rooms in the counselors' cabin. A cramped hallway with a mirror and four doors. It smelled like a summer cabin. Robin's was the last room on the left.

He went to the window and pulled down the shade.

"Sit down," he said, pointing at the bed.

It was messy, with his clothes and belongings strewn everywhere: on the floor, on the bed, on the small bedside table. Next to the bed stood Robin's half-open suitcase, and as I sat I peered curiously down at underwear, deodorant, and undershirts.

"Be right back," he said, vanishing into the hall again.

I sat on the bed and felt the beating of my heart. Soon I heard the flush of the toilet.

I'm not stupid. Sure, I was only fifteen, but obviously I knew what was happening. There wasn't anything Robin wanted to show me. I could have stood up and run away, and the thought did occur to me, but I wanted to stay. I wanted to hold on to the thrill.

And by then there was no risk that the guys would catch us in the act and throw everything into chaos. The worst that could happen was if they started looking for us and . . .

I sent off a quick text.

Abort! I changed my mind.

And received a thumbs-up in response.

A second later, Robin opened the door. There was something new in his face, something resolute, determined. His upper lip twitched as he pulled me close. Our lips met, his tongue found its way into my mouth, and we kissed.

I enjoyed it.

He pressed himself against me and that turned me on. I wanted him to keep going.

After a while, he rolled me onto the bed. I lay on my back and he let his whole weight rest on me, covering my mouth with his lips and sticking his tongue way down my throat.

It didn't feel good anymore. I couldn't breathe.

I flailed beneath him like a fish. Tried to scream. Didn't he notice he was hurting me?

I couldn't breathe, but Robin just kept going. There was no longer anything tender or loving about it. His motions were forceful, a demonstration of power and strength. I was prey and he had brought me down.

At last I realized it was pointless to resist. All I could do was close my eyes and wait for the hurt to stop. Hope it would be quick.

Robin yanked my underwear down over my hips and spread my legs. It felt like something broke inside me.

I was caught in his hold. I couldn't do anything.

Then suddenly everything was suspended.

I didn't know if I was dead or alive.

Robin flew up and paced around.

"Someone's out there," he hissed, his pants around his knees.

I filled my lungs with oxygen, again and again. Finally, I could breathe.

"It's Adam!"

Robin stared in terror at the window as he ran around looking for his shirt. He grabbed me by the arms and tried to pull me up off the bed.

"It's your dad!"

I closed my eyes and breathed.

Dad.

Thank God.

Dad.

52

I miss Mom and Dad so freaking much, but I don't know how I can ever look them in the eyes again. I miss Amina. I miss light.

This place will make you sick. My memories haunt me constantly and there's nowhere to run.

In the middle of the night I wake up because I'm about to die. I'm drowning.

I toss and turn in the bed. I pound at the walls, try to yank the door open. I kick it until my toes are numb. My screams tear through my eardrums.

At last Jimmy the Guard opens the door. There are four of them, and they rush into the room and I don't have time to think. They throw themselves at me and take me down.

Jimmy's meaty hand presses my face to the floor. My screams are muffled by his nasty reptile skin.

My memories of the rape are sharp as knives; the images clear as glass. Part of me will always be there on that bed in the counselors' cabin, gasping for breath.

They lock my hands behind my back and lift me up. I try to scream, but my mouth is clogged.

Four muscular men carry me out of my room. I fling my body around and they are forced to drop me in the corridor. I land on the floor with a crack and one of them hits me in the face. I don't know if it's on purpose.

It takes fifteen minutes for them to drag me to the elevator. Down in the observation cell, they receive help from a few more guards to lift me up on the restraint bed. The straps tighten around my wrists and ankles. I lie on my back, crying and shaking. I'm back in the counselors' cabin at confirmation camp. I'm drowning in Robin's panting breath. The sweat and tears blend together. The inconceivable horror of another person taking control of my body. Another person forcing their way into the innermost parts of me and robbing me of the dignity and right to self-determination I had taken for granted.

Anyone who claims that she would never consider revenge, who firmly believes bloody, violent retaliation can never be justified, has never been subjected to rape. It's even in the Bible: An eye for an eye, a tooth for a tooth. Before Jesus fucked everything up with that part about turning the other cheek.

53

Two days later, it's new-girl Elsa's turn to take me to the psychologist.

Elsa smells like vanilla. She seems to have a lot of questions in her head, but is far too professional or shy to say anything.

"Stella."

Shirine gestures at me to have a seat.

Her small Bambi eyes are full of sympathy and trust. It's hard to dislike Shirine as much as I'm trying to. She's the kind of person anyone would have trouble not loving. I really want to hate people like that.

"How was your week?"

"Like an all-inclusive trip to the Canary Islands."

She quashes a small smile. I look at the things on her desk and my eyes linger on a cute, flowery pencil case.

"I had one just like that in elementary school," I say.

She puts the pencil case away.

"My daughter picked it out."

Apparently it's a sensitive subject.

"So what did you think of this?" she asks about *The Catcher in the Rye*.

"You said it wouldn't be as depressing."

"Was it? It's been years since I read it. I just remember loving it."

"Well, he ends up in the psych ward," I say. "Sometimes I wonder if it's possible to end up any other way in this sick world. Suicide or the psych ward, there doesn't seem to be any other way out."

"It doesn't have to be that way," Shirine says. "Life can be pretty simple too. You don't have to make it so hard."

I stare at her. Is she suggesting that I have only myself to blame? That

Esther Greenwood and Holden Caulfield could have had an easier time and felt better if only they'd made different choices and hadn't made everything so fucking complicated?

"I was thinking about something," Shirine says. "What you said about how you've been to a bunch of psychologists before. What was it you didn't like?"

I know she's trying to coax me into sharing. This is just a way to get me to talk. And still I fall for it.

"You're so sold on diagnoses. You want to force people into ready-made templates. I don't believe in all that."

"Know what?" Shirine says. "Me neither. I promise not to diagnose you."

She sounds sincere.

"For a while I actually wanted to be a psychologist myself," I say with a snort. "Stupid, huh?"

"Not at all."

I lean back in the chair and cross my arms.

"Listen," Shirine says. "Couldn't you give me a chance? I like to say that everyone deserves a chance. I think it's a pretty fair proposition."

"Like you're going to give me a chance?"

"Of course." She smiles.

"Why did you become a psychologist?" I ask.

Shirine fiddles with the silvery button of her earring.

"My parents."

"They wanted you to?"

"No, no, the opposite." She looks down and runs her fingers through her hair. "They wanted me to become a doctor. My grandfather is a doctor, and so are both my parents. They believe that humans are biological beings first and foremost. They don't think you can cure illnesses by talking about feelings and other abstract stuff like that."

She still smiles, although her voice sounds dejected and her eyes are shiny.

"So that's why you became a psychologist? To rebel?"

"Not really. I'm sure I would have become a doctor if it weren't for my germaphobia."

"Germaphobia?"

Shirine nods.

"I've undergone therapy."

"Did it help?"

She gives a dubious smile.

"Maybe you should try drugs."

Then she bursts into laughter.

"I'm really curious about you, Stella. I want to get to know you."

"Because I'm a murderer?"

"I don't know anything about that. You're still awaiting trial."

Shirine is polished in a sneaky way. Somehow she's lured me into a conversation.

"Can I leave now?" I ask.

"Will you come back?"

I look at her in feigned surprise.

"Like I have a choice."

54

I didn't actually want to go out. It had been a long Friday at work, and the very thought of getting out of my sweatpants, fixing my hair, and putting on my face exhausted me.

"Come on," said Amina, who had lined up shots on the desk. "For once I don't have a match tomorrow."

She wanted to go to Tegnérs, but said she was open to other ideas too.

"Know what you need?" she asked, handing me a shot glass brimming with surface tension. "To get laid."

"Seriously? The only dudes I need right now are called Ben and Jerry."

I balanced the glass in my hand, hesitating.

"Cheers," said Amina, and we took the shots.

I did it to be a good friend. For Amina and the alcohol. After two ciders and several shots that were basically forced on me, my heart sped up and my body got warmer. I don't usually drink that much. Amina started our "Party Like an Animal" playlist on Spotify and at last we sat on our bikes on our way to Tegnérs. It was early June and the nights were still chilly. I had to grip my skirt, which blew up around my legs.

Brimming with giggles and expectations, we stumbled into Tegnérs. The flashing lights made the dance floor overflow. Cascades of color were flung at us from every direction and the vibration of the bassline rumbled like cannon fire in our chests. Amina and I went all in. Purses on the floor and hands in the air.

A few guys from our old high school showed up and were shockingly entertaining. As I shot the shit with them, Amina disappeared over to the bar.

"Need a glass of water," she said.

After quite some time, the guys had moved on and she still hadn't come back.

I found her at the bar.

She was standing on tiptoe. She's always wished she were a few inches taller. Her eyes sparkled, and between her lips she held a long straw that vanished into a toxically green drink. Next to her stood a guy in a paisley shirt, babbling as if he was afraid the oxygen was about to run out.

"So this is where you're hiding?"

Amina jumped. The guy stopped midsentence and stared like I had just ruined his night. He was one of those classic hunks with thick, slicked-back hair and bright blue eyes. I realized that he was also old. At least ten years older than us.

"Who's the grandpa?" I asked, dissecting him with my gaze.

Amina groaned, but Paisley Shirt chuckled, all laid-back.

"I'm not that old, am I?"

"It's all relative. Al Pacino is like seventy-five. And Abraham lived to be one hundred and seventy-five, right?"

"Abraham?" Paisley Shirt asked as he waved the bartender over.

"From the Bible," I said. "Like, the forefather of all religions."

He ordered a drink across the bar before he looked at me.

"So you're Christian?"

"Not at all. It's called being well-informed."

He laughed again. His teeth were a little too straight and white to seem natural.

"I apologize for her," said Amina. "She's not used to drinking."

"Blame the alcohol," I said.

"She has her good sides too. If you look really hard, for a long time."

"So how old are you?" I asked. "Because you *are* old."

He struck a pose: put his hand on his side and stuck out his chest as he fired off another smile.

"What do you think?"

"Thirty-five," I said.

He pretended to be offended.

"Twenty-nine?" Amina guessed.

"Nice. On the first try too," he said, touching her arm casually. "You've won the drink of your choice."

Amina turned to me.

"His name is Christopher."

He put out his hand, and after a moment of feigned hesitation I took it.

"Chris," he said with a wink. "You can call me Chris."

I wanted to dance again, and Amina promised to join me soon. As if.

I reached my arms high up in the air and pumped them to the beat. It felt like there was helium in my chest. I had wings.

Time flew by with no sign of Amina. I was sweaty and aching when I finally tracked her down at a table, her gaze sunk deep into Chris.

"We're drinking champagne," he said, offering me a glass.

I tried to make eye contact with Amina. What was this? Was she interested in this guy? Amina's not the flirty type. She would never go home with a guy she met at the bar. Last time she had a serious crush on someone was when we were in fifth grade. And this guy was ten years older than us. Almost thirty.

I filled my mouth with bubbles and got the feeling that there was something shady about this whole thing, that something was off.

"So what do you do?" I asked.

Chris flashed a big smile, as if he appreciated the question.

"A little of everything, actually. Business. Mostly real estate. I have a couple different firms."

This mostly sounded suspicious to my ears.

"Amina told me she's going to be a doctor," said Chris. "So what are your plans?"

I tried to attract Amina's attention, but she only had eyes for Chris.

"I used to want to be a psychologist," I said. "But I don't think I could deal. People have so fucking many problems."

Chris laughed again. I've always had issues with people who seem perfect. Seems like there must be some serious fault behind all that fantastic exterior.

"Maybe I'll get a law degree," I said. "My mom's an attorney, but I guess I'd rather be a judge. I like being in charge."

"My mom is a lawyer too," Chris said. "A professor these days."

"Exciting," I responded.

It sounded more sarcastic than I had been aiming for.

"Not at all," he said, laughing. "Jurisprudence is just a bunch of quibbling and splitting hairs."

"I don't believe that."

"You'll see."

"Nah," I said, stretching. "I'll probably just say fuck law school and go to Asia instead. For years I've been dreaming of taking a long trip to Cambodia, Laos, and Vietnam."

"She's totally obsessed with that trip," said Amina. "Ask her a question or two and she'll talk about it until your ears bleed."

"Wonderful. I like traveling," said Chris.

There was hardly a corner of the map he hadn't discovered. He'd been everywhere in Asia except Mongolia. He'd lived in New York, Los Angeles, London, and Paris. But Lund was his childhood, and his home. For some reason he always returned.

I wondered what kind of business he was actually involved in. He looked and acted like someone who didn't need to worry about money, and that made me both curious and skeptical.

"Still, it must be nice to have a law professor in the family when you're dealing with companies and business and stuff, right?"

Chris seemed to consider this.

"I have actually been able to use Mom's help a lot recently. But not business-wise. She doesn't interfere with that."

"So what happened?"

For the first time he stopped talking and looked down at the table.

"It's none of our business," Amina said primly.

"It's okay," said Chris. "I was subjected to . . . a lot of shit. But it's a long story."

"This place doesn't close until three," I said.

He looked at me. His smile was different now, his lips brushed with softness.

"I had a stalker," he said.

"A stalker?"

"Seriously?"

Amina raised her eyebrows.

"Yeah, a real sicko," said Chris.

55

Chris didn't like to dance, so when Amina and I returned to the neon sea of the dance floor, he remained at the table with his champagne and his smile.

"Be honest, Amina," I shouted on the dance floor. "Are you horny for him?"

"Quit it! What do you think?"

We held each other's hands and spun around. The bass vibrated pleasantly through my body.

"He's not ugly," I said.

"I've seen worse."

I laughed and twerked.

I'm not quite sure about what happened after that. I don't usually drink much. In time I've come to realize that I don't need alcohol, I get my kicks in other ways. Drinking mostly just makes me all hyped and annoying, and sick as a dog the next day.

Anyway, some guy dragged me off. We danced closer and closer, and soon his mouth was against my neck, his bulge against my ass. We'd met before, sometime last spring. The sex had been fine, but I didn't remember his name, what he did, what we had talked about.

"I have to find my friend," I said after a while.

"What the hell?"

He looked like I had just given him a fatal diagnosis.

I crowded my way across the dance floor, hunting for Amina. It was almost two thirty. Was she sitting with that Chris guy again, waiting for a slow dance? I staggered between tables, walked past the bar, but couldn't find her anywhere. When I took out my phone to text her, I saw I already had a message.

Sorry!!! I went home puked in the bathroom couldnt find you

I wrote back that it was cool, I understood, I was also heading home. I received a green puking emoji in return.

After downing a large glass of water at the bar, I wobbled my way to the sidewalk. The night was filled with birdsong, it smelled like liquor, sweaty perfume, and pollen. The sky was studded with stars.

"Taxi?" asked a male voice behind me.

I ignored him. I never take gypsy cabs.

"We can share one," he said, and I turned around.

It was Chris.

"Only if you want to, I mean. It'll be cheaper."

He smiled in that intimate, humble way again. The glow of a streetlight was reflected in his pale eyes.

"I don't know where you're going," I said, realizing I was having trouble standing upright.

Did I really want to take a cab with him?

"Pilegatan," he said. "Right by Polhem."

Well, we *were* going in the same direction.

Chris walked over to the nearest taxi and waved at me to follow. How dangerous could it be? We would only have to ride, like, five minutes together.

We slid into the backseat through opposite doors and I pressed my knees together.

The car took off with a jolt and my stomach turned. My mouth was dry as dust and I tried to ignore my dizziness.

"Are you okay?" Chris asked.

I tried to look at him, but everything was spinny and flickery.

"Do you feel okay?" he asked again, putting a hand on my arm.

"Like a princess," I said, hiding a burp with my hand. "It must be the Chinese food I ate. Fucking duck."

"Oh, bad duck. Been there, done that. Not my favorite memory."

I gazed out the window. Fumbled with my phone and texted Amina.

Taking a taxi with Grandpa Chris!

She didn't respond. What if she was mad?

No hard feelings, right? I wrote.

This time the answer appeared quickly.

Ha ha you can have grandpa to yourself no worries

Happy smiley face with sunglasses.

"Do you come here often?" Chris asked.

That repulsive perfect smile again.

"To Tegnérs? Well, there's not many options when you're too young."

"Or too old," he said.

That was actually funny. I appreciated his self-awareness.

The taxi braked suddenly and my stomach gave another worrying lurch. A thick clump stuck in my throat.

"Everything okay?" Chris asked.

I took a deep breath and muttered something about how he'd managed to choose the worst taxi driver in town, what were the chances?

"Have you tried Tinder?" I asked. "Happy Pancake? Those are full of people your age."

"Happy what now?"

"There's this new thing. The internet. A worldwide digital zone. Mostly for us young folks, maybe."

He chuckled, but soon a more serious expression passed over his face.

"I've had some bad experiences."

"With the internet?"

"With girls."

I laughed a bit, but Chris's smile seemed forced and sad. The taxi took a left and braked. More gently this time. Maybe the driver had heard my dig. My stomach was seriously upset, though, and I was afraid I might throw up at any moment.

"This is me," Chris said, and only then did I realize that the car had stopped. "I'll pay for the whole trip, so just tell the driver where to let you off."

He leaned between the front seats to swipe his American Express.

My phone buzzed. Another text from Amina.

Youve got your pepper spray right?? You never know!

What did she think? I began a response, but the puke was rising up and my cheeks filled with saliva and I couldn't wait any longer. I opened the door and staggered out.

With my eyes on the asphalt, I stumbled over to a bush, tossed my purse on the ground, and threw up.

It took a long time. I gagged and coughed and more came out. Until it was just bile. How had I gotten so drunk? I hadn't had all *that* much to drink.

This was why I hated drinking.

Surely no one had put anything in my drink, right?

When I was sure I was done, I tried to fix myself up a little using a wet wipe from my purse. Then I turned around, shame-faced, only to discover that the taxi was gone. Farther down the sidewalk was Chris, something hard in his gaze.

"Come on," he said. "You can come up and freshen up a bit."

I thought of Amina's text and felt for the pepper spray in my bag. Rummaging and rooting. What the fuck? I shoved half my arm in. Nothing. I always have that little bottle with me. Always.

But it wasn't there.

56

Chris lived one floor up in a yellow building pretty close to Polhem School. The door said *C. Olsen*.

What was I doing there? Drunk and dizzy and totally wrecked after puking out half my stomach.

As I bent down in the hallway to pull my shoes off, I nearly fell onto my head. Chris caught me and held me up, his hands on my hips.

"Lie down on the sofa for a minute," he said, guiding me gently into the living room.

I collapsed onto the sofa and lay there like a beached whale, staring up at the fancy plasterwork on the high ceiling. Meanwhile, Chris was clattering around in the kitchen. My eyelids were heavy and I was halfway into a fog.

"Are you asleep?" Chris asked.

He set a large glass of water on the coffee table.

"Drink this."

My eyes swam as I sat up. I took big gulps of the water.

Chris watched me expectantly.

When I put the glass back down, it struck me how ridiculously naïve I was. I knew full well that there were rape drugs you couldn't taste. Why was I being so careless? But, okay, we were in his house and at the moment I was northern Europe's least sexy pick-up. So there probably wasn't anything to worry about.

"That thing you said. About girls," I said. "What did you mean?"

"What did I say about girls?"

"You said you had some bad experiences."

"Oh, that."

He sucked at his lower lip and looked like he regretted mentioning it.

"It's fine," I said. "We don't have to talk about it."

Chris leaned back on the sofa and rested his hands in his lap.

"You know that stalker I mentioned?"

"Oh, right, the stalker."

The memory gradually returned.

"It wasn't just some random. It was my ex."

"Your ex?"

He nodded and scratched his chin.

"She couldn't deal with things ending between us. I didn't handle it well, I'll admit that. I met someone else and fell for her. Not a pretty story, but you can't help what your heart wants, can you?"

"Did you cheat on her?"

"Depends on how you look at it. Nothing happened between us, not physically, I mean, not even a kiss. But I cheated emotionally and I'm not proud of it."

I understood. I hate cheaters, but no one can control their feelings.

"Obviously I realized I would hurt Linda, which I suppose is why I kept putting it off. But I never would have dreamed that she'd flip out this much."

"What did she do?"

He scratched his chin even more. No doubt this was hard to talk about. I drank my water and felt a little more alert.

"Linda has a long history of being mentally unwell," said Chris.

"What do you mean?"

I've never understood that concept. You seldom hear people talking about being "physically unwell."

"I knew she was unstable. She'd had periods of depression before, and eating disorders and stuff like that, back when she was a teenager. She's a sensitive soul."

That just seemed silly. Whose soul isn't sensitive to being abandoned by the person you love?

"When I told her what was going on, she lost it. Violent outbursts, throwing things, and threatening me. Even though this is my apartment—I'd had it for three years when Linda entered the picture—she refused to move out. I had to stay with my mom for several weeks and threaten to bring in the police and stuff, before she finally gave in."

"That was when you got your mom to help?"

"Well, one of the times. It gets worse. Linda started harassing my new girlfriend. She sent messages, several hundred a day. Then she showed up outside my girlfriend's work, and followed her."

"That sounds just sick."

Like something out of a movie.

"I kept thinking that it would be possible to talk to her. We were together for three years, after all. My girlfriend wanted to file a police report, but I convinced her not to. Since I knew Linda."

"What a bizarre story. I understand why you're on guard now, when it comes to girls."

Chris nodded.

"But that's not all. Linda went to the police and reported me. She made up a whole bunch of awful accusations. I can hardly stand to think about it. She claimed I abused and raped her. It was absurd."

"Shit," I blurted.

"I had to sit through interrogations and listen to a ton of morbid things she claimed I had done. It was the worst thing that's ever happened to me. For a while I thought it was going to work. It seemed like the investigators believed her. I was about to be put away for terrible things, to be marked as a domestic abuser and rapist. My life was about to be ruined."

"Shit."

That's all I could manage to say. Chris looked shaken, as if it was all coming back to him, and I was ashamed that I'd been thinking about rape drugs. Really, though, I hadn't done anything wrong. Life has taught me to consider every man a potential rapist. Better safe than sorry. I had no reason to feel ashamed, but when I saw Chris's fear I couldn't help it.

"After a while things ended with my new girlfriend too. She said she supported me, sure, but I knew she had doubts. Maybe it's wrong to blame her; how could she know for sure? But I can't be with someone who even entertains the thought that I could hurt her."

His pale blue eyes gleamed and thoughts whizzed through my brain like fleeing birds.

"So that's why I'm single, and a little bit afraid of girls," Chris said, his smile edged with sadness. "It's probably going to take some time before I can trust anyone again."

"I understand."

He gave a heavy sigh and lowered his head. Out of sheer reflex I placed a comforting hand on his knee. Warmth radiated from him and traveled through my body. Tears glistened in his eyes.

I don't know what I was thinking. I suppose I felt sorry for him. The alcohol had turned my brain into mushy fruit.

"Hey," I said, putting an arm around his neck.

When he turned his face towards mine, I brought my lips to his.

"Stop," he mumbled, shoving me away.

I let go of him. My face went hot and my heart was pounding like a drum. What the hell was I doing?

"Not like this," he said. "Not now."

I just wanted to crawl under the sofa and disappear.

"I think it's best if you go home," Chris said, typing on his phone. "I'll get you a taxi. Where do you live?"

So fucking humiliating. I didn't even want to look at him.

I gave him my address and staggered into the hall as he made the call. When I looked at myself in the mirror, I had to squint. I looked like *come fucking help me.*

On my phone was a new message from Amina.

What's going on? Where are you???

Heading home, I wrote.

Chris followed me down to the street and hugged me. It felt stiff. I was convinced I would never see him again, and as I got into the taxi I regretted having given him my real address.

57

Michael Blomberg has a new shirt on: dolphin-blue with white buttons and rolled-up sleeves, and a sloppily folded handkerchief in his breast pocket. He leans way over the table with an oversized smile.

"I really want you to see your mother. We need to talk, the three of us."

"I can't," I say.

The very thought scares the shit out of me.

"What do you want me to tell her, then?" Blomberg asks. "That you don't want to see your own mother?"

Of course I want to see her. There's nothing I want more. But Blomberg would never understand.

"Tell the truth. I can't deal with it."

He sighs heavily.

"Or else lie," I suggest. "I'm sure you're competent enough to come up with a good lie."

The big lawyer shakes his head.

"I've known Ulrika for many years . . ."

"I know. You know Mom pretty well, right?"

Blomberg stiffens. This isn't the first time I've made such an insinuation, and it won't be the last. I'm happy to let him wonder. Ignorance is power.

"Do you know Margaretha Olsen too?" I ask.

"I don't exactly know her. She's a—"

"Professor."

He is startled and makes an annoyed grimace.

"Lund is a small . . ."

"Pond."

"City," he says. "Lund is a small city."

"Does she think I'm guilty too?"

"Who? What?"

"Margaretha Olsen. Does she?"

"I have no idea about that whatsoever," Blomberg says, scratching behind his ear. "What does it matter? Who cares what people think? The important thing is for us to demonstrate reasonable doubt in court."

"Is that really the important thing? Then why does it feel like everyone has already made up their minds about what happened?"

"What 'everyone' are you talking about?"

"The police, the prosecutor, like, the whole world."

Blomberg squirms, but sounds as certain as always.

"That's called confirmation bias. When you have a theory and ignore everything that contradicts it. It's extremely common. Doesn't have to be conscious at all. And likely isn't."

"But isn't an investigation supposed to be objective?"

He shrugs.

"We're talking about human beings here. We're only human, all of us."

Then he fingers the black beads of his necklace and seems to brace himself before dropping his little bomb.

"Linda Lokind."

He waits me out with his gaze.

"What about her?" I ask.

"Do you know her?"

"Not know, exactly. Lund is a small . . ."

"Pond."

Blomberg leans back and winks.

"Now tell me, Stella. You have had contact with Linda Lokind, haven't you?"

"Had contact?" It sounds so formal. "I mean, I know who she is."

"You do?"

Blomberg nods slowly. The question is, how much does *he* know?

"I met her once or twice. That's it."

"But you know she and Christopher Olsen were together for a few years? They lived together."

I try to act surprised, but Blomberg hardly seems convinced.

"I'm planning to present Linda Lokind as an alternative perpetrator."

"What? To the police?"

He nods.

"You can't do that!"

I feel dizzy and hot. My mind is spinning.

"But it could mean your freedom," Blomberg says.

Does he believe Linda is the one who killed Chris? I reach for a glass of water and accidentally splash some on the table when I go to pour. Blomberg follows my every movement with interest.

"Linda Lokind filed a police report on Christopher Olsen after they broke up last spring. According to her, Olsen was a real tyrant. But there was no proof, so the investigation was closed pretty quickly. A reasonable motive for revenge, right? And it doesn't matter whether it was true or not. In Lokind's mind, Olsen was a violent man who assaulted her in the most horrific ways."

"In Lokind's mind? You think she was lying?"

Blomberg waves a hand.

"It doesn't really matter. There's still plenty to suggest Lokind as the perpetrator. We've dug up quite a bit on her."

"What do you mean, 'dug up'? You're not the police," I say. "You're only supposed to defend my rights. Not play investigator."

He gives me a look that says, *oh, sweetie.*

"This is how it goes. When the police don't do their job, we have to fix it for them. It's not about pointing the finger at Lokind. I just want to make sure there's reasonable doubt about your guilt."

I'm sweating hard now. The air in here is stuffy.

"No," I say. "This isn't okay. Don't mix Linda up in this."

He looks surprised.

"But it might be your salvation, Stella. I'm going to have to talk to your mom."

"You have to fucking follow confidentiality. I could get you disbarred."

Blomberg rests his hands on his stomach. It almost looks like he feels sorry for me.

"You have no idea what Ulrika has been through for you."

"What do you mean?"

He scoots his chair back and stands up.

"What the fuck are you talking about?" I say.

My mom basically only cares about herself and her career. I was never good enough for her. What could she possibly have had to go through for my sake?

"I'll be back," Blomberg says.

He turns around and raps at the pane of glass.

"You believe it too, don't you," I say.

"Believe what?"

"You think I did it."

58

On Sunday after Tegnérs Amina and I met at a burger joint. The outdoor seating area was deserted, even though it was June. The sky was all gray clouds and the wind chilly. Inside, hungover college students sat crouched over their course literature, oozing trans-fats through their pores.

After we'd ordered, Amina took my arm.

"Did anything happen?"

I dropped my tray on the table with a thud.

"No, I told you."

"Come on, *something* must have happened," she nagged. "Just a little hookup?"

She sounded annoyingly curious, and not enthusiastic in the least.

"Are you jealous?"

"Quit it."

Amina is the only person I know who eats hamburgers with a knife and fork. She stuck her fork in the burger and sawed away with her knife.

"Sorry. I didn't mean to go to his place. We were only supposed to share a cab."

"Stop it. I'm not jealous."

"I swear, nothing happened."

Amina cut through her burger so hard that the knife squealed against the plate.

"You know that stalker he was talking about?" I said. "It was his ex."

"What?"

I told her the whole story of Chris's ex and how she refused to accept it when he fell in love with someone else. How she had followed and harassed

Chris's new girlfriend and then went to the police and accused Chris of assaulting and raping her.

"That's sick," Amina said, her face full of disgust. "You should seriously stay away from guys like that."

"Guys like that? It's hardly Chris's fault that his ex is a freak."

Amina didn't seem to agree.

"Are you going to see him again?"

"Why would I?"

I sounded much more certain than I felt.

I worked all day on Monday. I found my pepper spray in a jacket pocket and put it back in my purse. I got home late and changed into sweatpants, spread peanut butter on two slices of bread, and curled up in one corner of the sofa to look through my feed on my phone. That's when I discovered that Chris had sent me a friend request.

What did he want with me? A loaded, hot twenty-nine-year-old who ran several companies and traveled all over the world. Obviously I understood exactly what he was after. I knew I should follow Amina's advice. There was no reason to have further contact with this guy.

I hesitated for a moment, then accepted the request. It was only Facebook, after all. It wasn't like I was planning to marry him.

It only took thirty seconds for the first message to arrive.

I'm thinking about you, he wrote.

There was something about that. At the time I couldn't put my finger on it, but now I know. It was the verb, the present tense. Like he was always thinking about me, like he was doing so right now.

Stella? He wrote when I didn't respond right away. *That's a really beautiful name.*

I typed a short reply, erased it, tried again, and erased it once more. At last I sent:

It means star in Italian.

He sent a star emoji.

My dad loves Italy, I wrote. *He's actually kind of obsessed.*

Chris sent a thumbs-up.

Italy is sweet. Cinque Terre, Tuscany, Liguria.

I sent a yawn emoji in response.

The bubble with three dots let me know he was typing again, but no text showed up. I squeezed my phone. At last it appeared.

Did you know that when people are asked on their deathbeds what their greatest regret is, they never regret the things they did but what they didn't do?

What did he mean? Was this how twenty-nine-year-olds flirted?

I'm not planning to regret a fucking thing, I wrote.

He sent a smiley face.

I think we're the same, he wrote. *We're the kind of people who are never at peace. People like us have to find our way to one another to survive.*

He was trying to analyze me. I hate people who do that.

You don't know a thing about me, I wrote.

He responded: *I bet I know more than you think I do.*

This guy was just too much.

For example, I bet you sleep naked.

What? I read it three times.

I *wanted* to be furious, but I couldn't help being tickled. It was so unexpected.

Gotta go to bed now, I wrote.

He answered: *Sleep tight, little star.*

I called Amina right away. She sounded depressed.

"Do whatever you want," she said.

"Forget it, I'm not interested."

Even I could hear how much it sounded like a lie.

"I'm just so tired of how nothing ever happens," I said. "It's so fucking boring here."

"You'll be out traveling soon."

"Soon?" Amina and I have never experienced time in the same way. "That's months away. If I even manage to go."

"Of course you will," said Amina. "Time flies."

I lay down in bed with my computer. A few days earlier, I had found an American site about psychopaths that turned out to be a real gold mine. A ton of researchers and psychiatrists wrote long, interesting entries for it. I read that psychopaths are sometimes described as predators who manipulate those around them with their exceptional charm and charisma. Those who encounter the seductive flattery of a psychopath seldom realize they're being manipulated until it's too late. Psychopaths lie often and without guilt. Psychopaths lie for their own gain, to improve their self-image, and to get ahead in life.

I've always been a master at telling lies. Was that a psychopathic trait?

Psychopaths know they're lying. And so did I. And sure, sometimes I lied for my own benefit. I wasn't sure that I always felt guilty when I lied. What did that say about me?

I read about a woman whose whole life was ruined when she met a man who cheated her out of everything she owned. I felt sorry for her, of course, but at the same time I couldn't help but feel some disdain.

On Friday the sun came out. The city emptied quickly, everyone on their way to the coast or a park. I was at work when I saw Chris's message. I never check my phone when I'm at the store. Especially not when Malin is there—the store manager. She's the type who would fire you for using your phone during working hours. There are rumors that she stopped giving one girl hours just because she chewed gum at the register.

But I was on break when I saw the message from Chris. I was alone in the break room and maybe that was lucky, because my reaction involved maybe a little too much teen-girl cheering.

Can you be ready at 6? A limo will pick you up. I suggest a dress. Maybe pajamas. Oh no, that's right, you sleep naked.

My whole body got the butterflies when I read that.

On the one hand Chris was too much. On the other hand, my life was too boring. I'd never ridden in a limo and I confess I am both materialistic and easily impressed.

How dangerous could it be? A date. Who doesn't want to get dressed up and take a limousine to a fancy restaurant that serves dishes you can't even pronounce?

I held off on answering Chris for a while, but the truth is I never really hesitated. The offer was too good to refuse.

At six on the dot, I was standing on the sidewalk near my house in my newest, sexiest dress as the limo pulled up. It was one of those mega-huge ones with a white interior and a well-stocked bar. We opened a bottle of Moët and toasted as we headed across the bridge to Copenhagen.

"I'm so glad you wanted to come along," said Chris.

His eyes were glowing.

When we arrived, he ran around the car and opened the door for me. Then he guided me ahead of him, one hand resting gently on the small of my back. Apparently the restaurant had Michelin stars and was world famous. I've forgotten the name. The food was mostly just weird, and despite four courses I wasn't anywhere near full.

"Can we stop here?" I called to the driver when we passed an ice-cream stand on our way home.

I bought a giant soft-serve with whipped cream and fruit topping. Then we sat there at a folding table with gulls at our feet, and Chris watched wide-eyed as I got sticky with fruit and licked my fingers clean.

"I dig your style," he said.

I didn't get what there was to like, but naturally I was flattered.

We rounded off the evening at a rooftop bar with a view of the Sound; you could see all the way to Sweden. A ruddy guy played sad songs on the grand piano and Chris stared at me so intently, and for so long, that I almost blushed.

"Tell me your dreams?" he asked.

"Sorry, I was just thinking . . ."

"No," he interrupted, and tiny peanut-shaped dimples appeared in his cheeks as he laughed. "I mean, what are your dreams, what do you want to do with your life?"

"Oh."

I didn't laugh, not at all. My stomach twisted in a familiar way.

"I hate that question."

"Why?"

"Because I can't answer it."

Chris raised his eyebrows.

"It's true," I said. "All my friends know exactly what they're going to do; they've, like, planned out their whole lives. Travel, education, job, family. I can't do that. I just get bored."

"Me too. It sounds awful. That's not what I meant at all."

"I think it sucks having to plan next weekend ahead of time. I want to be surprised."

Chris's laughter made his eyes sparkle like diamonds.

"I'm exactly the same way."

I smiled at him. Despite the age difference, we had quite a bit in common.

"Most people my age live extremely routine lives," he said as the pianist played that Elton John song from *The Lion King*. "It started happening when we were around twenty-five. People were suddenly so damn boring. Every day is the same, they do the same things, watch the same TV shows, listen to the same podcasts, eat the same food, go to the same gym, follow the same Instagram accounts, and have the exact same opinions about everything."

"Ugh, I hope I never end up that way."

"No risk of that. You and I are different."

He hummed along with the refrain. *Can you feel the love tonight?*

"That's why I quit handball. I was actually really good, got to go to the national-team camps and stuff. But suddenly everything had to be so regimented. Every offensive had to be planned out ahead of time and if you tried to take any initiative on your own you'd get chewed out by the coaches. It wasn't fun anymore."

"They killed your creativity." Chris sighed.

"And the excitement. How exciting can it be when everything has been decided in advance?"

"You sound so wise."

"For my age?"

He laughed.

"Age is overrated. For most people, it's the same as empty calories. The years add up, but development stands still."

An hour later, our driver pulled up in the limo and opened the door for me. I caught a few jealous glances from the corner of my eye.

In the middle of the Öresund Bridge, Chris opened the sunroof and got up. We stood close together, the wind in our hair. It was like we were floating. I was exhausted as we sank back into the white leather again. We gazed at each other and it almost felt like we'd just had sex. Chris laughed with his face so close to mine that our lips couldn't help but meet. A quick kiss, and he let go of me.

"I'm sorry," he said, looking like he was guilty of an unpardonable violation. "It just happened. I'm sorry."

I leaned back, my arms behind my neck, and stretched out my legs.

"Stop apologizing. Kiss me instead."

But Chris's shoulders sagged and his gaze seemed to shrink.

"There's nothing I'd rather do," he said.

"But?"

I straightened back up, squeezed my knees together, and gathered my hair in one hand.

"I still haven't gotten over everything that happened with my ex. I swear, this has nothing to do with you. I just need more time."

"I understand."

I thought of Amina. In all our years as best friends, we had never ended up interested in the same guy. But we had anticipated the risk and promised each other never to let a guy come between us. This time it felt strange. Amina was the one who'd met Chris first, at the bar. And she'd sure seemed interested. I felt like I should back off, forget Chris and move on.

"Thanks for being so understanding," Chris said, placing his hands on my knee. "Our time will come."

59

"I can't read this," I say to Shirine, handing back the book she's just given me.

It's called *Rape* and is the thinnest, most modern book I've received from her, but the text on the back cover makes me feel nauseated.

"What do you mean?" Shirine asks.

"It doesn't seem like my kind of book."

Shirine shrugs her shoulders with a smile.

"For someone who's hardly read any books, you seem to have very firm views on what you do and don't like," she says.

"I'm happy to challenge my own views!" I say. "It's not that."

"Okay. Then what is it?"

She deserves an explanation.

"I can't read about rape," I say, turning away.

I feel Shirine staring at me.

"Oh no," she says. "I'm sorry. I didn't know."

"How could you know?"

I slowly turn around to see her sad brown eyes.

"No one knows," I say. "We never reported it."

"We?"

I take a deep breath and stare at the desk. I can't believe I'm doing this. So many barriers slam down inside me, shouting at me to stop, and still I tell her. This is not how I was raised. There are some things that are no one else's business. Some things that you keep within the family.

Despite that, I tell Shirine about the confirmation camp, about Robin and Dad, my idiotic plan to punish Dad, and everything that happened after.

"I'm so sorry, Stella."

I just nod. My voice won't hold any longer.

I've never even told Amina the whole story. For a few years, I thought it was because of who I was, because I was different. All those thoughts and feelings just brought shame. If I revealed my innermost thoughts to someone, they would probably lock me up on a psych ward and hook me up to a drip of their very strongest drugs.

Yeah, I know. Such a cliché. Show me a teen girl who doesn't think she's unique and that no one understands her.

But that's not why it took me so long to tell Amina about the rape. It was something else. I so desperately wanted to be the strong girl everyone thought I was, so I couldn't identify with the victim role. Was I even a victim? Mom and Dad said I was the one who would suffer the most if we reported it. For a week or so I went around thinking that I hadn't been subjected to an assault at all. I had willingly followed him to the counselors' cabin; I'd been into it too. After all, it was my plan from the start. I was mostly just furious at Dad for spying.

"Oh my god." Shirine raises her voice. "You were subjected to a horrific assault and your parents didn't take it seriously."

"But I understand why," I say. "*Now* I understand."

"What? You don't mean that."

"I'm glad we didn't report him."

Shirine is almost breathless.

"Was I supposed to sit through a trial and explain why I kissed him and followed him to his cabin? They would have questioned why I didn't resist or cry for help. People would have judged me even though I was the victim."

Shirine shakes her head.

"You have to trust the justice system."

"No, you don't. I wish I could, I really want to, but I don't *have* to. I have to protect myself."

Shirine raises her eyebrows as if she's just come to a realization. I'm afraid that I've said too much.

60

The sun stayed through Saturday. I stretched out on a blanket in the botanical gardens and soaked up the summer's first real warmth. That night we were sitting on Amina's balcony, discussing whether we should go out. One second Amina was super stoked, while I was hesitant. The next second I was the one who was dying to party, while Amina wanted to back out.

"I've got a match tomorrow," she said. "Don't you have to work?"

I did. I had to work basically every day all summer.

"It shouldn't be called work; my job isn't actually hard work. It's fun. Going to school was fucking hard, but working at H&M doesn't take any effort at all."

Amina laughed.

"Was school really that hard for you?"

"Maybe not so much for me, but it was for people who studied all the time."

Amina was one of them, of course. I made it through with decent grades thanks to a solid base of previous knowledge, good sense, and my gift for verbal diarrhea. Amina, though, she had something I was missing. I think maybe you could call it a sense of duty, that ability to just accept certain things, to just plow through without questioning or protesting. She says it's a second-generation immigrant thing, but I don't know if that's true. Anyway, she's always been like that. Amina nods obediently and does as she's told, only to vomit out all her feelings afterward, while I get all worked up and cocky and spew out all my resistance in the heat of the moment.

"Okay, let's stay home then," I say. "We'll sit around and wither away in pointlessness."

A group of girls was making a happy racket down on the street, and Amina topped off our glasses with wine.

"What's Chris up to tonight?"

"No idea," I said. "Whatever thirty-year-olds do. Couples dinner? Bank meeting? Weekly grocery shop?"

Amina typed his name into Facebook.

"Private profile."

"Not so strange, if you've been stalked before."

"One mutual friend," Amina said. "Stella Sandell. You'll have to check out his profile."

"Why?"

"To snoop, obviously."

I took out my phone and searched for him. In his profile pic he was looking right at the camera and smiling, with messy hair and a gleam in his eye.

His page was basically empty. A status update here and there, photos from a couple of trips, a restaurant recommendation. Only 187 friends.

"Scroll through his cover photos," said Amina. "People always forget to clean those up."

I clicked on his cover photo, which was of an endless white beach in an orange sunset. There were two more. One was the logo of Liverpool FC. In the last one, Chris was standing in front of a tall stone wall. He was sunburned and red-eyed and holding a woman's hand.

"Is that her? The ex?"

Amina yanked the phone from me.

"I don't know."

But it felt like I really did know. It had to be her. Linda.

The woman in the picture looked like a total supermodel. Curly blond hair, shining blue eyes, prominent cheekbones, and smooth peaches-and-cream skin.

"She doesn't *look* like a psycho," Amina said.

I didn't respond. I didn't like what I saw.

"Look at this," she said, pointing at her own screen.

She had brought up a page of personal information. At the top was the name Christopher Olsen. The address was right, Pilegatan, Lund. Further down it said that he was involved with four different companies. He was unmarried and his birthday was in December. He would be thirty-three.

"Thirty-three? Didn't he say—"

"He lied about his age."

Amina stared at me, a concerned look on her face.

I hadn't suspected a thing. Apparently Chris Olsen was a good liar.

I biked home in the warm night air. My purse dangled from the handlebars; all the windows were dark. Lund was slumbering.

When Chris called, my first inclination was to ignore it. I stood straddling my bike in the railway tunnel on Trollebergsvägen with the vibrating phone in my hand. His name called to me from the screen, and at last my curiosity won out.

"Can't you come over?" he said.

"Now?"

I looked at the time. Twelve thirty.

"Yes, now."

He'd been at some fancy dinner in Helsingborg and sounded a little tipsy.

"I miss you," he said.

It sounded like he meant it.

I was still plenty awake and up for some fun, slightly disappointed that Amina hadn't wanted to come out with me.

"Okay, I'm on my way."

What was the worst that could happen?

The door of the yellow brick building was open and I dashed up the stairs. Chris was wearing a checked shirt and a tie. He smelled like man and the air quavered between us.

"I've been in agony all day long," he said, taking my jacket. "I can't believe I . . . I really wanted to kiss you, Stella."

He took my hands and looked me in the eyes.

I hesitated. Why had he lied about his age?

"How old did you say you were?" I asked.

He responded immediately, with no reaction.

"I guess I said I was twenty-nine. I'm actually thirty-two."

"So you lied?"

He made a chagrined face.

"I was afraid of scaring you off. When Amina guessed twenty-nine, I just happened to say she was right."

A little white lie. Well, I'd been known to add a few years to my age now and then.

"Age is only a number, after all," I said.

Chris smiled.

"I had no idea you'd feel the same. But, I'm sorry, I should have told you earlier."

"It's okay."

I stood on tiptoe and kissed him. The tip of his tongue slipped gently into my mouth; I closed my eyes and everything spun.

My heart swelled. At last, something was happening.

Soon I was on my back on the sofa and Chris was stroking me slowly, gently—sometimes with his eyes, sometimes with his fingertips. It was heaven.

61

I'm back with Shirine. She looks cool and amiable, as always, and her Bambi eyes are Bambier than ever. Like in the movie, when the mom has just been shot.

"How are you doing?" she asks.

I can hardly manage a shrug.

"I brought this for you."

She hands me a brochure entitled *A Career in Psychology*. I take it and page through it without much enthusiasm.

"Thanks," I say. "But I don't think I can become a psychologist."

Shirine shoots me a look of exaggerated surprise.

"You *can't* or you don't *want* to? I think you would make an excellent psychologist."

"Right?"

I put the brochure aside and stare down at the table.

"What's this about?"

"What?"

"This resignation. As if you don't believe in yourself at all."

"Are you joking? I'm in here for murder. Even if I'm not convicted in court, I'm screwed. Guilty in everyone's eyes. Do you seriously think I could become a psychologist? Come on."

Shirine leans forward.

"You're not screwed, Stella. You're intelligent, funny, quick, and . . . attractive."

She's embarrassing me.

"Are you hitting on me?" I say.

Shirine laughs, breaking the tension.

"What do you want to talk about today?" she asks.

"Anything but myself."

"We can talk about someone else. It's up to you."

I think about Dad. I've been thinking about him a lot in the past few days.

"Anyone?" I ask.

"Of course."

"Control freaks. What do you know about them?"

"Control freaks?"

"Is it the same as having OCD?"

"No, not really," Shirine says, pushing the plastic pitcher of water toward me. "Being a control freak, or using coercive control, can be a compulsion, but it doesn't have to be. Many people associate the need for control with a pedantic sense of order, but I'd say it often has to do with the need to be able to predict the future."

I pour water into my glass.

"To avoid surprises?"

"Many people are frightened of the fact that reality is changeable. People seek security in their lives. So a person might feel that they're in control when they have the chance to predict what will happen, and when they can make good decisions based on solid knowledge."

I don't manage to swallow all the water down, and some trickles from the corner of my mouth.

"Good decisions? Is there such a thing?"

Shirine hands me a napkin.

"Well, the decision you think is best, the one you think will benefit you and your family."

That sounds reasonable. Of course there's a difference between making an objectively good decision and one you yourself believe is right.

"In today's society, when people become brands and everything has to be documented on social media, lots of people also feel a great need to look a certain way in the eyes of others. Of course, this can lead to an unhealthy need for control as well."

Dad's words echo inside me. *Keep it in the family.* He hates social media. *Some things are private.*

"The paradox is, you know, the more you try to keep control, the less control you feel like you have. It turns into a vicious cycle. You lose control, so you feel stressed, and you try to balance it out by being even more controlling."

Shirine scratches her ear and looks at me for a long time. She's good at looking truly concerned, as if she honestly cares, as if this isn't just a job.

Then her gaze clears. She places her hands on the table and her voice grows sharper.

"Are we talking about Christopher Olsen here?"

"Huh?"

It takes a moment for me to catch on.

"Did he try to control you, Stella? Was he jealous?"

I battle my impulses. They're hammering and pounding inside my skull, yanking and tugging at every fiber of my being. Christopher Olsen? Was this what Shirine was trying to get at from the very start? Is she trying to investigate me? Everything has just been a front.

"Fuck you!"

I plant my hands on the table and stare her down. Shirine scoots backward in her chair and one hand slips under the edge of the table. I know there's a panic button there.

"Go to hell," I say. "You're just like everyone else."

Then I stand up even as two guards storm in and lock my arms behind my back.

62

The two weeks that followed were fantastic. Summer was in full bloom. Chris and I ate ice cream on the long pier in Bjärred and he snuck his hand under my skirt and kissed the caramel sprinkles from my lips.

"Let's go to a spa!" he said over beers the next night when he met me at Stortorget after work.

"I'm working all weekend," I said with a crooked smile.

"I don't mean this weekend. I mean now!"

Of course. Why not?

He made me call Malin and say I was sick.

"Brutal cramps," I whimpered into the phone. "I can hardly stand up."

Then we walked around in bathrobes all day, having sex every hour, and when nightfall came we cuddled in a wicker chair with our limbs intertwined, enjoying champagne and strawberries, watching the sun sprinkle the Baltic Sea with twilight.

On Sunday Amina called while we were walking on the beach.

"I was worried," she said. "You're not answering your texts."

"Sorry!"

I realized that I'd completely lost track of time and space. Chris had occupied my world and I felt bewitched.

"Friday," I said to Amina. "Let's go to Tegnérs."

Chris winked and squeezed my hand.

I kept playing hooky from work. On Monday we took the train to Tivoli in Copenhagen and screamed ourselves hoarse on the roller coaster, checked into a hotel when it got late, and had sex in the morning until they called from the reception desk to say we should have checked out an hour earlier.

On Friday, Amina came over to my house with pizza.

We ate with our hands in front of Dr. Phil and discussed some of life's great questions. Such as whether it's to your advantage to mention, in your résumé, that you've been on a reality show (depends on which reality show and what job you're applying for), which quote we would have chosen to get as a tattoo and where (*I fear no evil* on the back of your neck or *It hurts to know, but wondering is just as painful* on your forearm), and obviously, whether Dr. Phil's wife had had even more plastic surgery, and how gross it was that she was sitting there in the audience in every episode and left the studio arm-in-arm with Dr. Phil when the show was over.

It didn't take long before I was texting Chris.

"Can I see?" Amina asked, yanking at my phone. "What did he say? Is it dirty?"

"Dirty?"

She laughed.

"Come on, though. Why so secretive?"

I don't know why. Normally I have no problem with the whole kiss-and-tell thing. Kind of the opposite—I like to dissect every last detail. There's not an erogenous zone on my body that Amina doesn't know about. But somehow it was different with Chris. It felt wrong to discuss it too exhaustively. Not just the sex, all of it.

"So, what? Are you together?" Amina asked.

"Of course not."

"But you like him?"

"Maybe? I don't know."

Most of all I didn't want to think about it too much. There was no way that could lead to anything good. I was not about to fall in love, especially not with a thirty-two-year-old.

"I guess a summer fling isn't so bad."

Really, it was just something I threw out casually. That's not how it felt. The problem was, those feelings I'd started to discover in myself were scaring the shit out of me.

"You player!" said Amina.

"You should get a summer fling too." I laughed.

I slept at Chris's after Tegnérs that Friday and woke to a breakfast buffet with fresh-baked buns and candles. Chris filled the juicer with oranges and massaged my shoulders as I drank.

"Can't you forget about work today?"

"No," I said. "Not again."

I needed my job. I needed every single krona to make my Asia trip happen. But I didn't mention that. I was afraid Chris would be disappointed, that he would launch a campaign to convince me to drop my travel plans. Or in the worst case, he would want to come along. I definitely wasn't ready for that conversation.

"But I get off early today," I said, stroking his arm. "We'll see each other soon."

He shook his head.

"I don't understand what you do to me. I feel lonely as soon as you leave."

We kissed several times at the door, and then I ran down the stairs and biked off like crazy. Panting, I stumbled into the store five minutes late. Malin looked at me and winked.

"Walk of shame?"

I'd been at the register for quite a while when Benita finally showed up and relieved me. The lack of sleep over the past few weeks was starting to put me a little out of balance.

"So will you be buying that?" I said to a customer who'd tried on four different blouses in similar colors.

She shot me a hateful look.

In order to get away for a while, I snuck up to the men's department and unpacked new shirts. I got lost in my thoughts and jumped when I heard a voice behind me.

"Hi, Stella."

A girl of around twenty-five, with blond curls, was right next to me, wringing her hands.

"Do I know you?"

There was something familiar about her, but I couldn't place it.

"We don't know each other," she said. "But you know Chris."

In that instant, I knew who she was. The same girl I'd seen in the picture on Facebook.

"What do you want?"

I took a step back.

"My name is Linda," she said. "I'm sure Chris has mentioned me. Is that why you look so scared?"

My heart was pounding. I looked around, but there was no one in sight.

"I think you should go now."

"I will. You don't need to be afraid of me, Stella."

She was small and thin, extremely pretty, and didn't show the slightest sign of being unstable or dangerous.

"I just want you to be careful," she said. "Chris isn't who you think."

I stuck out an elbow and crowded my way past her.

"Please, listen to me. Chris is trying to trick you."

I quickly headed for the stairs, but I could sense her following me. My heart pounded even faster.

"Look in the big cabinet in his room. The room he calls his office," she said as I swung down the stairs. "The locked drawer, at the top right. You'll find the key in the bottom left drawer."

I headed for the registers. I didn't turn around until I had reached the short line and could feel some degree of safety.

I just stared at Linda's back. She was heading out the glass doors.

"What's going on?" Benita asked from behind me. "You look like someone's been chasing you."

I tried to calm my breathing.

"Nothing," I said. "It was nothing."

I didn't know what to think.

63

"Seriously?" I say when Shirine arrives with more books. "Those are super thick."

Crime and Punishment. Six hundred and forty-six pages of nineteenth-century Russia.

"Listen," I say, paging through it with my thumb. "If I could choose between reading this or having cramps for two weeks straight . . ."

"You'll like it."

"I'll read it. To escape the stench in here for a while. Because there's nothing else to do."

Shirine smiles at me.

"And this one," she says, resting a finger on the next book.

It's called *Thérèse Raquin,* and it's also from the 1800s, but it's only 195 pages—hardly longer than an H&M catalog.

"I think I'll start with this one," I say.

As I read the foreword and the first chapter, Shirine sits beside me.

The book is pretty blah, tons of descriptions of Paris, and soon my mind begins to wander. I sneak a look at Shirine. It occurs to me that I don't know much about her.

"How many kids do you have?" I ask.

"Just one," she says, with a small, surprised smile. "Lovisa."

"Why?"

She looks puzzled.

"Because it's a beautiful name. My husband's aunt was named Lovisa."

"No, no, not that. I mean, why do you have a kid?"

"What?" she exclaims.

"Or was it a mistake? A broken condom?"

"It was not a mistake." She smiles. "It seemed like a good time. I . . . I really don't know."

I roll my eyes.

"I have a theory, Shirine."

"Go figure," she says, and sighs.

"I think a lot of people have kids for their own sake. Kind of like how when everything seems gray and boring you pop downtown to buy a new lipstick just to feel a little better for a minute."

"Are you comparing bringing a child into the world with buying lipstick?"

"Sure, maybe it's not the best analogy, but you know what I mean. People have kids to make themselves feel good, brace up their own identity, kill the boredom—you know, whatever."

"Or because it's the greatest thing that can happen to you, the most beautiful form of love that exists. The meaning of life?"

"Come on, Shirine! The meaning of life? Seriously."

She shakes her head with a smile.

"Are you going to have more?" I ask.

"More what?"

"More kids. Are you and your husband going to have more kids?"

"I think so. I think it's good to have siblings."

She still isn't looking at me.

"My parents felt the same way. They went at it like rabbits for years so they could have another kid. It didn't work. I don't know, maybe God wasn't really happy with how they were handling the one they already had. Anyway, sometimes it feels like half my childhood revolved around this sibling that never actually appeared."

Shirine looks uncomfortable.

"That sort of thing can certainly be a tragedy."

"I mostly just wanted us to move on. We were already a family, you know?"

"I understand."

"Don't do that to your little girl, to little Lovisa," I say quietly. "Promise me."

"I promise."

When Shirine has left I think about Michael Blomberg's idea, to place the blame on Linda. An "alternative perpetrator," as he put it. He has discussed it with Mom. He must have.

I know how it works in Sweden. If there are two potential perpetrators, it must be proven beyond all reasonable doubt which of them did what, or that both are equally guilty—otherwise neither one can be convicted. I've always thought this was messed up and ought to be changed.

My heart aches when I think of Amina. I miss her so much. Amina. Mom. Dad.

I think about when I was little and my dad was my favorite person in the world. Can it go back to being like that? Is it even possible? Or is everything ruined?

Maybe it would be best to confess everything. It would be simplest. For me to tell the whole story to the police and end this shit.

Then I look around. The smell, the walls, the boredom. Time that never passes, the nights that kill me. I'm not going to be able to handle it; soon I won't be able to deal with it anymore. I thump my head on my pillow and scream. I have to get out of here!

64

"This is just nuts," Amina said when I told her what had happened. "What if she's right? How can you be sure it's Linda who's the psycho and not Chris?"

"Come on. If there's anyone who would recognize a psychopath, it's me."

We were walking our bikes through the park as a big group of middle-aged women in running tights and colorful sneakers did fire hydrants on the nearby lawn.

"Did she seem . . . off?"

Amina looked at me and I didn't know what to say.

"Isn't it pretty 'off' to track down a girl who's dating your ex?"

"Maybe," said Amina. "But she said she wanted to warn you. If you don't have feelings for him anyway, maybe you might as well . . ."

I shot her a look of annoyance.

"I know Chris."

"You've known him for what, three or four weeks?"

"Long enough to know he isn't a psychopath."

Naturally I was curious what was in the drawer Linda had been talking about. But I decided not to mention it to Amina. It would only give her more fodder.

"Are you going to tell Chris?" she asked. "That Linda came to H&M?"

"I'm not sure."

I knew I should. But then again: one person's ignorance was another person's power.

"Promise you'll be careful," Amina said before we parted ways outside the arena. "You've got your pepper spray, right?"

I felt for it in my purse and nodded.

———

I biked to Chris's place, where I showered and changed clothes. He kissed me slowly, and the scent of his neck made my knees tremble.

"You twist up my brain," he said. "I wasn't supposed to jump into anything again so soon."

I wondered what he meant by "anything," but decided it was best not to know.

We drank wine and played Trivial Pursuit. Chris whistled when I knew which director had been married to Sharon Tate, one of Charles Manson's victims. I soaked up his praise, but I didn't think it was the right time to reveal that I'm a bit of an Aspie when it comes to psychopaths.

Anyway, in the end I let Chris win.

No, actually, he won fair and square. He could rattle off a whole ton of kings and dates from, like, before Christ. I've never liked history. I prefer the future.

"I'm getting tired," he said, shaking the last few drops of wine from the bottle.

We stood up at the same time and he rested a hand on my hip. His expression went hard and sharp. He guided me firmly ahead of him to the bedroom.

"Is something wrong?" he whispered into my ear.

I shook my head.

We'd hardly fallen asleep when Chris's phone woke us up again. He rolled onto his side of the bed and turned away as he spoke. It was something about a meeting, negotiations, and bidding.

"You're welcome to stay here and sleep in," he said, kissing the back of my neck. "I have to head to a meeting right away."

"Now? What time is it?"

"Five to seven."

"Fuck no."

I watched, eyes half closed, as he put on a ridiculously expensive suit and knotted his tie in front of the wardrobe mirror.

"Maybe I'll stay right here until you get back."

He turned around and pinched my big toe.

"Kids these days."

"I'm a teenager. I need lots of extra sleep."

He smiled and his eyes turned to diamonds.

"Don't you have to work today?"

"Yeah. Boo." I sighed. "But I don't start until ten fifteen."

He bent over and his tie dangled between my breasts as he kissed me.

"The door locks automatically. You can just pull it shut when you leave."

Once he was gone I tried to fall back asleep, but even though I'd hardly gotten a wink I felt wide awake. My skin was crawling; my feet itching to move. I gave it fifteen minutes or so, tossing and turning and fluffing my pillow at least a hundred times. At last I gave up and slipped to the kitchen with the comforter wrapped around me.

The fridge was full to bursting with delicacies and I set out a hotel-level breakfast for myself. Then I ate with my feet up on a chair and listened to Lund awakening through the half-open balcony door.

Linda's words echoed in my head. *The big cabinet, the top right drawer, the key in the bottom left.*

I walked into the hall. Stood before the mirror for a moment, considering.

I needed to pee. In the bathroom I snooped quickly through his medicines. Nose spray, allergy pills, pain relievers. Nothing exciting.

I washed up and went to the room Chris called his office.

Next to the window was a desk. On the wall hung an impressive painting; it must have been two meters wide. It was impossible to tell what it was supposed to be, but I had no doubt it was worth more than a year's salary at H&M.

The facing wall was taken up by a large filing cabinet. This was what Linda had been talking about.

I turned to look out the window, realizing that this was a betrayal of Chris. But it would be stupid *not* to check what was in that drawer. If only to do away with the minor doubts I was having. Chris would never know.

I crouched down and pulled out the bottom left drawer. Inside were two plastic boxes with lids. The first was full of little stuff: bracelets, key rings, old swimming-achievement badges. Keepsakes he apparently hadn't had the heart to toss.

The next plastic container was slightly smaller. The lid gave me some trouble, but at last I managed to pry it off. At the bottom were a dozen or so keys.

I considered the drawer at the top right of the filing cabinet. There were two keys that might reasonably fit that lock. I tried the first one, but nothing happened when I turned it. I decided to try out the other one too. There was a click from the lock as I turned it.

I pulled out the drawer and stared down into it.

What had I expected?

I stood there, gawking, unable to get my thoughts in order.

65

"Why did you react so strongly at our meeting the other day?"

Shirine pulls her colorful infinity scarf up to her chin and looks at me. She confronts my stubborn silence with question after question.

"Is it upsetting to think about? Do you think it might help to talk about it?"

I sigh. I don't know why I'm back here again. I could keep playing sick; I could protest wildly, physically resist.

"Are you familiar with the concept of thrill seeking?" Shirine asks.

I cross my arms and stare at a spot on the wall behind her. I don't want her to think everything is just fine now, back to normal quick as a wink. She promised not to have a bunch of preconceived notions about me, and yet she assumed I was talking about Chris when I asked about control freaks.

"Researchers have shown that some people need extra stimulation to experience joy. We often call them thrill seekers," she says. "For example, a person might pursue extreme sports like mountain climbing or bungee jumping. But it might also be the case that someone seeks out risky relationships and enjoys conflict."

I struggle to look as blasé as I possibly can, even though I'm actually listening attentively.

"Was he exciting, Christopher Olsen?" Shirine asks.

This time she is much more cautious about mentioning his name—her back is straight and her finger is probably on the panic button.

"Oh, lay off." I sigh.

"You like excitement, right? Isn't that true?"

I give a loud snort.

"I like your analyses. For real. If I ever need a therapist, I'm sure I'll be calling you."

I look her in the eye.

"Your sense of humor . . . ," she says.

"A defense mechanism, right?"

She doesn't respond.

Finally, I think. *Finally, she's giving up.*

Before leaving, I snap *Thérèse Raquin* shut so hard that Shirine glares at me. At first I identified with Thérèse quite a bit—her frustration over how bored she is and how nothing ever happens. Thérèse gets, like, married off to Camille, who isn't a girl, like I thought at first. Thérèse likes dudes, obviously, we're talking the 1800s here. Anyway, soon she meets another guy, Laurent, and she falls in love and has an affair with him. All three of them rent a little boat and the lover Laurent throws the husband Camille overboard and he drowns.

After the murder, Thérèse and Laurent argue about which of them is at fault. Both of them totally lose it and end up wracked with guilt and planning to kill each other. In the end they commit suicide together.

"I didn't like it," I say, mostly to annoy Shirine.

"It didn't make you think?"

"It did," I said. "That was the problem."

After lunch, I have an hour to myself at the gym. I increase the resistance on the exercise bike and pedal my thighs full of lactic acid, letting the sweat trickle off my forehead until it forms a little puddle beneath me.

Then I do a few rounds of chins and dips. My strength is the resilient sort. On the handball court, I loved catching the ball with a defender or two on my back. I was at my best when they were hanging on me like backpacks, struggling to keep me at the six-meter line. Five years in a row I was our internal high scorer.

Sometimes I miss it. I miss the sense of community, and the competition— setting a goal and fighting hard together to achieve it. But in the end I couldn't handle how planned it all was, how the coaches determined every step you took, every pass and shot. I felt like a game piece that was being guided by other people, and all the joy of handball disappeared.

After the workout I stand in the shower for an extra-long time, standing as straight as an arrow, letting the water envelop me in a deafening tunnel. I can honestly feel the smell running off me.

I think about Thérèse and Laurent in the book. Anyone is capable of murder. Is that what the writer was trying to say? No doubt he is right. If a person is violated deeply enough, there is no limit to what she might do. This is something I know from experience.

I step out of the shower like a freshly lit sparkler, then dry off and get dressed before the guards tug at me.

"You almost smell good," Jimmy says, a nasty grin on his face. "But remember, you're still a murderer whore. You can't wash that off."

66

Amina, best friend that she was, immediately came to my rescue.

"This isn't normal, Stella. It's not healthy."

We were sitting in the living room, our feet on the edge of the sofa, and I had just told Amina about the things I found in Chris's drawer. Mom and Dad had gone to an Italian food festival and were going to spend the night at a castle in the countryside.

"Lots of people like that stuff," I said. "Bondage and S&M. Tying each other up and things. It's more common than you think."

"But honestly. Could you do something like that?"

"Not me."

The very thought of not being in control, of being restrained while having sex, made me shaky.

"Why did Linda want you to see those things?" Amina wondered.

I didn't know. In the locked drawer I had found a black leather gag with that ball thing that gets stuffed in someone's mouth. A plastic bottle full of transparent liquid, a dark-gray rag, and a pair of sturdy metal handcuffs. At the bottom was a jackknife, its blade glaringly sharp.

"I suppose she wants to scare me off. It's not exactly proof that Chris is a psychopath."

"But the knife. Why does he have a knife?"

"You tell me."

I hardly dared to think about it.

"Are you going to ask him?"

"What the hell would I say? That I *happened* to find the key to his locked drawer?"

He'd already sent three messages I hadn't responded to. I didn't know which way was up anymore.

"He lied about his age," said Amina.

"It was only a white lie."

Amina sighed.

"Can't we do something else?" I asked. "Go somewhere?"

Too many thoughts were buzzing in my brain.

"Jerker Lindeberg's having a party," Amina said, swiping her thumb across her phone screen.

"Lindeberg. Doesn't he live in Bjärred?"

"Barsebäck."

Even worse. That was like fifteen kilometers away.

"I guess we could borrow Dad's car," I said. "They rode with some friends."

Amina's nose wrinkled.

"Just for a little while. If it's lame we'll leave right away."

This wasn't the first time I'd "borrowed" Dad's car. It's one of those big cars, unnecessarily big if you ask me; it feels like driving a delivery truck. I really prefer to practice for my road test in the driving school's little Fiat.

I drove us through town, past Nova Mall, and toward the coast. Amina plugged her phone into the stereo and turned the volume to max. We were ironically digging some sax-heavy dance-band song about high mountains and low valleys when out of nowhere a tiny but flashy Audi TT pulled out in front of us.

I rammed the passenger side of the little German car, sending it flying off the road into a strawberry field. The driver was a wrinkled man in a toupée who rolled up his pant legs to keep from getting strawberry stains on them before chewing me out and informing me that he'd always said women were horrible drivers and, why, here was proof.

Dad and Mom had to drop everything to leave the party at the castle. They met us at the police station. Dad's expression was dark and I sobbed inconsolably.

Luckily enough, it never went to court. I signed an order of summary punishment and had to pay a fine, and went home to curse at my own fucking stupidity.

The incident with the car, Dad called it.

The police called it driving without a license and reckless driving. Increased insurance premiums and income-based fines. Thirty thousand kronor right down the drain.

I was so furious at myself that I locked myself in my room and cried. Thirty thousand. That was half of my savings. There was no longer any chance I'd get away in the winter.

I was back to being stuck.

I lay in bed with music on my headphones, reading about psychopaths and sex. I knew I had read more or less the same stuff before, but I had to refresh my memory.

For a psychopath, sex is all about power.

In the beginning, the psychopath often places all the focus on their partner during the act of sex. But psychopaths are drawn to excitement and variation. Soon he will want to spice up their sex life, often with activities that seem uncomfortable to the partner. The psychopath slowly pushes the partner's limits and in this way gains power over her. If the partner refuses to give in to his suggestions, he responds by making her feel guilty or threatening to find someone new.

Suddenly there was a bad taste in my mouth.

I thought about our walk along the beach, how Chris smelled when I rested against his chest, how he fed me strawberries in the sunset, how his hand squeezed my knee firmly on the roller coaster.

It couldn't be.

When Chris called, I froze and stared at my phone as if it was a red-hot coal.

"What happened?" he asked.

I held the phone away from my cheek as I told him about the accident.

"I got fines," I said. "And the insurance premium is going up."

"It'll be okay, Stella. It's just money. The important thing is that you and Amina are okay."

"But you don't get it. For years I've been dreaming of this trip to Asia. It's been my main goal. I've been saving and saving."

The line crackled. Chris fell silent.

"And now I can't afford it," I sobbed.

"It's going to be okay, Stella. Of course you'll make it to Asia."

67

"It feels like I don't have anything to look forward to anymore."

Amina thought I was exaggerating, of course. She scrunched up her nose at me from across the table.

"Stop being such a drama queen."

She had just finished practice and we were in the café at the arena, surrounded by sweat and the smell of coffee.

"Easy for you to say. You've, like, always known what you're going to do. Medical school, marriage, two kids, a house in Stångby, a summer home in Bosnia."

"That sounds so freaking boring."

We both laughed, and Amina sucked up her protein shake.

"I've been looking forward to getting away for so long."

"I know," said Amina. "But you can still go. Worst-case scenario, you have to postpone it a few months."

I gave a heavy sigh. A few months? She made it sound like life lasts a whole damn eternity.

"I'm so tired of how nothing ever happens! Is this just how it's going to be now? Fifty years of gloom, and then you die?"

"Fifty?" Amina shook her head. "You should probably count on another sixty or seventy."

"Sigh," I said, rolling my eyes. "Although my parents seem to have a better time the older they get. It's like a totally different vibe at home."

"I've always liked your parents."

I suppose she thought she knew everything. Didn't Amina realize she'd never been let into the inner core of our family?

"Next week Mom and Dad are going on a couple's getaway," I said. "They rented a cabin on Orust."

"Ooh, so romantic."

"You have to come keep me company."

"What about Chris?"

"Oh, I don't know," I said, running my hands through my hair. "I really just want to get out of here, go on my trip."

"You will," Amina said, smiling. "Sooner or later."

She absently said hello to a passing teammate. Then she stood up and aimed her empty bottle at the closest trash can.

"It seems so easy to be you," I said.

She looked at me like she wanted to kick me in the crotch.

For once Dad didn't make Italian food for dinner. Mom was shooting these little loving glances across the table, and Dad kept smiling. Once we were done eating he wanted to show me something on the computer.

"Your birthday's coming up."

He had found a pink Vespa. Pretty fucking cool, but it cost a shit-ton of money.

"So you won't have to *borrow* the car," he said.

"But Dad, thirty thousand! That's so much money. I told you, all I want is cash for my trip."

He stared at the screen.

"We'll see. I like this one."

"But you're not the one having a birthday," I said.

I spent the rest of the evening between Mom and Dad on the sofa. There was a harmonious energy between them. An unusual calm. We didn't talk much, but we didn't need to. I felt secure.

I sank into the sofa and rested my eyes. When I woke up, it was past midnight. Dad was snoring with his mouth open and his cheek resting on a book. Mom was in the other corner, her knees drawn up, tears on her face.

"What happened?" I asked drowsily.

"The dog . . . ," she said, pointing at the TV. "The dog died."

I patted her shoulder.

"Mom, Hollywood always kills the dog. Haven't you learned?"

I dug out my phone from under the pillows.

Four missed calls from Chris. One new text.

I opened the message and found it had been sent from a number that wasn't stored in my contacts.

I'm sure he's being wonderful to you right now. He was to me too, at first. It took two years for me to figure out who he really was. I don't want you to make the same mistake as me. Be careful.

For God's sake. Was Linda so disturbed that she still hadn't gotten over Chris? Was she trying to control who he spent time with? To destroy everything that might make him happy?

I read the text one more time, then deleted it and blocked Linda Lokind's number.

On my way up the stairs, I called Chris.

"Finally," he said. "I was actually starting to worry."

There was buzzing in the background. Cars, a horn.

"Sorry, I fell asleep on the couch."

"You have to come out," he said. "I'm in the car. I booked the suite at the Grand Hotel."

68

Elsa unlocks the door for Shirine, who lingers just inside of it.

"Are you better?" she asks cautiously.

"Yes?"

I may be lying on the bed, but I'm fully dressed.

"You missed your appointment yesterday. They said you were sick."

"Oh." I'd almost forgotten about that. "I'm a bit better now."

Shirine picks up *Crime and Punishment* from the table.

"So what did you think of this?"

I wrack my brains for a moment.

"It was long."

Just think, I voluntarily plowed my way through a never-ending, nineteenth-century Russian novel. Without even hating it.

Raskolnikov is just over twenty years old and thinks he's smarter and better than everyone else. He needs money, so he decides to rob and kill an old pawnbroker, who he describes as a horrible, evil person who doesn't deserve to live.

"What do you think?" Shirine asks. "Are all murders equally heinous, or can there sometimes be extenuating circumstances?"

I gaze at her thoughtfully.

"Of course there can be extenuating circumstances," I say.

"Is it that straightforward?"

"There might not be any in these books, but of course. Hypothetically speaking."

"Hypothetically," Shirine repeats warily, as if she's never heard the word before. "Such as? What could possibly justify taking another person's life?"

"Not *justify*. That's a different story. We're talking about extenuating circumstances."

"Give me an example," Shirine says, gesturing with one hand.

"Self-defense."

"But that's different. In that case it's not murder. Everyone has the right to defend themselves. Give me another example."

I scratch my cheek.

"Some people don't deserve to live."

Shirine's eyes narrow.

"I don't mean that anyone can just go around killing people," I say. "But some people have exhausted their right to life. One solution to the problem, obviously, would be a functional justice system. If killers and rapists were properly punished . . ."

"Are you saying you're pro–death penalty?"

"I think most people are. It's awfully easy to be against the death penalty as long as you aren't personally affected. Ask anyone who has lost a family member to murder and I bet the answer is pretty obvious."

"But don't you think people deserve a second chance?" she says.

"After raping and killing?"

I don't know if she's purposely trying to wind me up, but if she is, it's working.

"The man who raped me," I say. "Are you saying he deserves a second chance?"

"I . . . well . . ."

"I was fifteen. Fifteen! He trapped me and held me down so hard I couldn't breathe. I fought for my life while he shoved his disgusting cock inside me."

Shirine's face is stuck in a grotesque grimace.

"There are extenuating circumstances," I declare. "I would have been happy to watch that pig die."

Shirine is smart enough not to argue. She blinks a few times and looks down at her hands.

"I could have killed him myself," I say.

69

I woke up in the suite at the Grand Hotel. Chris had sunk into the easy chair across from me, a cup of coffee in his hands and his ankles crossed on the ottoman.

"Good morning, hot stuff."

I smiled and padded past him to the bathroom, where I washed my face in the sink and sat down on the edge of the bathtub, which we'd soaked in a long time the night before. A thick clump of regret was bubbling in my stomach.

"What time do you have to work?" Chris called from his chair.

"Quarter to ten."

I was already cutting it close.

I dressed and made an effort to look happy and grateful as I hugged Chris.

"Don't forget this," he said, handing me the map.

It was a present. He'd given it to me while we were drinking bubbly in the bed, right after we got the room keys. It was an A3-sized piece of paper, rolled up like parchment and secured with a lovely velvet ribbon. I had un-rolled it and felt my heart leap. It was a map of Asia, and Chris had marked special spots with gold stars. Places he wanted us to experience together. I didn't mention that I already had a map, much bigger and full of pushpins.

I should have been happy as I took the elevator down and turned onto Lilla Fiskaregatan. The problem was, all these feelings. I didn't want to have them. There was no way I could go to Asia on the trip of my life in the company of a thirty-two-year-old man. It was unthinkable. And yet it was like something in my chest was aglow, telling me to stop analyzing everything so much and just let stuff happen.

As I crossed the town square with two minutes max until the start of my shift, the heavens opened and rain poured down. It was the first time in weeks.

It was still raining when I left the store that evening. My plan was to slip around the corner and get the bus at Botulfsplatsen. I had timed it so I wouldn't end up soaking wet.

But I only made it a few meters.

At the edge of my field of vision, which was limited thanks to my hood, I caught sight of two people under a big umbrella.

"Stella!"

Amina took my arm.

"Come here, you have to hear this."

Her hair was wet and her eyes were wild.

"What's going on?"

"Let's get out of the rain," she said, tugging at me.

Beside her was Linda Lokind, holding the umbrella in one hand and trying to keep the neckline of her shirt closed with the other.

"What the hell, Amina?"

My fury was all systems go. Had she and Linda Lokind been waiting to ambush me? Were they ganging up on me? I pulled away and stared at her.

"Please, you have to listen to what Linda has to say."

The rain was streaming down her face. There was something desperate about the whole situation.

"Okay," I said, looking at Linda. "Make it quick."

We huddled under the bus stop shelter and Amina swept wet tendrils of hair from her cheeks and urged Linda to tell me what she'd apparently told Amina.

"I was with Chris for three years," said Linda Lokind. "I thought I had the perfect life. I didn't even notice that things had started to change."

She looked at me, her eyes shifty.

"Keep going," said Amina.

"It happened gradually. A few tiny things at a time. I told myself it wouldn't keep happening, wouldn't get worse. I wanted so badly for everything to be okay."

The rain pattered against the roof of the shelter. A few boys ran to catch a bus, hanging on the door until the driver let them in.

"The first thing I noticed was his jealousy," said Linda. "At first I thought it was sort of cute, like it proved he really loved me. But it just got stronger and stronger. Once he was about to punch a guy in the face because he thought I'd been flirting with him."

I looked her straight in the eye. Most people suck at lying, but there was no sign that Linda wasn't telling the truth.

"I was a student when we met, but he convinced me to drop out. He said it would be better for me to work at his company. I didn't need an education. That's about when my parents started to worry, and he got me to break off contact with them. After a while we stopped spending time with my friends too. There was always some excuse. Like if I said someone had invited us over, Chris had just been planning to surprise me with a weekend in Prague. And it kept on like that. In the end I hardly had anyone left. Just Chris."

I thought of the picture on his Facebook. They'd looked happy. Was this all just rationalization? A grim way to plot her revenge?

"I shrank my whole life until it was all about Chris," said Linda. "Exactly as he wanted me to. He was slowly breaking me down."

A bus turned onto the street, water splashing high around its tires. I turned to Amina. I knew she was doing this out of concern, but it was still difficult to accept. What was she thinking? Just showing up out of nowhere, with Linda Lokind in tow. Did Amina trust this woman?

"He's going to do the same thing to you too," Linda said, shaking off her umbrella. "He was pathologically suspicious. I didn't understand at first, but after a few months he showed his jealousy. He wanted to know every detail about what I did, and where, and who with. And in the end, he was still the one who cheated."

I thought of what Chris had said. *I cheated emotionally, but nothing happened.*

"I found a text on his phone. From a girl both of us know. Someone I thought was my friend. It was super obvious what was going on between them, but when I confronted Chris, he shoved me up against a wall."

She closed her umbrella and gazed out at the street.

"He ruptured my spleen. At the hospital we made up a story about how I fell off my bike."

That couldn't be true. Chris wasn't violent.

"When was this?" I asked.

"Last winter. Right before Christmas."

According to Chris, he hadn't met someone new and ended things until last spring.

"Why didn't you leave him?" I asked.

"It's not that simple. I can't explain it, but it was like he owned me. I was constantly afraid. After he hit me the first time, it just snowballed. Each time I swore to myself that I would never let it happen again. But he . . . I'll never forgive myself for staying."

She squeezed her eyes closed. Were those raindrops or tears on her face? Amina touched my arm gently like an apology of some sort.

Did I have any choice? Whether this was true or not, I couldn't keep seeing Chris. In fact, it was disturbing that I'd let it go this far. Sure, he was thrilling and sexy and loaded, but enough was enough. I couldn't take any more drama.

"Did you open the drawer?" Linda asked.

I nodded.

"Chris made me go along with stuff I didn't actually want to do. He said if I truly loved him I would show it. When I finally dared to put my foot down, he was enraged. He tied my hands behind my back and stuffed a ball gag in my mouth. I could hardly breathe."

I gasped for breath automatically. Memories struck me like lightning.

"He raped me. I suppose he must have wanted me to resist. That was how he liked it. I realized that then."

I thought of Chris's gentle hands in the bathtub at the Grand. The water lapping rhythmically against our bodies. Nothing that Linda said seemed to match the Chris I knew.

"Why didn't you go to the police?"

"I did, but they closed the investigation. Chris's mom is a law professor and knows every prosecutor and judge in this country. Chris is a successful entrepreneur and a millionaire. Why would anyone believe me?"

"When did you file the police report?" I asked.

Linda shifted side to side.

"In April."

"After you left him?" Amina asked.

Linda nodded.

"After *you* left *him*?" I said. "Or was it the other way around?"

She closed her eyes for a brief moment and dried her cheek.

"The other way around," she said quietly.

I spat on the sidewalk. Ahead of me, another bus pulled up and a woman with a suitcase jumped aside as the water splashed over the sidewalk.

"That's my bus," I said, running after it.

70

I stretch out on the bed in my cell and stare at a stain on the ceiling until it starts to grow and come to life and float into an optical illusion of blurry colors and patterns.

I think about Chris. Maybe there is something to Shirine's chatter about brain chemistry and emotions and the need for stimulus. But does that mean I shouldn't blame myself? In the end, I suppose everyone has to take responsibility for their own actions. Dopamine and serotonin and adrenaline can never be held accountable. Extenuating circumstances? I don't know.

I knew who Chris Olsen was. At least I should have.

Impulses and feelings only exist for a moment. I've always thought that love is different, a choice you make. A crush flames up and fades out. Jeez, I fall in love, like, ten times a day on any given random Tuesday in October. But I didn't choose to fall for Chris. Or did I? Was I even capable of choosing?

Why does my stomach hurt when I think about it?

Everything comes back around. Confusion and disgust.

Betrayal.

When I think about Amina, it's like my skin starts to split. The sorrow and guilt swell up and give me total motion sickness.

I think about Esther Greenwood and Holden Caulfield. Is it even possible to survive this life with reason intact?

I'm not at all prepared when Shirine shows up. I fly to the edge of the bed and hide my tears behind my hands.

"What is it?" she asks, putting her leather briefcase down on the desk.

"Nothing," I mumble. "Just tired."

She bends down and places a reassuring hand on my shoulder.

I slowly turn my face up toward her and let the tears come.

71

On Friday, Amina and I split a kebab platter on the sofa, even though Mom and Dad had made me promise only to eat in the kitchen or at the dining room table.

"Don't disappoint your father" was the last thing Mom said before they left.

Story of my life, in some ways.

"I can't believe you inflicted that psycho on me," I said, glaring at Amina.

"What was I supposed to do? I couldn't get rid of her."

"Honestly, Amina. That Linda Lokind found out who you were and tracked you down. She must have stalked you. Just like she stalked Chris."

Amina bit her lip. She so clearly wanted to protest, but I guess she realized it wasn't the right time.

We'd searched online for more info about Linda, some sort of proof that she was a few sandwiches short of a picnic, but Linda Lokind was as good as invisible.

"You've got something there," Amina said, pointing with her plastic fork. "No, there. Higher up."

I moved my finger up my cheek and wiped away a smear of sauce.

Amina sighed. She gets embarrassed whenever I'm messy and sloppy. She uses her utensils like surgical instruments, making tiny mouse-sized portions that slip into her mouth so she hardly needs to open it. You can never see her chewing.

"Tegnérs tonight?" she said. "Please, please, please."

"No way."

I'd had a headache all afternoon and all I wanted to do was crash on the couch and sleep for ten hours. This day was made for a crappy night in. And I didn't have to worry about Chris. He'd texted to say he was going to meet up with an old friend and we would talk another day. For some reason I was trembling at the thought of having to break up with him. I didn't know whether I should take the bull by the horns and tell the truth or let it just kind of fade away.

"Please," said Amina. "I'm begging you."

She wanted to dance, party, meet people. She said she was feeling more stoked than ever. And, of course, like the best friend I want and try to be, I rallied. We goofed around, dancing to old Eurovision songs, crowding in front of the mirror in the hall, changing and exchanging outfits. Just before midnight we got on our bikes and breezed down the hills toward Tegnérs.

We tossed our hair and sweated beneath explosions of light on the dance floor. Amina held my hand as we slalomed between whirling nightclub bodies, and we soon landed at the bar, breathless, to order ciders from the bearded bartender.

I was drenched with sweat and my head was pounding.

"Look at that!" Amina said, pointing across the bar. "Wasn't he supposed to be with an old friend?"

Chris was standing with his back to the bar, leaning slightly over a bare-shouldered girl with silver earrings. They were laughing, and her hand gently brushed his elbow.

"Who is she?" said Amina.

I grabbed my cider and rounded the bar. Chris was just about to turn around—he was still laughing when he discovered me.

"Stella! You're here too?"

I tensed my whole body in protest when he hugged me. The girl with all the earrings looked at me in surprise.

"This is my friend Beatrice," said Chris.

I sized her up as we shook hands. She was around twenty-five, or maybe thirty, and wore a lot of makeup. She had big lips and a tight body.

"Sorry," I said. "When you said 'old friend,' I thought . . ."

"*Old?*" Beatrice said with a laugh.

Chris faked a look of shame.

"So how do you know each other?" I asked.

"Originally through Chris's ex," said Beatrice.

Chris pretended not to hear and said something about how much he liked my top. He didn't seem into this conversation at all, but I wasn't about to let it go.

"You mean Linda?" I asked.

Beatrice looked at Chris, who yielded to her with a shrug.

"Linda and I became friends back in school," said Beatrice. "I was actually there the first time she and Chris met. We hung out quite a bit back in the beginning of their relationship, before she . . . got sick."

She lowered her head a little.

"Sick?" I said.

Beatrice nodded, but didn't elaborate.

"Linda tracked me down," I said, turning to Chris, who face-palmed.

"Seriously?"

"She even found Amina. She wanted to warn us about you. She claimed you did some pretty sick stuff."

"Jesus Christ," said Chris. "I've had enough of this. She's out to ruin my life, no matter what it takes."

"It's so sad," Beatrice said, patting Chris's arm. "Linda was the sweetest girl in the world when I first got to know her. So kind and considerate. Yeah, maybe she was a little paranoid and jealous even then, but who would have ever thought things would end up like this?"

"Can't she get help?" I asked. "Like, from a psychiatrist?"

"Linda's been seeing therapists since she was a teenager," said Chris.

"Unfortunately it's only getting worse," said Beatrice. "When Chris broke up with her, she totally lost it."

More or less as I had suspected. Linda Lokind wasn't entirely right in the head. I shot Amina a meaningful look.

She placed a hand on my shoulder.

"Bathroom," she said.

"But . . ."

"Now please. Before I pee myself."

———

We closed ourselves into a stall and took turns peeing. I felt warm and out of sorts; my head was heavy. Was it some sort of virus? Maybe I had just been working too hard.

"What's up with you?" Amina asked.

"I don't know. I'm beat."

Really, all I wanted to do was go home and crawl into bed.

"*Now* do you believe me?" I asked. "Do you get that Linda Lokind is totally disturbed?"

She slapped her forehead to illustrate how dumb she had been.

"How was I supposed to know? I didn't want to take the chance."

"It's fine," I assured her.

"He's awfully yummy," Amina said with a sly smile.

"Who?"

"Your summer fling."

I smiled, but an instant later I was struck with an urgent sense of unease. I didn't know where it came from or what it meant, but it crept through my body.

"Now, come on!" Amina said, opening the stall door. "I'm so freaking hyped!"

We wound our way to the center of the roiling dance floor. I battled my sleepiness as Amina put on a show. She pumped her arms and laughter rose from her mouth like soap bubbles.

I looked for Chris in the crowd and found him standing at the bar. Amina followed close behind me as I walked up to him.

"Where is Beatrice?" I asked.

"She went home to her boyfriend."

My head was heavy. The beats throbbed in my belly and my legs felt weaker and weaker.

"I'm not feeling well. I think I need to leave too."

Both Chris and Amina looked at me in concern.

"Should I come with you?" Chris asked.

"No, stay here with Amina. I'll bike home and go to bed."

I gave him a quick peck and hugged Amina.

"You sure?" she said.

"Sorry," I replied.

The fresh air did me good. My head didn't feel as heavy any longer and I felt new strength in my legs as I biked home through town. After two Tylenol and a Hydralyte, I collapsed in bed with my phone and was out like a light.

I woke up because my pillow was vibrating; I flew up and tracked down my phone, which had slipped between the headboard and the mattress.

"Hello?"

Amina was gasping on the other end.

"I have to tell you something."

"What's going on?"

"I went home with Chris."

I felt a stab of pain in my chest. What did she mean?

"It just happened. We shared a taxi. I forgot I had my bike at Tegnérs." She took a breath. My heart was pounding.

"Did anything happen?" I asked.

"No, no, nothing."

"Nothing?"

I flopped back down on my pillow.

"Of course nothing happened. What the hell did you think?"

"No, of course not."

"I just wanted to tell you I went home with him."

I said something about how that was just fine, no problem, nothing had happened.

I had made up my mind to end things with Chris. But now I wasn't so sure.

"Are you feeling better?" Amina asked.

"I think so."

I checked the time. Four thirty in the morning.

"Now get home and into bed before Dino starts to worry."

Amina laughed nervously.

"He's already called twice."

"Talk tomorrow. Love you."

Five percent battery. I found the charger on the floor and was just about to plug it in when I realized I had a new text from a number I didn't recognize.

Please, stay away from Chris. He's dangerous.

72

I wake in a cold sweat, no idea what time it is. It might be before midnight, or almost morning. In here, the passage of time means nothing.

Something is chasing after me. I vault out of bed and spin around the room. The smell is just as pungent, just as strong as when I first arrived.

I pound hysterically on the locked door as terrifying images press into my mind. So true to life that the boundary between dream and reality is erased.

"Let me out!" I roar at the door, still beating at it although my fists throb and ache.

In my mind I see Chris's blood-drenched body on the ground. How it jerks and writhes even as fresh blood pumps from the cuts in his stomach.

"Open the door!"

I bang my forehead against the hard metal and sink to my knees as my fingernails tear desperately at the door.

At last the hatch slides open and a frightened eye stares down at me. It's Elsa.

"Help," I croak.

I'm drowning. My body just keeps sinking even though I'm already in a pile on the floor. I force my way upward and reach out my arms, but the air is too thick. It's like trying to swim in cement.

"Mom! Mom!"

Elsa orders me to back away from the door and slowly I manage to crawl away as I hear Elsa calling for help.

I lie on my back and stare up at the ceiling as they examine me. Their voices are far away, like faint whispers in the distance.

The image of Chris dying comes back over and over. That pulsating, bloody body on the ground.

A medic slaps my face. I explain that I'm having trouble breathing, that there's something wrong with my throat. He brings a glass of water to my lips, but most of it ends up running down my chin and cheek. He gets help from a guard to sit me up.

There are several strange hands in my face. Rubber gloves feeling inside my mouth. Someone shoves two pills into me and says I'm going to sleep.

"No!" I roar, flailing my limbs.

Sleep is dangerous. I don't want to go back there.

"I don't want to!" I scream.

They're behind me, restraining me.

I take a deep breath and hold it. I can actually feel the oxygen streaming into my blood and my pulse starts to calm down.

I see Elsa, backed into the corner and trembling, looking like a lost child.

"The police," I manage to say. "I want to talk to the police."

I don't know what I'm going to tell them: the whole truth, part of the truth, or something that has nothing at all to do with the truth. I just know I need to talk. I have to tell, before I explode.

73

Chris wanted to come over to my house.

I want to see how you live, he texted. *I'd love to meet your parents too, but maybe we should hold off on that. Anyway, it'll be perfect since they're off on their trip.*

I looked around. Clothes, bags, and random objects were strewn all over. The kitchen smelled like something had died in there and I had built a mountain of underwear and tank tops in the laundry room.

Okay, I responded. *But give me two hours.*

I had to talk to him. This couldn't continue. Even if I enjoyed his laid-back attitude and his desire to live in the moment, I had to make sure that we were on the same page about what we were doing. I was afraid someone was going to get hurt.

After the incident with the car, it sure couldn't hurt to make the house look nice before Mom and Dad came home on Friday. I started with the living room. I straightened, vacuumed, and scrubbed the table. On to the kitchen. I emptied the dishwasher and reloaded it, put stuff away in the cupboards, and scrubbed the counter until it gleamed.

At last I had a whole pile of garbage bags in the entryway. The stench prickled my nostrils as I lugged them through the door.

I absolutely adore those warm summer nights when the sun has set, but there's still a little bit of light left in the sky, when the air stands perfectly still and the birds are singing lullabies.

After I'd dumped the garbage bags in the bin, I lingered on the driveway, just enjoying a rare sense of peace in my body.

Suddenly something flapped around in the bushes. A quick movement. A bird, maybe?

I walked over to check. More flapping. A large shadow against the wall. My heart flew into my throat. I didn't dare breathe.

"Is someone there?" I asked out loud.

Five meters away, the bushes moved again. Rustling leaves, the crack of a twig.

"Who is it?"

I dug through my pockets for my phone but realized I must have left it in the house.

I ran back and pulled the door shut behind me. I flipped both locks and listened to my own gasping breath.

Was I imagining things? Was I becoming paranoid?

Maybe it was just a bird. A large bird. Or some other animal. A cat?

Or was someone sneaking around out there?

Chris brought a bouquet of roses. I didn't mention what had happened when I was taking out the trash.

He walked through the house like a museumgoer. The first thing he did in my room was sit on the bed and bounce as if he wanted to check its durability. Then he caught sight of the wall with my map of Asia on it, with pins in all the spots I wanted to see.

"You had a map already?"

It was pretty awkward. I hadn't been able to say anything when I received the present from him, and I didn't know what to say now either.

Chris made a gesture that meant *it's fine.*

"Know what?" he asked. "I've arranged things so I have February and March off next year. That's a great time to visit Asia."

I just smiled. What could I say? That I preferred to go by myself? That there was no chance he would be coming with me?

Chris pressed up against me. He gently swept my hair out of the way and kissed me slowly. His hand slid along the hem of my underwear; I closed my eyes. No one else had ever turned me on so much.

"Where do your parents sleep?"

Without letting go of me, he backed out through the door.

"There?" he said, pointing at Mom and Dad's bedroom.

He guided me through the hall in a reluctant dance. Obviously I wasn't about to lie down in their bed. I pushed Chris away but he came right back. The door opened and we stumbled into their bedroom. I tensed my body, grabbed the handle of the door and struggled.

"Not here."

Chris laughed and let go of me. He stood there motionless, looking down at my parents' double bed.

"So this is where Papa Pastor sleeps."

When he looked at me, I felt the sting of his smile.

"Come on," he said, putting his arms around me. "I want to have you in Mommy and Daddy's bed."

"No, stop it."

I struggled against him. He made an attempt to tip me over onto the bed, but apparently he underestimated my strength. I filled my feet with energy until they were stuck to the floor like suction cups, then used my upper body to push him off. I'd been through much tougher wrestling matches on the six-meter line of the handball court.

"Okay, okay," Chris said, laughing, trying to disarm me with his expression. "It was just a thought. An experiment. Don't you like to experiment?"

I thought of the objects in the locked drawer of the file cabinet.

"Not like this, anyway," I said.

"No?"

All my desire was gone.

"Let's go sit on the couch for a while."

Chris made a wounded face and waited a moment before following me down the stairs. I turned on the TV and rested my head on his shoulder. My thoughts were going a mile a minute.

What was keeping me with Chris? I had been so goddamn tired of how nothing ever happened, so when Chris showed up I had thrown myself head-first into the unknown. But now? I didn't want a boyfriend, much less one who was thirty-two. I wasn't about to experiment in my parents' bed. Above all I just wanted to take off on the journey I'd been dreaming about for ages. No fucking guy was going to stand in my way.

I looked at Chris. He was, without a doubt, one of the most beautiful beings I'd ever been in the vicinity of. But what did that matter? I wasn't even eighteen yet—I had my whole life ahead of me.

Chris gazed at me for a long time. His smile was back to being all kind and adorable. All the hard edges had been erased.

I didn't know what to say. I didn't know how to say it. I only knew that something had to be said.

74

The next morning, Chris had to hurry off to a meeting. I did a walk-through of the house with a spray bottle and a rag so I could rub out every trace of him.

I messaged Amina:

Think I have to dump Chris.

Why??? she responded.

I kept fiddling with the wording, saving draft after draft, erasing it all and writing it again. At last, I sent something:

Think he's starting to fall for me.

Amina didn't answer for almost an hour. Then she wrote that it was probably for the best.

Later that afternoon, Mom and Dad returned home from vacation.

"It looks so nice in here," said Mom.

I asked if they'd had a good time, and they both smiled and nodded.

"You should have been there," said Mom.

Or not.

They were in high spirits. Dad joked around, making a fool of himself. As Mom tried to unpack her suitcase he tickled her midsection, wrapped his arms around her from behind, and kissed the back of her neck.

"What did you do to him?" I asked.

"What do you mean?" Mom giggled.

"Yeah, what do you mean?" Dad said, poking his tickle-fingers into my side as well, until I had to flee to the kitchen.

"Is he on happy pills or something?"

"I am the only happy pill your dad needs." Mom laughed.

I biked to the arena to meet up with Amina after practice. It was starting to get dark but City Park was still full of people enjoying the summer warmth. Someone was singing and playing guitar; one group was playing soccer; some people seemed to be on dates.

Near the indoor pool, a mother duck came waddling along, her babies trailing behind her. I braked and stepped off my bike so they could pass safely.

As I stood there, grinning at the ducklings' wobbly journey across the gravel path, I heard steps approaching behind me. I moved my bike to the side, carefully, to keep from scaring the ducks.

"Please, listen to me."

When I turned around, I found Linda Lokind standing two meters behind me.

"Jesus Christ," I said. "Leave me alone. There is nothing serious between me and Chris. You can take it easy."

She looked at me like I was speaking a foreign language.

"I know all about you," I said. "You need help. Medication or something. If you don't leave me alone this instant, I don't know what I might do."

I was being loud. I didn't care that people nearby could hear.

"Of course," said Linda. "Chris says I'm sick. A mental case, right?"

I shook my head.

"It's not just Chris. The police didn't believe you either. And I've met your old friend Beatrice."

Linda's hand flexed and landed near her pants pocket. She turned aside so I couldn't see what she was doing. Did she have something in her pocket? I started walking, pushing my bike.

"I told you about the girl he cheated with," Linda said. "I found a text from her on his phone."

I walked faster, but Linda followed me.

"It was Beatrice, my best friend. He slept with my best friend. Then he brainwashed her. She still believes it was all my fault, that I had some sort of mental breakdown."

I stopped and turned my bike so it formed a barrier between us.

"You're lying."

I couldn't take this anymore. Chris and Linda and Beatrice could all go to hell.

"I swear, it's true."

"I don't care," I said.

A few families had laid out picnics on flowered blankets on the grass nearby. Two girls of about five years old were galloping around on hobby horses, clacking their tongues. One of them looked just like I had at that age.

"One day last winter, I was going to hang a picture in the bedroom," said Linda. "It had fallen down when Chris threw a bottle of beer at the wall. After I nailed it back up, he walked over and took a look at it. *It's fucking crooked. The nail is crooked.* I apologized and promised to fix it right away."

Her words flowed like blood from an open wound. I didn't dare take my eyes off the laughing little girls on the lawn.

"I reached for the hammer, but Chris got there first. He threw me down on the bed and swung the hammer through the air. *You can't even hang a fucking picture right!*"

My skin was crawling. Linda stood before me as the girls on the lawn shrieked with joy.

"He raped me with the hammer."

A wave of disgust washed over me.

"That's enough!"

Linda shoved her hand into her pocket.

"I would like to hurt him. I want him to suffer the same way I did."

Her cheeks were scarlet; her neck was thrust forward and her eyebrows lowered. She was scaring me.

"I could kill him."

I got on my bike and set off for the arena. Before Amina even came out from practice I had looked up Chris in my phone and deleted the contact.

75

Michael Blomberg is sitting in front of me in a sky-blue shirt that's unbuttoned almost to his navel. He places his giant paw of a hand on the table and looks at me as though he's my dad.

"Why do you want to meet with Agnes Thelin?"

"I'm going to tell."

"Tell what?"

I shrug.

"What happened."

He waves his huge hand dismissively.

"Listen. I've spoken with Ulrika and we've decided you have to keep mum as long as possible."

I make fists under the table.

"Are you still fucking?"

Blomberg looks like someone has just kicked him in the nuts.

"You don't have to answer," I said. "I'd prefer not to know."

Blomberg runs his hand over his mouth.

"That was a long time ago," he says quietly. "Before this, I hadn't seen Ulrika for several years."

He wipes away the sweat that's trickling down his neck and behind his ears. Then he lifts his laptop onto the table. He stares at the screen and types noisily at the keys before finally looking at me again.

"The prosecutor's hypothesis is that Amina and Christopher Olsen were seeing each other behind your back."

"What? Seriously?"

"The prosecutor believes that Olsen was unfaithful to you with Amina, and that you found them out, so to speak," says Blomberg.

The words drum out of him mercilessly. I know this has to do with me, but it sounds so foreign, like something you'd read on Reddit.

"Unfaithful?"

He nods.

"They believe that you discovered them and made up your mind to kill Olsen."

"Hold on. The prosecutor thinks I killed Chris because he and Amina . . . what . . . had sex?"

"Yes."

"Because I was jealous?"

"Jealous? Betrayed? What do I know?" he says.

"That's totally fucked up!"

Rage flares in my chest. I have to tell. Let everyone know what really happened.

"Do you care about Amina?" Blomberg asks.

"What the hell are you talking about? I love her!"

"Then you will listen to what I have to say."

I snort, but force myself to listen.

"For Amina's sake," Blomberg says.

I can picture her, the fear in her eyes, her crushed dreams, and it's like I collapse, like my whole body crumbles. Without Amina, I don't know where I would be today, *who* I would be. I will never let her down.

"The prosecutor will likely claim that you went to Olsen's apartment with the intention of taking his life. But their argument is based on a weak chain of circumstantial evidence," Blomberg says. "They have the witness testimony from the neighbor who says she saw you outside the building, of course. But that girl is a fragile little thing, not exactly a dream witness."

He looks straight at his monitor.

"Then they have the shoe print and traces of pepper spray. Strands of hair, flakes of skin, and fibers from clothing. But there is no direct evidence that you were the one who killed Olsen."

"Okay."

He turns the screen toward me, but I don't have the energy to read the tiny letters.

"They have found evidence on Olsen's computer too, messages and chats. They have a few phone records here and there."

Blomberg's voice is calm and stable and makes me feel a little more composed.

"The most important thing right now is your alibi, Stella."

"Okay?" I say, not sure what he means.

He looks at me again.

"The prosecutor's timeline doesn't hold water, because you have an alibi for the time the medical examiner says the murder was committed."

The words spin in my head.

"I have an alibi?"

That seems unlikely.

"According to the ME's report, Olsen died sometime between one and three in the morning."

I still don't get it.

"You were already home then, Stella."

"I was? No . . ."

"Your dad looked at the clock. He is one hundred percent sure that you came home at quarter to twelve that night."

Dad? Quarter to twelve?

My basic understanding of time is out of whack. I can't get a handle on it.

"That can't be right," I say.

"Of course it is. If your dad says he's sure, then it is definitely right."

I hardly hear what Blomberg says after that.

I'm starting to understand what is going on.

"Surely you don't think your dad would lie?"

76

On the second-to-last Friday in August I turned eighteen. Dad was the one who chose the restaurant. Italian, of course. He's obsessed with Italian food and anything that has even the slightest thing to do with that goddamn spaghetti nation, and he takes for granted that Mom and I feel the same way.

All those vacations in Italy. Honestly: bruschetta and pasta, *birra grande* and *vino rosso*, and all those flirty, greasy-haired waiters with their fucking *"Ciao, bella"*? Gag me.

In other words, I didn't exactly have high hopes for my birthday dinner, but Mom and Dad had been nagging me about it all summer and considering the incident with the car, I didn't want to disappoint them too much.

The evening began on a low note. The restaurant had managed to book us for the wrong day, or maybe it was Dad's fault; I don't know. Then he didn't want to let me order wine.

"I'm turning eighteen," I said. "The law is on my side."

"The law is not perfect," Dad said.

At least he was smiling.

"What does our legal expert say?"

As luck would have it, I had Mom on my side too.

"Of course she can have wine."

Not that it mattered much what I drank with my food. It was the principle of the thing.

When we were finished eating, they gave me a card that included a little map I was supposed to follow out the restaurant and around the corner. There stood the pink Vespa with a big ugly bow on the handlebars. I couldn't believe my eyes! Dad had completely ignored my wish for travel money and instead blew thirty thousand kronor on a Vespa.

"But I said . . ."

"A 'thanks' will do," said Dad.

I hated myself. Of course I should have been grateful, should have thrown my arms around Dad's neck, but there I stood, rooted to the spot, my body full of conflicted emotions. What was wrong with me?

After dessert we sat there, quiet and full, staring at each other across the table. At regular intervals I checked my phone. The congratulations were streaming in on Facebook, but I hadn't heard from Amina yet.

"I think I have to take off soon," I said.

Dad was annoyed, of course. Here they had organized a birthday dinner for me, and I was just going to leave.

"I'm going out with Amina," I said, putting on my jacket. "Thank you so much for dinner and the present."

"Are you taking the Vespa?" Dad asked.

I looked at my wineglass. Was that it? He knew I couldn't drink if I had the Vespa.

"Don't worry," Mom said. "We'll find a way to get it home tonight."

She stood up with a melancholy smile and I closed my eyes as we hugged. Suddenly I felt so fucking unhappy. Regret, longing—a deep ache burned inside me, and I held on to Mom for a long time.

Dad didn't get up from the table. Our hug was an awkward, cold number. I saw how they gazed after me as I left.

The heat of late summer has a certain smell. When the hot weather has stuck around long enough, it penetrates the air in a way that only a steady rain can get rid of.

I crossed Fjelievägen and walked past the sporting fields. It smelled like apples and sauna, and someone was bouncing a ball against the concrete wall of the nearby running track. Cheerful voices and unbridled laughter rose above the monotonous traffic buzz on Ringvägen.

I didn't really have any plans at all. When I'd spoken to Amina on Thursday night, I'd said I didn't feel like doing anything. I would go out to eat with Mom and Dad and then head home and chill.

But now it felt wrong to waste the night. The wine had pepped me up and I had traded my Saturday shift so I could sleep away the whole next morning if I wanted to. I texted Amina, but when she didn't respond within a minute I called instead.

"What are you up to?" I asked.

There was a crackle. A small thud.

Amina disappeared for an instant, but soon returned with a clearer voice. She was panting slightly and seemed worked up.

"I'm with Chris," she said.

"Chris?"

Something hardened in my chest.

"What are you doing with Chris?"

She was slow to answer.

"Oh, just . . . we're, like, hanging out."

For a moment no one said anything. What was going on? Were Amina and Chris spending time together without me?

"We were going to surprise you."

That sounded like a white lie.

"Are you at Chris's apartment? I can be there in five minutes."

"Five minutes?" Amina said.

Next thing she hung up on me.

What was going on? I knew Amina would never go behind my back. She would never do anything with Chris, not a chance, not without talking to me first. But I could hear in her voice that something wasn't right.

I thought of the sick story Linda had told me in City Park and started walking faster, past Polhem, down toward the community garden. For a brief time in ninth grade I was dating a guy who was in his last year at Polhem. Amina and I cut school after lunch a couple times, just to sit on the hidden playground at the corner, chain-smoking and doing away with our teen angst as we waited for the guys with driver's licenses and their daddies' cars, which gave them enormous status among kids our age.

My phone rang as I turned onto Chris's street.

"Hey," Amina said breathlessly. "Wait outside. I'll come down."

"Why?"

I scrutinized the yellow building at the end of the street and saw the flicker in the stairwell before the lights came on.

"I'm on my way," Amina panted.

"What's going on?"

She hung up. An instant later, the door flew open and she stormed onto the street.

I took a few quick steps and met her halfway.

Her eyes were huge and her breath came in small, violent bursts.

"Let's forget about him."

She stared down at the asphalt. Her mascara was all smudged and her shoelaces were untied.

"What?" I said.

"Let's just forget that piece of shit Chris Olsen."

77

For once, I'm more or less well rested when I wake up. It gives me a fresh, healthier outlook on everything. You don't understand how important sleep is until you're unable to sleep undisturbed.

The police have arranged for another interview right after breakfast. I slowly chew my dry slice of bread and wonder what I will say to Agnes Thelin.

Elsa and Jimmy take the elevator with me, down to the interrogation room, where Michael Blomberg is waiting.

"Good morning, Stella," he says.

He seems nervous. Is he afraid of what I'm going to say? He huffs and puffs as he wrestles his way out of his tight jacket. His shirt is navy blue.

Agnes Thelin rattles off a few pleasantries before settling down across from me and starting the recording.

"You've had some time to think since we last spoke, Stella. Is there something you want to tell me, or clarify?"

"Well . . ."

Agnes Thelin smiles patiently.

"I don't think so," I say, peering at Blomberg, who's messing with his tie.

"It's just that your activities on the day of the murder . . . ," says Agnes Thelin. "We can't quite get a handle on them, Stella."

"No."

She watches me for a long time without a word. A little too long. At last I just have to say something, anything, to get out of her grasp.

"Blomberg says Dad gave me an alibi."

The lawyer's eyes widen. He scratches his nose.

"Well," Agnes Thelin says, with a look at Blomberg. "It might not be quite that simple."

"Oh? Why not?" I ask.

"It's nearly impossible to pin down the exact moment of a human death."

"What about the neighbor? Didn't she hear screaming at one?"

Agnes Thelin doesn't respond. I still don't know how much to tell her.

"Can you try to recall exactly what you did after you left the restaurant that night, Stella?"

I breathe deeply, heavily.

There's nothing wrong with my memory. I remember exactly what I did.

"What does Dad say?" I ask.

Agnes Thelin looks me straight in the eye.

"Your dad says you came home at exactly eleven forty-five on Friday night. He claims to be one hundred percent certain of it."

I still don't get it. Is Dad planning to lie in court? Why?

"He says he spoke with you. Is that right?"

I shift, but don't say anything.

The next look Agnes gives me seems to carry an appeal.

"When did you really come home that night, Stella?"

She leans toward me, but I look past Agnes Thelin, past everything, into the bare wall behind her. I think about Amina. I can still hear her terrified breaths. I can see her broken gaze.

"Is your father's information correct, Stella? Did you come home at quarter to twelve that night?"

"Mm."

"I'm sorry?"

The room falls dead silent. Everything is holding its breath.

"I didn't come home until two."

It feels good in my heart.

Blomberg's eyes are about to pop out of their sockets, but Agnes Thelin exhales and now I'm looking only at her.

"What happened that night, Stella?"

"I biked over to Chris's."

I think about Amina. I picture her before me, in a doctor's coat. She is beaming, as usual. She must have started med school by now. I think of all the years we shared, everything we made it through. I don't feel any dread; the smell is gone; everything is fine.

"What happened after that?" Agnes Thelin asks.

Blomberg wipes sweat from his forehead.

I think of what he said about Amina. *If you care about Amina, you won't say anything.*

I think of Shirine; I think of my trip to Asia. I think about Mom and Dad.

I think of the rapist.

I can't keep quiet any longer.

78

Amina hesitantly brought the glass to her lips.

"We were going to surprise you," she said. "We were going to think of something together. He wanted me to come over to his place."

I fixed my eyes on her. She took a quick sip.

"He kissed me," she said then, almost in passing.

"What? Chris kissed you?"

I took a huge gulp of rosé.

"I swear, I wasn't expecting it at all. Suddenly he was just there, totally on top of me, and his lips . . . I tried to shove him off. You have to believe me."

I stared at her and downed the rest of my wine. We were sitting in the outdoor seating area at the Stortorget restaurant; it was Friday night and full of people. Even so, it felt like we were all alone in our little bubble, just Amina and me. The rest of the world was canned elevator music.

"You trust me, right? You know I would never do anything with him," said Amina.

Her giant pupils darted back and forth. It was a point of honor, of course. We were best friends.

"Obviously," I said, since I knew what a horrible liar she is.

"He's a jerk, a total fuckboy," she said. "Jesus, you just don't *do* that. He knows we're best friends. It doesn't matter that you . . ."

She stopped, apparently regretting her words.

"That I what?"

She looked down and fiddled with her necklace, the one with the silver ball I'd given her for her eighteenth birthday.

"That you were going to dump him."

"But he didn't know that," I said.

"No, of course not."

She kept messing with the silver ball.

"You told him?"

She really does suck at lying.

"I'm sorry. He just kept nagging me about it. He said he'd texted you a bunch of times but you never responded. He knew something was wrong."

I couldn't produce a single word. I didn't even want to look at her.

"He was a bad summer fling," Amina said, attempting a half smile. "Maybe it was for the best that it ended up like this. Now we know what a jerk he is."

I couldn't smile. Nor could I see any plus side to what had happened. I was still having trouble taking it in.

I really wanted to be angry. I wanted to call Chris and tell him what a pathetic pig he was and that he could go to hell. But my rage was forced into the background by other emotions that were new to me.

Above all, I felt betrayed.

The next day, he sent more messages over Facebook and Snapchat. I resisted the impulse to respond and blocked him everywhere instead. I never wanted to have anything to do with Christopher Olsen ever again.

During that week, I stopped thinking about him. Or, well, at least long periods passed without him infiltrating my brain. Several hours without an ache in my heart. I decided it would simply take time, that I had to withstand it. It was like quitting smoking.

When I got home after work that Wednesday, as August was panting its last hot breaths, I realized that Chris had hardly been in my thoughts since early that morning. I was already moving on; I had buried whatever feelings might still be there under the surface, and I wasn't going to dig them up again. It was actually going faster than I'd thought.

Neither Chris Olsen nor Linda Lokind would be part of my future. Just like thousands of other people, they had passed through the fringes of my life. They'd had nothing more than brief cameos. Soon I would have forgotten them. In ten or twenty years, I would recall this crazy story and tell it to new friends with a smile full of horror and delight: the guy fifteen years my senior who took me to Copenhagen in a limo and booked the suite at the Grand for us; his mentally unstable ex who stalked me. I would only have vague memories of what they looked like, who they were, and what actually happened. I would definitely laugh at the whole mess and people who listened to it would question its accuracy.

If only it hadn't been for Amina.

79

Friday was the last day of August. The end of this summer had been magical and there was nothing to suggest that the spell was about to break. The sun was shining and the sky was blue.

I thought about my Asia trip. In a few weeks, when the darkness blew in across the plains around Lund, I would finally have my one-way ticket to sun, heat, and adventure in my back pocket. Finally. I would scrape together enough money even if it meant toiling from open to close seven days a week.

Last night I had listed the Vespa for sale online. I felt horribly ungrateful, but I had made myself clear. I didn't want a Vespa—I needed money for my trip.

In the morning I messaged Amina to ask if she had time to meet up that night. We had to talk. I was disappointed about what had happened, but I also couldn't shake the feeling that I was making a mountain out of a molehill. What did it really matter that Amina had revealed to Chris that I didn't want to see him anymore? In some ways, she had done me a favor.

Amina wrote back that she had practice, but that she'd love to get a glass of wine afterward.

I kept Chris out of my mind all day. I found there was a new lightness in my chest and walked around smiling and humming Disney songs all afternoon.

When we closed the store at seven, I tagged along with my coworkers to grab a bite at Stortorget. Amina's practice wouldn't end until eight anyway.

At eight thirty she sent a text.

Too wrecked to go out match tomorrow

No problem, I responded. *Xoxo.*

Sorry youre not mad right

Course not, I wrote.

We can talk tomorrow love you xoxo

I had to get up for work too, and I wasn't planning to stay out very long. Also, I was coming more and more to terms with what had happened, and I accepted it as a good thing. I really didn't feel like having a deep conversation about trust and shit.

I ordered a glass of sparkling wine, put on my sunglasses, and leaned back to enjoy the sun.

My colleagues started chattering about their usual topics: diapers, doo-doo, baby food, and BabyBjörns, and even though I fake-yawned as wide as I possibly could, they didn't seem to catch on. We needed a better topic of conversation, something more acute, something to get people riled up a little.

Malin said that the preschool her children went to was focusing on the lesson "each person is of equal worth" and the others chimed in, in unison, about how important and good that was.

I saw my chance.

"Come on," I said. "Do you really think everyone is truly equal?"

They stared at me like you do when you're not sure if someone is trying to make a joke or if they just said something unusually stupid.

"I'm totally serious." I turned to Malin, the manager, since she's the easiest to get worked up. "If you had to choose, either fifty kids in Syria have to die or else your Tindra does, what would you do?"

"Oh, lay off," Sofie whined. "You can't say stuff like that."

But Malin wanted to answer.

"That example has nothing to do with people being equal. Of course Tindra is worth more to me, because she's my child, but from a purely objective standpoint she isn't worth more than any other person."

I hadn't expected anything else. Malin isn't dumb.

"Would you say that Tindra is worth the same as a pedophile?"

Malin made a face.

"Pedophiles don't even deserve to be called human."

I smiled triumphantly.

"What about murderers? Rapists?"

"Those are extreme examples," said Sofie. "Ninety-nine percent of people are neither pedophiles nor murderers."

"What about someone who beats their wife or kid? A racist? Someone who writes hate messages online, a bully? Is that person worth the same as an innocent child?"

Sofie started to respond, but she was interrupted by Malin, who thought that the "discussion was pointless." I tried in vain to goad her back into it but soon the mommy chatter was back in full swing again. The step from moral dilemmas to vitamin drops and Pull-Ups is not as far as you might think.

I couldn't take it anymore.

"See you tomorrow," I said, hugging them one by one. Then I strolled across the town square to get my bike.

You could tell it was a payday weekend. It was ten thirty, but people were streaming through town, excited at the chance to treat themselves to an extra drink, happy about the nice weather, pumped about sucking up the last few drops of warmth as fall was approaching.

At the bus stop I lifted my bike out of the rack and had just swung my right leg over the frame when something caught my eye.

There she was, right across the street, her back to a brick wall and her eyes roving the bus stop, wearing a floral, summery yellow dress, boots, and a beige coat with her bag held tightly over her shoulder.

I had to look again to make sure.

My arms turned to spaghetti and the bike tipped. I lost my balance.

80

Shirine's eyes are glistening with tears.

"Get ahold of yourself," I say.

Sentimental farewells are, like, not my thing. So obviously I'm crabby.

"I'm sure I'll still be here when you get back."

"I don't think so," Shirine says, biting her lower lip.

She's leaving tomorrow; she'll be gone for three weeks.

"It's going to trial, right?" she says.

"Seems like."

I don't really want to talk about it.

"The Canary Islands?" I say instead, a skeptical look on my face. "I'm sure you can still change your mind. You got cancellation insurance, didn't you?"

It works. Shirine's teary sad-face transforms into a sparkling smile.

"You're just jealous. Eighty degrees in the shade all week long."

"Don't forget your sunscreen." I laugh.

She nods, wrinkling her nose.

"Can I ask you something, Shirine?"

"Of course."

I hesitate. I try to find the right words, but it's not easy.

I lay awake all night, thinking about Dad. Why did he claim I came home much earlier that night than I actually did?

"How far would you go to protect your daughter?"

"I'm not quite sure what you mean," Shirine says. "I would do anything for Lovisa. I think any parent would."

"Perjury?"

"Huh?"

Shirine shoots me a look of suspicion.

"It means lying under oath."

"I know what it means, but I'm pretty sure you can't be forced to testify under oath against your own child."

"No, but forget the details. Would you lie in court to protect Lovisa?"

"That's a tough one," she says, apparently thinking it over. "It depends . . ."

"Come on."

"Okay," she says, with resolve. "I'm sure I would do everything in my power. Even lie. In court."

"Good."

"I bet a parent could do the most unimaginable things to save their child."

"But my dad does things for his own sake. Or so that other people won't find out that he and his family aren't as perfect as he wants them to be."

A prominent wrinkle appears on Shirine's forehead. She doesn't say anything for a minute.

"Know what? I don't think that's so unusual. I suppose we all want our families to appear a little more harmonious and faultless than they really are."

I shake my head. Shirine doesn't get it; she can't even imagine what it's like.

"My dad didn't want to raise me. He wanted to create me, as if he was God himself. He wanted me to be exactly like him. No, wait, he wanted me to be the way he imagined a daughter of his would be. And when it didn't turn out that way . . ."

That's all I can manage. My voice gives out and fades away.

"I actually don't believe that your dad would lie about just anything to protect himself or his family's reputation."

I turn away from her. What the hell does Shirine know about my father?

"Then why is he doing it?"

"Because it's what dads do. Because he loves you."

I won't look at her. I want to say something mean, something hurtful, something to poke a hole in this sentimental mood, but I can't muster a single word.

"It's going to be okay, Stella."

I feel her gentle hand on my arm and all I want is for her to leave.

"Hey," she whispers.

The tears make my eyes overflow. Jesus, just go!

She slowly strokes my back. It makes me feel safe and hopeful, but at the same time I know she's about to leave me. Soon she'll be sitting on a lounge chair by the pool on some Canary Island, tickling little Lovisa until her sides split.

I shove her hand away without meeting her gaze.

"I have to go now," Shirine says.

I still have my back to her.

"I really have to go now, Stella."

"Okay."

I turn around and see her at the door. She's peering back over her shoulder and shifting slowly back and forth from foot to foot.

"Okay," I say again.

Then I take two steps forward and put my arms around her neck.

I'm crying again. Letting everything pour out of me.

Shirine hugs me hard, for a long time.

"Good luck now," she whispers.

I don't respond. I have no voice.

81

I straddled my bike in the alley by the deli. It had gone too far. Too damn far. Linda Lokind was still following me, even though I'd broken up with Chris. Cautiously I peered over to the bus stop, but I couldn't see her anywhere.

I shook off a shudder, took out my phone, and called Amina. When she didn't answer, I tried text, Messenger, and Snapchat, but it was radio silence everywhere.

Each noise and movement made me twist my body. My heart was pounding. I felt hunted, and I didn't want to be alone.

As I quickly led my bike toward the cathedral, I weighed my options. Obviously I could rejoin my coworkers at Stortorget. I wouldn't need to say why I was back, and it would still make me feel safer to sit with them for a while.

Or else I could bike home. The downside to that was, it would take at least fifteen minutes. It was getting dark and the streets were empty. I needed people around.

I checked my phone again. Amina was offline everywhere. She was probably sleeping.

Someone else?

There, among the little profile pictures across the top of Messenger, I caught sight of his face. His big smile and diamond eyes. A green dot glowed in front of his name. *Online.* I had forgotten to remove Chris from Messenger.

Shit! I had decided to forget him, delete him from my life, but now that I thought about it Chris seemed like the best option after all. He knew Linda. Maybe he could explain that there was nothing between us anymore. Maybe he could convince her to leave me alone. If there was anyone who could calm me down, it was Chris.

I looked at his picture again, and in that moment I realized how much I missed him. Tears burned behind my eyes as I headed into Lundagård Park.

Here and there a bike skidded past on the gravel paths, and an older lady was dragging her scraggly dachshund around by the statue of Tegnér, but for the most part everything was quiet and still.

What should I do?

I called Amina again. Still no answer.

I made a hasty decision and messaged Chris.

Are you there?

I stared down at the screen, but nothing happened. Several times I spun around to look over my shoulder, thinking I'd heard footsteps, seeing glowing eyes in the bushes.

Still no response on Messenger.

I looked up Chris's number and sent a text. I waited five minutes, then called multiple times in a row. Nothing.

What was I going to do?

I parked my bike outside Tegnérs and sent even more messages, to both Chris and Amina. I wrote in all caps that they had to get back to me ASAP. It was important.

I headed into the club to hide in the crowd. After dashing around aimlessly, in the hopes of finding a familiar face to take my mind off Linda Lokind, I stood at the bar sipping at a pear cider and checking my phone at least ten times a minute. Still nothing.

People were giving me strange looks. A guy with Ronaldo hair attempted to flirt out of habit, but I waved him off like a gnat. I surfed the net for a while and texted Amina for the eleventh time.

When I came back out, the darkness was just about impenetrable. I got on my bike and pedaled through the park, swerving around a puddle and nearly crashing into two rivet-studded dudes who asked if I had a light. I didn't respond, just looked around in the dark and decided to bike home. Just as I took a right onto Kyrkogatan, I glanced over my shoulder, wobbled, and almost toppled over.

Linda Lokind was standing across the intersection, looking like a ghost in the dull yellow umbrella of light cast by the streetlamp. Both hands were shoved into her pockets, and she was staring at nothing.

With that, I veered up onto the sidewalk and climbed off my bike. There's this little pub at the end of Sandgatan, I think it's called Inferno—the door was wide open and music and laughter were streaming out, so I shoved past a couple tattooed guys with full beards and into the dim bar.

It had to have been Linda. This time I was sure of it.

Or was I? Could I have been mistaken after all?

Hunched over a glass of wine in a deep corner, I lingered. My heart was pounding. Was it really Linda? Now that I thought about it, I hadn't really gotten a good look at her face.

I recalled her words in the park. How she threatened to hurt Chris. What if he was in danger? Or worse? She could have hurt him already. And now . . . was she out to get me too?

Where was Amina? Why hadn't she gotten back to me?

I glanced at the dimly lit bar. No Linda. People were drinking beer, bullshitting, laughing like nothing was wrong. I finished my wine and got the hiccups as a result. At last my phone vibrated.

Everything's ok. Sleeping. See you tomorrow. <3

It had come from Amina's phone.

I read it over and over.

What the fuck was this?

Amina and I have been texting each other since preschool. I know how my best friend writes as well as I know her voice.

Amina doesn't use punctuation when she texts.

Amina does not shorten okay to ok.

That text had been written by someone else.

82

I pedaled so hard I couldn't feel my legs beneath me. Nothing else existed; it was just me and my bike. Traffic, cars, and people whizzed by at the periphery. I saw nothing, heard nothing. My thoughts flew by without taking hold.

All I could see ahead of me was Amina. I had to get a move on. I had to get hold of Chris.

On my way up and out of the railroad tunnel on Trollebergsvägen, I saw the police station up ahead and it occurred to me I could turn to the police. This was serious. Someone wanted to make sure I thought Amina was fine. Someone who wasn't Amina.

As I passed the station, though, I decided to keep going. It would only take me a few minutes to get to Pilegatan.

Linda Lokind's words echoed in my head. I pictured Chris. Amina. What was going on?

My bike flew those last few meters over the asphalt. The wind socked me in the face and I saw stars.

When I reached the building, I flung my bike up against it and stared up. The blinds were down in all of Chris's windows. It was completely dark.

I went up the stairs on numb legs. My pulse was throbbing; my brain nothing but one big shriek.

I pounded on the door. Rang the bell. Not a sound.

I pressed my ear to the door, then opened the mail slot and yelled through it. "Chris! Amina!"

Nothing.

I knew something had happened.

I had no idea what was about to happen.

PART THREE

THE MOTHER

There is no such thing as justice—in or out of court.

Clarence Darrow

83

Main proceedings are called to order in Courtroom 2.

Outside the windows, the snow is falling in large diamond flakes and every time the door to the courthouse opens, a chill sweeps through the building, making the hair on my arms stand straight up.

When I enter the courtroom, the district court judge Göran Leijon meets my gaze and nods grimly. We have met on several occasions throughout the years, and I have never had reason to be dissatisfied. Leijon is not just a competent judge. He is also sharp and nuanced, a courteous person with great integrity.

The courtroom has in many ways become a second home for me over the years, but this time I feel anything but at home. Everything I usually find attractive—the solemn atmosphere, the gravity of the situation, and the tension in the air—provokes nothing but anxiety in me now. The room, the air, the walls, the faces—they all seem threatening and make me dizzy.

The past several days are a blur. Places and moments crisscross in my mind like brambly patterns. Impressions flash by here and there, all out of order in time and space. It's like walking around in an endless, foggy dream.

I was just in a meeting with a client in Stockholm. I no longer have any notion of what was said or why I was there. I know I dozed off on the plane home. A flight attendant asked if I was feeling okay. I can still see her worried face.

I was so recently at the height of my career, with a bounce in my step, clad in Dolce & Gabbana from head to toe, admired for my straightforward manner, my skill, my industriousness. Now I'm sitting in a courtroom and awaiting the proceedings that will determine my daughter's future, the future of myself and my family.

Until so recently, we were a perfectly ordinary family. Now we are prisoners under a merciless spotlight.

There before me, Presiding Judge Göran Leijon whispers something to the lay judges. Two of them are women in their seventies, one from the Green Party, one Social Democrat—rather typical lay judges. By all appearances they are empathetic women who bring to the court great understanding of how socioeconomic factors may influence criminal acts. The type of lay judges I have myself encountered in hundreds of cases, and who, nine times out of ten, mean good news for me and my client. In this particular matter, however, I'm not entirely convinced that the effect will be positive, a worry I have brought up with Michael. Partly this is because Stella is a woman; partly it's because her appearance will work against her. What's more, she must in every respect be considered a member of the white upper middle class. To make matters worse, she has a tendency to refuse, under any circumstances, to live up to the norms of how a well-brought-up young lady is expected to present herself. With any luck, Michael has helped her come to understand what a crucial role her courtroom behavior might play.

I feel more confident about the third lay judge. He is a man in his forties, retired on disability, a Sweden Democrat—according to Michael he seldom shows any great interest in the legal process.

It is often not worth expending too much worry on the lay judges. In reality, their role in the courtroom can be considered window dressing. No one gives much weight to their opinions, and should they have the poor taste to disagree with the presiding judge's decision, he will squash them flat without batting an eye. In that aspect I can rely one hundred percent on Göran Leijon.

The door on the far end of the room opens and each head in the gallery swivels. Everything stops. The open door gapes before me. It feels as if I am caught in a narrow tunnel. I twist my body, squirming and trying to breathe normally.

First, a uniformed security guard appears in the doorway. He turns around and says something. My vision is limited and blurry and the tunnel keeps closing in around me.

At last I see Stella. Tears squeeze from my eyes, further clouding my vision.

She is so small, and everything hurts so frightfully much. It feels like just yesterday that she fit on my lap, when she would sit with me to be petted like a doll. Her pacifier and security blanket, the first time she stood up and ran. Stella neither crawled nor walked—she ran right away. I remember chicken pox and scraped knees, strawberry stains on her summer dress, her freckles, and how I fell asleep in her bed night after night with a book on my face.

I think about all her dreams. She wanted to change the world. What could otherwise be the point of living? At first she wanted to become a pastor like her father, and later a police officer or fireman. She was so enraged that people said *fireman*—she was going to become the first firegirl.

Are there any dreams left? As I watch her being led into the courtroom it all becomes so clear, like a blow to the face. My failure is as thorough as it is unforgivable. Stella is eighteen years old and all her dreams have been crushed.

She has always wanted to help people. She was going to see the world, swim with sharks, climb mountains, learn to dive and fly, go skydiving, and ride a motorcycle across the United States. For a while she dreamed of becoming an actor or a psychologist.

What is a human being without dreams?

Our gazes meet for the briefest of moments before she sits down next to Michael. Her eyes are tired and empty; her hair is lank, her skin full of spots. She is still a frightened little girl. *My* frightened little girl. And I rise slightly from my seat, balancing on my toes and stretching out my arm. To fail to be there for your own child. There is no greater betrayal.

84

Here in my seat in the gallery, I cling to the walls of my tunnel. Should my gaze deviate in the slightest I risk encountering accusations, blame, and hatred I cannot face.

Adam is waiting out in the corridor, because he will be testifying. I realize I miss him. I have never needed him the way I do now.

Since I'm seated closer to the prosecution, I can't help but catch a glimpse of Margaretha Olsen at the edge of my tunnel. In the nineties, I had her as an instructor in a few courses during law school; these days she is a professor of criminal law. But today, she is first and foremost the mother of a man who was robbed of his life. Next to her sits the injured-party counsel, a red-haired woman in her fifties whom I think I recognize but can't quite place, and a male assistant prosecutor with slicked-back hair and round glasses. And last but not least, the prosecutor herself: Jenny Jansdotter.

I know Jansdotter is my age, but she appears much younger, possibly because she's so short. Her hair is secured in a severe bun and her gaze is narrow and focused as she slips on her glasses. I think of all the times I've found myself in this very situation: the tension and suspense when you've just stepped into the courtroom at the start of a new trial.

In the gallery, the atmosphere is entirely different. I squirm and fight back tears, trying to find something to do with my unwieldy hands. Here, concentration is exchanged for confusion and concern. Sweat trickles from my underarms and my tongue crackles, dry against the roof of my mouth.

I look at Michael. I wish he would glance in my direction, but he is fully consumed with his preparations. We have gone through the indictment together a number of times.

This case is based on nothing but circumstantial evidence. The prosecutor has based her account of the deed solely upon circumstances that cannot prove criminal wrongdoing on their own, but together they form a chain that is meant to rule out any other possible explanation.

The evidence in question consists of a shoe print that demonstrates that Stella was at the scene of the crime on the night of the murder, phone records and chat transcripts between Stella and Christopher Olsen, and forensic evidence from Olsen's apartment and clothing in the form of flakes of skin, strands of hair, and fibers of fabric.

Beyond this, the prosecutor has called witnesses: My Sennevall, a resident on Pilegatan, will attest that Stella was at the scene at the time of the murder. Stella's colleagues from H&M, Malin Johansson and Sofie Silverberg, will testify that Stella had pepper spray in her purse. Jimmy Bark, an employee of the jail, will confirm that Stella has demonstrated violent behavior on repeated occasions during the last few weeks.

The defense has called two witnesses: Adam and Amina.

Jenny Jansdotter clears her throat and looks straight at Stella. I want to shout at her to stop, to leave my daughter alone. She delivers her opening statement without blinking, without taking a breath, without stumbling over her words at any point.

"Stella Sandell got to know Christopher Olsen in June of this year. They met at the restaurant Tegnérs, where they initiated a conversation. After a relatively short time, they began a sexual relationship."

Stella looks vacant. She is staring straight ahead at Jansdotter, and it's impossible to spot even a flicker of protest against the prosecutor's version of events.

"Eventually, Stella's friend Amina Bešić, whom we will hear from today, began to see Christopher Olsen behind Stella's back. Amina, too, had a sexual relationship with Christopher, which Stella soon discovered."

I think I see a nearly invisible nod from Presiding Judge Göran Leijon. Beside him, the lay judges are following the prosecutor's story with intense interest. Thus far, there is no other narrative. Thus far, what she is presenting is the truth.

"Christopher Olsen chose to end his relationship with Stella Sandell and for one week they had no contact. But on the night of August the thirty-first, just hours before the time of the murder, Stella tried to call and text him again, and she went to his residence on Pilegatan. At eleven thirty, witness My Sennevall, a neighbor of Olsen's, saw Stella arrive at the residence by bicycle and run up to Christopher Olsen's apartment. Thirty minutes later, My Sennevall saw Stella once more. This time, she was standing on the sidewalk across from Olsen's residence, apparently waiting for something."

The structure of these proceedings gives the prosecutor an undeniable advantage. There is a psychological benefit to being the first to present a series of events. The narrative one is first given simply appears to be the truth; any subsequent versions must meet a much higher threshold of believability to change one's original understanding of said chain of events. And unfortunately, both judges and lay judges are only human, no matter how much they strive to rise above and ignore prejudices and all the other psychological mechanisms that affect and guide us.

People are typing away at keyboards in the gallery. Some are taking notes by hand. Journalists and reporters, who naturally have their own neatly prepackaged ideas about what happened, ready to be shared with every soul who has access to a TV antenna or an internet connection. I extend my hand toward a bearded guy in the seat next to mine. *There is another truth; you haven't heard everything yet. Both sides must have the chance to speak.* The bearded man looks at me in surprise between his strikes of the keyboard, raising his eyebrows as if to ask if I want something from him. I retreat back into my tunnel. I can smell the odor of my own sweat rising.

"Sometime between midnight and one o'clock on September the first, Christopher Olsen arrives at his residence," the prosecutor says. "Stella has been waiting on the street outside, and he lets her in. An argument breaks out in the apartment, in all likelihood linked to Olsen's relationship with Amina Bešić. During the argument, Stella takes a knife from the wall of Christopher Olsen's kitchen. Olsen flees his residence and goes out to the street. He runs to the playground at the corner of Pilegatan and Rådmansgatan. As he reaches the playground, Stella Sandell catches up with him and brutally attacks him, stabbing the defenseless Christopher Olsen with the knife. He is struck in the chest, stomach, and neck, but none of the wounds are immediately fatal and Christopher does not die right away. Stella Sandell leaves him to bleed to death."

It all plays out like a movie in my mind. I see the knife in Stella's hand as she raises it back over her shoulder and stabs.

I have to stand up. People stare at me; everyone knows who I am, of course. The journalists have long since identified me. One last shred of professional honor and respect for others is the only thing that stops them from assailing me with questions and blame. I look around and take a few steps to the right, then a few steps to the left—and then I duck back down onto my chair. Everything is spinning.

"Are you okay?" the bearded man asks.

I shake my head. I am far from okay. I press my hands to my belly and breathe, my lips trembling.

I know Adam is sitting right outside the door, but even so I feel thoroughly, deeply abandoned. I don't understand. Usually, when people talk about the fact that humans are social animals, part of a mainland and never an island, I have trouble relating. For my entire life I have felt cut off from the rest of humanity. This has never been a great cause of sorrow for me, possibly because it's impossible to miss what you never had, but the strong bonds that united other people, whether or not they were symbolized by rings or blood or something else, have always appeared to be looser, thinner, less meaningful for me than they are for others.

The first time I realized this was a few years ago, when I observed Stella and Amina's friendship and saw something I longed for. It was a thoroughly unnatural feeling, to feel jealous of one's own daughter's relationship with a friend. It took quite a bit of time, resentment, and tears—a full-fledged catastrophe around the corner—before I realized that even if I have strong feelings about Amina, even if I see myself in her and feel a great kinship with her, what I really longed for was my own family.

I longed for Stella. I longed for my beloved little girl.

And I missed Adam.

85

I think it was Adam's humble image I fell for first. I had seen him gliding past me in the hallways of Wermlands dorms before, but I never really noticed him. One late December night, we happened to end up sitting across the table from each other in one of the shared kitchens, and a few years later we had made a family.

It sounds ridiculous in hindsight, but I was hardly aware that men like Adam existed. I'd had many boyfriends back at home, but there was seldom anyone worth keeping more than a few months. The guys I was interested in were attractive, outgoing, and confident, which often meant that as soon as you scratched the hard outer surface you found a scared little boy.

For a few weeks in the last semester of my third year of high school I dated a guy named Klabbe, who did arms and chest in the gym four nights a week whenever he wasn't driving back and forth between the two city squares in the BMW that ate up half his salary from the bread factory. He liked to call me Princess because I made him rinse the tobacco from his teeth before we kissed.

Certainly there had been other men like Adam in my vicinity, but they passed under my radar since their position and status were practically non-existent in the small town I came from. In Lund, everything was different. Other characteristics and attributes were of value here. I was absolutely determined never to return home.

Adam offered thrilling perspectives on both our little world and the wider one. More often than not, the starting points of our discussions were our diametrically opposed views, which eventually led us to fresh insights and some form of consensus. He was in possession of an incomparable ability to treat others' thoughts with such dignity and respect that it was impossible to become angry with him. And that made me angry.

"You can't just acquiesce, Adam! *On the one hand, on the other hand, everyone is right in their own way.* The whole point of a discussion is to win!"

"You think so? I think the point of a discussion is for us to develop as people. Every time my views are questioned, I learn something new."

We sometimes spent half the night sitting in his small dorm room: Adam on the bed, his knees drawn up beneath him; me on the floor below him, my legs outstretched. A bottle of wine and a bag of chips.

"All this increasing relativism makes me nervous, Adam. Certainly some values must be absolute. Isn't that true of religion? Are you really allowed to believe as little of it as you like?"

"Of course. That's why it's called 'believing,' not 'knowing.'"

This whole idea of belief was new and rather frightening. Without quite knowing why, and as a matter of routine, I had judged all religion to be dogmatic and the enemy of individuality. There was no room for such things in my liberal, secular worldview. I came from a place where it was as natural to christen your children in church as it was to scorn and ridicule those who called themselves Christian.

"I don't think it's a good thing to be driven by conviction, no matter what sort," said Adam. "It has nothing to do with religion or a belief in God."

"Stop sounding so sensible," I said, stuffing more chips into my mouth. "I want to have a discussion I can win!"

"You're going to make an excellent lawyer."

We laughed and kissed and had sex. This was all new to me. Adam touched me with new hands; he looked at me with a kind of gaze I had never experienced before. He put his heart on the line for me, laid his soul bare, and sat before me, absolutely fearless, in his sloppily made bed that smelled of Axe body spray and sour cream chips.

I saw it as a stormy relationship. Somehow I assumed all along that it would end as unexpectedly and explosively as it had begun. That was my image of romantic relationships: they were brief, intense, and hastily forgotten. You should enjoy them while they lasted but get out before everything was reduced to rubble.

People around me always reacted strongly when I mentioned Adam's education.

"Is he really going to be a pastor?"

Each time, I recoiled too. I usually defended Adam by pointing out that he wasn't at all like a pastor. Not a real one.

"But he believes in God and the Bible and all that?"

I couldn't deny that.

"But it's not like you think," I said sometimes, though I wasn't able to express how it actually was.

It was perfectly natural for our relationship to continue. Now, almost twenty-five years later, it might sound trivial and boring, but my and Adam's relationship was first and foremost based on security, solidarity, and the strong sense of having found our proper places in life. And that was exactly what I needed.

The future was never particularly present in our everyday lives. We were too busy with everything that was going on. In that sense I don't think we were all that different from other people our age. It wasn't that we refused to consider what lay ahead of us, decisions we would have to make about family and careers and so forth. It was just that we couldn't see over the horizon.

That line on the pregnancy test a week or so before Christmas changed everything in one fell swoop. At first I went around in a captivated state that most closely resembled being newly in love, but once that state of dizziness passed it didn't take long before I was beset by anxiety the proportions of which I had never before come close to. It began with doubt about our decision to have a family—wouldn't it be better to wait a few years?—and ended in hopeless frustration about a deteriorating world imbued with violence and misery. I was aghast and found myself in tears over the future that seemed inevitable for my unborn child.

It's horrid to think of now. As if I knew, even back then. A terrifying premonition deep inside me, warning me about bringing Stella into the world. The guilt twists and tears at my insides.

I was far too young. I allowed myself to be persuaded.

86

The presiding judge turns to Stella.

"Would you like to speak about these events and what, if anything, you have witnessed?"

Stella glances at Michael, who nods at her. I am so grateful that he's the one sitting there.

When he called that Saturday night in the beginning of September to tell us that Stella had been taken into police custody, I knew I would be able to make him listen to reason. He owed me that much, after everything that had happened. It was, of course, a torment to sit in his office with Adam, it was a constant balancing act to keep from giving anything away, but none of this would have been possible without Michael.

"Where should I begin?" Stella asks, looking at the judge.

The whole court is staring at her. Göran Leijon's eyes may be warm and kind, but I see Stella's hand trembling on the edge of the table. I wish I could sit beside her and hold her. The tunnel is closing in around me, and I gasp for air. The bearded journalist looks at me.

Stella knows exactly what she must and must not say. Michael has run through it with her several times. The important thing now is that she—for once—does as she's been told. Please, my darling Stella!

This part of the proceedings is so tremendously important. The defendant's first and likely only chance to make an impression on the court. I know Michael's technique inside and out. Most of what I've learned has come from him. It's crucial for the defendant to create trust, to present herself as both strong and vulnerable. It is best to agree with the prosecutor's narrative to the greatest extent possible, and only depart from it on the points that are absolutely necessary in order to object to that version of the crime. It is important to appear cooperative. Stella must show that she is human; no more, no less.

"Are you acquainted with Christopher Olsen?" the presiding judge asks. "I suppose we can start there."

Stella takes a deep breath and looks at Michael. He nods at her as if giving her the green light, then twists his body to the side, away from the audience, away from me.

I feel a stabbing sensation in my belly. A flash of doubt. I can trust Michael, can't I?

"We met him at Tegnérs," Stella says in a subdued voice. "Me and Amina."

I don't dare move a millimeter; I hardly dare to breathe.

"It was sometime in June. I thought Chris was charming, and . . . you know, exciting. He was so much older. He was thirty-two and I was seventeen."

The female lay judges glance at each other.

"He told me he traveled a ton," Stella continues. "He had been, like, everywhere. And you could tell he had money. He seemed to have a super-eventful life. Kind of like I dream of having."

She's using the present tense: dream. Not dreamed. She's still dreaming.

"After that night he texted me and wanted to meet up again, so we did."

Her voice sounds stronger now. Every so often she lifts her head and looks straight at Leijon and the lay judges. Michael straightens up and encourages her to go on with a pat on the arm. Naturally he's wearing one of those blue shirts he special-orders from a tailor in Helsingborg. Many years ago, when we worked together, he confessed that he usually tosses each shirt after a day in court. The sweat is impossible to wash out.

"We went to Chris's apartment a few times," Stella says. "We took a limousine to Copenhagen and went to a fancy restaurant. We went to the spa in Ystad and one night we got a suite at the Grand Hotel."

It's ridiculous how little you know about your own child. Here I had convinced myself that Stella and I had grown closer in recent years. Yet I know only a fraction of what goes on in her life. I consider whether this is strange, or even wrong; if it's characteristic of our relationship in particular or if mothers of teenagers generally believe that they know more about their children than they actually do.

"Sometimes all three of us hung out. Chris, Amina, and me," Stella says. "I mean, Chris and I weren't in a relationship. We had sex a few times, but we weren't a couple."

The lay judges exchange glances again. The two women cringe, and the Sweden Democrat's face glows red. I don't want my daughter's sex life laid bare either, but it takes quite a bit more than this to shock me.

"It was nothing serious, nothing like that. For me or for him. To be perfectly honest, I don't think Chris wanted to be with a seventeen-year-old, and for me it was unthinkable to start anything. I was going to leave soon on a big trip. To Asia."

My eyes sting and I carefully dab at them with a tissue. In my mind I see Stella under a palm tree on a beach in paradise. I hardly dare to imagine the alternative. Several years in prison. And presumably a life sentence from society—on the job market, among friends and acquaintances. How would Adam and I manage to go on? How would Stella manage?

"I know Amina was with Chris too, a few times," Stella says. "It didn't bother me."

Göran Leijon scratches his head.

"Can you be more precise on that point?"

"Which?"

"What do you mean, exactly, when you say Amina was *with* Chris?"

For the first time, the court gets to see a different side of Stella. Her eyes flash and the veins in her neck stand out.

"I mean they spent time together. That's it! Amina didn't have sex with Chris, if that's what you're implying."

Göran Leijon's cheeks turn red and he takes a sip of water as Michael places a calming hand on Stella's arm.

"I was in total shock when I found out . . ." Her voice trembles and Stella scratches near her lips. "When the police told me what had happened. I couldn't believe it. I knew Chris had received threats, but for him to die . . . I still haven't come to terms with it."

Faces are slowly changing in the gallery. The journalists' typing starts to slow. Behind me, someone's whisper is a little too loud as he wonders what threats Stella is talking about. Is it the ex-partner? I close my eyes and breathe. The tunnel has widened a bit.

"Before the prosecutor asks her questions, perhaps you would like to tell us what you were doing on the night of August the thirty-first," says Göran Leijon.

His voice is gentle, his eyes empathetic and trust inducing.

"I worked at H&M until we closed at seven fifteen," Stella says. "Then I went with some coworkers to the Stortorget restaurant. We hung out at the outdoor seating there for a few hours. It was probably around ten thirty when I went to get my bike."

Michael has sunk back into his chair slightly and his shoulders have relaxed. This makes me feel relieved and worried at the same time.

"Just when I was about to get on my bike, I caught sight of Linda Lokind on the other side of the street. Chris's ex, that is. She had followed me another time too. She's pretty creepy, so I tried to call Amina, but she didn't answer. I didn't know what to do. That was when I tried to get hold of Chris."

I tried to put myself in her shoes. What would I have done? It's so easy to believe you know exactly how you would react in different situations, but I have learned, not least through my work, that such notions don't mean a thing when the chips are down. It's simply not possible to predict how you will handle certain situations.

Stella explains that Linda Lokind had been following and harassing her for several weeks. She was scared; she knew Linda was unstable and perhaps even dangerous. That was why Stella slipped into Tegnérs, mostly to surround herself with people while she waited for Amina or Chris to respond.

"They never did, so once I had calmed down a little, I decided to bike home. I only made it to Kyrkogatan, the intersection by the library. And there stood Linda Lokind again."

The lay judges are startled and a buzz goes through the gallery. The only person who doesn't seem affected in the least is Jenny Jansdotter. She is sitting ramrod straight, perfectly still, as if she's just waiting for her chance to crush Stella.

"I was terrified," Stella says, and she explains how she darted into the pub Inferno, right at that intersection.

She hid in the back of the pub and hoped Linda Lokind wouldn't follow her.

"Amina still wasn't answering and I couldn't get hold of Chris, so I decided to bike to his place. It was all such a nightmare. I didn't know what to do."

Stella's breathing is the only sound audible in the room. All eyes are on her.

"They weren't there," Stella says.

Beside me, people turn their heads. Someone scrapes their shoe against the floor. A gal from the TV news chews her gum.

"I rang the bell and banged on the door. Then I pressed my ear up against it to listen, but they weren't there."

Stella lifts her water glass. Her hand is quaking and as she leans forward, her hair falls in front of her face.

Something seems off. What if she tells the whole story? Stella has always loved drama. She used to dream of becoming an actor, and here she has her stage, her audience, her big number. I desperately extend one arm toward her.

"I biked home. I biked home and went to bed," she says, brushing her hair to the side. "I don't know what happened after that."

87

"With that, the prosecutor has the floor," says the presiding judge.

Jenny Jansdotter doesn't move. Every muscle in her severe face appears to be in deep concentration. The whole courtroom is waiting for her.

Then she gives a start and turns toward Stella.

"Who wasn't there?"

Her voice is sharp and authoritative, not at all in keeping with her stature.

"What?"

"You just said 'They weren't there.' Who were you referring to?"

Stella makes a gesture that's meant to seem blasé.

"Chris," she says. "Christopher Olsen. He wasn't in his apartment, so I went home."

"But you didn't say 'he.' You said 'they.' Plural. More than one person. Who was it, besides Chris Olsen, that wasn't there?"

Stella shoots a quick glance at Michael.

"Amina, I guess."

"Amina Bešić?"

Stella nods.

"I must ask you to respond verbally to the prosecutor's questions," says Göran Leijon. "For the sake of the recording."

Stella glowers at him. Her upper lip trembles.

"Yes," Stella says, her voice exaggeratedly loud.

When I turn my head, I discover that the bearded journalist is watching me. He hastily turns away as soon as our eyes meet.

What is he thinking about me? I look around at the spectators. What are they thinking? Maybe they feel sorry for me. Surely some of them blame me. Others probably feel that a parent bears partial responsibility for the actions of their child. Especially in my case. Partly because I'm a woman and a mother; a man could never be burdened to the same extent. Partly because I'm a hard-boiled defense attorney, while my husband is a charming pastor who preaches God's love and the Golden Rule.

Should I also be sitting in the defendant's seat? Side by side with Stella, accused of having an inadequate aptitude for parenting and being an accessory to murder. I am convinced that some people think I should be.

Jenny Jansdotter aims a meaningful look at the presiding judge before going on. I have no idea what the prosecutor is thinking, but I consider it highly unlikely that she regards me as thoroughly innocent.

"Why did you assume Amina would be at Chris's residence?" she asks Stella.

"I don't know. I don't know if I did assume that."

"But that's what you just said."

Jansdotter has orchestrated an effective silence in the court. Stella doesn't know where to look.

"Why did you believe that Amina was with Christopher Olsen on this particular night, the thirty-first of August?" the prosecutor asks. "Wasn't it true that you had broken off all contact with Olsen? Both you and Amina?"

Stella's forehead is sweaty. Her fear creeps through this confining room and attaches to my skin like a sticky goo. Desperate, I scratch and tear at myself.

You can do it, Stella. Don't lose courage now!

"We had stopped spending time with Chris," she said, looking at the prosecutor.

"You had?" Jansdotter stares at her for a long time, but Stella won't give in. "You had an agreement?"

"Something like that."

Jansdotter hardly listens to this response. She's already on to her next question.

"You say that you biked home when no one answered the door at Chris's apartment. What time was it then?"

"I don't know," says Stella.

She glances at Michael. It's so quick that most people in the room likely don't even notice. But I see it. And I know that this is a critical juncture. If Stella continues to claim that she came home at two o'clock, that's the end of Adam's testimony. He can't sit before the court and contradict Stella. My chest feels like it's filling with cement.

Michael tugs at the knot of his tie. Sweat is beginning to soak through his shirt. We are about to learn whether he has succeeded in his task.

"You have no idea whatsoever what time it was?" Jansdotter says.

Stella's lips purse slightly.

"I suppose it was around eleven thirty, midnight. That seems reasonable."

The cement block in my chest feels a little lighter. Air trickles into my lungs.

"During police questioning you said you came home at two o'clock," Jansdotter says sharply. "Isn't that correct?"

Stella looks down.

"I said that to punish Dad."

Jansdotter seems genuinely surprised.

"Please explain."

"When I learned that Dad had given me an alibi, I wanted to make him seem like a liar."

Not an ounce of hesitation in her voice. I breathe calmly, peacefully.

"Are you saying that you lied in a police interrogation to punish your father?"

Stella nods.

"Why would you want to punish your father, Stella?"

"He's always been so overprotective. Sometimes we have a rough time. I was being childish."

I'm glad Adam can't hear this. I knew he wouldn't get to hear it, otherwise I'm not sure it would have been possible.

"I'm sure you understand that this sounds strange," Jansdotter says.

"It is what it is."

"Is it really? Are you sure you're not lying right now, Stella? To protect your father?"

She looks up and shakes her head firmly.

"No!"

Jansdotter pages through her documents.

"When did you arrive home that night, Stella? When the police questioned you, you said you came home at two o'clock . . ."

"I was home before midnight. Between eleven thirty and twelve."

The prosecutor sighs loudly.

"So you and Amina Bešić had an agreement that neither of you would see Christopher Olsen again," says the prosecutor. "Have I understood this correctly?"

"It wasn't an *agreement*. We just said we wouldn't."

The prosecutor moves her eyes as if to suggest that Stella is splitting hairs.

"Why did you say so, then? Why would you stop seeing Christopher?"

"We found out that he was lying. It was as if he was trying to play me and Amina against each other, and we would never allow anyone to do that, ever."

"Wasn't it the case that you knew Amina and Christopher had a sexual relationship?"

"They never had a sexual relationship."

"Did you discover that Christopher was going behind your back, Stella?"

"Absolutely not."

I recognize that sharp tone in her voice. Her patience is wearing thin.

"Isn't it true that you found out that your best friend and the man you had just begun a relationship with were spending time together without your knowledge? Surely you couldn't have believed that everything was strictly platonic between them."

I hold my breath.

Stella gazes around the room. For a fraction of a second we look at each other. It's enough.

Does she know that I know too?

"Platonic means . . . ," Jansdotter begins, but Stella brushes off her explanation.

"I know what platonic means," she says. "At least I think I know what you're getting at. Actually, though, Plato never meant that true spiritual love can't involve physical closeness and sex, but it's a very common misunderstanding, so don't feel stupid."

A man in the gallery laughs and the bearded man next to me gives me an encouraging smile.

"Plato is my favorite philosopher," Stella says.

"I've always preferred Socrates, myself," Jansdotter responds.

"That doesn't surprise me."

Michael hides a chuckle with one hand. The lay judges turn to each other and a small smile appears even on Presiding Judge Göran Leijon's lips.

"Amina didn't sleep with Chris Olsen," Stella says, and the merry atmosphere dies out as quickly as it appeared.

Jenny Jansdotter is about to formulate another question, but Stella isn't finished yet. She raises a hand. Her voice is thin and shaky.

"Amina never slept with anyone. She was . . . is . . . a virgin."

88

I dig through my handbag for a wet wipe. My heart is in my throat and the sweat keeps coming even though I dab incessantly at my forehead. It's as if the heat has forced its way into my brain and is making my thoughts boil.

Stella is slowly shrinking before my eyes. I don't know if it's an optical illusion or if her shoulders are dropping and her body is curling in on itself.

What are her motives? For eight interminable weeks, Stella has been locked up in jail with full restrictions.

Naturally she is doing this for Amina's sake. But that's not a sufficient explanation. There would have been other paths for Stella to take. Simpler paths. The only reasonable conclusion is that she is doing all of this, that she is sitting before me now with sunken shoulders and glassy eyes, not just for Amina but also for us. For Adam and me. For our family.

I have wished many a time that I too had had a friend like Amina. Ever since preschool she and Stella have been more or less inseparable. Certainly they have had their share of conflict and discord, but in the end their unshakeable solidarity has overcome every imaginable obstacle. At least until now.

I cannot imagine anything that could feel more secure than having an ally in life the way Stella and Amina have always had each other. Perhaps my life would have been different if I had been open to such an intimate friendship. To be sure, I had a few best friends in middle and high school, but even then I had begun to erect walls around the deepest parts of me. I have always considered it a weakness to show my emotions in front of other people.

I pat my forehead again and try to look poised. The bearded man beside me rustles a bag of candy and chews with his mouth open as the prosecutor presents the forensic evidence. A lab technician is called in and explains to the court that there can be no doubt that the shoe print discovered at the scene of the crime came from Stella's shoe. The print was found just a few feet from Christopher Olsen's body and there was a bit of blood spatter in it, which indicates that the print was made before Olsen was stabbed. Since there were rain showers on Friday morning, one can also draw the conclusion that the earliest Stella could have been at the playground was lunchtime on the day leading up to the murder.

When My Sennevall takes the stand, there is a change in the atmosphere. It's as if everyone is afraid that this frail girl, with her guarded gaze and unkempt hair, is about to go to pieces right in front of them. Both the prosecutor and Michael lower their voices when they pose questions. My Sennevall shoots paranoid glances around for some time before responding.

"You say you heard shouting at one o'clock," Michael says. "Can you describe how it sounded?"

My Sennevall looks at him for a long time.

"It sounded like someone was getting stabbed. He screamed several times, like someone was stabbing him with a knife."

Naturally, Michael questions her on this. How could she possibly know that the screams were coming from someone being stabbed?

"If he'd been shot I would have heard the gun," My Sennevall says.

The bearded journalist rolls his eyes.

"Would you like to tell us a little about your health?" Michael says. "Is it true that you see a psychiatrist regularly?"

I'm only listening with one ear as My Sennevall shares her sad life story. When she leaves the courtroom, she does so as an even more broken woman. The door sounds like it gives a sigh of relief as it closes behind her.

The testimonies that follow are quick and without sensation. Stella's colleagues from H&M, Malin and Sofie, confirm that Stella always has pepper spray in her purse, and that she had the purse with her that Friday night. The prosecutor displays a spray bottle and both witnesses verify that the one Stella owns is exactly the same.

The police technicians present the same spray bottle to the court and explain that, by way of chemical analysis, it has been confirmed that the traces of liquid found on Christopher Olsen's body are identical to the brand of pepper spray that Stella owned.

After this, correctional officer Jimmy Bark says that, during her time in jail, Stella has been violent on more than one occasion. Jimmy Bark gives a plainly unsympathetic impression, answering the questions briefly and nonchalantly, and I reflect that someone like him could likely provoke aggressive tendencies in the Dalai Lama.

The bearded journalist wrinkles his forehead during the correctional officer's testimony. Then, just like that, he holds out his bag of candy to offer me some. I'm so nonplussed that I take a caramel, even though I don't like them.

He smiles at me. Have I misjudged him?

I have always received other people with doubt. A healthy skepticism. All my life, I have dreaded appearing gullible. My father once said that only submissive dogs bare their throats to their adversaries. Only recently have I begun to understand that I don't need to consider other people adversaries.

During my time at law school, my entire existence was one big competition.

"I'm collecting As, not friends," I might say when turning down a social invitation.

It was as if I had built myself into a capsule, the shell of which grew harder every day. Every imperfection must be hidden by smarts and success, even as the fear that my true self would be revealed just kept growing. In spite of this, I often ended up in the spotlight at all sorts of gatherings. I had difficulty being in a situation without taking action, being an influencer. People were drawn to me and were eager to get to know me, but the only one who ever really understood me beyond arguments, exam points, and superficial mingling was Adam.

Now he's waiting outside the courtroom door. Very soon, it will be his turn. At any moment the clerk will call him in via the PA system. I am still uncertain about what will happen.

At first I didn't think it would work; didn't believe we would get this far. Adam has always been unyielding when it comes to his moral standards. The idea that he would lie to the police seemed remote, if not unthinkable. But I underestimated the significance of family. People are prepared to put aside everything in the way of ethics and morals to protect their families. The most rigid of principles can be easily pulverized when it comes to defending your own child. Lies, guilt, and secrets. What family isn't built on such grounds?

In the moment a person comes into the world, two other people are transformed into parents. The love for our children does not obey the rule of law.

Last night Adam and I sat in the kitchen with silence and a bottle of wine.

"I don't know if I can do it, honey."

I pray to God that he can do it. It feels odd, but I actually fold my hands and send up a prayer to God. An instant later, the clerk summons Adam into the courtroom.

89

Adam walks slowly through the room. He never takes his eyes from Stella as the presiding judge welcomes him and tells him where to sit.

He takes the witness's seat, his back to the gallery. The bearded man looks at me the way you look at someone who's critically ill.

Then the judge gives Michael the floor.

"Hello, Adam," he says. "I understand that this is incredibly hard for you, so I'll try to keep it brief. Can you begin by telling the court about your work?"

Adam still hasn't taken his eyes off Stella.

"I'm a pastor in the Church of Sweden."

At Michael's urging, he explains that he was a prison chaplain for many years but is now a pastor for one of the city's largest congregations.

His voice falters a bit.

"Can you briefly describe your relationship with Stella?" Michael asks.

Adam and Stella look at each other.

"I love Stella," Adam says. "She means everything to me."

My heart ties itself in a knot. More than once, over the years, I have reproached Adam for the state of my relationship with Stella. When she was little, I constantly heard about what a wonderful dad Adam was, and how lucky I was to have had a child with him. That was certainly true. Adam was and is a fantastic family man and I love him dearly for it. I am ashamed of the envy I have sometimes felt. Why did I react to my own failures with Stella by further distancing myself? I worked too much instead of dealing with our relationship, spending even more time on something I knew I was actually good at. I was clearly deceiving myself; it was a betrayal of Stella.

Next Michael asks for an account of Adam and Stella's relationship over the years.

"It hasn't always been perfect," Adam replies. "There have been ups and downs. At times it was very difficult."

Michael gives him a chance to elaborate and Adam hangs his head slightly.

"Nothing is as difficult as being a parent. Naturally I fell short many times. I had so many hopes and expectations about what it would be like. What sort of dad I would be; what sort of daughter Stella would be. What our relationship would be like."

"It didn't always turn out the way you'd hoped?" Michael says.

"I don't think the problem is how it turned out—more like what I had expected. I've had trouble accepting some of Stella's life choices. Sometimes you forget what it's like to be a teenager."

I look at the presiding judge. There's a flicker of understanding in Göran Leijon's expression. He knows. He has teenagers himself.

"Adam," Michael says, "can you tell us what happened on Friday the thirty-first of August?"

Adam turns his body to look at Stella again. I lean forward to catch a glimpse of his face.

Adam doesn't say anything. Why isn't he saying something?

Naturally I should have allowed him more into the loop, but I was terrified that he wouldn't understand or that his firm morals would stand in the way.

What if it's too late? If he changes his mind, if he takes it all back? That would be devastating.

"I worked pretty late that day," he says, drawing out the words.

His voice unsteady, he talks about the funeral of a young person. It had been a rough week, and by Friday Adam felt generally tired and run-down. After work he made dinner, after which we played games on the sofa and went to bed.

"Did you know where Stella was that night?" Michael asks, fingering the knot of his tie.

Adam's cheeks are pale.

"She had said she was going to meet up with a friend. Amina Bešić."

"Okay," Michael says calmly, "so you and your wife went to bed before Stella had arrived home?"

"That's correct."

"What time was it then?"

I sit up straight in my chair.

Please, Adam. Think of your family!

"Around eleven," he says. "I didn't actually check."

"Did you fall asleep right away?"

"No, I lay awake for a few hours."

"A few hours?"

"Yes."

I take a quick sip of water, but I fail to properly screw the lid back onto the bottle; water spills in my lap and I dry it with the back of my hand. The bearded man glances at me.

"Were you awake when Stella came home that night?" Michael asks.

I lean even further to the side. Adam raises his chin and his clerical collar shines white as innocence in the direction of the judges.

"I was awake when she came home," he says.

His voice is stronger now. Clear and firm. I sink back in my chair.

"Do you know what time it was?" Michael asks.

"It was quarter to twelve. I looked at the clock when I heard her come in."

One of the lay judges brings their hand to their mouth. The rest of the court stares at Adam in silence.

"And you're absolutely certain about the time?"

"I'm absolutely certain. I swear to God."

90

"How can you be so sure?" I asked Adam.

This was, of course, one of his hang-ups: he was always doubting. And right now, there was absolutely no room for nuance. He had made up his mind.

"It's going to be wonderful. You're going to be the most fantastic mother in the world."

He merely brushed off all my misgivings. According to Adam, my anxiety was a natural part of the process. Becoming a parent meant comprehensive adjustments that would change our lives forever. It was no wonder I was full of doubt and hesitation that made me feel ill.

In actuality we were too young to have a baby. I had just been assigned my post for my law clerk position, and Adam was in the middle of his program. Just six months earlier we had been living in the student dorm, spending several evenings a week hanging out at bars, low-key disco clubs, and fancy student dinners, but during the summer, against all odds, we had managed to come across a relatively spacious one-room apartment on Norra Fäladen. Furthermore, Adam was convinced that the rental agency would agree to upgrade us to a two-room place if there were to be an addition to our family.

"I love you," Adam said multiple times per day, bending down to kiss the growing bump of my belly. "And you too, in there."

Gradually the worst of my end-of-the-world mentality abated and my anxiety was exchanged for swollen elephant feet. Some days I couldn't get out of bed, and I felt like a huge failure of a woman.

Adam served me homemade soup, brought me compression stockings and warm rice pillows, and gave me massages. Although I questioned the timing, whether it was really the right moment for us to bring a child into the world, I never doubted that Adam was the right man to father my child.

I spent quite a lot of time working when Stella was little. Sometimes I wondered if there was something wrong with me, whether I was somehow constructed differently from other new mothers, because I couldn't put the rest of my life on standby and get all my strength from the fact that I was now the mother of a child.

Without Adam, it wouldn't have been possible. He was constantly there, a safe harbor where I could land. He never denied me anything. Adam supported me at any price.

I soon found that the successes I was denied in my family life could be won instead in my career. By the time I was twenty-nine I had become a full-fledged attorney, and, considered an up-and-comer, I was recruited to a major firm with offices in all three Swedish metro areas. As Adam taught Stella to ride her bike without training wheels and put Band-Aids on her skinned knees, I commuted between high-profile clients in Stockholm and quick briefs in front of kids' shows and a microwaved dinner plate. I hardly think I'm alone in saying that I craved stimulation from both career and family. Even though I happen to have been born without a penis.

Being a devoted mother always seemed to collide with my egotistical desire for self-affirmation and success in other parts of my life, and although I truly did try, I never managed to reduce myself enough to become the mother I was expected to be, the mother I believed I wanted to be. Meanwhile I saw men constantly getting away with the same shortcomings that plagued me and made me feel worthless as a parent.

At first, I considered the bond that developed between Adam and Stella to be entirely a good thing. Stella was Daddy's girl. I might come home late, my brain full of statutes and precedents, to find them cuddled up in a sea of pillows, having bedtime stories in pajamas. Stella held her Dad's hand through all of life's little forks in the road. It was an Astrid Lindgren world, and I felt tiny leaps of joy in my heart every morning when our daughter's miniature feet came romping across the bedroom floor.

———

The transformation happened very slowly. I can't say when it began, but things that had once warmed my heart were soon sending cold shivers down my spine. I found new triggers for irritation everywhere. When someone pointed out what a wonderful father Adam was and what a lovely relationship he seemed to have with Stella, I no longer experienced pride; rather, I felt alienated. When Adam related long, colorful descriptions of his fairy-tale days with Stella, I welled with guilt and shame and envy.

We spoke early on about expanding our family. I suppose our desire for another child was grounded in a vague disappointment that neither of us would ever have given voice to. Against all reason, I convinced myself that my relationship with Stella would benefit if she had a sibling.

We tried to conceive again for over a year. We never talked about why it didn't work. I suspect this was due to some sort of mutual but utterly misplaced respect. Sooner or later, the test would be positive and until then all we could do was try as often as we could manage, and, in Adam's case, perhaps also pray to God for some sort of aid.

On Walpurgis Night the year Stella was four, we finally broke the silence. We were lying in bed and the whole world spun as soon as I opened my eyes. The bonfire smell had penetrated our skin.

"Honey," Adam whispered. "Something must be wrong."

"Wrong?" I repeated, although I knew what he was talking about.

"What should we do?"

I couldn't produce a single word. Tears stung behind my eyelids, but I kept fighting them back.

"I love you," Adam said.

I was unable to respond.

91

"Does the prosecutor have any questions for the witness?" the presiding judge asks.

"Yes, I do."

Jenny Jansdotter confers briefly with the assistant prosecutor before turning to Adam.

"How was your state of mind on the Friday in question?"

I think I glimpse a shrug, but Adam doesn't have time to formulate a response before Jansdotter continues.

"You said earlier that you felt tired and worn out. It had been a tough week. You had just had to bury a young man."

"That's right."

"And yet you couldn't sleep that night?"

"Well, sometimes that sort of exhaustion has the opposite effect," Adam says calmly. "You can't fall asleep, even though you feel dead tired. I was also worried about Stella, of course. Terribly worried. I don't like going to sleep before she gets home."

Jenny Jansdotter picks up a pen and twirls it between her fingers.

"So you claim you were awake when Stella arrived home that night?"

"Yes."

"And what time was that?"

"I said that already."

"I'd like you to repeat it."

"Quarter to twelve," Adam says, annoyed.

Jenny Jansdotter tilts her chin up and juts her head out over the table like a bird of prey.

"Curious," she says.

There is an alarming hint of triumph in her voice.

"Very curious," Jansdotter says, unfolding a piece of paper on the table in front of her.

What is this? Is there something we missed?

"I have here a list of your text messages, Adam. Each text that was sent from your phone on the night of the murder, and each text you received, is included. Two messages were deleted from your phone, but the evidence technicians were able to recover them. I'm sure you are aware that deleted texts can be recovered?"

Adam bows his head.

Dammit, this cannot be true. How could Michael have missed the phone records? We knew the police had taken Adam's cell phone into evidence, but it never occurred to me that there could have been any compromising information on it.

"At eighteen minutes after eleven, the following text was sent from your phone to Stella's number: *Are you coming home tonight?*"

The prosecutor holds the list up and points with the tip of her pen.

"Okay?" Adam says.

"Do you recall sending such a text?"

His shoulders squirm and he looks thoroughly uncomfortable.

"Yes, I suppose I could have. My wife said Stella might be spending the night at Amina's. That's why I texted her to ask."

"*Are you coming home tonight?*" Jansdotter repeats. "Did you receive a response from Stella?"

Adam scratches his chin. I try to catch Michael's attention, but he refuses to look in my direction. Sweat is running down his face and he tugs at his tie as if he can't breathe.

"I don't remember," Adam mumbles.

"Are you sure? You don't remember whether you received an answer?"

Adam swallows hard and shakes his head rapidly.

"Probably not."

Jansdotter waves the list. Beside me, the bearded man sucks air through his teeth. I'm getting an inkling of where this is going. How could we have missed it?

"Stella did in fact send a reply," the prosecutor says.

"Oh?"

Adam just sits there as if waiting for a death blow. I want to shout at him to hold his ground—he can't give up now.

"The technicians have managed to recover that one as well. The fact is, you deleted both of these messages on Saturday, when you learned that Stella had been taken into police custody."

"I did?" Adam says.

He doesn't sound like he's very good at lying. No one is buying this.

"Stella wrote, *On my way home now.* The message was received by your phone at twenty minutes to two. When Stella had already, according to your story, been home for almost two hours."

92

Adam doesn't respond to the prosecutor's statement.

"Do you have any explanation for this text?" Jansdotter says. "Why would Stella send a text to say she's on her way home at twenty minutes to two when you claim she was home by eleven forty-five?"

Adam is silent. The seconds are ticking by.

A woman in the row behind mine tugs at my blouse and gestures at me to sit down. But I have to go to Adam. He needs me. This is all my fault!

"I'm sure there can be delays," Adam says at last.

The bearded man hisses *psst* at me and nods toward the end of the row, where a security guard has puffed up his chest and is staring at me.

"What do you mean, Adam?" Jenny Jansdotter says.

"Sometimes texts can get stuck out in cyberspace," he says, obvious doubt in his voice. "Just because I received a message at a certain point in time doesn't necessarily mean it was sent right then."

I sink down on my chair and a sigh of relief goes through my body. Naturally, Adam is right. He may not have a clue about all these technicalities, but he's smart and quick on his feet. Common sense would dictate that he's not wrong. The fact that the prosecutor has proof of when a text arrived means nothing in practice unless she can also prove when it was sent. And in order to do that she would need access to Stella's phone.

Jenny Jansdotter makes a pained face.

"Isn't it the case that Stella in fact came home much later than you claim?"

I sneak a look at the security guard and find that his interest in me has abated.

"No," Adam says firmly. "Stella came home at eleven forty-five."

Michael swipes the back of his hand over his sweaty forehead. Next to him, Stella is staring at the table with glassy eyes. She looks so small and fragile and I hate myself for what I am subjecting her to.

In the past few weeks, I have found myself explaining time and again to both myself and Michael why we can't tell Stella everything. I have felt my doubts gnawing at and burrowing into me, but it would be too risky to tell her. Stella has far too much trouble controlling her impulses. One too-strong emotion, one stray word, and that would be the end of it.

Furthermore, Stella has always loved being contrary. When her handball coaches told her to aim low she lobbed high instead; when Adam's mother admired her waist-length hair she shaved her head.

My chest fills with pain as I look at her.

"Do you know where Stella's cell phone is?" the prosecutor asks Adam.

"No idea."

"Why have the investigators been unable to locate it?"

"I don't know."

Adam's voice sounds calmer now.

"When did you last see Stella's phone?"

"I don't remember."

"Isn't it the case that you found it, Adam?"

"No," he says firmly. "Stella always has her phone with her."

"You mean she had it with her at work, at H&M, on that Saturday when she was taken into police custody?"

"I assume so."

"If that were true, the police would have found it, wouldn't they?"

Jansdotter stares him down, but doesn't manage to make him lose his cool.

"Isn't it true that you found Stella's phone on Saturday? The day she was brought in to jail."

"Absolutely not."

Adam jerks his head and glances over his shoulder; for a split second we look straight at one another.

"I don't know anything about Stella's phone," he repeats.

This is closer to the truth than the prosecutor suspects. Adam doesn't know what happened to Stella's phone. Only I do.

For a brief moment, the prosecutor loses her train of thought. She does a good job of hiding it, but it certainly doesn't escape me or the other experienced lawyers in the courtroom. I allow myself to relax ever so slightly; I lean back and take a few sips of water. The bearded man looks at me and I get the sense that he knows, that he can see right into my thoughts.

Once Jansdotter has collected herself and conferred with her assistant, she continues her examination.

"Did you speak to Stella when she returned home that Friday night?"

"Yes," Adam says. "As I've already stated."

"What did the two of you say?" the prosecutor asks.

"I opened the door and said goodnight. Stella said goodnight too."

"So you saw her?"

"Yes."

"What was she wearing?" Jansdotter asks.

"Underwear."

"Just underwear? Does she usually undress before going up to her room?"

"It happens, I guess. If her clothes need washing she puts them in the laundry room."

"According to Stella's colleagues, those who were with her at the Stortorget restaurant that night, Stella was wearing dark blue jeans and a white blouse. The police found the jeans when they searched the house, but the top hasn't been located. Did you see the white blouse when Stella came home?"

"No," Adam says. "I don't know anything about a blouse."

To some extent, this is true.

"Are you sure? You didn't see the white blouse in the laundry room?"

"No."

"On Saturday either?"

"Not that I can recall," Adam says. "But if I had seen it, I probably wouldn't have committed it to memory."

"I think you would have, actually," says Jansdotter. "Because I believe that blouse was covered in stains. From blood. You really didn't see the bloody blouse?"

"Definitely not!"

Now Adam is so firm that he sounds angry. That's not good. Not good at all. Michael sends him a small signal.

Jansdotter lunges again.

"You have a woodstove in the house?"

"Yes?" Adam says.

"During the search of your home, the police noted that a fire had recently been lit in the woodstove. Who lit the fire that Saturday?"

Adam scratches behind his ear.

"It could have been me. Or my wife."

He's smart. Obviously he understands what's happening here. All he has to do is keep a cool head. Think of your family, Adam. Think of Stella and me.

"You don't know?" Jansdotter asks.

"We have a fire pretty often."

"In the summer? The first days of September? When it's seventy degrees outside?"

"We think it's cozy."

The prosecutor sighs loudly.

"Isn't it true that you found Stella's bloody blouse and burned it in the woodstove?"

"Absolutely not," Adam says. "I did not burn any blouse."

No, he didn't.

93

When the presiding judge concludes the first day of proceedings, I stand up and manage to catch Stella's eye before the guards take her away. We look at each other for a second or two. I reach out my hand; it fumbles in the air. This is the moment when I must be a real mother; I must compensate for what I never managed to do when Stella was little. This time I'm doing what I'm best at. Please, Stella, you have to trust me.

In the past few years, our relationship has slowly improved. While Adam found it increasingly difficult to understand Stella's various life choices, I have become closer to her; I have come to understand my daughter better and better. To some extent I have Amina to thank. It was through her that I was finally able to meet Stella on her own terms. Through Amina, I learned to understand.

Naturally, it has pained me to find that I have an easier time talking to Amina than to Stella. That guilt has constantly lain at the bottom of my soul like a heavy layer of sludge. At times when I found it impossible to make sense of Stella's actions, reasoning, and motives, I have seen my own driving forces reflected in Amina.

"Stella's not like you and me," she once said. "Stella's just Stella."

This was soon after Stella quit handball. One day she was at a gathering with the national youth team, where she was predicted to have a dazzling future; the next she was putting her handball shoes up for sale online. Adam and I were befuddled.

"You can't understand Stella unless you start to think like Stella," Amina said.

It sounds so simple, so obvious—and yet it's not.

"Stella can't deal with other people trying to control her," Amina said. "At this level, handball is so much about running preplanned plays, stuff we've practiced over and over. Stella can't handle that."

I think Adam was the one who suffered most for never having more children. He has his crosses to bear. He bashed himself bloody, trying to force Stella to live up to our expectations instead of accepting her for who she is. It's a wonder our family didn't crumble to pieces. I try to see what is currently happening as a chance to start over, a new opportunity I intend to seize at any price.

"Why can't you be more like Amina?" I once said when Stella had gone off the rails, turning the world around her upside down for the umpteenth time in a row.

For once she had no withering response. She just fell silent. She looked at me, and although her eyes were perfectly dry, it was as if she were crying.

She knew what I meant, of course. The words just slipped out of me—only one time, never again—but Stella saw right through me. She saw the way I looked at Amina, the way I talked to her, how we shared something.

I caught Stella up in my arms and cried on her shoulder.

"I'm sorry, sweetie, I'm sorry. I didn't mean it like that."

It was pointless, of course. We both knew exactly what I meant.

As I walk out of the courtroom, Adam is nowhere in sight. The benches in the lobby are occupied by strangers. I take a few steps down the hallway, but there's no Adam.

Where is he?

Just a moment ago he was sitting in court, swearing before God that his daughter was at home when that man lay bleeding to death on a playground in another part of the city.

He has to be on the verge of a breakdown.

My heart pounds and I take a few long strides into the next hallway. I find him outside the bathrooms. He's hunched on a bench, looking as if every bone in his body is broken.

"Honey," I whisper, "I'm so proud of you."

I put my arm around him. His body feels hard and cold. I cautiously lean against his shoulder and a gentle warmth branches through my chest. Stella and Amina aren't the only ones I'm doing this for.

"What if it doesn't help?" His gaze is a desperate plea. "What have I done?"

I stroke his nape, his back.

"I'm here," I whisper. "We're together."

It's not much, but it's the best comfort I have to offer. During these past weeks I have always thought I understood his agonized suffering; I have equated it with my own anguish. Just as Adam has violated the ethics of his profession, I have gone against everything I believed in. The law has been my religion. It certainly has its faults, rather extensive ones in some respects, but still I firmly believed the law to be the pillar and guiding light of a modern society. I believed the law to be the optimal means to regulate a democratic society. Now I don't know what to believe. Some values are impossible to explain or to measure in statutes. And just as with life, the law has no regard for what ordinary people call justice.

When I look at Adam, I understand that this must be taking a greater toll on him than on me. In the worst-case scenario, he himself will face charges: trespassing, violence against a public officer, unlawful influence.

At last we stand up. I keep my arm tightly around his waist all the way through the courthouse, past the reception desk, and out to the steps.

"You did the right thing, honey," I say. "Tomorrow it's Amina's turn."

We take a taxi home and Adam grills me about everything that happened in the courtroom prior to his testimony. When I tell him about the footprint and the analysis of the pepper spray, an expression of concern appears on his face.

"But there's no concrete evidence," he says.

"It's up to the court to evaluate the evidence. In a case based on circumstantial evidence like this one is, one cannot judge each piece of evidence individually; one must look at the whole picture. After that, the court will test the prosecutor's narrative of the crime against alternate hypotheses. If it's not possible to rule out other explanations, there is reasonable doubt and the court must acquit."

"Aren't there always other explanations?"

"Typically the minimum requirements are that the defendant was at the scene of the crime, the person in question had the opportunity to commit the crime, and that other potential perpetrators can be ruled out."

Adam gazes out the window and I take out my phone to see what the newspapers are reporting. *Sydsvenskan* and *Skånskan* have brief pieces on the first day of trial but haven't said much. *Aftonbladet's* crime section bears the headline "Father Squeezed Hard by Prosecutor." The article is full of insinuations that question Adam's testimony. *One hundred years ago it would have been completely unthinkable for a pastor to lie in court, but after today's proceedings in Lund County Court there is every reason to wonder if this is still the case.* I can hardly believe my eyes. Under no circumstances can I allow Adam to read this. At the top of the page is a byline and a photo of the writer. It's the bearded man I've been sitting next to all day.

The taxi turns onto our street. A few neighbors are standing in a tight clump, looking in our direction.

"Have a good night," the driver says as I pay.

"Mmhmm."

I walk around the car and take Adam by the hand. Neither of us looks at the neighbors.

In the entryway, Adam goes stiff.

"Was it . . . was she the one who did it?"

I don't like lying to him. Just one last time.

"I don't know, honey."

94

The courtroom is my home and my fortress. I have almost spent more hours in various courtrooms than at home with my family. But I have never felt this lost and exposed here, choked with anguish, tormented by regret.

Adam stays close by my side as we walk through the courthouse hallway. At first, as we enter the courtroom, I only see strange faces among the spectators. Journalists, I assume, perhaps a curious onlooker from the so-called general public. I look for the bearded reporter, but he's nowhere in sight. Perhaps *Aftonbladet* sent someone else today? Christopher Olsen's suit-clad business acquaintances, at least, form the same phalanx as yesterday. They're whispering loudly. Apparently a few of them were investigated for their involvement in the massive ring of shady business deals and illegal labor Michael uncovered.

In the back row of the gallery, I spot a familiar face. Alexandra has just bent down to take something from her purse, and her bangs have fallen over her eyes.

My eyes dart back and forth for a moment. Then Alexandra brushes her hair away and looks at me. We exchange brief nods and I exhale when I realize Dino isn't here.

I've always thought well of Alexandra. In many ways I see myself in her. A strong woman with a successful career and a relaxed outlook on life. Good food, a few glasses of better wine, and a good laugh in the company of friends have united us. At the same time, I can't deny that I have envied her at times, when I have seen how easy Amina is—there have been moments I wished we could change places.

———

The clerk calls in the day's first witness and the door opens.

Amina walks straight to the witness's seat and sits down without raising her eyes even once. She is pale and without makeup; her cheeks have become slightly sunken over the past few weeks.

Michael glances anxiously in my direction.

"Do you understand what it means to act as a witness?" Göran Leijon asks.

Amina nods and whispers, "Yes."

Then she repeats after Leijon.

"I, Amina Bešić, swear and affirm on my honor and conscience that I will tell the whole truth and nothing but the truth."

I put a hand to my chest and concentrate on breathing. Unease is eating its way through my body. A horrific sense of looming catastrophe forces me up against the back of my seat.

"We'll begin with questions from the defense attorney," says Göran Leijon.

This is it.

Michael speaks slowly and gently. Next to him, Stella has raised her chin and is looking straight at Amina. It's been several weeks since they last saw each other.

"Can you start by telling us how you and Stella know one another?" Michael asks.

Amina looks down at the table.

"We've been best friends since preschool. We were in the same class from first through ninth grades and we were on the same handball team."

There's a burning sensation in my chest. In my mind, I picture the two girls.

"How would you describe your relationship today?" Michael asks.

Amina continues to stare at the table. Time passes, and I can sense Michael's growing doubt.

"She's still my best friend."

Michael nods. In the ensuing silence, I glimpse a cautious light in Stella's eyes. What has she been thinking? What did she assume was going on? If it had been up to Amina, we never would have left Stella alone in that prison of thought and anguish. It was my decision, what we did, and I'm the one whom Stella will have to hold accountable—whatever happens.

"How would you describe Stella's personality?" Michael asks.

"Well, she . . . she's just the way she is. She's *Stella,* there's no one else like her."

I can't help but smile. In the midst of all of this, I'm actually sitting there with a smile on my face.

"She's really brave. She always says what she thinks and does what *she* wants to do. Peer pressure—it's like she's never even heard of it."

The two best friends look at each other. The bonds that link Stella and Amina are stronger than anyone in this courtroom could imagine.

"And she's really smart, too," Amina says. "Not everyone gets that until they truly get to know her. And she's easily the most stubborn person I know. Very impulsive and forward. A go-getter. Some people think she's too much. I think Stella's the kind of person you either love or hate."

Michael is just about to ask the next question when Amina interrupts him.

"And I love her."

Her voice cracks and she buries her face in her hands. Giant tears run down her cheeks. There's a lump in my throat. Even Michael seems moved.

"Can you tell us a little about Christopher Olsen?" he says. "How did the two of you get to know him?"

Amina looks at Stella. My heart is pounding at my chest; sweat makes my underarms sticky. It feels horrible, no longer being able to influence what's happening. Now I have to trust in Amina. Now everything is in her hands.

95

"Tell us about Christopher Olsen," Michael says. "How did you two get to know him?"

He pushes a box of tissues across the table and Amina dries her cheeks.

"We met Chris at Tegnérs one night."

I sneak a look at Adam, who appears deep in concentration. I'm terrified about what's coming.

Amina tells the same story Stella did yesterday. The girls saw Christopher Olsen a few times, both out and about and at Olsen's residence, but that was it.

"Would you say that Stella and Christopher Olsen were a couple?" Michael asks.

"Definitely not. Stella and Chris messed around a little, that's all."

Michael nods.

"Would you like to elaborate? Did they have a sexual relationship?"

"They had sex, but it wasn't a relationship."

Amina sounds confident and convincing.

"Yesterday we heard allegations that Stella sometimes acted violently. Is that true? Have you ever felt that she has been violent?"

Amina draws up her shoulders. My heart leaps.

I don't understand why Michael is asking this question. To forestall the prosecutor?

"No," Amina says.

But she doesn't sound nearly as convincing anymore.

Michael wipes the sweat from his brow.

"Does the defense have any further questions?" Göran Leijon asks.

"No, thank you."

"Then I give the floor to the prosecution."

I bring my hand to my heart. I can't feel my heartbeat anymore. Adam is looking at me, wide-eyed.

Jenny Jansdotter takes her time. She does it on purpose—it's a technique to throw Amina off balance. She places documents in stacks before her, meticulously straightening their edges, and stretches slowly.

Michael and Stella observe her in suspense.

When I found Stella's cell phone on her desk that Saturday, I was immediately struck with desperate alarm. How could she have forgotten her phone at home?

I've actually never been the type to snoop. Gossip and juicy secrets seldom interest me. I'm someone who finds appeal in cold, hard facts and reliable proof. If anyone was spying on Stella, and to a certain extent even infringing on her right to a private life, it was Adam. I don't know what would have happened if he had been the one to find her phone.

As the hours passed and we didn't hear from her, I decided to go through the phone. It wasn't to snoop. I was beside myself with worry. And when I read the messages, it dawned on me that something really had happened, something truly terrible. I immediately attempted to contact Amina, but she refused to speak to me. She had closed herself up in her room, claiming to be too sick to talk. I knew she was lying.

Now she is sitting before the prosecutor, testifying under oath. Jansdotter's voice is sharp as a scalpel, and Amina recoils.

"What do you mean when you say that Christopher Olsen and Stella were not a couple?"

"I . . . I mean exactly that. They weren't a couple."

"Can you define their relationship? Describe who they were to each other?"

Amina looks at Stella, as if she's asking permission.

"According to Stella, Chris was a summer fling."

"And what did you think about that?" Jansdotter asks.

"About what?"

"About the situation. That Stella was having a sexual relationship with Christopher Olsen, even though she wasn't seriously interested in him."

Amina bows her head. The seconds tick by in silence.

"How did you really feel about Christopher?" Jansdotter asks.

"I liked Chris. He was charming and cool. It was fun to spend time with him."

"Were you attracted to him?"

"Maybe."

I look at Stella. Her expression is vacant. What thoughts are going through her head right now? I don't even know how much she knows.

I feel sick. What kind of mother puts her child through this? There must be something seriously wrong with me. An emotional dysfunction? Some sort of failure to bond? I view myself from the outside and see a person I don't want to be.

Would I have done the same if the roles were switched, if Amina were the one in jail? I'm far from certain. Presumably I would have just let Amina decide from the start. I should have listened to her. We should have done as she suggested. Now it's too late.

Jenny Jansdotter squeezes Amina with her gaze.

"Did anything sexual happen between you and Christopher Olsen?" she asks.

Amina's shoulders slump.

Everything is spinning, going blurry.

"Yes," Amina says. "Things happened."

96

It became clear to us early on that Stella liked to be in charge. She often played Adam and me against each other. The first to capitulate was showered with love, while the other wasn't worth a fig. It could turn on a dime—one second you were the best mom in the world; the next, a pariah for who knew how long.

Happily, Amina was always present as a neutralizing force, an intermediary between our obstreperous daughter and the rest of the world.

Handball, too, functioned as a way for Stella to vent. On the court she had an outlet for all the energy bubbling and fermenting insider her; her pigheadedness and explosive nature were enormous assets on the six-meter line.

Handball was good for Adam too. As a pair, he and Dino became well-liked coaches who soon attained great success with their team. It often seemed as if Adam forgot himself on the sidelines of a sizzling match. He was thoroughly consumed by the game—the shouting, cheering, and gesticulating.

One Saturday a few years ago, as I sat in the bleachers at Borgeby watching Stella pelt in goal after goal, I experienced something that still affects me. My thoughts had wandered off, but suddenly Amina was lying on the court and writhing in pain—I had completely missed whatever had caused her injury. But since Alexandra wasn't there, it seemed natural that I should be the one to trot down to the court and prop Amina up as we went to the locker room.

"Do we need to go get you checked out at the hospital?" I asked.

We were sitting across from each other on the benches, looking down at her hastily bandaged knee.

She shook her head.

"I just can't do this anymore."

She sounded utterly resigned.

"Do what?" I said.

"Swear you won't say anything to Dad! He would never understand. Neither would Mom! Promise?"

Unaware of what I was doing, I gave her my word.

"Didn't you see I messed up the defense? Two times, the exact same feint?"

I had to confess that I hadn't noticed anything.

"And then I fumbled that last pass to Stella. You saw that, didn't you?"

"But you're ahead twelve to four," I objected.

"Dad doesn't care about that," Amina said, staring down at the floor as she unwound the bandage from her knee with a few hasty movements. "I can't handle being the best all the time. I just can't deal with it."

This struck a painful chord. I thought of how I had spent a whole life toiling away to keep from being a disappointment to others.

"It's only handball," I said. "It doesn't mean a damn thing. Not really."

"But it's not just handball." She gazed at me with glassy eyes. "It's everything. School, friends, at home. I can't do it anymore."

Without thinking it over, I moved to sit beside her and opened my arms. Amina curled up like a small child and I rocked her slowly back and forth.

I had such powerful feelings for Amina, and I wasn't sure how to act upon them.

Several years later, on a hellish Sunday in early September, I was faced with the impossible choice between Amina and my own daughter, and I chose both of them.

I'm afraid that choice may cost me everything.

97

Jenny Jansdotter patiently waits for Amina to speak. The entire courtroom is waiting for Amina. She is about to reveal everything.

"One night when we were at Tegnérs, I think it was in the middle of August, Stella got a headache and left early. I ended up going home with Chris."

She takes a long pause and looks at Stella.

"We were really just supposed to share a taxi, but . . . we'd had quite a bit to drink, and . . ."

Amina swallows the last word and hangs her head. Stella looks at her in confusion.

"We sat on his sofa, chatting. I'd had too much to drink. It just happened."

Stella glowers at her best friend, who is speaking down at the table.

"What happened?" Jansdotter asks.

"He tried to kiss me."

"And what did you do?"

This is painful. Stella and Amina mean so much to each other. Can their friendship survive this?

"I let him do it." Amina's voice is faint. "He kissed me several times, until I panicked and said I had to leave. I ran out of there and on the way home I called Stella."

"Did you tell Stella about the kissing?"

"No. I was going to, but then . . . I couldn't."

Stella slowly brings her glass of water to her lips and lets it hover in the air for a moment before taking a sip. Jansdotter is rolling her pen between her fingers.

"Did you see Chris again after this?"

"He called me, like, a week later. We were supposed to plan a surprise for Stella, because it was her birthday. So Chris picked me up in his car and we brought sushi back to his apartment."

She stops, her hand to her forehead.

"Go on," Jansdotter urges her. "What happened at his apartment?"

"He kissed me again."

I watch Stella deflate and recall how we hugged that night, after her birthday dinner. Only recently have we begun to embrace each other that way. Naturally and sincerely. Adam was snoring on the sofa, his mouth wide open, and we were careful not to wake him. Stella sniffled out a brief account of what had happened after she left the Italian restaurant. And that was when it hit me. While I am far from a relationship expert, I figured out what Stella herself refused to see. The more she told me, the clearer it became. She'd had her heart broken. She was in love and had been betrayed.

"What did you and Christopher talk about that night?" the prosecutor asks Amina. "While you were alone?"

Amina sighs deeply.

"Chris said he liked me. I'm the one he noticed first at Tegnérs. He said he liked Stella too, but not the same way. He had begun to see her downsides. He realized that there would be problems, but he said you can't help your feelings."

Stella is twisting her hands, around and around. I long to give her a hug.

"Did you believe him?"

"He was very convincing," Amina says. "And I knew Stella wasn't interested in him anyway. Not that it matters, but still."

"So you betrayed your best friend?"

Amina sobs and shakes her head.

"I mean, I was, like, in love. Or . . . I thought I was."

I take Adam's hand and see the confusion in his eyes. Around us, a symphony of scratching pens and tapping keys. I glance quickly over my shoulder at Alexandra. She has mascara on her cheeks and fear in her eyes.

"Didn't you ever see Stella that night?" Jansdotter asks. "You said you were going to celebrate her birthday."

"Yes, she called. It was pretty late. She said she was on her way to Chris's place. I seriously panicked and shouted at Chris that Stella was out on the street and then I rushed down to see her."

"Did you tell Stella what had happened?"

Amina sighed.

"I told her that Chris had kissed me. I honestly regretted it, I felt totally worthless, and then we agreed that Chris was a pig and we would never see him again."

"Did you stick to that agreement?" the prosecutor asks.

Amina turns to look at Stella.

"No," she says. "I didn't."

98

I expect it's easiest to hang your concerns on something concrete. When you can't find the root of the problem, when whatever is making you itch and chafe can't be seen, it's extremely convenient to be able to focus on something tangible.

Is that why people turn to God? A world that's impossible to understand demands explanations one can comprehend. An image of a man, an absolute ruler.

For a long time, my and Adam's view of the world revolved around a child who never arrived. The egg that would not be fertilized became the emblem of our stalled life, which would never transform into the life we had imagined. As the distance between us widened, I experienced a desire for spiritual closeness I didn't recognize. It was at its worst when I had just concluded a case. It was as if a vacuum opened up inside me, a bottomless loneliness. I would sit on a plane, heading home to my family in Lund, feeling my insides come crashing down.

It's a dreadful experience, being unable to identify with your own child. I often felt powerless and resigned about my attempts to reach Stella.

"She's like you," Adam said after a fight that lasted a whole evening.

"What the hell do you mean?"

It started when we learned from Stella's teacher that she was bullying a few girls in her class. When we confronted her, Stella threw a tantrum and hurled a glass of milk at Adam. She refused to discuss the situation at school. We wanted to know how she was truly feeling, but she went berserk all over the kitchen and Adam had to pin her arms behind her back until she was hanging over the floor like a wrung-out rag of screaming and tears.

Two days later, Amina was standing in our entryway in her handball shoes and knee socks, a burgundy backpack on her shoulders. As Stella slipped away to gather what she needed for practice, Amina looked at me with a grave expression that made her seem much older.

"It's really not Stella's fault," she said.

I looked at her, puzzled.

"What's going on at school, I mean. They provoke Stella. They know exactly what to say to get her to flip out. Then they tattle to the teacher."

A mountain of shame rose in my chest.

"It's the other girls who are the mean ones," Amina said.

Her brown eyes looked almost black in the dim light of the entryway.

I thought of what Adam had said. *She's like you.*

The summer Stella would turn fourteen, we traveled to a handball tournament in Denmark. The girls and the coaches had lodgings in a school, while Alexandra and I shared a hotel room.

One evening we went out to a smoky bar and people bought drinks for us. Alexandra got way too drunk and threw up outside the hotel. After I'd forced a shower on her, she lay down on a chaise in the hotel room and cried over how worthless her life was. She wailed about Dino, who only cared about handball and refused to lift a finger at home. But she also complained about Amina, who never had time for anything besides schoolwork and her goddamn handball practice. I didn't say anything, of course, but a thorny irritation began to grow inside me. I personally never had the privilege of feeling that my parents were completely satisfied with me. There was always an even higher grade, someone else who did better, someone smarter and more attractive.

A few weeks later, on a sunny morning, Amina came to our house. For once I was managing to relax—I was in the yard with a coffee and a novel.

"Stella's not home," I explained. "She went to Landskrona. I thought you were going too."

Amina didn't respond. She stood there in her shorts and tank top, under the cherry tree, gazing at me with a grim expression.

"Is something wrong?" I asked, putting down my book.

She gestured as if to say she wasn't quite sure.

"Do you have a minute?" she asked.

"Of course!"

Once I'd brought out soda and a cinnamon roll, she began to appear more comfortable.

"I feel like the worst friend in the world right now."

"Why? What's going on?"

She squinted across the yard and told me in a restrained voice that she had put this off until the last moment. She really didn't want to be a bad friend, but fear had taken over. She was worried about Stella.

"Those guys she's with in Landskrona. They're not good people. They get up to a bunch of bad stuff. Smoking and drinking."

"Alcohol? You're only fourteen."

"I know."

"I'm glad you told me, Amina."

She bent forward.

"You promise not to say anything to Stella, right? If she finds out I . . . You have to promise me!"

I promised.

I wasn't really thinking about Stella very much at that moment, however strange that may sound. I was mostly thinking of Amina. I admired her courage, her natural instinct to do the right thing.

"I'm so glad you came to me," I said.

We stood facing each other for a long time before she leaned forward and hugged me.

During the week that followed, Adam and I had a serious talk with Stella. It was the start of a long, horrible period for us. The more we tried to reason with her, the more Stella lashed out.

"Stop interfering in my life! Living with you is like being in prison!"

Later that fall, when it came to light that Stella was smoking dope, Adam and I realized after a lot of "ifs" and "buts" that we needed professional help.

It was torture to sit through those meetings with principals and teachers, nurses and counselors—not to mention all the social workers and psychologists. I have never felt so vulnerable and violated, so belittled as a person. No failure in the world is comparable to being an inadequate parent.

Michael Blomberg offered a way out, a bit of solace.

99

I turn around to look at Alexandra again. I see my own mother in her. My stomach knots as I think of how ungrateful she has been toward Amina.

Alexandra meets my gaze. So far, she still doesn't know. I'm sure Amina hasn't said anything.

Ever since she told me what happened, I've taken pains to ensure that as few people as possible find out.

Not even Adam knows. Not even Stella.

In time, they will all understand.

Jenny Jansdotter's sharp treble rips a hole in the silence of the courtroom.

"So you violated your agreement with Stella and continued to see Christopher Olsen?"

Amina shakes her head.

"That's not quite what happened."

The prosecutor makes a baffled expression.

"No? Isn't that what you just said?"

"I only saw Chris once after Stella's birthday. He contacted me several times that week, but I told him we couldn't see each other. He was really persistent. He wrote that he was so curious about me and it would be a waste not to explore what might happen between us. And stuff like that."

"So you agreed to meet him?"

"I was honestly planning to tell him to go to hell. I didn't meet up with him because I wanted us to be together or anything. I just wanted to get rid of him. I swear."

She takes another tissue and blows her nose.

"On Friday he texted me again. I'd made an agreement with Stella. I didn't want to see Chris again."

"But you did?"

"He wrote that he had a surprise for me," she continues. "He was going to pick me up in a limo. I told him my dad would beat him up if he showed up at our house. But anyway . . . he wouldn't give up, so we decided he would pick me up at the Ball House after handball."

"Did he arrive in a limousine?"

"No, he had his own car. Something got messed up with the reservation."

Stella is watching Amina intently. How much of this does she know?

"And this was on the thirty-first of August, the same night Christopher Olsen was murdered?" Jansdotter asks.

"Yes."

"What did the two of you do then, Amina? After Chris picked you up in his car?"

"We drove out to the sea. I don't know exactly what the place is called. But you could see Barsebäck from there, anyway. The nuclear power plant. We sat on a grassy hill and Chris had brought a basket with wine and bread and a bunch of cheeses."

Amina falls silent.

"Go on," says the prosecutor.

"We ate and drank the wine. We watched the sunset and then . . ."

Amina loses herself again. A journalist in the row ahead of me drops their pen and the whole courtroom hears it land on the floor. Stella whirls around and stares. She looks straight at me, her eyes black.

"Then what?" Jansdotter says. "What happened next?"

I watch as Michael places a reassuring hand on Stella's arm.

"Then he kissed me." Amina gulps. "We kissed."

100

The chance to work with Michael Blomberg was a dream. One of the country's most prominent defense attorneys. I knew it would involve a lot of business trips and nights in hotels, but Adam supported me wholeheartedly and it was a chance I couldn't pass up.

What would have happened if I'd declined Michael's offer? I know there's no point in such thoughts, but it's hard to stop myself from wondering.

As Amina talks about Christopher Olsen in the courtroom—how she couldn't resist him, how she was swept up and felt like she was falling for him, even though in reality something totally different was going on—it's hard not to relate.

Maybe sometimes all it takes to believe you're in love is being appreciated and valued. Being seen for who you are, admired for your existence rather than your actions. That's exactly what made me fall for Adam. His natural way of looking beyond my accomplishments. The way he captured my soul with his gaze.

Fifteen years later, Michael Blomberg did the same thing.

My relationship with Michael went hand in hand with my increasing inability to deal with Adam. The man I had once fallen for, the romantic idealist with a heart the size of a star and eyes full of nuance no longer seemed to exist. I hadn't been present enough to know how it had happened, but Adam had gradually developed a neurotic temperament that was well on its way to turning into a manic need for control.

Adam had imagined an entirely different life for himself than what he was now stuck with. The images he had created of his future and his family were diametrically opposed to reality, and his increasing need for control was, in that sense, nothing more than a desperate but potent method of maintaining his dream of the life he had pictured for himself. But just because I understood what had happened didn't mean I had any intention of accepting it.

Adam crossed the line one night when he forced his way into Stella's room after smelling smoke through the door. I had just flown in from Bromma on the last flight of the day, and I landed in our kitchen around midnight, a total wreck.

"You have to let Stella make her own mistakes. Weren't you ever a teenager? You are violating her privacy."

Adam was pacing back and forth, muttering in despair. When I saw him in that state, I made up my mind.

"I love you," I said, putting my arms around his neck. "I'm going to spend more time at home with both of you."

"I'm sorry," said Adam. "It's all my fault. You don't have to . . ."

I battled back my guilt.

"I've been working too much," I said, promising to decrease my hours. "There are things I can take care of from home."

"I have to try to calm down," Adam said. "To talk to Stella without losing my temper."

"Count to ten first."

He smiled and we kissed.

On Monday I sat down with my phone as soon as Adam had left for work. Naturally, I was flattered by Michael's attention, but I had never fooled myself into thinking that it would lead to anything but brief moments of self-fulfillment. I knew Michael well enough to understand that we would hardly have a future together, or even anything exclusive.

He sounded neither surprised nor disappointed when I called to tell him that from that point on, our relationship must be kept strictly professional. I have to confess that my heart ached when he ended both the conversation and the relationship with the phrase "no problem."

As I hung up, I collapsed on the kitchen table. A dam was crumbling down. My tears were a cleansing bath as the drawn-out tension was finally released. I never noticed Stella walking in. Suddenly I just felt her hand on my shoulder.

"Who was that?" she asked.

"God, you scared me! How long have you been standing there?"

Stella stared at me.

I knew she had heard everything.

"It's not what you think. It was work. That was Michael, my boss."

I reached for her, but she turned on her heel and walked back through the hall and out the door. I ran after her, my heart in my throat, and just as she took her first step down the stairs I threw my arms around her from behind and pulled her close.

"I love you, Stella."

We held each other for a long time, and as sad as it sounds, I hadn't felt so close to my daughter for years. I was bubbling with grand words and promises, but I couldn't manage to produce a sound. And in that moment, all we needed was to be close.

A few months later, I left Michael Blomberg's firm for a different job closer to home. Things slowly improved between Adam and me, and Stella seemed more well-adjusted. She and Amina soon found their way back to one another, and I started to think of what had happened as a phase, a rough patch—sure, it may have come close to breaking us, but we had made it through and in the long run, with any luck, it would make our family stronger.

Little did I know that the real catastrophe was waiting around the corner.

101

Prosecutor Jansdotter twirls her pen as she waits for Amina to blow her nose yet again.

"So you went down to the beach with Chris Olsen and you kissed again?"

"Although I was starting to have doubts," Amina says. "I felt horrible about what I was doing."

"And this was the same night Chris Olsen died? What time could it have been?"

Amina shrugs.

"Stella means the world to me," she says, as if she didn't hear the prosecutor's question. "I'd never let a guy come between us."

"But you kissed him?" Jansdotter says. "What time was this?"

"I regretted it right away. It was like I was watching it all from outside myself, almost like it was a movie. I realized what I was doing and told Chris to stop."

Jansdotter interrupts her.

"You have been questioned by the police twice, Amina. Why didn't you mention any of this? During the interrogations you consistently stated that you never saw Christopher Olsen at all after Stella's birthday."

"I couldn't bear to explain. I thought Stella would be released anyway."

I scrutinize the lay judges. The Sweden Democrat has leaned back slightly and pushed out his belly as if he's just eaten a large dinner. My immediate sense is that he's already made up his mind. Next to him, the women are hunched toward each other, whispering.

Jenny Jansdotter sounds honestly curious as she asks the next question.

"Why would we believe you now, Amina? You've had many opportunities to tell the police what happened."

I slip my hand into Adam's, but I don't have the courage to look at him.

"He didn't stop," Amina says. "I kept telling him to stop."

Jansdotter drops her pen, but her fingers keep twirling as if she hasn't noticed.

"He just kept going," Amina says.

The prosecutor is gaping. Now it's dawning on her. She opens her mouth several times, trying to say something, but she seems to keep drawing a blank and starting over.

"I told him I didn't want to," Amina says. "I screamed at him."

"Why didn't you mention this during the police interrogation?" the prosecutor asks.

The words come in starts.

"I—was—a virgin."

Jansdotter falls silent.

"I tried to shove him away, but I couldn't. He pushed my arms to the ground. I couldn't . . . I struggled and clawed and screamed, but I couldn't get away."

I release Adam's hand, then turn around and look at Alexandra again. It's enough to drive away any lingering doubt. I am now sure that this is the right thing to do. We couldn't have done it any other way. There is no justice anyway.

Amina has to fight for her voice to hold out. She takes a sip of water and clears her throat.

Then she looks straight at the presiding judge.

"Christopher Olsen raped me."

102

In reality, it was an idiotic idea from the start. Stella's attitude toward the church was overtly hostile. What business would she have at a confirmation camp?

"I think it would be good for her," said Adam. "She might feel left out if she doesn't go."

"Amina's not going either," I pointed out.

"But she's Muslim."

"Her dad is Muslim. And Stella's an atheist."

I wish I had stood my ground. This terrible regret I have had to live with. Why did I let her go?

Adam had finally started loosening the reins and becoming gradually more permissive and sensible in his relationship with Stella, and I wasn't eager to cause a setback. So despite my misgivings, I gave in and, when I saw the joy on Stella's face, I thought I had made the right decision.

Later, when Adam called from camp and tried to explain what had happened, what that pig had done to our little girl . . . At first I couldn't put it all together. I had just arrived on the evening flight from Stockholm.

"You're at the confirmation camp? What are you doing there?"

Adam rambled something about responsibility and how the reason didn't matter right now.

"Do you realize what has happened?" he shouted through the phone. "Stella was raped."

My head was spinning. The phone trembled against my ear.

"You have to call the police. Take her to the hospital, Adam."

His response was evasive.

"Adam! It's crucial that she be examined by a doctor."

"We'll talk about it later. We're on our way home now."

I was sitting at the kitchen table when the car sped into the driveway. I ran out; my head was about to burst.

Stella landed in my embrace and I carried her into the house as if she were five years old again. She sat in the kitchen, paralyzed, her face devoid of emotion.

I cried and hammered my fists against Adam's chest.

"How could this happen?"

"Calm down," Adam said, holding my arms tight.

"Why didn't you call the police? Why did you come home?"

He didn't want to look at me.

"What were you doing there? Were you spying on Stella?"

"It's my job."

"Your job?" He hadn't said a word about visiting the camp. "I'm calling the police."

I pulled my phone from its case, but Adam grabbed it from me.

"Hold on! It's not as simple as you think."

"What do you mean, it's not simple?"

He glanced at Stella and gestured at me to follow him into the hall. He lowered his voice.

"Stella went with Robin to the counselors' cabin. It even seems like she initiated it."

I couldn't believe my ears.

"She initiated it?"

"Some of the other confirmands said that she was planning to seduce him."

"Seduce? Can you hear yourself? She's fifteen."

"Of course. I'm not defending Robin."

"Then what are you saying?"

He took my shoulders and gazed at me with sorrow in his eyes.

"I guarantee that he will never, ever get another job with the Church of Sweden."

"But?"

"But moving forward with this . . . it will only hurt us. Hurt Stella."

A void opened up inside me.

"We have to, Adam. We have to!"

He shook his head.

"Everyone will find out. People will judge her. She'll have to live with this forever."

My head was spinning. I gave a harsh cough, scared I might throw up. To some extent, I understood Adam's point. I myself had defended men accused of rape. I myself had posed all those unpleasant questions to the victim, about clothing, alcohol, previous experience, and sexual preferences. In some cases, I really had doubted the victim's account. In others, I had only been doing my job.

"She's a victim," I said, sobbing over the sink. "None of the guilt here belongs to her."

"I know, honey. Of course she's not guilty of anything. But the rape happened, and we can't change that. All we can do now is protect her so this doesn't get any worse."

He put his arms around me and I burrowed into his chest. Our hearts were racing, completely out of sync.

So this is how our lives turned out, I thought at the time.

Now I think there's still a chance to change it. There's still a chance to save our family, to be the mother I always wanted to be, a mother who would do anything to protect her child.

103

On Sunday the second of September, the same day that the police technicians searched our home, Adam was brought in for initial questioning. I had
begged him to remain strong, to weigh each word carefully. Meanwhile I
was contemplating how much to reveal to him. There could be no doubt
Adam was prepared to walk through the fires of hell for Stella, but in this
case I suspected that his unshakeable morals would weigh him down like a
burdensome cross on his back.

That night the prosecutor had decided to remand Stella and the only
bright spot I could see was that Michael Blomberg had been assigned as her
public defender.

I asked a contact with the police to call as soon as they were finished
searching our house. Then I walked through our rooms on shaky legs, trying to ferret out what the technicians had found. It couldn't be much.

Before Adam and I took the taxi to the police station on Saturday night,
I had staggered in among the bins at the neighborhood recycling station
around the corner. I pretended to vomit noisily as I stomped Stella's phone
to pieces and tossed them in the metal-recycling container. The SIM card
was already safely tucked in my purse. I still didn't know what had happened,
but I knew that Stella's texts might contain compromising information. Anguish chafed in my chest, but it was easier than I'd expected. You may think
there are things you're incapable of doing, but they suddenly seem natural
when it comes to protecting your child.

Later that night, I rooted through every corner of the house and discovered the bloody blouse, which was hidden rather sloppily under a pile of
clothes in the laundry room. It was still damp. Had Stella hidden it there?

Or had Adam emptied the washing machine? I was of two minds about what to do for a bit, but when Michael called to say that the police were on their way I threw the blouse into the woodstove to be on the safe side. I watched sparks fly around the crackling fabric.

I was full of conflicting emotions. As a lawyer, I was guilty of the most horrific violation of the law one could imagine. As a mother, my choice was the only correct one. I still had no idea what had happened on Friday night, but I knew with certainty that it was my duty to protect my daughter.

On Sunday afternoon, Adam called as soon as his interrogation was over. When I realized he'd lied to the police to give Stella an alibi, I was flooded with warmth. It was an act of love, perhaps the ultimate proof of how much he loved Stella and me. From that moment on, I knew that I would do anything for our family.

I told Adam that the police technicians were still in our house. He couldn't return home for a few more hours. I needed to buy time.

A few minutes later, there was a knock at the door. I stole to the window of the laundry room and peeked out.

All I could see of the person at the door was a black cap pulled so low on their forehead that it hid their face. A pair of feet in dark sneakers were shuffling nervously on the stone steps.

I cracked the door, just wide enough to grab her arm and pull her into the entryway.

"I didn't want to call anymore," she said.

I peered out the small window mounted in the door and concluded that the street was deserted. No one had seen her.

"Come in," I said.

She walked to the kitchen without removing her shoes. I hurried past her to the window and flicked the curtain over it.

"What happened?"

My voice quaked.

Amina looked at me with her beautiful brown eyes, which had gone red and runny.

"I can't believe it . . . Stella . . . I . . ."

She was shaking as I took her hand. We hugged each other tightly; it felt as if she wanted to cling to me. After a while I had to work my way out of her arms.

"I know," I said. "I read Stella's texts."

"You did?"

She stiffened. I stroked her arm and brushed a strand of hair from her cheek.

"Stella forgot her phone at home."

Amina gasped. I held her with both hands and found myself struggling not to break down.

"We're going to fix this, sweetie. We'll fix it."

She cried like a child.

She *was* just a child. She and Stella were both children.

I was the adult here. I was the mother. I was the one who had to save them.

All of a sudden, the tears stopped. Amina heaved silently.

"He wasn't supposed to die."

104

"It was self-defense," said Amina. "Wasn't it?"

I tried to absorb what she'd just told me. There was so much, all at once, so many emotions and details.

"I was planning to run as soon as he stopped the car. I even had my hand on the door handle, ready to jump out. But he had locked the doors from the inside. I couldn't go anywhere."

She looked at me as if she were dangling from a cliff and I was the only one who could extend a helping hand.

"You must have been so scared," I said.

Amina nodded.

"It was self-defense, right?"

"I don't know," I said truthfully. I still hadn't quite formed a clear picture of what had happened. "Where did the knife come from?"

"It was in the basket. Chris had brought it to our picnic."

Amina had gone on a date with Christopher Olsen, somewhere at the seaside. I understood that much.

"The knife was on top, in the basket. Between the seats," she said. "I saw it and just took it. I wasn't thinking."

He had forced himself on her. That brute had raped Amina.

"What about the pepper spray?" I asked.

"I always carry that. Stella has one too. You can buy them online."

I knew that, of course. I was the one who had urged Stella to purchase it. I had even paid for it.

"So first you sprayed him and then you grabbed the knife?"

Amina nodded and I gently stroked her swollen, pale cheek.

"But he figured out what I was doing before I hit the spray button. He put up his arms and turned his face away. Some of it must have hit him, though, because he roared like an animal. Then I tried to unlock the car door, but the button was in the wrong spot, on the dashboard. I had to lean over his lap, but at last I managed to get the door open. That's when I saw the knife."

"And you ran away from the car with the knife in your hand?"

"Yes."

I tried to picture it.

"He followed you?"

She nodded again.

"Obviously I didn't want to use the knife. Why the hell did I take it with me?"

"Stop," I said. "There's no point in that. You were terrified. You did the right thing. Anyone would have taken the knife."

Amina swore at herself.

"What about Stella?" I asked. "What was Stella doing there?"

"I don't know. She was . . . angry . . . worried. She had called and sent a bunch of messages."

"She didn't know you were with Christopher?"

"I lied to her. I betrayed my best friend."

Amina doubled over, sobbing. And I tried to comfort her, to embrace and stroke her. Even as my mind was gearing up.

"Stella had blood on her blouse, Amina."

She shuddered and turned her face up to me.

"He's dead! Don't you get it? Dead!"

I squeezed her arms hard, holding her the way you hold your baby to keep it from plunging to the floor.

My thoughts slowly turned down a new path.

You have no idea what you're capable of doing for another person until you are faced with a true threat. I still didn't realize what I was prepared to sacrifice for Amina's sake.

"Stella is in custody under suspicion of murder," I said. "The police were here and searched our house."

Amina sobbed.

"I'm sorry! It's all my fault! Can you drive me to the police station so I can tell them? They have to let Stella go."

Naturally, she was right. That was what we had to do. It was the right thing. Amina would lay out the truth for the police and Stella would be released from jail. Justice would be served, eventually, in some form. If there was such a thing as justice. Either way, there were extenuating circumstances. Amina would presumably be convicted of manslaughter, but she was young so her sentence would be reduced. It wouldn't be out of the question for her to be released in just a few years.

But she would never become a doctor. She would always carry that conviction with her. Her bright future had suddenly gone fuzzy at the edges.

"We have to get Stella out," she said. "Can you come with me? Please, can you give me a ride?"

I pushed back my chair and took the car keys from the silver dish on the kitchen island.

Was there any other option?

"The police will figure out that one of us did it," Amina said. "They're going to figure that out, right?"

I stopped midstep.

Of course there was another option. There always is.

Amina's words swirled around in my head. *They'll figure out that one of us did it.* But that is not enough for a conviction.

I looked at Amina; I thought of Stella. My heart ached.

A person cannot be convicted of murder if there are two potential perpetrators and it's impossible to prove which one of them committed the murder or, alternately, that they were in collusion.

I put my car keys back in the dish.

105

I pulled Amina over to the sofa and told her to sit. Her motions were mechanical. It was clear that she hadn't had time to work through what had happened. It was my job to be strong and rational, to think like a defense attorney.

"Aren't we going?" Amina asked.

I sat down right next to her and placed my hands on her knees.

"You have to trust me."

"But . . ."

Her knees were trembling. Her dry lower lip hung toward her chin like a flap of skin.

"Both you and Stella were there when Christopher Olsen died, right?"

"Yes."

"Here in Sweden the burden of proof is high," I said, even as I tried to figure out where I was going with this line of reasoning. "If there are two potential perpetrators at the scene when a murder is committed, the prosecutor must be able to prove either that one of them was without a doubt the killer, or that they committed the murder together."

The strong beats of Amina's pulse spread through my palm and turned my body into a single throbbing thing.

"What are you saying? Should I tell the police that Stella and I were both there?"

"Oh, I don't know."

Maybe I was a raving madwoman. The idea had sprung from sheer desperation; I had formed it without examining it deeply. What would it involve? Could I save both Stella and Amina? And was I prepared to subject them to everything it would take?

"Presumably that wouldn't work," I said. "If you tell the police, they will do everything in their power to convict you both. For this to work, you have to wait until the trial."

"Why?"

"It has to come as a surprise to the prosecutor. Suddenly the possibility of a second perpetrator appears, and the court cannot deny that there is reasonable doubt. And once there has been an acquittal, a great deal of new evidence is required for the prosecutor to bring a new indictment in a case. No prosecutor wants to lose the same case twice."

Amina stared at me, her mouth open.

"A trial? Doesn't that take a long time? Do we have to let Stella . . . ?"

No, of course, we couldn't do that. We couldn't allow Stella to remain behind bars.

"I don't know," I said.

"It's better if I just confess."

"But your education, Amina. Your entire future . . ."

At the same time, I was picturing Stella in a shabby jail cell. What kind of mother even considers letting her child stay locked up? It might take weeks, even months, for the indictment to come.

"We have to make sure Stella doesn't say anything," I said.

"What do you mean?"

"We can't tell her. You know Stella. We have to get her to keep quiet. At the same time, we can't reveal too much."

"Are you nuts? We're going to let Stella stay in jail without saying anything?"

"There's no other way, if you're both going to walk free. I know Stella's attorney. He'll help us."

"No, we can't," Amina said.

I took her hand.

"We love Stella, and she knows that. She'll know it more than ever once this is over."

Amina gave a sob.

"This is all my fault."

I wondered if this was really true. If it's ever true. Is there any sort of situation where you can say with certainty that a single person is responsible for what happens? Everything in life is dependent on so many different factors that interact in so many different ways.

Whose fault is it that our family turned out the way it did?

Sometimes I wish I could believe in a god, a higher power of some sort. Perhaps it would be simpler to have something to blame. On the other hand, not even the most dogmatic fundamentalists seem inclined to blame their omnipotent gods for the misery that strikes us all sooner or later. To be born human is to carry blame.

"What do you think Stella would want us to do?" I asked. "Let's let her decide."

Amina looked at me in despair. I was holding both of her hands now, like a bond, a promise.

There is no justice. All that exists of justice is what we create together.

"Stella would convince us to do it," Amina said.

She went out to the entryway to get a plastic bag. I knew immediately what it contained.

106

Amina buries her face in her hands and all that remains are the shaking shoulders of a little girl.

"Would you like us to take a break?" Göran Leijon asks.

Michael nods at the suggestion. Both he and Leijon seem seriously shaken by the story they've just been forced to listen to.

After Stella was raped, she and I were finally able to be closer to one another, in a way that had previously been impossible. I was the one she came to in the middle of the night when she was sure she would never wake up again if she fell asleep. I was the one who sat on the edge of her bed, wiping tears from her face with my fingertips. And as she slowly opened up to me, I became aware of how much we shared once you dug under the surface. Our shared fear of showing weakness. The constant worry that we weren't good enough. And not least, the paralyzing feeling of being incapable of connecting—either to our own emotions or to other people.

"Sometimes I wish I could be more like Amina," Stella said. "That I knew who I am and what I want, like her. I hate that my brain is like a fucking pinball machine."

"I don't want you to be like anyone else," I responded, a lump in my throat. "You're perfect the way you are."

I stroked her cheek but couldn't bring myself to look her in the eye. The shame was such a burden, the shame I felt because I, too, had wished Stella was more like Amina.

———

Stella whispers and gestures at Michael. She seems annoyed and confused. I wonder how much she understands.

"I don't need a break," Amina says, crumpling yet another tissue.

Adam grabs my arm.

"What is going on?"

I shush him without looking at him.

"Then the prosecutor may continue her questioning," says Göran Leijon.

Jansdotter is consumed with paging through her documents. The assistant prosecutor hangs over her, pointing and discussing.

"I don't understand, Amina," the prosecutor says. "Why didn't you tell this to the police?"

"I couldn't."

"But now you can?"

"I have to," Amina says. "For Stella."

The prosecutor picks up her pen again and brings it to her chin.

"What happened after . . . ?" She swallows the last word. "What happened afterwards, Amina? Did you come back to Lund with Christopher?"

"I cried the whole way in the car. But I didn't have a choice."

"Why didn't you have a choice? You could have—"

"I was so damn scared!" Amina interrupts. "I understood that everything Linda Lokind had said was true. Chris *was* a psychopath. I tried to text Stella, but Chris noticed and he took my phone away. I figured if I could just get back to town I could run away as soon as I got the chance. I had my pepper spray in my purse and I thought if I sprayed him when he stopped the car I could jump out and escape."

Jenny Jansdotter leans forward, propped on her elbows.

"Why did you have pepper spray in your purse?"

"I always carry it. As a girl, you have to be prepared to defend yourself."

Jansdotter doesn't seem convinced, but she lets it go. She clicks her pen and makes a brief note in her papers. Then she asks Amina to describe what happened when Christopher Olsen stopped the car outside his building.

"As soon as he turned off the engine I sprayed him. I grabbed my phone and threw myself at the door, but I couldn't open it. Chris was screaming. *My eyes, my eyes.* Finally, I found the lock button and then I ran as fast as I could. I've never been so scared in my whole life. I was sure he would kill me if he caught up to me."

"Which direction did you run?"

"No idea, I was just trying to get away. I remember I saw Polhem ahead of me, the school, but otherwise it was all a big blur."

"What about Christopher, what did he do?"

"When I turned around the first time, he was still in the car. But then I saw that he had gotten out. I knew he was after me, so I just ran as far as I could."

Jansdotter tries to ask another question, but Amina won't give her the space.

"I saw a bunch of guys in the parking lot at the Ball House. So I slowed down and walked right behind them, all the way to the station. I kept turning around, but Chris wasn't there. It seemed like he had given up."

"Did you call the police?"

"Obviously that was my first thought, but then . . ." Amina shook her head. "Then I started thinking about what would happen."

"What do you mean?" Jansdotter asks.

Amina is breathing heavily. I see her back moving slightly.

"There was one week left before I would start medical school. I've been dreaming of that since I was little."

"So you didn't tell anyone you were raped?"

"I didn't dare to. I was thinking about Dad. I know how stupid it sounds, but it would destroy Dad if he found out. I was afraid of what he would do. Plus, Linda Lokind had already reported Chris, and it never led anywhere. Guys like him always get off."

I can hardly bring myself to listen any longer. I just want this to be over now. Adam is glaring at me from the next seat, and I'm afraid of how he's going to handle hearing the truth.

Amina raises her voice a notch.

"Stella was raped too."

It takes a moment for the words to sink in. My gasp is so loud that the journalist in front of me turns around.

What are you doing, Amina?

"She was only fifteen."

A buzz goes through the room. I slouch down in my seat. I just want to keep sinking.

"Her parents didn't report it," Amina says.

All eyes are on Adam and me. I feel myself crumbling to pieces.

"Stella's mom is a lawyer. She knew what a trial would involve. A rape trial."

Please, Amina. Stop!

I shrink into myself, trying to disappear. Adam is staring at nothing. His eyes look like they're made of porcelain.

"I wouldn't be able to deal with that kind of trial either," Amina says. "I realized that right away. Having everything questioned, being blamed, and then having to watch Chris go free or at most get a few months in prison. I saw how Stella felt when it happened to her, and I saw how destroyed Linda Lokind was."

I know what Amina is up to. She's smart. She's sacrificing my reputation for Stella's sake. She knew I would never go along with this, so she didn't say anything. As I peer over at Göran Leijon and the upset lay judges, I realize it's working.

"When did you tell Stella?" Jansdotter asks.

Amina's shoulders rise slightly.

"I didn't. I just couldn't."

I can see how Stella is looking at her. She's trying to summon up a rage that is completely overshadowed by sadness.

"You didn't say anything to your best friend?"

A moment passes before Amina can bring herself to respond.

"I had betrayed Stella. Obviously I wanted nothing more than to talk to her, but I couldn't. It was impossible. I would have to tell her that I betrayed her trust and went behind her back and I just couldn't stomach it."

"So you had no contact whatsoever with Stella, on the evening and night Christopher Olsen was murdered?"

"Stella texted me and called several times, but I didn't answer."

As Jansdotter confers with her assistant, I once again dare to sit up tall. A quick glance at Adam and I suspect, from how he's looking at me, that he's come to a certain understanding.

"Stella herself said that she biked to Christopher Olsen's residence that evening," the prosecutor says. "She rang the doorbell and banged on the door. Did you see Stella there, at Olsen's residence?"

"No."

"Did you see Stella at any point during that evening or night?"

"No."

Jansdotter sighs. The assistant points at something in her documents.

"Did Christopher Olsen bring a knife to your picnic?"

Amina answers quickly, with no hesitation.

"Yes, there was a knife in the picnic basket."

Jansdotter asks her to describe the knife.

"How long was it?"

Amina holds her hands ten to twenty centimeters apart.

"Where did this knife end up afterwards? As you were driving back to the city?"

"It must have stayed in the basket."

"But it didn't. The police have not found a knife like that."

Amina hesitates for a moment. All three lay judges are on tenterhooks.

"I don't know what happened to the knife."

I find myself nodding. I don't mean to.

Both Stella and Amina were there when Christopher Olsen died, and each has a motive. But there is no murder weapon.

They will never find the knife.

"Were you the one who killed Christopher Olsen?" Jenny Jansdotter asks.

Adam makes a sound of surprise. Amina looks straight at the prosecutor.

"I didn't kill him," she says. "I sprayed him with pepper spray and ran for my life. I don't know what happened after that."

The prosecutor looks at her assistant. Adam looks at me, and I take his hand.

"I would never be able to kill someone," Amina says.

107

I hardly hear what is said during the closing arguments. The voices turn to vacant, tinny echoes in the distance. Foreign languages I don't understand.

One moment I'm convinced that everything will be okay. The next I fear that we have made a terrible mistake. Stella will be locked up, forever stamped as a killer, and Amina will be sentenced by the court of public opinion; her career as a doctor will be over before it can even begin.

Prosecutor Jansdotter is having a hard time keeping her voice steady. She loses her place a number of times and glances down at her notes or discusses something with her assistant. But in any case, she claims that she has proven Stella was there when Christopher Olsen was robbed of his life. She also considers it clear that Stella had a motive to kill Olsen. Stella was jealous and out for revenge because Olsen had initiated a relationship with Amina. According to the prosecutor, Stella had plenty of time to think through a plan. She went to Olsen's apartment with the intent to kill him. Jansdotter therefore maintains that Stella must be convicted of murder. She says there is far too much doubt surrounding the information given by Adam and Amina. There are, according to Jansdotter, solid reasons to question Amina's entire story of rape, not least because she had neglected to inform anyone about the incident earlier, during the investigation. Thus the court ought to find Stella guilty of murder; the prosecutor calls for a sentence of fourteen years in prison.

My mind is spinning. In fourteen years, Stella will be thirty-two. I think of all the things she would miss out on. One can experience so much of the world in fourteen years! When I was thirty-two, I was midstride in life. Stella might never have the opportunity to become a mother, create a family, or have a career.

Fourteen years is a long time. Fourteen years in prison is an immensely long time. A goddamn eternity.

I look at Stella and am struck by how small she looks. She is still twelve years old with blue eyes full of longing, the same snot-nosed seven-year-old whose bad dreams woke her up, sneaking in to sleep between Mom and Dad. Maybe I'll always see her that way. In my eyes, she remains a child. My child.

My guilt is eating deeper and deeper into me. What have I done? Why didn't I put Amina in the car and drive her to the police station?

On several occasions I have felt that this is my way of repaying my debts for neglecting my family, but what if, in fact, I have sacrificed my own daughter to save Amina? I don't know if I can live with that.

Michael adjusts the knot of his tie before beginning his closing arguments. He is quick and to the point as he breaks down the prosecutor's evidence point by point until nothing is left.

"The only thing the prosecutor has succeeded in proving is that my client was in the vicinity of Christopher Olsen's residence on the night he was attacked. Meanwhile, during today's proceedings, we heard that Amina Bešić was there as well, at that point in time."

He looks at the presiding judge and his tone is confidential, almost as if he is addressing the judge personally. As if there is no one else in the room.

"Both Amina Bešić and Stella Sandell were there, then, when Christopher Olsen died. Furthermore, it seems both of them had a motive to want to hurt Olsen. But naturally, that proves nothing. It is in no way proven beyond reasonable doubt that my client was the one holding the knife that caused Christopher Olsen's death."

And then it's over. Everything that happens after this is beyond my control.

Göran Leijon casts the hastiest of glances at his lay judges and then turns to the gallery to declare the proceedings closed.

"The court will now deliberate, and then a decision will be delivered."

I sink far down into my seat again. It feels like I'm hanging over a cliff, a gap in time and space, my feet kicking desperately.

Stella is guided out through the basement door along with Michael, to avoid confronting the crowd of journalists and photographers that have gathered in the hallways of the courthouse.

People in the gallery are crowding each other, shoving and muttering, eager to get out. Meanwhile, I gather my belongings. My purse, coat, shawl.

Adam tells me to hurry up. I don't know why he's in such a rush.

When I stand up, it's as if all of my blood pools in my feet. I can't feel my own body, my head, my arms. I lose my balance and fall back into my seat.

My hand on my heart, I sit there like I've cracked down the middle and concentrate on breathing.

Adam takes my hand and helps me to my feet again. He tenderly leads me out of the room. My legs are heavy; the air is thick. We walk through the corridor, past all the curious faces and voices.

"I need something cold to drink," I say, pointing at the vending machine in the corner.

I paw through my purse for some change. My hand is trembling; I dig and dig. I bring up a pack of gum and some hair ties and toss them on the floor. My hand keeps moving until everything in my purse is rotating like it's in a cement mixer.

"Take it easy!" Adam says, grasping my arm.

My purse falls to the floor and I stand in front of the flashing vending machine, a quivering mess. Adam hands me two gold ten-kronor coins and fishes my bag from the floor.

"What just happened in there, honey?"

I know I have to explain it all to Adam, and soon. I don't know whether I can.

"The court will deliberate," I say, sipping the water.

"How long will that take?"

I look at him. My heart is one big, throbbing wound. What have I done to my family?

"I don't know," I say. "It could take anywhere from five minutes to several hours."

Adam looks around in bewilderment.

"I don't understand. Was Amina the one . . . ?"

I put a finger to his lips.

"I love you," I say, taking his hand.

It comes straight from my heart.

Adam and Stella are everything to me. I know Stella and I are everything to him.

"I love you too," he says.

I hold his hand. No, I squeeze it, embrace it, cling to it.

I have to tell him.

108

For a long time I feared that Adam would give away the whole thing. He would never allow me to carry out my plan if he knew what was going on. It was uncharacteristic enough that he had likely hidden the bloody blouse and then lied to the police about what time it was when Stella had returned home. I couldn't let him find out any further details.

He had begun to suspect Amina that very Saturday. After our lunch at her parents', he hinted that Amina had been lying about spending Friday night with Stella. I'd been forced to put up several smoke screens.

When we returned home from the police station late Saturday night, I lingered out on the street to speak with Michael, who had given us a ride home. He believed that Stella would soon be released, but I had read the messages on her phone and feared that the situation was quite a bit more complicated than we knew. As we waited for further information, I tried to insinuate to Adam that Stella was in need of an alibi. I couldn't say too much; he must under no circumstances suspect that I knew more than I was letting on, but I hinted that he was the only one who could exonerate Stella by claiming that she had come home earlier than she actually had done. Of course, I could have lied to the police myself to give Stella an alibi. But the statement would hold much more weight if Adam did it. Who dares to question the honesty of a pastor who has spent his entire life campaigning for the truth?

Furthermore, I strongly preferred not to testify. It wouldn't be particularly exceptional for me to lie under oath considering everything else I had done; my professional honor no longer exists anyhow. At the same time, it was important for me to follow the entire trial as an onlooker. I wanted to see it all. I suppose it has to do with feeling in control.

It was impossible for me to sleep on that Saturday night; the thoughts tore through my mind like galloping horses, but after a few hours I discovered that Adam was sinking deeper and deeper into his chair. He blinked several times, his head drooping to his shoulder, and I sat perfectly still without making a sound until deep snores came rattling from his throat.

Then I quickly tiptoed up to my office and called Amina. She was agitated and almost incoherent. We decided to meet as soon as we had the opportunity, but that very night she had to call Adam and confess that she had lied. She must not continue to claim she had been with Stella on Friday night.

Adam, however, was not so easily mollified. He has always been good at uncovering lies, and he could tell that Amina was hiding something. In fact, there are only two people who know how to lie to Adam. One is Stella; the other is me.

On the Thursday after the murder, Amina called me again. Thus far everything seemed to be going as we'd hoped, but suddenly Amina was frantic and out of breath on the line. Adam had been waiting for her outside the arena, trying to squeeze her for information. She was sure he knew. Somehow, Adam had figured out that Stella and Amina were involved in Christopher Olsen's death.

I had never intended to reveal to Adam that I, too, was awake when Stella arrived home that night, but as his behavior became increasingly desperate I realized something had to be done. This was also the point at which I had the idea of moving to Stockholm.

I love Adam. Our relationship has sometimes been shaky, to say the least; it has crashed and burned, but they say that broken vases last the longest. Two people who have gone through everything we have together, who have come through an ordeal like ours in one piece, belong together in a way that is hard for others to comprehend.

In Stockholm we would be able to build something new from the ground up. At the same time, the preliminary investigation was dragging on, and I had to find a way to get Adam out of Lund before disaster struck. Although in the end I was forced to confess to him that I was the one who made sure

Stella's phone disappeared, and although he must have realized I was the one who had taken care of the stained blouse, I succeeded in getting Adam to follow through with his lie and give Stella an alibi.

The moment I discovered that Stella had left her phone at home, I realized that something was wrong. Stella never forgets her phone. With each passing minute, my worry grew. In the end I saw no other way out than to read through her texts.

I read Stella's last, desperate message to Amina in horror. For a fleeting minute I considered showing Adam, but I quickly realized that would be disastrous.

I was sitting on the sofa, my eyes glued to Stella's phone, when Michael called.

"I'm so sorry, Ulrika, but the police have Stella in custody."

It was a shock to hear his voice again after all these years.

"She has requested me as a public defender."

"What?"

I was bewildered. Stella had requested Michael as her attorney?

"Does she know who you are?" I had asked as he drove Adam and me home later that night.

"Of course."

This was so typical of Stella. She knew that my relationship with Michael had extended beyond the professional; she had heard us speaking on the phone, and that was why she had now requested him as her defense.

Because surely it wasn't the case that she *knew*? That she realized Michael would break confidentiality and involve me?

It was a dreadful decision, leaving Stella in the dark about all that was going on, abandoned in a jail cell. I felt so sick about it that I finally asked Michael to arrange a visit so I could explain, but Stella refused and I didn't dare to entrust Michael with making her understand. There was no other way out. If I were to succeed in saving both Amina and Stella, this had to go to trial. The stakes were terribly high. I was risking my daughter. My family.

———

On Sunday afternoon, just after the police searched our house, Amina came to see me. Adam was being interrogated by the police, and when he called I bought time by claiming that there were still technicians in the house.

Once we'd made our decision, Amina took out a plastic bag she'd had hidden inside her jacket. She explained that she had found the bag in a trash bin at the playground, and I knew at once what it contained.

We got in the car and drove straight to the quarry in Dalby, where I stopped and turned off the engine on a small gravel road.

I looked around anxiously before emptying the contents of the bag on the ground. Amina stood next to me, sniffling as I stomped Christopher Olsen's phone to pieces.

"Yours too," I said.

She looked at me, wide-eyed. Then she handed me her phone and I pried the SIM card loose with creeping-spider fingers before stomping it to pieces as well. I was wracked with agony, but there was no time to hesitate. At last I knew what was important, what really meant something. Here was my opportunity to prove it.

I stepped onto the cliff above the quarry, to the very edge, where the wall of rock plunged into the dark water that was so still it looked like a deep, black hole. I pulled on a pair of gloves, then threw the knife that had killed Christopher Olsen over the precipice. It sailed in a wide curve through the air, and the edge cleaved the silent water. The deep lake opened up and swallowed it with a slurp.

109

Adam takes a step back and almost crashes into the vending machine.

"Do you realize what you've done?"

The pain is enormous. At that moment, I regret everything. Not only do I risk losing my daughter—Adam won't be there either.

"I did it for you. For my family."

"And Amina?"

I nod.

"But I don't understand. I saw with my own eyes that Linda Lokind had the same shoes as Stella. And she followed her that night."

I drink up the last splash of water, crumple the bottle, and toss it in a trash bin.

"Linda Lokind didn't kill Christopher Olsen," I say. "Everything Linda said when she was trying to warn Stella off was likely true. Olsen subjected her to atrocious abuse."

I take pains to really emphasize this last part. Perhaps I do so to convince Adam that he did the right thing? Perhaps it's mostly to convince myself?

Adam still looks confused.

"But what about those Polish guys?"

"The ones from the pizzeria," I say with a shrug. "They're certainly petty thieves and swindlers, but they have nothing to do with Olsen's death. They just wanted to keep their pizzeria in his building."

Adam shakes his head.

"This is crazy," he says. "Why didn't Amina say anything? How could she let Stella endure this?"

I open my mouth, but my voice has vanished. Adam will never forgive me. He'll never understand.

"And you?" he says. "You, too?"

This mostly sounds like a statement. I don't hear any accusation in his voice.

"What won't a person do for their child?" I say.

Adam gazes into my eyes. *Maybe,* I think. *Maybe he can understand after all.*

"I love you," I whisper.

At last I know it's true. That's what I do. I love Adam. I love Stella. I love our family.

Then the loudspeakers crackle and we are summoned back into Courtroom 2.

Adam and I are holding hands. The benches of the gallery are nearly empty now. Many of the journalists appear to have assumed that the deliberations would drag on, and so have left the courthouse. Others must have expected no surprising news, reckoning instead that Stella would have to remain in jail pending sentencing at a later date.

She is so thin. Her hair is hanging in tangled clumps and her gaze is dull and empty. She doesn't look in our direction. Like everyone else, her eyes are on Presiding Judge Göran Leijon.

"The court has deliberated," he says, looking at the lay judges. "We are prepared to deliver the verdict."

My heart stops. They have a verdict already? Although not even twenty minutes have passed?

Adam squeezes my hand and looks puzzled.

"They've decided already?"

I nod and lean forward.

The only thing that exists in my world is Göran Leijon's voice. I don't hear everything that is said, but the important parts make it through. The essential words find their way through the roar and hit me like a blow to the face.

I can't move. It's as though my brain is registering the information but doesn't want to accept it.

After a moment I turn to Adam. He's staring at the floor.

This isn't true. I can't believe it's true.

"Stella Sandell is exonerated of the charges, and with that the court lifts the detention requirement."

A buzz goes through the courtroom. My brain is chaos. Can it be true?

"What's going on?" Adam asks.

He looks at me, his eyes huge.

"The charges were exonerated." It's not until I say it out loud that it dawns on me what this means. "Stella is free!"

Meanwhile, Michael has stood up to embrace Stella. People in the gallery begin to move. Everyone is suddenly in a rush. A large guard puffs out his chest and readies his eagle eye. Only now can each part of my brain finally accept what is happening as real.

"Stella!" I cry, forcing my way between the chairs, passing under the sharp gaze of the guard, and butting my way past Michael's teary smile.

As if on a bridge spanning the shit that has happened, through a tunnel of brilliant, streaming light, I dive right into Stella's arms.

Behind us I hear Adam's astonished voice.

"Is this real? What happened?"

"The chain of evidence broke," Michael says with such pride in his voice that one might think this is primarily thanks to him. "After your testimony, and Amina's, there was far too much doubt. They were forced to free Stella."

Adam stares at Michael.

"I apologize for questioning your methods, but I didn't know what was going on," he says. "I understand now what you've done for my family."

Michael looks almost overwhelmed. He nods at Adam and then, when he sneaks a look in my direction, I catch a glimpse of a smile. It looks like he's enjoying this. Is that why he does it?

"I'm sorry, Stella," I say, moving a lock of hair away from her pale cheek.

"For what?"

"For this. For everything."

She looks at me for a long time.

My little girl. I stick to her trembling body like a Band-Aid. I tighten my arms around her; I never want to let go of her again. Her heart beats against my breast and the longing in our eyes calms, finding peace.

"Mom," she whispers.

It doesn't matter if she's eighteen years or four weeks old. She is always my child.

I would do anything for her.

"I love you, Mom."

I try to respond, but it all gets caught in my throat. Like a clot of emotions. Years of pent-up yearning forming a dam in my throat. And when it breaks, it feels as if my whole body turns to liquid.

Time doesn't exist; space has no meaning. We flow together in eternity, my little girl and me. Slowly, she leans forward and whispers in my ear.

"I sure picked a good lawyer, didn't I?"

My body goes hard and stiff. As Stella pulls away, I can see myself in her eyes. She turns to her father.

Adam looks wrecked. As if something fundamental has broken.

I have let him down one time too many. If Adam finds out about Michael and me . . . I would never be able to repair that.

Michael smiles at me again. I turn toward Stella.

"Thanks," she whispers to her dad.

Adam is crying like a child. He just lets it all come out, absolutely uninhibited and stripped bare.

Stella extends a hand to touch him. Adam watches her hand move, sees the fingers stretching out and meeting his skin. The tiny hairs on his arm stand up.

"Does it feel good in your heart now?" Stella asks.

Epilogue

After I'd rung the bell at Chris's place and pressed my ear to the door, I rushed back down the stairs. I got on my bike and pedaled around the neighborhood aimlessly as I tried to figure out what had happened. Had Linda Lokind really been following me, or was it all in my mind? Was I losing it?

I've always been different and I've never really seen myself reflected in other people. What if I'd always been heading for this: a psychosis just waiting to blossom?

After a few random rounds, I parked my bike outside Polhem and sat down on a bench. My legs were shaking and I could feel my pulse pounding at my temples. I couldn't just bike home and leave Amina.

For the hundredth time I read her text.

Everything's ok. Sleeping. See you tomorrow. <3

I could buy the heart at the end. But *ok?* Periods in a text? No, not a chance. I frantically scrolled through the mile-long thread of texts we'd exchanged and found that sure enough, Amina had never ended a single text with a period. She hadn't written that text.

It must have been Chris. He was refusing to answer my calls or texts. Had Linda Lokind been telling the truth after all? What if Chris was holding Amina prisoner? Or even worse . . . ?

I paced up and down the street, impatient, walking into the schoolyard and up to the roundabout and back again. I went along the hedge, over to the building where Chris lived. I stared up at his window, but noticed a shadowy figure in the window next door and hurried back toward the school. As soon as I stopped, sat down, or leaned against a tree, that creeping sensation came back, tiny insect feet on my skin, unrelenting twitches of muscle that forced me back up and off again.

When the silence broke, I was in the middle of my course between the schoolyard and the playground, fifty meters from Chris's building. Out of nowhere, the night filled with the patter of tottering footsteps, repressed screams against the asphalt.

She was running down the middle of the street. Her shirt was pulled down off one shoulder and her hair was wildly mussed like a black halo that had fallen down around her neck. Her eyes had that warrior gaze. On the handball court, people often compare her to a pit bull.

"Amina!" I cried.

She was panting hard; she glanced over her shoulder and her mouth formed a wordless scream.

At that moment, Chris came dashing around the corner behind her. One hand to his face, the other surging at his side like a sprinter.

He was chasing her.

"Run!" Amina shouted at me.

But my feet were stuck to the asphalt. Amina soon reached me and I saw her face twist.

"Run!"

I tried to find an escape route as Chris came closer and closer.

Just as I turned around, I saw the knife. A tiny movement of Amina's hand made the blade flash in the glow of the streetlights.

Chris's feet thundered against the asphalt.

"Come on!" I cried, dragging Amina with me.

We rounded the hedge and entered the darkness of the playground. The gravel crunched under our feet. Amina was shuddering and panting, gasping for air. It smelled like sweat and adrenaline and something else, something strong. Pepper?

"What the fuck is going on?"

Amina didn't respond. Her gaze seemed shrouded in a thick fog. I shook her, trying to reach her, but she was completely out of it.

I took her by the wrist and forced her to look at me.

"What did he do to you?"

Her mouth opened and her lips quivered like a fish.

"I'm—sorry," she stammered. "I broke our agreement."

"What the fuck did he do, Amina?"

"He . . . he . . ."

The steps were coming closer. In a few seconds, we would be eye to eye with Chris.

"He raped me."

Amina's voice was like a kick to my gut.

"He raped you?"

An instant later, Chris rounded the corner and towered up before us. He was only a few meters away. He skidded to a stop and stood there with a hand over one eye.

I backed away. Two quick steps. I had let go of Amina but assumed she was following me.

My body tensed, my skin tightening to the breaking point. I should have been scared, I should have been terrified, but instead every cell in my body was riddled with fury. I hated him. I hated Chris Olsen so much I was about to break.

Again and again I was forced to relive my own rape: the pressure on my throat, the weight on my body, and the burning pain when he forced himself in.

How the fuck could I have let the same thing happen to Amina? If only I had listened to Linda.

Chris Olsen grunted in between gasps. He made a terrible face and rubbed his eyes with the back of his hand. I looked at Amina and realized that she hadn't backed up at all. Instead she took a big step closer to Chris. The knife was trembling, threatening, in the shaky hand she had raised toward him.

"People like you don't deserve to live," she hissed between her teeth.

"That's enough," Chris said.

His voice revealed neither regret nor fear. He looked completely blank.

"Stop, Amina."

It was my own voice.

I don't know if she heard me. She was in another world, one where only she and Chris existed. She and her rapist. And the knife, shaking in her hand.

"Get out of here!" she said.

Chris stared at her.

"Get the fuck out!"

I stepped up beside her. The sharp blade of the knife quivered in the air right beside me. Inside, my hatred coiled like a snake, it twisted around itself, a fist about to pop.

I saw the devastation in Amina's eyes and knew it was my fault, every last bit. If only I had listened to Linda Lokind's warnings. How could I have been so blind?

And then Chris Olsen laughed.

I looked at my best friend and took the knife from her hand.

Acknowledgments

Thanks to Pastor Markus von Martens, who both gave me a wife and read the manuscript. Thanks to Birgitta Ekstrand and Monika Wieser for invaluable insights. Thanks to Zackarias Ekman for general brilliance and legal expertise. Thanks to everyone at Bokförlaget Forum and Bonnierförlagen. Thanks to Astri, Christine, Kaisa, Marit, and Kajsa at Ahlander Agency. It's an honor to work with you. You're all shining stars. Thanks to Karin and Peter at Kult PR.

Thanks to everyone at Celadon Books. I am so delighted to work with your brilliant team. Thanks to Deb for everything! And thanks to Vicki at Pan Macmillan! You both made this book even better.

Without my editor, John Häggblom, this novel would not be what it is. Thanks for your meticulousness and your wisdom, and for believing in me from the start. Without my Swedish publisher, Karin Linge Nordh, everything would have been worse. Thank you for everything. Without my agent, Astri Ahlander, this book probably wouldn't exist. I'm so happy and thankful for everything you do for me. Without Kajsa, Ellen, and Tove, there would have been no point.

CELADON
BOOKS

Founded in 2017, Celadon Books, a division of Macmillan Publishers, publishes a highly curated list of twenty to twenty-five new titles a year. The list of both fiction and nonfiction is eclectic and focuses on publishing commercial and literary books and discovering and nurturing talent.